Holding
SOMEDAY

A Novel Inspired by Actual Events

Mike Williams
W. R. Ponder

FIDELIS
PUBLISHING

Fidelis Publishing ®
Winchester, VA • Nashville, TN
www.fidelispublishing.com

ISBN: 9781956454789
ISBN: 9781956454796 (eBook)
Finding Someday
A Novel Inspired by Actual Events
Copyright © 2024 Mike Williams

Order at www.faithfultext.com for a significant discount. Email info@fidelispublishing.com to inquire about bulk purchase discounts.

Cover designed by Diana Lawrence
Interior design by Xcel Graphic
Edited by Amanda Varian

Manufactured in the United States of America

10 9 8 7 6 5 4 3 2 1

To all of those who are trying to make tough decisions.

PROLOGUE

The day Jayla entered the world was the day her father exited hers. To say he lacked the commitment necessary to be involved wasn't true. He had ample ability to commit, often going above and beyond to dedicate himself to several women around the almost dead city of La Cienega, while also living with Jayla's mother, Amarika. Surprisingly, he was there as she went into labor and held her hand as the nurses told her it was too late for an epidural. But when the ice chips were running low, he sprang up to grab more and never returned.

From time to time over the years, he would drop by the old apartment he and Amarika once shared and peer beyond the steel bars, through the half-parted curtains, to look for a few minutes, but Amarika had moved on after being evicted shortly after Jayla's birth due to months of unpaid rent. The same rent money hatched in Amarika's hands nested in his deepening pockets and flew at the heels of his many lovers across the city. Countless women in La Cienega unwittingly share two things in common—the love of the same man, and his child.

While most women would hide this reality from their children, for Amarika, it was a topic that needed to be aired daily with her rapidly growing daughter. The younger she was, the more expedient Amarika thought it was for her daughter to know all her father's flaws without ever knowing his name. Amarika only ever referred to him as "that man" or "good for nothing" in the stories she told. Jayla knew he was white, worked as a day laborer most of the time, and loved women of color. Many women of color. "Anyone who walks out on their family doesn't deserve a name," Amarika would say whenever Jayla asked. "And if you don't watch out, you'll become just like him." There were never any Father's Day festivities in the ramshackle apartment they shared on the corner of squalor and outlawed hope. Instead, twice a summer, Amarika made sure she alone was recognized for her constant sacrifice and commitment to raising Jayla.

This was not to say Jayla's life was devoid of men, only devoid of fatherly figures. A parade of men ran through their apartment in the neighborhood called "The Bricks," each relationship sustaining as long as the other could help keep up with their share of the rent. Some of these men took a seemingly sincere interest in Jayla, some couldn't care less about her, and a few let their eyes and hands linger on her longer than was proper.

"I'm doing this for you," Amarika would tell Jayla every time a new man moved in, or when she picked up an extra shift at one of her two part-time jobs. "All of this I'm going through is on account of you. And where's my thank-you?" This weighed heavily on Jayla growing up, and she carried the bitter seeds of guilt within, watered with her tears, and blossoming into full-fledged resentment.

With Amarika out of the house for much of the day, Jayla grew up playing on the street with other kids from The Bricks. Around the complex, there was no shortage of mischief to get into. Spotting potential friends was always easy but keeping them proved a challenge to Jayla. Her face was more winsome than it was initially beautiful, and her arms and legs were husky from the junk food she was constantly being fed at home. "A bag of chips is cheaper than a bag of apples, and the chips will last longer," Amarika would say to Jayla at the grocery store as they passed the produce section.

The fewer friends Jayla had, the more she ate, and the more she ate, the more ridicule she endured around the neighborhood. And when they weren't jabbing her for her weight, they were redirecting their hateful words toward the dingy cycle of unwashed clothes she often wore for days on end.

The rejection of the kids around The Bricks and the constant rotation of men paying her no regard at home combined to create a deep-seated need within her young heart. She so wanted to feel valued, to have worth, to matter. So starved for positive attention, Jayla would give herself, heart and soul, to anyone who gave a hint of approval or interest, like a withered sapling craning and twisting toward the promise of sunlight.

This yearning for value was stoked further by the verbal assault she received from Amarika. The exhaustion of working multiple jobs to make ends meet, the compounding hate for the men whose bad habits she had to endure and whose endless physical appetite she had to fill— all this toxicity and pain needed an outlet. An outlet who couldn't fire her from work for an outburst. An outlet who wouldn't withdraw financial assistance, paying a share of the blizzard of bills that flurried the beginning of each month. An outlet like this young little girl who looked and sounded more and more like the father she never met with each passing day.

Fear of bearing the brunt of undeserved scoldings cultivated a deceptive side to Jayla. More than just concealing a favorite snack in her room or sheltering a favorite toy from getting pawned, she learned to hide herself away. Anytime the pungent smell of smoke wafted under the front door to alert her of Amarika's arrival, she would stow herself in her room or camouflage herself within the sprawling maze of The Bricks complex. Thriving off respect in the absence of love, Jayla learned to get attention by being fearless in front of the other kids her age. Anything they wouldn't try, she would, as long as they watched and applauded.

This cynical and aggressive behavior bled into her life when she started going to school. She wanted to gain the approval of her teachers. She possessed a proven intelligence, and her principal would remind her of that whenever she got into trouble. But the same kids who expected a performance from her at The Bricks were the same ones watching her in the classroom.

When Jayla entered second grade, she was moved into an ESE class for having what her teachers called "behavior modification disorder." In that environment, bored from unchallenging schoolwork and disinterested temporary teachers, her character rotted and soured as the outlandish defiance of yesterday became the standard expected behavior today from her classmates. By fourth grade, she was exhausted, angry, and empty, and there was nowhere to go but down. That is, if it hadn't been for Mrs. Neidringhouse.

Mrs. Neidringhouse cared about her students and looked for creative ways to help them learn. She was kind and patient, quick with a compliment while being firm and having high expectations for those in her class. In this teacher, Jayla found the one thing she hadn't been able to find in her peers—love. This love wasn't earned but was freely given. Jayla's grades soared, not from the feeding of her intellect, but the nurturing of her soul.

Over the next year, Jayla stayed in touch with Mrs. Neidringhouse. Whether it was a school or home problem, she knew Mrs. Neidringhouse would answer the phone whenever she called. She was the mother Jayla always wanted—the mother she never had.

Meanwhile, Amarika's personality became more and more resentful, pickled from the bitterness of her circumstances. And the more Jayla talked about the perfect and wonderful and immaculate Mrs. Neidringhouse, the more Amarika despised the woman. Here Amarika was slaving away for a child who didn't appreciate her, who didn't like her, and who never thanked her. A softening child on the verge of being swallowed by the same world that chewed up Amarika and spit her out. There was no way she could just sit idly by and watch this happen.

So Amarika wrote a letter, signed it from Mrs. Neidringhouse, and slipped it under the door to their apartment. In that letter, Amarika poured out in ink all the vile backlogged in her heart. And after everything was written out, all the paragraphs of how disappointing and fat and stupid and worthless Jayla was, she added the most devastating blow, a demand to never hear from or see Jayla again. And then Amarika left for work, sickeningly excited to see Jayla broken by the weight of the words. Not simply for the sake of the hurt but for what she could build from the ashes of that ambush. For how she could carve a more appreciative daughter from the sharp edges of each letter. For how she could save Jayla by ruining her and reforming her in Amarika's own likeness. She would do everything in her power to prepare her daughter for the real world, whatever it took, however many times necessary, even if Jayla hated her in the end for it. Wasn't that what real love was, after all? For better or worse, to protect a loved one by making them impervious to harm, even if it took some hurt to get them there. To love them, not as merely a teacher, but as only a mother could. And Amarika was up for the challenge.

CHAPTER 1

RESIDUE OF A FORMER LIFE

Jayla Cadel's Apartment
July 2, 2022

Jayla tossed another three chalky tan pills into her mouth before chasing them down with a swig of tap water. It had been a little over fifteen minutes since the first tablet entered her empty stomach. She floated, welcoming the drowsy effects the drug gave her.

Lying on the bed, she gazed at the wallpaper, the peeling mess of picked-over wallpaper scabs from former tenants. Her eyes traveled to the week-old carnations perfuming the air around her with a sick sweetness that turned her stomach. They rivaled the more rancid velvet-textured violets delivered personally by the governor. The feel of his leathery cheek, hot with the sting of a fresh slap, still warmed the palm of her otherwise icy hand.

With effort, Jayla guzzled the rest of the water as the beginning stages of cottonmouth weighted her tongue. The back of her throat burned as she swallowed. She fumbled with the remote and found the volume button, pressing it until the television with its cracked screen blared full blast.

Regret mingled with the sticky sweat on her clammy brow. Inside, her intestines felt scrambled as the ache of emptiness, more terrible than any physical pain, nestled in for what promised to be a long sleep. Only sleep didn't come. Minutes seemed like weeks on the merciless mattress as Jayla fought against the current of abdominal pain, trying to get comfortable. Overly exhausted, her mind raced, unwilling to wholly accept the mantra she repeated since before she opened the tawny pill bottle.

Life is always going to be like this. Life is never going to get better. You're worthless. You're weak. You're a waste of breath. You're a waste of space. Once you go to sleep, do everyone a favor, and don't wake back up.

Insufficient to distract herself from her rambling thoughts, Jayla reached for her smartphone, lingering as she stared at the locked screen. The picture, though taken just a few weeks prior, revealed a version of herself that seemed alien to her now. In the image, she looked at peace, surrounded by the closest family she had ever known. Wedged between her best friends, she had an unmistakable glow as they fought to outdo one another with fun glamour poses.

Memories flooded her mind as hot tears welled in her eyes. Jayla reached over to the bedside table and exchanged her phone for the tiny bottle of circular blue promises. Swallowing the last of her prescription, she waited once more. The container tumbled out of her tingling grasp. By her estimation, she took enough capsules to erase the memory she was trying to evade and, if she had any control left in her life, this last dose would deliver her into long-eluded peace.

Jayla closed her eyes and listened to sounds around her. A car alarm ricocheted along the cracks and crevasses of the worn apartment complex outside. Low bass thuds caused the faux wood headboard behind her to rattle as a muffled baby cry worked its way through her ears, into her heart. Every few seconds a synthetic laugh from the sitcom next door mocked her sorrow at full volume. What always sounded like slamming doors echoed up and down the dingy hallway.

Embedded within these sounds was a punctuated vibration beckoning from her bedside table. With blurred vision, Jayla fumbled with her phone; pin-pricking sensations jabbed up and down her thin fingers. With her eyes at half-mast, she brought the screen within view, her movements growing more sluggish as the medicine permeated her system.

Focusing intently to counteract the drowsiness, Jayla saw she had a missed call. While the digits had not been recognized within her contact list, Jayla knew the number by heart. It was LifeLine Pregnancy Center where she once worked, where the screensaver of her and her sisters-in-uniform was taken. Where she would be at this very minute if not for the lies, the deception, and the manipulation she'd spouted.

A second call from the same number began to ring through. She managed to press the green button to answer the call but lost her grip on the vibrating phone, sending it tumbling to the floor. Jayla wanted to scream, but no sound would form.

A subdued voice came from the floor. "Hello? Jayla, it's Renee. Can you hear me?"

The room tilted and spun. As she twirled, she fell into herself. Her lungs strained for air.

"Renee," Jayla mouthed, unsure if the whimper of her voice originated in her thoughts or on her tongue. "Renee?"

It was there in the consuming darkness of her mind, drowning in the quicksand of desperation, Jayla came face-to-face with the reality she had been repressing. It was gnarled and unrelenting and stole into a memory now months passed. The memory of how she came to lose everything she loved, herself included. The unwanted residue of a former life.

CHAPTER 2

TWO BLUE LINES

LifeLine Pregancy Center
March 6, 2022

"For real?" Jayla said, shaking her head in disbelief.

Ahead of her, on the asphalt, the lines of her favorite parking spot had been repainted periwinkle with a matching handicap image and signpost to complete the ensemble.

"How many handicap ladies do we have getting pregnant?" she asked aloud, moving her 2003 Honda Accord to another spot.

Closing her door emphatically, Jayla huffed through the parking lot toward the LifeLine Pregnancy Center, navigating around a minefield of small potholes. *I guess this is penance for going to a Community College Job Fair*, she thought to herself, remembering how this had to be better than her only other offer that day, to wave at people while wearing a shiny green Statue of Liberty costume in front of the tax place on route 284.

The LifeLine Pregnancy Center was located at the outskirts of the city and was, itself, fairly nondescript, sporting certain earmarks suggesting it might have initially been built as a mini warehouse. After some basic cosmetic remodeling and retrofitting, the bland-colored stucco still sported the routed-out signage holes of past businesses, as though a capitalist shotgun blasted the entrance in search of bigger game many times before.

Pulling out her wireless earbuds, Jayla reached for the outdated copper latch and pulled. The door wouldn't budge.

"Every day with this," Jayla mumbled to herself as she flung her arms in view of the two camera bubbles hanging in the entryway. Ringing the bell in short, rather aggressive spurts, she heard a long buzz and pulled at the door a second time.

"What? You didn't see me out there?" Jayla barked at Brittany, the receptionist, as she entered.

"Coffee or Jesus?" the plump woman at the front desk inquired.

"What?" Jayla asked, stomping through the empty waiting room.

"Is it coffee you need more of? Or Jesus? Because honey, you need one of them."

Rolling her eyes, Jayla stood impatiently in front of an internal set of locked doors restricting access from the lobby to the rest of the building, until it let out a courteous buzz. Pulling the door handle, she entered a long beige hallway lined with Bible verses, pictures of mothers holding children, and large whiteboards filled with encouraging notes handwritten from one team member to another.

Rounding the corner, Jayla hurried into the supply room to clock in, knowing each second delayed translated into less money in her pocket.

"Hey, Jayla," a soft but firm voice called from the doorway. Jayla turned to see Renee, the center's director, standing with one foot straddling the room and the other hovering in the hall. "If you have a sec, can you come to my office?"

Jayla's already queasy stomach dropped to her knees. "Yeah, okay," she said, putting her purse into her designated cubby.

Following Renee felt a little like walking single-file at elementary school, but with the child leading the teacher. Despite her height, Renee's five-foot two-inch stature cast a giant shadow over Jayla as she personally greeted every employee and volunteer by name heading into the office at the rear of the building. As they entered the small, cramped space, Jayla's eyes connected with the large motivational plaque frosted with gold leaves and dried flowers that hung over the doorway, inscribed with a quote from someone named Roland Warren, which read, *Say hard things in a soft way.*

The faux leather seat sharply exhaled as Jayla sat, her body instinctively positioning itself for a brawl, as Jayla was always ready for a brawl. Renee took a seat in her oversized office chair, her straight black hair parting perfectly around her heart-shaped, tan face.

"Jayla, I want to start by telling you you're doing a great job in reception," Renee began, pulling down her hand-sewn face mask exposing a big smile, "Before you, I had never hired anyone from a job fair. Normally our staff comes from a supporter's referral and is well vetted from a church we know, but with Covid and all—but it's all good. We trust God." As if to motivate herself to believe the words she just spoke, she continued, "I'm sure you remember me sharing how, statistically, guests know in less than five minutes of being here whether they can let their guard down and be open to all the options of their pregnancy. So, what you do in front, even the little things, amount to a big impact on the women coming here. In many ways, you and Brittany are the face of our ministry."

Jayla allowed her shoulders to loosen a little at the foreign sound of a compliment, but her jaw remained clenched in anticipation of criticism packed between niceties.

"That having been said, I've noticed on your timesheet you've been coming to work progressively later each day. Normally, we allow a measure of flexibility with our staff, but as your employment with us has been for less than a month, I see a negative trend starting that, if it continues, will jeopardize your longevity with us. I don't want that. I know you don't want that, either. Jayla, I realize three days of work a week at minimum wage is not much, but we are working for a cause and not a check here at LifeLine Pregnancy Center. I hope you know that. You can make a difference here."

Renee paused to allow Jayla to vocalize her thoughts, but simmering silence was the only reply. Jayla sat, eyebrow arched, arms crossed, press-on nails tapping against her light-brown skin.

"Today, for example," Renee continued, "you arrived fifteen minutes late. You missed our daily time of prayer and devotion. That time is a very important part of what we do here."

"Well, if the parking spots were not all turned handicapped, maybe I would have got in on time—plus I had to go back for a mask. Why do we have to keep wearing these worthless masks? Hasn't it been proven they do nothing?" Jayla quipped in a sarcastic tone.

"None of our other employees seemed to have a problem with the special spot. And for the masks, we just don't want to do anything that could possibly harm our clients. If the client wears a mask, then we do; if not, we don't," Renee responded without flinching. "We actually discussed both of these issues in the last meeting we had."

"I don't remember that," Jayla said.

"You missed it because you were late," Renee replied, allowing the comment to linger in the air. "Jayla, I like you. I see a lot of potential with your involvement here. But if you allow this streak of tardiness to continue, you will rob yourself of a future with our ministry. Understand?"

"Understood," Jayla answered, biting her lower lip.

"Excellent. And in that case, it looks like we still have—" Renee paused to check the clock on her ancient desktop computer, "forty-five minutes until we are officially open. Let's make sure the reception area is ready for our guests."

When Jayla returned to the lobby, Brittany was bent over, sorting the magazines on the end tables to ensure the newest issue was on top. "Everything okay?" Brittany asked.

"Yeah, it was nothing," Jayla replied, guardedly.

"That's good. Hey, I got you something while you were gone," Brittany said with a mischievous smile. Then, walking over to the front desk, she pulled out a large steaming paper cup.

"I figured you'd like some coffee," Brittany chuckled.

"I will never say no to coffee," Jayla said, beginning to thaw.

After a few deep sips, Jayla joined her coworker in their morning routine. First, she began with setting out fresh snacks, juice boxes, and hand sanitizer. Then she restocked the never-ending, ever-growing, series of pamphlet racks mounted on the wall. On cue, the clock chimed, and Brittany unlocked the front door, flipping over the sign in the window to read *OPEN*. Jayla took her place behind the front desk, busying herself by pairing patient intake forms with clipboards, hoping she would appear too busy to take the first client of the day.

Within a few moments, a girl, around sixteen years old, entered the lobby. She was light-skinned with checkered acne smattering her forehead. Her eyes were arenas of competing emotion, looking at once relieved and terrified, youthful and worn.

"Good morning," Brittany greeted the young woman warmly.

The girl didn't reply other than with a winced half-smile, then, keeping her eyes glued to the floor, advanced toward Jayla.

"Hello," Jayla said with a grin to conceal her frustration in taking the first client of the day.

"Hi, I, umm—" the girl said hesitantly, shooting a glance to the door behind her as if she were considering bolting back into the safe anonymity of the parking lot. "I . . ."

"Would you like to talk to someone?" Jayla replied, trying to fill in the blanks.

The girl nodded her head, her blonde hair bouncing on her shoulders.

"Because you're pregnant?" Jayla inquired, trying to decide which intake form to grab.

Tears glazed over the girl's eyes as she slowly nodded her head before casting her countenance to the floor, looking as though the act of public admission made the truth more real.

"Okay, sweetie, have a seat, fill out our intake form, and we'll have one of our client advocates meet with you to discuss your options," Jayla said, sliding the clipboard over the counter.

The girl nervously took the forms and sat near the television to begin the entry process. As she filled out the forms, Jayla studied the guest, defaulting to the internal game she played with each new client.

High school cheerleader, she thought to herself. *No wait*, she reevaluated, *Marching band. One month along. Boyfriend doesn't know. And parents . . .*

As if rehearsed, the young woman pulled a ringing smartphone from her pocket. "Hello?" she whispered. "No the app must be wrong, I'm in class. Uh-huh, okay, Daddy."

Parents definitely don't know, concluded Jayla.

Jayla buzzed Brittany in the inner office area where she emerged shortly thereafter with Samantha, a client advocate, in tow. Samantha slowly made her way over to the guest. "Hello," she greeted with a slow Southern drawl. "I'm Samantha, one of the client advocates here. If you're ready, I'd love for us to discuss your options in one of our private counseling rooms, Miss . . ."

Alice—Allie—Anna, Jayla thought.

"Ashley," the fair-haired girl replied.

Knew it, thought Jayla, subduing a look of satisfaction.

"Well, Ashley, if you're ready," Samantha said, allowing her hand gesture to finish her sentence.

As the two strolled past the office area and into the counseling rooms, the front door opened hesitantly, and another bleary-eyed guest trickled in. It wasn't long before the morning was in full swing with guests coming and calling. It was a steady churn of varying faces, races, ages, swelling to a peak by noon. When Jayla's late lunch hour finally announced itself, she had personally dispersed multiple intake forms, some to teens sitting with their parents, a few moms who brought their kids with them, one lady who looked to be in her mid-forties, and a few women with loosely worn wedding rings.

"You ready for some lunch?" Brittany asked as the lobby gradually cleared.

"Well, I was going to eat leftovers, but they were messing my stomach up, so I threw them out," Jayla said while grimacing. "Don't worry, I'm not contagious or anything. I think I just ate something bad."

"Are you *late* for anything—other than work today? If I see a bunch of pregnancy test boxes in the staff bathroom trash, I'm gonna be telling Reverend Pastor Steve about it," Brittany laughingly quipped as she shuttled down the hallway, oblivious to the impact of her words.

Jayla stood and smoothed her blouse. "I am *not* pregnant," she mumbled between gritted teeth before stepping into the hallway. *So then take the test!* Jayla thought to herself.

The very idea of being pregnant made Jayla nauseous. In her head she thought about her queasiness; as she retraced the thought, she instinctually moved her hand over the tender bruise on her shoulder.

Later in the day as her shift was ending, Jayla walked over to the supply closet, preparing to clock out when she suddenly stopped, her fingers not entirely sure why. She glanced over to the back corner of the room at the bin of pregnancy tests and then looked around to see if she was truly alone. Seeing no one within sight, Jayla grabbed a few pregnancy tests, and, taking her purse from its cubby, shoved them inside. Then, composing herself, Jayla clocked out and walked briskly toward the front of the building, smiling at colleagues to mask her inner turmoil.

As she threaded through drive-time traffic back to her apartment, Jayla's thoughts weaved from topic to topic. She shuffled through songs on her smartphone, but no amount of distraction or volume was enough to uproot her mind from the idea planted earlier that afternoon.

Arriving at her complex, Jayla quickly latched the door to her apartment and rushed to the bathroom. She tore open the package and urinated onto the test strip. She waited in silence as the longest five minutes of her life slowly steamrolled over her. The wall clock took its own sweet leisurely time as she paced the tile floor, sporadically laughing to herself over how ridiculously she was acting. After several eternities passed, she picked up the test and squinted, her jaw slacked, her mind trying to process what she was seeing.

"For real?" Jayla said, shaking her head in disbelief.

Two blue lines.

CHAPTER 3

WHY ME, LORD?

Never before had Jayla been so doubtful of her vision or critical of her ability to distinguish between one blue line and two. But there they stood, twin harbingers, resilient against the arsenal of doubts she launched against them. Three positive tests back-to-back.

"Pregnant?" Jayla laughed to herself, "come on now." Instinctually, she found herself inside the small kitchen, reaching into an overhead cabinet for a small silver-rimmed glass. Pulling an ice-cold bottle of vodka from the freezer, she poured herself a generous amount.

"No, no, no, no," she muttered as she walked to her sofa, her mind working overtime. Jayla set the glass of alcohol on the coffee table. She stared at it as the condensation gently trickled down from the penetrating southwestern heat. Inclining forward she reached for the glass then hesitated. In her mind flashed the videos she saw at the clinic of babies born with alcohol-related disabilities. She thought of her own mother who drank herself into having a miscarriage. On the edge of her seat, Jayla was suddenly eight years old again, listening to her mother saying between gulps of paper-sack whiskey, "I'll drink it out of me. I'll drink it out of me."

Jayla rolled her eyes, fell back into the couch, and groaned. More than protesting the possibility of being pregnant, she refused to be anything even resembling her mother. Actually, being pregnant would be awful, but discovering herself in the image of her mother would be worse.

More than horizontal blue lines, these results appeared to Jayla as equal signs. This pregnancy equaled single motherhood and loneliness. These lines equaled spiraling backward into the poverty she was working so hard to claw her way out of. "I can't believe this happened to me," she sighed.

But this hadn't been her choice. Jayla felt again the bruise on her shoulder. Still tender to the touch despite the nurturing of time, she ran her fingers across it again and again, as though the more she felt it the more callused it would become. The deeper and harder she stroked over the bruise, her memory was heightened of that horrible night.

This pregnancy was not her choice. There was no choice in what happened to her, in what he did to her. The right of consent was one of the many things stripped from her that night and now, just as that initial freedom was obstructed, so too would all her subsequent freedoms for the next eighteen years and nine months.

He did this to me, but what does he get? Jayla thought to herself, her eyes darting to the mirror ahead. Nothing. Nothing happens to him. She did nothing wrong, yet she was expected to bear the punishment. A mandatory sentence for a crime she didn't commit, an unbelievable, unbearable price for an experience she never wanted in the first place. *Nothing happens to him*, she thought, *so why should it happen to me?*

Rage frothed over all Jayla's thoughts. She had no choice in what happened to her, but she could choose what to do about it now. Of all the things she couldn't control, she could control this outcome. Of all the wrongs she couldn't reverse, she could at least do right by herself this once.

I gotta take care of me, Jayla thought. *I'm gonna get it taken care of.*

CHAPTER 4

ACCIDENTAL APPLICATION

Through the night Jayla tossed and turned on her rickety bed. When her alarm sounded at six in the morning, it was met with a relieved apprehension, as if the ringside bell of a boxing match signaled the start of the final round.

Grabbing her phone, Jayla activated her maps app and found two abortion providers nearby. The closest was only twenty minutes away, depending on traffic, but the business wouldn't be open for a few more hours. *I should probably call Renee*, she thought to herself, briefly entertaining the idea. Immediately a dread came over her.

Getting up from bed, Jayla walked toward the kitchen, stopping by the bathroom along the way. When she reached the kitchen, she opened the upper half of her pantry, where twelve tuna cans and eight instant macaroni and cheese boxes sat neatly in rows, alongside a half loaf of hardening white bread and a jar of generic peanut butter. Everything was pulled toward the front and bunched together, leaving a foot of empty space in the rear, a uniform wall of silver and brown sealing off the barrenness within. It is not just art that imitates life.

Can't wait till payday, she thought, imagining for a moment the delicious snacks she would soon be stocking. Some fresh and decadent hors d'oeuvres, some salty-sweet guilty pleasures, all her favorites, especially the ones *he* would never let her eat.

Jayla could practically taste the delights on her tongue when she remembered her appointment. All that food money, gone, quicker than it could hit her bank account. *Oh well, better a few hundred dollars now than who knows how much later.* For good measure, Jayla glanced at the lower half of the pantry, which was filled with empty packaged boxes of her favorite things. Pausing from her search, she stooped and rearranged the cartons until any evidence of poverty was gone.

As expected, the options in Jayla's barely functioning refrigerator weren't much better. There were half empty condiments, a few yogurts, some questionable microwave bacon strips, and freshly bought fizzy waters she had strewn about the shelves in a way that made the little she had look like much. As her eyes panned from top to bottom, she made eye contact with a quarter-eaten can of his expired potted meat. Instantly the tangy, rancid smell hit her nostrils and overwhelmed her senses. Her stomach reeled and clenched as bile rose in her throat.

Jayla threw herself over the sink and vomited. Wiping her lips with the kitchen rag, she turned on the faucet, first rinsing out her mouth, then spraying down the metal basin. The smell from her open refrigerator sucker-punched her again, sending her gagging and retching back into the sink, her sense of smell inordinately heightened from the pregnancy.

Plugging her nose, Jayla took the can with her index finger and thumb, touching it as little as possible, as she hurried to the large window in her living room. Prying it open, she threw the gelatinous meat through a rip in the screen. Jayla slammed the window closed, muttering, "I am not going to miss this," she said, wishing her hypersensitivity to smells and accompanying morning queasiness away.

I really should call Renee, Jayla considered again, checking the clock. Instead, she decided to take a nice, long shower.

With towels wrapped around her torso and hair, Jayla stared into her closet. It was surprisingly difficult for her to pick the exact manner of dress to fit the unique occasion. Nothing too uncomfortable or tight-fitting, but nothing so loungey she would look unkempt, she settled on wearing her favorite long gray comfy pants and a flowing painted T-shirt.

As Jayla left her apartment, she grabbed her earbuds, scrolling through songs as she gingerly walked down the crumbling brick stairs to the ground level. Climbing into her decaying Honda, she pulled up the map app, noticing her scheduled work time was rapidly approaching.

Reluctantly, Jayla scrolled through her phone contact list until she found Renee's personal cell phone number. Her long press-on nail hovered over the call option with bated breath, weighing and second-guessing her decision. She knew she couldn't put it off any longer.

After three rings, Jayla heard a familiar peppy, barely Hispanic accent from the other end, "LifeLine. We are women helping women, Renee speaking, how may I help you?"

"Renee," Jayla replied, clearing her throat, "This is Jayla."

"Jayla! Hello! How are we looking on time this morning?"

"That's what I wanted to talk to you about," Jayla began, forcing a shallow cough, "I'm actually not feeling too good and wanted to let you know I won't be able to come in today. Maybe I do have the flu or something?"

There was a brief silence on the other line, uncomfortable enough Jayla felt prompted to continue after a dramatic sniffle. "Yeah, you know, I don't want to get anybody sick, especially since we got all those pregnant ladies and I'm supposed to be the face of the ministry and all," she said, unable to miss an opportunity to passive-aggressively quote her boss back to her.

"I see," the response slowly trickled in. "And how many hours will you be needing?"

"All day," Jayla said without inflection.

"All day—alright. Well, feel better, and we'll get someone to cover for you."

"Okay," Jayla coughed, "I will."

"Oh, and Jayla, why don't you come in a few minutes early on Wednesday so we can chat," Renee added, her voice accompanied by the crinkling of papers.

"Okay," Jayla replied meekly and disconnected. *She doesn't know my life*, she thought to herself as she started her car.

Maneuvering the winding desert roads in unusual stop-and-go traffic, Jayla's nerves ramped with each passing mile. *I'm a victim, not a villain*, she repeated to herself in defense against mounting reservations and doubts. *This isn't wrong. What happened was wrong, and this is undoing that wrong. This is right.*

Jayla saw her destination come into view. There it was, a recently updated tall brick building. Its new and modern appearance stood in stark contrast from the older storefronts in the adjoining strip mall. Their neighbors were a hodgepodge of business ventures, a Cash Advance, a Water Purification company, a real estate service, and another Discount Liquors. A large *U.I.* logo was the only advertisement shown on the clinic, and the address above the door, 13 Madeleine Street. They didn't need to advertise their services, as everyone knew the diversity of the services they provided for women of the area, sex-education, condoms, breast exams, and, well, everyone knows what else.

As she pulled into the plaza, Jayla's heart began to race. Although she was convinced what she was doing was the best choice for her, the thought of anyone she knew seeing her in this place gave her twinges of guilt and jostled nerves. The parking lot was pretty much empty. Aside from a homeless man pushing a shopping cart and some parking lot maintenance workers, the coast was clear.

Jayla took in a deep breath. With a final smoothing of her shirt, her head down and her eyes focused, she made her way to the Unplanned Incorporated entrance. A laminated paper sign read: MASK WEARING IS PREFERRED WHILE INSIDE BUILDING. Jayla hoped she had one in her purse.

Reaching for the door, she gave a tug. But the door didn't open. Instead of sliding into the clinic undetected, she hit the closed door with her foot with such undeterred force it shook the industrial grate that had been rolled up to the ceiling, its metallic clatter shattering the quiet of the corridor.

Jayla was stunned. She felt her cheeks warming with embarrassment as she gave the door handle another unsuccessful pull. Glancing from left to right, she saw the maintenance workers halted in their golf cart, staring at the source of the commotion. Jayla turned forward and peered into the glass, the seconds feeling like hours.

Finally, there was movement inside the lobby as a female employee slowly broke away from a conversation to attend to the entrance. A wave of relief rushed over Jayla as she smoothed over her outfit again, unfurling wrinkle and nerve. Suddenly, Jayla caught a reflection in the window of a person behind her, staring at her.

"Jay?" she heard a raspy, weathered voice say.

Jayla clenched her jaw, debating for a moment whether or not to admit her identity.

"Jay? Is that you?" the voice said again, sounding more like the seething of a smokestack than a woman.

Mortified, Jayla slowly turned. There were only three people in her life who called her by that nickname; two of them were deceased, and the other was as good as dead to her.

"Amarika," Jayla said contemptuously.

"Amarika?" the small neon-clad woman mimicked, pulling her mask down around her neck. "All this time and that's how you're gonna talk to me?" she scoffed.

"What do you want?" Jayla asked impatiently as the door behind her gradually unlocked.

"What do I want? Shoot, I just want to see how my baby's doing, since she's too good to stop by and help her ma around the house."

"Well, now you see me, so—" Jayla said as the door opened behind her with a jingle.

"Woah, woah, woah, Jay. What you doin' here?" Amarika asked as Jayla turned her back. The woman holding the door open gave an awkward smile and then let it close to remove herself from the conversation.

"What?" Jayla responded, not because she didn't hear the question, but because she needed time to think.

"Ooowee," Amarika snickered condescendingly. "You got something to take care of, Jay?" she asked, tugging Jayla's shirt up.

Jayla swiped her mother's hand away. "First of all," she snapped, waving a finger in the air. "You do not touch me. Second, what I'm doing here is none of your—"

"You was so high and mighty," Amarika cackled. "Always too good for us, talking about how you were not gonna be like me. And here you are. Like ma like child, ain't that right?"

"I'm never gonna be like you," Jayla exclaimed through clenched teeth. "And I'm not here for that."

"Oh, okay. Then why you here, Jay?" Amarika asked sarcastically. "You grabbin' some of those free condoms?"

"I'm here, uh," began Jayla still unsure where the sentence was heading, "I'm here—for a job."

Amarika appeared shocked. "A job?" she asked with an intonation as surprised as Jayla felt on the inside. "Wearing that?"

"That's right, I'm here for a job. So you can take all that attitude and assumption and go back to cleaning up trash," Jayla said, spitting her now flavorless gum onto the asphalt.

With that, Jayla spun, feeling self-satisfied. She pulled the door open and strutted inside. To her delight, no one else was in the lobby as she entered, so she was able to make her way directly to the front desk without any waiting.

"Good morning," Jayla said to the blonde behind the reception counter, the same one who unlocked the door for her.

"Good morning," the young woman said cheerfully. "How may I help you?"

"I'm here for—" Jayla paused, hearing a jingle from the front door.

Turning back, Jayla saw her mother limping into the entrance. "Don't mind me. I'm just looking for trash," Amarika smirked.

Jayla postured herself again toward the front desk, seething, humiliated, anxious, and on the verge of tears. "I am here for an application," she said, her voice quivering as she switched her speaking manner from street to sweet.

"Applications for employment can be found online," the employee replied, probably thinking herself to be helpful.

Sensing Amarika still behind her, Jayla persisted. "I would like to fill it out here if it's all the same," she replied, hoping the unwanted guest would leave halfway into the paperwork. "I wanted to be here in person to make the best impression."

"Oh, okay. Is there any position in particular you're wanting to apply for?"

"Just whatever is available is fine."

"Right, okay," the receptionist replied. Then, rolling her chair to a filing cabinet, the woman rifled through a nest of manilla folders before returning to Jayla. "Here you go," she said with a smile as she handed the application over to Jayla on a dark blue clipboard. "This is for our Tuesday and Thursday Patient Recovery Service position. It's the only opening we have right now. Just fill this out and bring it back up, and I'll make sure one of our managers gets it."

Jayla nodded and took the paperwork back to a seat strategically facing away from where Amarika hovered. The application was the easiest Jayla had ever completed, not because of the content or the questionnaire, but because she didn't care what she wrote down. As her hand moved along the page, her mind searched for the best next step. If she waited and came back, perhaps she would miss another run-in with Amarika. But the later it got, the more cars would be on the road, the more clients in the plaza, the higher the likelihood of someone else seeing and recognizing her. What else could she do?

Without clear direction, Jayla returned to the reception area and turned in the application. "How late are you open?" she asked in a hushed voice. "You know, if I get the position, would I have to work nights?" she clarified in the event her voice carried further than intended.

"Umm, no. No nights. We close at 5:00 p.m. to the public, but we stick around a little after to get everything ready for the next day."

"Five o'clock. Okay. Thanks," Jayla responded, weighing her options.

"Best of luck!" the employee chimed as Jayla turned to leave. Amarika was still at the entrance with a look of Lady Liberty, pleasantly opening the door for the huddled masses trickling inside, yearning to breathe free. Jayla brushed past her as she exited without any words exchanged.

"Jay! Jay!" Jayla heard a hurried voice behind her call as she neared her car.

Jayla pivoted with arms crossed and an arched eyebrow.

"You really were here for a job, huh, Jay?" Amarika said. "I hope you get it. Maybe then you can afford to take your ma out to lunch."

Jayla rolled her eyes and got into her car, locking the door.

"You remember what I said now, Jay," Amarika's muffled voice seeped through the window like carbon monoxide as Jayla hurried to activate her earbuds. "Come help around the house sometime. I'm where I've always been."

And always will be, thought Jayla, as she sped away.

CHAPTER 5

FUNNY THING ABOUT THE MIND

Jayla drove aimlessly for a few blocks, enraged, violated, and vulnerable. For reasons she couldn't explain, she kept checking the rearview mirror, half expecting to see the snaggle-toothed grin of her past wrapped in a wreath of smoke. The more she replayed the conversation, the more the car reeked with nicotine-stained memories of her mother, the harder it became to breathe.

Leaving the main road, Jayla veered into a parking lot and slammed on the brakes. She turned the air conditioning as high as it could go as heat pulsated across her body. Slowly she felt a single tear trickle down her cheek, followed by another. She slammed her hands into the top of the steering wheel over and over, screaming without noise, as tears streamed into expanding stains on her blouse.

Her thoughts were hampered by shame and rage. *Can't go back. I can't see her there again like that,* Jayla thought in snippets of cohesiveness.

At that moment, her stomach entered the conversation with a sharp growl, reminding her of her nonexistent breakfast as well as her current need to eat for two. *I ain't got time for this,* Jayla said to herself. The fizzy tingle of acid flecked in her throat, each wave climbing higher as the odd combination of hunger and nausea swam laps around her belly. Her head felt like it was on a swivel as she became drunk with stress.

The jaw-clenching, hands-trembling, heart-fluttering, skin-tingling kind of stress Jayla knew, if unattended, would lead to another panic attack.

Okay, okay . . . she took a deep breath and closed her eyes, attempting to deescalate her emotions. She settled her focus away from her racing thoughts and onto her immediate physical senses. Jayla felt the lukewarm air kissing against her sweat-dribbled face, neck, and arms. She listened to the continuous, truncated rhythm of the air conditioning as her car spluttered and stammered from being parked for too long. She cleared her mind with deep breaths and long exhalations, just like her grandmother taught her to do when she was young.

Softly and soothingly, Jayla found her voice and began to shakily speak out loud. "First, I'll eat."

With the air conditioning still on full blast, Jayla drove to the nearest drive-thru. Finding the least objectionable option, Jayla paid for her steaming bag of regret and parked under the struggling shade of a rare Live Oak, its lanky graffitied arms casting a random net of shade. It was there, with a dollar breakfast biscuit in one hand and her smartphone in the other, she began to search the city for alternative locations.

Swiping up and down on her screen, it seemed her choices were limited. There was the location she just visited, with another U.I. in Albuquerque, and a third in Phoenix. She scrolled down further, hoping to reveal less geographically extreme options, but her search was in vain as all she viewed were pregnancy centers whose Google Ad budgets worked to drive pregnant women to their doors for counseling—counseling for an option she was well aware of, but rejecting.

How am I gonna drive all the way up there and back after a procedure? she wondered to herself between soggy bites of breakfast. Jayla knew with how much the procedure would be, she wouldn't be able to afford a taxi or Uber all the way there and back. *Maybe they would give me that pill . . . I don't know?*

Jayla's thumb toggled back and forth between locations as she evaluated her dilemma with sighs. As her finger hovered over her screen, her phone began to ring. The incoming call was identified simply as *Unplanned.* Jayla's head tilted in confused curiosity. *How did they know about this?* she wondered. Like most people, she had experienced instances of talking about a product just to find it magically advertised on a website she was browsing, but this seemed to be taking it to the extreme. Against her better judgment, Jayla tapped to answer the phone.

"Hello?" she asked.

"Good morning. Is this Jayla?" responded a deep female voice, husky with experience and authority.

"It is," Jayla answered hesitantly.

"Jayla, this is Lynn Maddox with Unplanned, Inc. You filled out an application for us this morning."

"Yes, ma'am," she said as if trying to extract details from a long-faded dream.

"I know this is short notice and very unorthodox—very, very unorthodox. But would you possibly be available for an interview later this afternoon?"

"An interview?" asked Jayla, stunned.

"I know, I know. Typically, this kind of thing takes days, if not weeks to process. And believe you me, I'm just as surprised as you are I'm calling," Lynn chuckled to herself in what seemed to Jayla as an uncharacteristically frazzled tone. "But, as it stands, one of our employees was, uh, let go this morning and, as lady luck would have it, *you* are the only application we have physically on file. Kudos for coming to us in person and dropping it off. I admire that kind of initiative."

"Thank you?" Jayla said, still not sure what was happening.

"How does three o'clock this afternoon sound for an interview?"

Jayla thought for a moment. "Will, will those parking lot cleaners still be there, then?" she asked, trying to mask her timidity. There was a pause from the other end of the phone before Jayla decided to clarify, Lynn's silence as commanding as her speaking. "One of the cleaners—"

"The black one?"

"*Excuse me?*" inquired Jayla, almost offended.

"Was it the old black one? The parking lot cleaner?"

"Yes."

"Freakin', that woman. She scares off more people than the protesters. With that attitude and that horrid smell! Don't you worry, she won't be here anymore. I've had enough." Lynn regained her professionalism and said, "It is two days a week, Tuesdays and Thursdays, and it pays twenty-five dollars an hour and even comes with some great benefits after you have been here for six months. So, Jayla, see you at three?"

"Yes, yes, I'll be there and thank you." Jayla could barely get the words out as a new plan formed in her head. In seconds she knew what she would do. It couldn't be that hard, could it? And twenty-five dollars an hour was twice what she was making at LifeLine.

CHAPTER 6

REVERSAL SOUNDS BETTER

"Do the interview, get the job, pocket some of those expensive abortion pills," Jayla said, rehearsing the plan to herself again as the Unplanned, Inc. building came into view. The closer she got, the more adamant she became regarding her final decision. *I could even do some reconnaissance for the pregnancy center.* At least that is what she told herself to improve her peace of mind, and it would make a really nice extra part-time paycheck in the process. It wasn't a perfect or even entirely reasonable next step. Still, for Jayla, it was the best move out of the emotional stalemate she stalled into.

Despite having hours to prepare, Jayla somehow still arrived late for her interview. Stepping out of her vehicle, she felt like a different woman than the one who entered the parking lot that morning. Gone was the baggy, flowing T-shirt and gray comfy pants, along with the meekness and insecurity accompanying them. Instead, like a purple-bloused phoenix with press-on talons, she rose from the ashes of her Accord.

Entering the building, Jayla was relieved the clerk behind the counter was different than the one she engaged with earlier that day. Rather than the scrawny blonde woman who assisted her that morning, there was a man, toned and handsome, who looked like he spent more time perfecting his hair than she had.

That's a nice bonus, Jayla thought to herself as she locked eyes with the man. "Hi," she grinned, indulging the nervous habit of smoothing over her outfit.

"Hey," the man replied smoothly, his biceps rippling as he reached for a blue plastic clipboard.

"I'm here for an interview with Lynn," Jayla said.

"You must be Jayla," he said. "Please have a seat, and she will be with you momentarily."

"Jayla?" an authoritative voice called from the doorway leading beyond the reception area.

Jayla recognized Lynn the moment she saw her. A tall, pale brunette, with an expensive gray business suit and a power stance expressive of the hunger of ambition and the satisfaction of already having reached the top of her field.

Lynn didn't wait for Jayla to verbalize her identity before strutting over, her arm extended for a hearty handshake. "It's a pleasure to meet you," Lynn said as perfect brown ringlets bounced against her shoulder pads.

"It's a pleasure to be here," Jayla responded with a smile as she stood. As the two shook hands, Lynn gave Jayla a quick once-over as she cupped her left hand on top of their grip in a quiet move of dominance.

"I'm so relieved you decided to come back, especially given the terribly rushed timing of it all."

"Of course," Jayla replied, her hand lost in the constricting grasp of her hostess. "It's no trouble."

"Right. Let's continue this conversation in my office," Lynn suggested, her curls twirling as she turned.

As she followed in Lynn's footsteps, Jayla shot a glance back over to the chiseled receptionist who winked at her as she passed. They walked down brightly colored hallways, and past cozy patient rooms fitted with the finest medical equipment the government had to offer. As they moved deeper into the interior, Jayla internally logged the building's layout, evaluating which offices were most likely to harbor the prescription-only pills she needed.

Turning a final corner, the duo reached a glass wall corner office with the name *Maddox* etched in black onto a gold nameplate. Lynn held the door open for Jayla to enter.

"Have a seat, Jayla," Lynn commanded as Jayla walked toward an enormous glass desk with the most expensive office chair she had ever seen. Obediently, she sat on one of the twin leather love seats perched symmetrically at either end of the desk, while admiring the wall ahead of her upon which hung three awards for every missing family photo. "Can I get you something to drink?"

"No, thank you," Jayla said, tightening her jaw to keep her teeth from chattering. For a woman who grew up without air conditioning and kept her apartment at a balmy eighty degrees, this was the closest to frozen she had ever been.

"So, Jayla," Lynn began, rigid in her office chair as though it were a throne. "When you think of Unplanned, Inc., what comes to mind?"

Jayla thought for a moment. "Umm, well . . . you provide abortions—"

"I'm going to stop you there," interrupted Lynn. "The answer you just gave is the perfect, quintessential response we get from victims of right-wing brainwashing. Which is just about everyone watching Newsmax these days; are they crazy or what? But what they don't want you to know is we believe in the fundamental right of each individual, throughout the world, to manage his or her fertility, regardless the individual's income, marital status, race, ethnicity, sexual orientation, age, national origin, or residence. We also provide other services like breast exams at many of our offices. That saves women's lives."

"Oh," replied Jayla, feeling a little overwhelmed at the amount of information. "That's awesome."

"It *is* awesome, Jayla, and so much more than just helping young girls have a life and a future through our pregnancy prevention and reversal programs."

"Absolutely. So much more," answered Jayla, wary of answering another impromptu question, while wondering what a "reversal program" was.

"What those religious bigots and political elephant extremists on the right don't want you to know is *we* are an unparalleled force for good for the women in our community. We provide contraceptives for women who can't afford them. We provide breast cancer screenings and examinations, as well as pre-cancer screenings. Do you know how many lives we save with that alone? You sure don't see any church groups doing that. We offer emotional support to local women without judgment. And we fight firmly for the rights of these women, unlike those pseudo-medical Crisis Pregnancy Centers. Our free contraceptive program prevents ten times more unplanned pregnancies than those religious abstinence-only so-called pregnancy centers could ever hope to. If we stopped promoting and providing condoms, they would see what the baby count could be."

Jayla cringed, her stomach clenching at the mention of her workplace.

"But, yes, to your point, we are the leading pregnancy reversal organization in the country."

"Pregnancy reversal?" Jayla asked.

"Abortions," Lynn clarified. "But don't you just love the way *pregnancy reversal* sounds? It has a certain poetic ring; plus, it fits our narrative better, don't you think? Abortion is a controversial word these days, but pregnancy reversal is so wonderfully generic and peaceful."

"It really does," Jayla bluffed as she silently wrung the warmth out of her hands.

Lynn nodded with an intense stare before whipping out Jayla's application from an upper drawer. "Now, it says here you are working on your associate's degree in nursing assistance, but you have completed your Certified Nursing Assistance certification. Is the certification current?"

"Yes. And I intend to continue school to become a registered nurse."

"Right, and have you had much real-world experience in using this degree?"

"Some," Jayla replied, resisting a shiver.

"Care to elaborate?"

"I worked at a nursing home for a bit, but that wasn't really for me."

"Heritage Park?" Lynn inquired as she fact-checked the résumé.

"That's right."

"What about it made you feel like it wasn't for you?"

Jayla quietly sighed as she mentally revisited the worst moments of her former workplace. "I helped clean and change the guests, get them bathed and make sure they took their pills, but sometimes, if they had Alzheimer's or something, they would get pretty aggressive and—"

"So it wasn't the care-taking side of the job that made you leave?" Lynn interrupted.

"No," replied Jayla. "No, I'm used to taking care of people. I just don't like gettin' my hair pulled out tryin' to do it."

"I see. Correct me if I'm wrong, but it sounds like, if an opportunity were to open itself for a position in the field of patient care, you would be interested?"

"Yeah, I'd be interested."

"The reason I ask is because the position we are looking to fill is in our recovery room. Surprisingly, it would be very similar to your former job at Heritage, but without the hair-pulling or unruly patients. We're looking for someone to care for the women who have undergone a surgical pregnancy reversal. This associate will need to have experience in a related field, which you do, and know how to give the brave women who come here the best post-op experience possible."

"I can do that," said Jayla confidently, thrilled to think she would most likely have access to the same resources she would need for her own—reversal.

"I believe you can! And you meet all the requirements for the job. But, just so we're clear, this is a part-time job. We would only need you to work Tuesdays and Thursdays. Just those two days a week. It pays twenty-five dollars an hour and comes without any insurance. You would have to get that yourself. I will not promise you any more hours than those at this point, and don't come asking. Well, if *Roe* is overturned, we will need to be open 24-7 for a while, we'll be slammed, but don't think about that. That will never happen."

"Okay . . ." Jayla said, her voice trailing off as she calculated the impact sixteen hours times twenty-five dollars would have on her life. This was more than twice what she was making at the pregnancy center. If she could pull this off, she would be out of that rat hole apartment and have a new car by the end of the year, and of course, her own reversal.

"So you need somebody working the recovery room. That's it?"

"That's it," Lynn said as she leaned back in her leather chair. "That, as well as the perk of opening the door for future positions within the company as they arise, which is great, because we like to promote internally whenever we can. And then there's also the plus of having the fee waived for a yearly mammogram."

Jayla wanted to inquire about the abortion pills, but it seemed a little too early to ask about those.

Lynn paused for a moment as if caught off guard, before continuing. "Of course, abortion services are not free for our workers unless they qualify for the government-funded programs. Unfortunately, I think our twenty-five dollars an hour starting salary, even at part-time would disqualify just about any of our paid staff. Just grab some free taxpayer-funded contraceptives and stay out of the chair," Lynn laughed.

As Jayla sat leaning forward to appear fully engaged, her knees were bobbing and knocking. And yet, despite all this, she was relieved for the first time since discovering her pregnancy.

"Do you want the gig?" Lynn asked coolly.

"Without a doubt," Jayla said with a smile. "How soon can I meet the doctors? How soon can I start?"

"Just one doctor, Molech is his name, and he is, ah, well, we all get used to him. Tomorrow is covered, I'll see you Thursday at 8 a.m."

CHAPTER 7

SPINNING PLATES

The LifeLine Pregnancy Center building looked incredibly cheap and shabby to Jayla the day after visiting Unplanned, Inc. The pockmarks on the exterior of the building seemed more accentuated, the paint looked faded and crumbly. Checking in, she made her way to the New Mothers Support Area, which doubled as a makeshift conference room for the team's pre-service huddle. She strolled through the interior like an inspector, revisiting her workplace with fresh eyes.

Though kept pretty clean, in Jayla's eyes, flaws gushed from every corner of the office space. As Renee took prayer requests, rejoiced over the soon-to-be-reached Total Center Makeover Fund, and addressed interdepartmental etiquette, Jayla tapped her pen against her notepad creating a new blemish with each strike. Colloquial posters with edges curling toward the center hung over gray refurbished couches. A few slightly water-damaged ceiling tiles jumped out this morning. Even her coworkers looked outdated by comparison, as gray-haired retired volunteers replaced college-aged receptionists.

As her coworkers took notes and gave input, Jayla couldn't help but think how the place would change if she were in charge. For a moment, she pictured herself in a glass office of her own, sitting in a custom-made oversized chair, being served rather than serving others for the first time in her life. Naturally, she began to compare her vision to Renee's current cramped office with the bowing wood paneling and musty hand-me-down furniture.

The more she thought about it, the more she could smell that dank, soured stench of used couches and chairs. Jayla's thoughts were interrupted suddenly by an acidic, bile reminder of pregnancy rising in her throat. "Excuse me," she blurted out as she rushed to the bathroom, breaking into the heartfelt prayer Renee had begun to lead. Launching herself into the bathroom, Jayla hurled into the sink, seconds away from not reaching her destination in time. With her forehead on the faucet and vomit on her chin, Jayla was simultaneously disgusted, fatigued, embarrassed, and angry. *That's it*, she thought, *I'm gonna do it. I'm going to get this taken care of the first chance I get.*

Turning on the faucet, she cupped her hand, bringing tepid water to her mouth before sloshing and spitting it out again. She rinsed the evidence of her sickness down the drain and splashed some water on her face for good measure.

Coming out into the hallway, Jayla saw her coworkers busy about their business as Renee stood by the breakfast bar, stirring a steaming cup of tea while staring in the direction of the bathroom. Before she even heard the words, Jayla knew what would come next.

"Jayla, can you come with me to my office for a minute?" Renee asked in her tender yet tenacious accent.

"Sure," replied Jayla, *But it never takes a minute with you.*

With a curt smile, Renee blew on her tea and started toward her office. Jayla followed after, imperceptibly wiping her teeth with her tongue, observing—of all the times she had been called into Renee's office—she had never been waited on to walk *beside* her.

Entering the confined office, Jayla plopped into the outdated faux leather chair and waited passively as Renee took her seat, readying herself to say whatever lie was required.

"Jayla—I don't know how to ask it without just coming out and asking it." Renee continued, "Are you pregnant?"

Jayla froze. Her heart raced as her stomach twisted and squirmed within her. Internally she was a wreck, but her face never flinched.

"What?" replied Jayla with a defensive bark.

"Are you pregnant?" Renee asked a second time, calmly, unaffected by Jayla's tone.

"Of course not. I'm not pregnant. What's wrong with you?" Jayla asserted, the rush of adrenaline underscoring her nausea. For her, it wasn't a matter of truth or falsehood, but of honor or shame, partly because she was considering terminating the pregnancy, but also because of the violent way the baby was created.

"Someone on staff suggested it was a possibility," answered Renee as she folded her hands, "which, as you know, would be against our company policy and in violation of your contract with us."

"Who said that?" inquired Jayla with fire in her breath, thinking, *So rape victims can't work here?* but she couldn't speak it without giving up the secret.

"I'm not at liberty to say."

"Oh, so I guess anyone can just say anything about anybody here, and you just believe it, huh? Even in a court, you can face your accuser," Jayla said scowling, a cocktail of bottled emotions spilling over.

Renee was patient to respond, shooting instead a sharp look to Jayla, appearing to censor herself. "You know that's not how it is, Jayla. And I'm sure if you were the one who—"

"Lied," Jayla interrupted.

"Voiced their concerns," Renee continued, unfazed, "you would want to be anonymous as well."

Jayla quietly let the words sink in as her brain sifted through a backlog of her coworkers to determine which one would have speculated to management over a possible pregnancy. Then it hit her.

"It was Brittany, wasn't it?" she asked, less as a question and more as an accusation. According to what Jayla pieced together, today was the first day she was back at work since finding out, and she hadn't told anyone. With no weight gain, no hormonal breakdown, no accidental slip-ups, no one knew to suspect anything, except for Brittany. Brittany, who first suggested the possibility of a pregnancy. Brittany, who was only too happy to pressure Jayla into taking a pregnancy test.

"We are not discussing a 'who' right now. We are discussing a 'what,' and that 'what' is whether or not you are, in fact, pregnant."

"Well, in fact, I am not," Jayla glowered, noting a curious absence of denial over Brittany's involvement.

"Wonderful," Renee responded with the kind of smile that heaped coals onto Jayla's already fuming head. "I'm glad to get that behind us," she said as she slid paperwork across the desk toward Jayla. "This is a copy of your contract," stated Renee. "I want you to take time today to re-read it, particularly the last paragraph on page two."

"Why?"

"It's the clause on sex outside of marriage. I want to make sure we're all on the same page about what is and is not appropriate while working in this ministry."

"Are you making everybody else read this clause too? Or just me?" Jayla asked wryly.

"Alright," Renee replied after muttering something in Spanish, her patience evidently wearing thin. It was the same tone Jayla noticed many people had when on the other side of an argument with her, a vocal cue she came to relish. "Read it, don't read it, it's up to you. As long as you know sex outside of marriage is a violation of your contract with us, and any associate found in violation of their contract will be recommended for termination."

Jayla opened her mouth to respond when she remembered she needed to discuss her schedule with Renee, one that would assure she would not be needed on Tuesdays and Thursdays. She was hoping to catch her boss at the right time to make the request, a moment when she was feeling gracious and good-humored, a moment Jayla had pretty soundly destroyed in their first interaction of the day.

Knowing the best way to move forward was to backpedal, Jayla shifted in her seat and instantly changed her demeanor from defensive to respectful with a dash of reluctance. "You're right. I know you're just trying to do what's best for me, and for the Center," Jayla said, fishing for the right combination of words Renee needed to hear. "It's not on you that somebody thought I was pregnant—and putting that on you was—I just grew up surrounded by wrong accusations. That is so wrong," Jayla paused, choking on the word, "wrong."

Renee pursed her lips, which meant Jayla was on the right track. Intuitively, Jayla picked up the contract and her eyes floated across the page, picking up on keywords and phrases. Turning the paper over, she saw the concluding paragraph Renee referenced regarding premarital sex. *Who wrote this, some mad virgin or something? This is 2022. People survived the loneliness of Covid by finding someone to get close to.* She made affirmation noises to indicate she was soaking everything in, and that's when she saw it.

Sitting there, hovering above the pregnancy paragraph, was a sub-heading that read *"Noncompete Clause.* No associate working for the pregnancy center shall directly or indirectly engage with a business that is competitive with the Company's current line of business, primarily, but not limited to, Abortion Clinics."

Jayla let her eyes linger on that last phrase before continuing, any associate found in violation of this stipulation will render this contract void and will be terminated immediately.

Suddenly Jayla grasped the gravity of her choice to work for Unplanned, Inc. Up until this point, the opportunity seemed like an easy way to earn an extra paycheck and secure a free abortion. But now, revisiting her decision through the stark, fine print filter of her contract, she saw the beginnings of the tightrope she was committing to walk for the foreseeable future. A duplicitous balancing act with no financial safety net to catch her if she fell.

"Something the matter?" Renee asked.

Jayla's eyes darted away from the page as she folded the papers onto her lap, reacting as if she had been caught for a crime that hadn't yet happened. "No—we're all good," she said, pondering her first precarious step on her way off the platform. "By the way—I need to put in a request for a schedule change."

"More time off?" Renee inquired with a slight scowl, turning to her computer, punching the thick black keyboard with enough force to puncture through the jostling plastic letters.

"Yeah, I need to know that I will not be scheduled on Tuesday and Thursday. When I started, it was supposed to be Monday, Wednesday, and Friday, but lately you have been adding an occasional Tuesday or Thursday," Jayla replied, her mind already scouring for a follow-up lie legitimate enough for Renee to accept and favorable enough for her to endorse.

"Full days for both?" Renee asked, turning away from the flickering screen. "That's going to really put us in a bind, I thought you wanted extra hours. Brittany has been doing a great job, but we're hurting when both of you aren't here."

"Actually," Jayla said, gently treading further onto the tightrope, "I need every Tuesday and Thursday off for a—"

"That's a big ask, Jayla," Renee interrupted, sighing as she rubbed her fingers soothingly where the bridge of her nose met her eyes. "Why do you need it off?"

"I need it because . . ." Jayla's mind rummaged the bottom of her brain for the best untruth she could think of, "you know—I'm just . . ." Jayla looked around the room, her synapses firing full blast as she searched for some clue into what Renee viewed as valuable. And that's when she saw it. There was the framed photo on her desk of Renee, roughly the same age as she was now, in a green cap and gown with a sea of relatives of all ages, shapes, and sizes. *Family*, Jayla thought, *and education.*

"I'm going back to school," answered Jayla confidently. Immediately she could see the surprise on Renee's face.

"Going back to school?" Renee asked with fascination.

Jayla nodded her head. "I know it will be hard, but I think it's worth it. Education's important, you know?"

"Oh, absolutely," Renee said, sounding the right mixture of being impressed and intrigued. "So you need Tuesdays and Thursdays to go to class?"

"Yeah, I mean, I figured it would be smart to get all the classes on the same day," Jayla answered, "that way I can still come to work. And I know that if I don't do my homework right after my classes, it will take me twice as long to do it. I just don't remember all the material any other way. You remember how it was back in college? You are just living on Ramen noodles and hanging on for future life."

Renee nodded her head, her eyes scanning back and forth like she did when she checked inventory or evaluated donations the Center received.

Not enough, Jayla thought to herself, looking for a kicker to secure her request. "It's okay if you can't change the schedule. Lots of folks told me not to even try to go back to school anyways—born poor—die poor."

A sudden look of determination and compassion swept over Renee's face. "People told me the same thing. They told me I was too old, too far out of school to go back and get a degree."

"Mmm, yes, girl. Same here," Jayla bemoaned convincingly.

"But you know what? I proved them wrong. It was hard, but I proved them wrong, and you will prove them wrong as well!" said Renee enthusiastically.

"You think so?" replied Jayla, milking Renee's emotions.

"I know so," Renee said with a confident smile. "If I could do it, you can too! Don't let anyone tell you otherwise."

"Right on! So, you'll approve the change?"

Renee's smile dissipated as she turned her attention back to her old box-style computer. "Well," she exhaled after a long pause, "you wouldn't be able to keep your position at Reception."

"That's okay!" replied Jayla, only regretting the possibility of not fully repaying Brittany for her betrayal if she left the area.

"You know what? We will make this work," Renee said, rediscovering her smile. "I'll find you a position somewhere. Create one, if I have to."

"Perfect," Jayla grinned, allowing herself to feel relief.

"What school is it?" asked Renee unexpectedly.

"What was that?" asked Jayla, not because she hadn't heard the question, but because she hadn't constructed that part of the lie yet.

"Which school are you enrolled in?"

"Oh, uh . . . just community college right now," Jayla answered, not even remembering the first name of the school.

"Huh—didn't you do your associate degree there?"

"Yeah, that's why I'm going back—to get my bachelor's," responded Jayla, starting to feel queasy again from the heightened tension only she felt.

"I didn't know they did a four-year degree," commented Renee, crossing her arms.

Jayla felt a flash of heat as those nine simple words threatened to derail her plans, ripping up the roots of her alibi. *How much does she know?* Jayla wondered to herself. Was this a test? An opportunity to come clean before things got out of hand? Has Renee known the whole time this was a lie? And would coming clean help at this point, or would just it cast doubt on her other assertions, like not being pregnant?

"Well, they offer a bunch of classes that can transfer forward," replied Jayla, doubling down. "They may be starting a full four-year program real soon, the advisor lady told me. No one else in my family has ever gotten their bachelor's," Jayla blurted, hoping to redirect Renee's attention with a familial lure.

"Mine either. I was the first," responded Renee with an air of camaraderie. "Tell me, what would you think about becoming a client advocate?"

I think that's a terrible idea, is what Jayla wanted to say, but found herself instead speaking only affirmations of the prospect. "Amazing. That would be great!"

Renee's demeanor brightened as she authoritatively clacked a few strokes on her keyboard. "Starting tomorrow, you will begin shadowing Samantha as a client advocate."

"But tomorrow's Thursday . . ." Jayla winced, hesitant to disrupt the positive traction of her request.

"Right. We will make it Friday then," Renee said as she input the new information into the system. "I'll let Brittany know you'll be leaving her. She's going to be sad to see you go!"

"Don't worry," said Jayla, masking a smirk, "I'll have a heart-to-heart with her before I leave."

As Jayla hastily made her way out the door, Renee momentarily retreated, "I really hate that you're missing Tuesday and Thursday. We always have special prayer those mornings, as those are the days the abortions are performed at Unplanned. Has anyone told you all about them?"

CHAPTER 8

JUST LUNCH

Jayla popped her knuckles as she stomped through the hall, just as her ma taught her to do before a fight. Whether the reason for the act was medicinal, superstitious, or compulsory, she wasn't sure. Still, after years of indulging the habit, the action signaled to the rest of her body an altercation was imminent. The beating of her pulse in her ears drowned out all other sounds. Her brow was furrowed, her muscles tense.

She felt like she was heading to her first fight. She was five years old in the alley behind The Bricks, the apartment complex she grew up in. The memory revealed itself in bursts. The glistening patchwork of broken bottles, the combined reek of stagnant swill and urine, the tattooed shirtless man flashing a toothless grin as he flicked the beaded bottoms of her braid, filled her memory. After all these years, she could still remember her ma standing behind her, not to hold her back from the fight, but to ensure she couldn't go anywhere but into the loosely woven circle of residents clamoring for a cure for their boredom. Here she was, a grown adult, somehow transported back to a time she hated the most, yet it drove her.

Rounding the corner, Jayla could see the door leading to the waiting area propped open. Brittany was bending to restock the snacks. Jayla rolled up her sleeves as she approached, not entirely sure of what she would do when she reached Brittany. Her thoughts—crazy and scattered as they were—focused on what she would say to Brittany and what she would do if it escalated into a true fight.

"Jayla? Jayla? Could you not hear me?" Renee asked, catching her breath, "I've been chasing you down the hall."

Jayla's body froze at the unexpected sight of Renee, the fear of being exposed as instigating rather than self-defending filled her mind.

"Oh, sorry. I was just thinking about something," Jayla apologized with a huff of insincerity.

"I was curious if you had any lunch plans for today?" Renee inquired, giving a wink and thumbs-up to Brittany, who stood behind Jayla.

"Me?" inquired Jayla, pausing to look back at Brittany as she tried to calm herself.

"Yes, you," Renee chuckled.

"No, I don't have any plans. Why?"

"In that case, would you be interested in having lunch with me?"

What's she playing at? Jayla wondered as she struggled to rein in her desire to fight. Attempting to look casual, she breathed in through her nostrils and out through her mouth to slow her heartbeat, but it wasn't working.

"Lunch would be on me, of course," Renee added, sensing Jayla's hesitation.

Ain't nothing really free, Jayla mused to herself as she began focusing her attention less on her own de-escalation and more on Renee's motives behind the spontaneous lunch offer. And then a concern surfaced in her mind undoing all her self-soothing. *What if she knows I'm lying?* Jayla thought.

Shifting her weight, Jayla placed her hands on her hips, her eyes automatically racing to the exit. "Okay," she replied uneasily.

I gotta get out of here, she thought. Maybe she could repay Brittany a different way. Perhaps, given enough time, an opportunity for betrayal or career sabotage would present itself, and she could dispense her revenge in a less incriminating manner. But the longer Renee lingered, the larger the realization loomed this was neither the time nor the method of retribution.

"Excellent! Let's do noon. You can ride with me," encouraged Renee, placing a friendly hand on Jayla's arm.

The touch was light and affectionate, the kind of airy gesture that happened on a hundred different occasions when someone referred to Jayla as Kayla by mistake. But this time, the brush against her skin was the friction of a match being struck, triggering Jayla. If she didn't leave now, there was no telling what she would do.

Without a word Jayla bolted to the front door, balling her fists at her side. Uneasy step after uneasy step, she raced to the exit as life around her began to block itself out.

"Sounds like somebody gets to have the talk today," she heard Brittany jest in muffled tones behind her. Through the door, beams of light cascaded down on Jayla, their brightness unnaturally brilliant within the frame of her heightened emotions. She walked to the rear of the building where the dumpster and air-conditioning unit lay in repose.

Finding some empty diaper boxes near the rear exit, she began stomping their seams, thrashing them. She bent low, snatching one from the ground, ripping it apart with her hands until flecks of cardboard filled the air like a miniature snow flurry. *Slam, crunch, pop, scrape*; with each strike she could feel her endorphins flaring as a steadily climaxing high replaced her inner rage. Then, when enough boxes were destroyed, she panted, giving a few final kicks until exhaustion slowed her temper to a halt. The burn of lactic acid in her joints mirrored the vomit-graded rawness of her throat as she doubled over to catch her breath.

"Everything alright, miss?" Jayla heard a graveled Southern voice call to her.

Shocked, she popped up and looked around. Two dingy men were standing on the opposite end of the dumpster, straddling the property line where the pregnancy center meets Dale's Pawn & Gun at its rear. A cloud of tobacco haze lazily fogged out of their open mouths as they alternately took long drags off their nubbed, unfiltered cigarettes. One was tall and skinny, the other was stout with a camouflage cap; both wore identical beige uniforms.

"Yeah," Jayla answered, catching her breath, then with a nod of her head toward the pregnancy center continued, "They got me breaking down these boxes."

"So you work at that Baby Center. That's some real good work y'all are doing in there, miss," said the stout one looking serious as he spit onto the dirt, narrowly missing his gangly beard. "Real good work."

Jayla nodded, her mouth attempting to impersonate a smile. The uneasiness of being alone with two strange men worried her as she covertly scanned the corners of the building for security cameras.

"The lives you save. Y'all the real deal over there," the big man continued with a long Texas-sounding drawl.

"You must know my missus—she works there too. Name's Darla," the thinner man said. Before Jayla could respond, he started a rant: "Up to me, I'd close every one of those government-sponsored slaughterhouses they got across our state. Across the country!"

The smoke from their cigarettes coalesced with the rancid stench of the dumpster, making Jayla take a few steps backward, enlarging the safety space between them. "I—gotta be getting back," she said semi-apologetically, moving toward the building without turning away from the men.

"Be seeing you, little lady," the stout one said as the two men continued their smoke break.

As Jayla yanked open the Lifeline door, a deluge of cold, manufactured air rushed over her, which she hoped would air out the stink of her backlot encounter clinging to her.

"You okay, Jayla?" Brittany asked, buzzing Jayla through the inner door. "You just up and left. You look like you've seen a ghost. Renee got worried when you left so fast, but I told her you probably forgot something in the car. What was it? Your phone? Your purse?"

Jayla straightened and smoothed over her outfit. Then, regaining her composure, she lifted her chin snidely and walked past her coworker without any acknowledgment or answer.

"Well, while you were gone, Renee told me you're leaving me to become a client advocate. That's exciting! Y'all talk about anything else this morning?" Brittany asked enthusiastically, allowing ample time for Jayla's response. But none came.

Instead, Jayla smacked a stack of colored pamphlets onto the table as she pulled a bag of rubber bands from a desk drawer, then slammed it shut. Out of the corner of her eye, she saw Brittany open her mouth and close it several times without ever speaking. Instead, the larger woman hummed something and shook her head in amusement as she rolled her chair to the counter.

"That's how it is, huh?" Brittany asked eventually.

Jayla sucked her teeth loudly in reply, her eyes never flickering off the page.

With that gesture, the tone of the shift was set. Morning clients arrived and departed with Jayla overly energetic and helpful to each one, amplifying the silence of her disfavor when she and Brittany were alone. And slowly, in the constant churning of clients, the clock bloated, one minute expanding into the next, steadily swelling into the afternoon.

CHAPTER 9

CHIPS AND SALSA

"Hey there, Jayla! Ready for lunch?" a peppy voice called out behind her in concert with the jingle of keys.

Jayla was anything but ready. In fact, she had almost forgotten all about their lunchtime rendezvous. She would have preferred a catnap in her car, the exhaustion of propping up her pointed silence wearing her thin.

Jayla swiveled in her chair, stomaching the bitterness of her disappointment. "Can't wait," she said, smiling through tight lips. Then she rose, ironed her outfit with the palm of her hand, and walked out following Renee, whose keys cheerfully jangled in her hand. Wondering which vehicle would be her boss's, it was clear to Jayla when she saw a cream-colored, decade-old minivan.

"This is us," Renee said as she pressed a button on her key remote. With a few beeps, the van unlocked, and Jayla climbed into the passenger seat.

"Do you have kids?" Jayla asked as she buckled her seatbelt, noting the cleanliness of this vehicle compared with her own.

"No, no," Renee laughed as she turned over the ignition, the small woman swallowed up by the large interior of her van. "I bought this because I needed to have a way to pick up girls who called in asking for a ride to come here. A lot of them needed medical check-ups and didn't have anyone who supported them beyond getting an abortion. We used a ride-sharing company until one of the drivers got a little fresh with a young mother. So I traded in my car for the minivan. Problem solved. But I would sure love to find a service we could trust. When we provide the service, we are liable for anything that happens on the drive."

"What was your car before this?" asked Jayla.

"A midnight blue little BMW convertible."

Jayla stared at Renee, not knowing if this was the most selfless or stupid exchange she ever heard. "You traded a BMW convertible for *this?*"

Renee looked at Jayla and, seeing her expression, laughed. "Oh, don't look at me like that. It was worth the trade. This way I can pick up a guest and her kids, if she has any, or her partner, or even take multiple mothers to our clinic at once." And then, with a small sigh, she added, "But on days like today, I really do miss that convertible top."

Jayla pictured herself for a moment in a BMW convertible, with the top folded back and the wind teasing her hair. She imagined the looks she would get from people, especially the ones she knew, seeing her so visibly successful. "I couldn't do it," Jayla said, recentering the tepid stream of air-conditioning on her face.

"Yes, a lot fewer guys check me out at red lights, that's for sure," Renee said with a wink.

A few stoplights later, the ladies pulled into the parking lot of a Mexican restaurant. "Have you been here before?" Renee asked as she checked her makeup in the rearview mirror.

"No," Jayla answered, wondering how well spicy food would sit on her stomach. The bustling mariachi music from the outdoor speakers was already seeping in through the windows.

"Oh, you'll love it. It's fantastic! And the great thing is, the owners support our ministry, and their food is so good! I try to bring people here every chance I get, and they give me a 20 percent discount."

Walking inside, the savory smell of piping hot tortilla chips splashed against Jayla's nose as the aroma of freshly cut jalapeños, onion, and bell pepper hung in the air with fragrances so colorful they might as well have been the vibrant fiesta garlands on the walls. Jayla felt her insides gurgle. Looking around at the meals on the tables she passed, she was unsure now if the rumble in her stomach was hunger or nausea.

Naturally, Renee greeted all the waiters and waitresses she encountered on their way to an empty table, calling each by name and pausing to ask a few about personal matters recounted on a prior visit. Then, finding an empty corner booth in the rear, the two ladies took a seat.

Immediately a waiter came over to their table with salty corn chips and a chunky, deep ruby salsa. Renee took no time ordering, never once cross-checking the menu. But Jayla took her time perusing her options. She wanted to get a big meal, a huge meal—a meal big enough she could use it to fend off a few hunger pangs over the coming days.

Her eyes hopped from picture to picture, price to price, as she did when she was younger and her kindly grandparents took her out for dinner. At that time, with so little food at home, storing up for herself became a survival feature she assumed all children experienced growing up. Unable to keep the food in the refrigerator without her ma finding it and eating it herself, she would hide it in her room, unaware of the effects of food sitting for hours in their window-only cooled apartment. She would bury it under dirty clothes, exhuming a bit of the souring food at a time, until the leftovers stank and bugs swarmed. Even now, though she had food in her apartment, she ranked the entrees based on how many projected portions she could parcel out from it and into a doggy bag.

"You must have quite the appetite," Renee said, impressed as the waiter left to put in their order. Jayla lifted her eyebrows and nodded, purposefully not returning her gaze.

"So, Jayla, can I ask you a question?" Renee said, scooping salsa onto a chip the size of her tiny hand. "Is there possibly a different reason why you're wanting to lessen your hours with us?"

Jayla's eyes darted down to the coffee-colored table. *I knew she knew something,* she thought, her mind auto-populating with the details of her lie. "Other than going back to school?" she asked innocently.

"Yes, other than school. Anything else you feel might be factoring into it?"

Jayla moved her eyes from left to right in mimic of thought. "No, nothing comes to mind."

"Let me phrase it another way. Are there any emotional factors that might be causing you to want to be around our ministry less?"

"Like what?" asked Jayla. Like a swan taking to water, her visible half above the table was calm and collected while her hands, under the surface, were fidgeting, with her leg bobbing up and down anxiously.

"Gracias," Renee said to the waiter bringing drinks. Then, taking a swig of sweet tea, she continued. "Emotional factors like stress, or anxiety, or—depression? It could be any number of things. Covid has affected so many people in so many ways."

"Anxiety?" Jayla asked, grabbing a handful of chips and submerging them into the salsa bowl before cramming them into her mouth. "About what?"

"You know, I've been at the pregnancy center for six years now. And do you know what I've learned? There's a trend among our employees that starts to show itself a few weeks into the job. Something happens to them—a type of emotional fatigue—that ultimately results in their stepping back from serving with us. There have been cases where the fatigue has been based on things going on outside of work, but mostly, mainly, it's the wear and tear of participating in our ministry. We save 80 percent of the babies, but we still mourn the 20 percent we lose. Some people can't take that."

Jayla nodded her head. *Maybe she doesn't know after all*, she thought.

"People don't often think about it before they come and work for us, but we deal with life and death every single day. There aren't a whole lot of jobs out there with that kind of strain, that gravity to it. Our nurses doing the ultrasounds meet every baby who comes through our doors. They see their little hands and feet, hear their heartbeats, sometimes even look into their eyes, knowing that in a matter of days, this gift of God might be terminated. Knowing the baby they just saw doesn't exist anymore—not in the way we think about it anyway, and that no one in the world will ever have met that child but them—wears on anyone. And then that scenario plays all over again with a new baby. And again. And again. Things like that, you can't train for. You can coach and encourage, but you can't ever prepare someone for that. Not really. And then there's the lying."

Jayla's ears perked up as she crammed another fistful of chips into her mouth.

"I'm sure you've seen what I mean," Renee continued. "To sacrifice day and night, to serve these brave women, to have all the medical experience and equipment, just to be told you're a fraud and your clinic is fake. We have spent over a hundred thousand dollars training ultrasound nurses over the years. Real education and real money! Just because these abortion clinics have more money—government money at that, and political connections—they think they can spread rumors to scare these already afraid new mothers away from getting help. That, on top of the spiritual warfare of dealing with forces of good and evil—it can be too much for a person to handle."

Jayla nodded in both understanding and relief.

"And so here you are, Jayla, you're working so hard against this darkness, and you're facing life and death every day. All the while, you're being berated and lied about for your efforts, and that's what I'm talking about. That's when stress and anxiety, and depression step in. It all usually starts coming to the surface around the one-month mark, which is about how long you've been with our ministry. So, after you left my office this morning, a red flag came up in my mind. I said to myself, *Here's a young, bright woman, been here a few weeks with us, exhibiting early signs of anxiety and irritability, wanting to cut back her hours*, and it all just seemed interconnected, you know?"

Renee stopped talking to munch on a few tortilla chips, and Jayla got the feeling she was being waited on to chime into the conversation, so she responded, "I don't know—I think that could be a part of it," trying to be non-committal in her response.

"It's very, very understandable. Tell me, Jayla, what have you been feeling?" Renee asked, visibly concerned.

Jayla blinked a few times, sipping soda through her straw, as she thought about the best response. "Just so much, you know?"

"Of course. Of course. And you can share with me anything. I'm here for you, Jayla. Only what you're comfortable with sharing, of course."

"It's just a lot," Jayla fabricated. "A lot of emotions, for sure. And, like you said, it's just hard to take, sometimes."

"Jayla, the last thing you'll ever hear me tell you is you shouldn't go back to school. It's a good thing to do for your future and will enrich you as a person. All I ask is you don't use school as an escape. Don't use it as an excuse to leave. Promise me, if you ever start to feel this emotional fatigue again—the stress, depression, anxiety—you'll come and talk to me. Don't make any rash actions, don't quit just because things have gotten hard, come talk to me. I have a list of great counselors in the city I can refer you to, and even help pay for, if necessary. Just don't quit. Our work in this city is too important to let any wounded soldier die."

Jayla nodded, feeling Renee's compassionate stare boring into her soul. Thankfully Jayla spotted their waiter coming to the rescue with enough food to feed five. "Food's here," she chirped, pushing her straw wrapper and used napkins to the side to make room for her meal.

The aroma of the sizzling chipotle chicken, tangy pico de gallo, fire-roasted corn, and fried jalapeños made her nose tingle and her mouth water. Grabbing her fork, she scooped up a huge helping and shoveled it into her mouth, when Renee interjected, "I'll bless the meal, or would you like to do it?"

"You can," she mumbled through a mouthful of cilantro rice.

Renee folded her hands, leaned forward, and closed her eyes. "Father, thank You for this meal. Thank You for Jayla and her role in our ministry. Please bless her as she goes back to school. Please bless the young mothers who come into our ministry today and bless the food. Amen."

Almost before the prayer was over, Jayla was into her second bite. Her fork plowed across the plate like a miser raking money into his wallet, every scrap accounted for. A minute or two passed in silence like this when Jayla got the overwhelming impression Renee was going to ply the dead air with questions unless she beat her to the punch.

"What did you do before LifeLine?" Jayla asked, scrambling for a conversation starter.

"I finished my degree while I worked with my family. They did this and that—mostly home repair stuff like fixing drywall or pulling up carpet. That kind of thing."

Jayla was surprised. She couldn't picture those tiny hands ripping glue from a foundation any more than she could imagine Renee in the WNBA. "You got a BMW doing that?" she joked.

"No, that was the benefit of making good investments. I never made much working for my family, but, then again, I never did it for the money."

"Mmm, pulling carpet is hard work," Jayla said with a shake of her head.

Renee nodded. "It sure is. But it makes you feel like you've earned your sleep at the end of the day, you know? Unfortunately, being paid next to nothing for a job became the norm. My parents are immigrants, and people used to take advantage of us and skimp on payments. Because we made so little, my family relied on one another to pitch in so we could take on more jobs and even out. Which is why they weren't pleased when I told them I was going to college."

Jayla remembered the photo she saw on Renee's desk earlier. The sea of relatives piled around her on her graduation day, each smile bigger than the one before. "They weren't happy about it?"

"Not when I told them, no. Certainly not when they took fewer jobs because of it, despite my working between classes and weekends. To see my family so disappointed was hard, and there were a couple times I almost quit. I love my family and would do anything for them, but I just couldn't let go of my dream. Slowly they came around. But I don't think it was until they saw me in my cap and gown, as the first one in my family to ever do that, they understood. My dad even, who was the most disappointed one of them all, was trying to talk me into getting my master's degree before I told him about my desire to take the job working at the New Life Rescue Center. That is what we called it when I first came there."

"I bet you're glad to not be pulling carpet no more," Jayla said, cracking a smile Renee returned in full.

CHAPTER 10

NEW FRAN

Jayla pulled into the parking lot of Unplanned, Inc., anxious and expectant. She paused the music playing through her earbuds and scrolled through her contact list for Lynn's number, which she saved under the name *Unplanned Lynn*.

"Lynn Maddox speaking," a gruff voice growled after a few rings.

"Hey, this is Jayla. I'm here," she said, pausing to recheck her breath to see if this morning's latest vomit session left its mark.

"Jayla! Oh, that's perfect. Just perfect. I'll be right out," Lynn said and without waiting for a response, disconnected the call.

Jayla got out of her vehicle with her brown sack lunch under her arm and a lurch in her stomach, the smell of day-old guacamole, ranchero beans, and chipotle chicken sashaying out of the paper seams. She smoothed over her blouse—a nervous habit that began in kindergarten. In her household where doing laundry was parsed as frequently as encouragement, Jayla was always out of clean uniforms. She would watch as her white short-sleeve shirts became yellowed and then gradually brown with age and spills and dandruff and dirt. Her sleeves and neckline stretched and sagged, crusted with white residue from countless nose wipes when her allergies were especially bad. And it was one particular day, as she was mindlessly brushing the crumbs off her two-week-old uniform, she realized something.

The more she brushed, the more the crumbs cracked and broke smaller and smaller until they were crushed into a thousand minuscule pieces that could hardly be seen. Likewise, the spills, when wiped all over, turned little deep bruises of stain into larger slight tinges of shade. Jayla found that with enough smearing and dusting and brushing, she could just nearly absorb or scatter any blemish out of others' casual view, though she could never quite deceive herself.

Standing there in the wake of her reflection in the tinted glass of the office building, she was that little girl brushing off her unwashed blouse the invisible grime of a lifetime, hoping with each flattening a swath of who she was, who she feared she would always be, would fall off like scales.

"There she is," Jayla heard a sing-song tone trill from out of her periphery. "First day here and the first one to arrive. I wish I had ten more like that," Lynn said with a demeanor in stark contrast with the way she sounded over the phone.

"Are you a morning person, Lynn?" asked Jayla as she walked through the door Lynn was holding open for her.

"Ah, no," Lynn replied, "But I have a friend who helps me with that. And that friend is called Café Cubano," she chortled, referring to her favorite espresso drink. "I'm simply a mess without it," Lynn said, standing in her Gabriela Hearst pantsuit with each tootsie roll ringette painstakingly in place. Then, peeking down into Jayla's arms, she chimed, "Sack lunch, huh? That looks fun. I remember those days. If only I had that kind of time on my hands now."

"No, I didn't make it. It's from that Mexican El Nortino's."

"Oh, I love them. I positively love them. You know, if you mention that you're one of ours, they'll give you a 15 percent discount."

"Mmm," Jayla grunted, remembering how convinced Renee was of their support of the pregnancy center because of their discount.

"Oh yeah. They're very supportive of what we do here. If you cut them, they'd bleed blue. Good people. Which is not always the way the colors run in the Hispanic and Latino communities on issues of repro-ductive choice."

Jayla wordlessly nodded her head.

"Well," Lynn sighed, "while we still have time, why don't we get this bad boy in the fridge, and then I'll show you around the Recovery Room?"

The Recovery Room was white with a long periwinkle accent wall playing host to seven dark leather recliners. Between each recliner sat a fashionable wastebasket and a small white cart topped with tissues. As the two walked in, Lynn handed Jayla a pink set of scrubs that had been strewn over a recliner, encasing it like a festive body bag.

"From now on, I'll need you to wear these," Lynn said as she swiped her finger over the chair top, inspecting for dust.

"Okay. How many employees are there?"

"Back here, none. It's just you," Lynn replied, as she scrolled through her phone before putting it into her pocket. "But we have two who work front of the house, a handful of operating room nurses, and, of course, Dr. Molech, who I've arranged for you to meet after your shift. He absolutely insists on it."

"And how many patients do you think I'll have back here today?" Jayla asked, peeking back toward the seven empty chairs.

"Today, hmm, hard to say. Not every woman who comes to our clinic is here for a pregnancy reversal. I'd say less than twenty."

"So, when the patients come in today, do I go and get them?"

"Yes, when the nurse has finished with the patient, she'll call you over the intercom. Depending on how that patient is doing, you might need to use one of the wheelchairs we keep in the utility closet. And always make sure to give them your undivided attention," Lynn said, her face twisted with agitation as she reached back into her pocket. "And definitely be on the lookout for patients who need help getting in and out of their chairs. We don't want anyone falling, especially after all they've been through, and we certainly don't need the litigation or the press."

Lynn's face then became serious, and, with the phone lighting up her face like she was about to tell a campfire ghost story, she stared at Jayla. "I can't remember if I mentioned this before, but you always need to make sure these women have someone else giving them a ride home. They cannot ever—I repeat—cannot ever—under any circumstances—drive themselves home. All we need is somebody leaving here and getting into an accident to start a conservative feeding frenzy. And believe me, a wolfpack is nothing compared to what *Fox & Friends* can do. Do that, and you'll be fired. Just kidding! But seriously, it cannot happen."

"So, help them into their seats, wait for their ride to come, then what?"

"So many questions," Lynn said passive-aggressively before putting her phone down and clopping over to the corner of the room where she pulled out a white rectangular cart with pink drawers and quizzed Jayla saying, "Do you know what this is?"

"It's a medical supply cart like we used over at Heritage Park."

"Right. Good. So once your patient is in her seat, you'll take her vitals. There's this really nice pulse oximeter in the top drawer you can use for that. Expect her blood pressure to be a little off, but if anything is really off, go get a nurse. Otherwise, we don't necessarily need the numbers documented, just checked. Once that's been done, if the patient is cognizant enough, give her a baggie with birth control and self-care information from the second drawer and, if she asks any questions you can't answer, go get a nurse. And then just hang out with her until her ride arrives. Some ladies might start to get sick, which is totally understandable. Make sure you help them get to the wastebasket in time and hold their hair whenever they get sick. Trust me, when the puke hits the fan, you will be glad you're wearing scrubs. And if anyone gets too sick, feel free to—"

"Get a nurse?" Jayla asked, finishing Lynn's sentence to her instructor's delight. "That's a lot to keep an eye on."

"Well, it is, and it isn't. I'm betting it takes you all of an hour before you have a routine worked out. And Jayla, honestly, at the end of the day, I just want you to make our client's stay here comfortable. Like Obama used to say, 'Do unto others as you would have them do unto you.'"

"Okay . . ." Jayla said, feeling unsure of herself, trying to keep her mind from getting tangled in the endless possibilities of how her first shift would go.

"I'll be in my office if you need anything!" Lynn advised as she turned around and began to walk away. "Waters and juice bottles are in the fridge, and there are animal crackers in the closet if the ladies need them," she called out behind her, "We have an open-door policy, so feel free to come on in any time—any time that my door is open, that is."

Jayla nodded and kept nodding even after the door closed behind Lynn. Immediately, she walked over to the cart and opened each bin, acquainting herself the contents. There was something familiar about it. Something in the scent of plastic and sterilization swabs brought her back to the middle school clinic, conjuring up old memories long buried. Like how on some mornings, she would purposefully pick a fight to create an alternative alibi for the bruises she received the night before. Or how she would sometimes feign lightheadedness to get an extra snack when she knew it could potentially be her last meal of the day.

Shaking off her memories and pulling the pink scrubs over her clothing, Jayla walked the room's length, ensuring everything she needed was within reach. Then, smoothing the pink scrubs with her nervous fingers, she pulled out a black-gripped wheelchair and waited for her first guest to arrive. Then after what seemed like a long time, a thin, blonde-haired girl in blue scrubs came through the door.

"Oh, I'm sorry," the young woman bristled, startled, "I didn't know anyone was back here."

It only took Jayla a moment to recognize her as the same receptionist who helped her earlier that week with her application. Back then, she was more focused on avoiding her past than engaging with the present, but now she was able to truly take in her new coworker.

"My bad," Jayla apologized, "I'm just waiting like Lynn told me."

"Oh, wait, I remember you!" the blonde said in throaty astonishment. "From the other day, are you the new Fran, then?"

"Fran?"

"Right, sorry. The new Recovery Room person?"

"Oh, yeah. Lynn's got me doing that for now. Jayla is my name."

"Hailey," the blonde giggled awkwardly as she gestured to herself. "So, New Fran, have you given in to temptation and raided the snacks yet?"

"I haven't. I didn't think I was supposed to?"

Hailey giggled and then, grabbing a package of animal crackers from the bin, stated in a very factual tone, "I like you, New Fran. You and I are destined to be great friends. I just know it. Make sure to save me a seat at lunch!" In a flash of blue, Hailey was gone.

Twenty minutes after opening, the round white intercom sounded with a static, disembodied voice. "Patient ready for recovery at OR one," it said before silence again draped over the room. Standing and smoothing her scrubs, Jayla took a deep breath and rolled the clunky wheelchair through the door.

Maneuvering through the brightly colored hallway, Jayla arrived at Operating Room one, where a middle-aged nurse with pecan skin and bright blue scrubs was waiting for her.

"Who are you? Where's Fran?" the nurse asked from outside the doorframe, peering on either side of Jayla as if she expected Fran to pop out at any moment.

"I'm Jayla."

"Shamice Jackson. Now that we're on a first-name basis, where's Fran?"

"I'm not too sure. I'm her replacement."

Shamice sighed frustratedly. "You spend all that time going and getting someone just how you like them, and then they just go and quit on you," she mumbled to herself. "Well, Kayla, welcome."

"Jayla."

"This one in here is still out of it from all the anesthesia we had to give her," Shamice continued, steamrolling over Jayla's correction, "so I'll take one side, and you take the other, and we'll walk her to the chair. Make sure you grab her at the elbows and not at the hands, or else she's gonna collapse. Okay?"

"Okay," Jayla responded as she started to walk away from the wheelchair.

"No, we're gonna need that old grocery cart in there," Shamice interjected impatiently, "you bring that with you."

Silently, Jayla maneuvered the wheelchair, inching it forward, squeezing the color out of the grips in her frustration. How often had she done this same rigmarole at Heritage Park? Enough times it was committed to muscle memory as much as breathing and blinking. Silently she berated herself for the incompetent way her nerves and indecision made her appear.

"Make sure you lock those wheels in place when you get in there, or this thing will shoot backward faster than you can say *lawsuit, lawsuit, lawsuit.*"

Jayla nodded and slowly maneuvered the wheelchair through the narrow entry, careful not to knock a notch out of either the doorframe or Shamice Jackson's ankle. Then, squeezing around the corner, Jayla's eyes lifted and she saw her.

The woman was thin, looking to be in her late thirties, with feathery blond wisps of hair. A white gold necklace with an askew cross pendant swung across the top of her purple blouse, her neck craning down with it as if inside that cross was the weight of her entire world. Clutching at the purse sitting on her lap, with big green eyes glazed with thick, gluey tears, she sat motionless, crinkled, and shriveled. Undoubtedly the wrapper of the woman who came through the doors of the clinic that morning.

"Honey," Shamice called to the woman, over-enunciating each syllable. "This here is Kayla. She's gonna help take care of you 'til your ride gets here." Then, turning to Jayla, she mouthed, "*elbows.*"

I know, Jayla bemoaned internally. Gripping the woman at the crease of her arm, Jayla and Shamice half balanced, half dragged her to the wheelchair. *Just another patient*, Jayla thought to herself as she reached within herself for enough strength to own the moment. *Like I've done it a thousand times.*

Backing out of the room, Jayla pushed the wheelchair through the hall, unsure as to whether she should make petty conversation or silently absorb the pop music coming out of the overhead speakers. *What would I want someone to do if I were in their situation?* She wondered before remembering she could very well be in the same position with the passing of enough time.

Entering the Recovery Room, Jayla pulled the wheelchair up to the first chair and doublechecked the wheels were locked before helping the patient up. She was able to help the woman into the chair just as she did for so many at Heritage Park.

"Anything I can do for you, miss?" Jayla asked, stalling, so she could mentally check off her to-do list.

The woman shook her head softly, the feathery locks of her hair gently swaying off her brow. "No," she whispered, still clutching her purse.

"Okay, has your ride been notified to pick you up?"

The woman wordlessly nodded her head.

Is she going to throw up? Jayla thought, trying to read the woman's body language. "Perfect. There are just a few more things we need to do before you're ready to go."

Jayla checked the woman's vitals with a warm smile plastered on her face, working as fast and as gently as possible. Then, grabbing a birth control baggie, she lightly said, "This is for you to read when you get home."

Jayla extended the sack, rigid with pamphlets, toward the woman and waited for her to take it, but she didn't. Her eyes never moved past her purse as she slowly swayed side to side as if the designer handbag sitting in her lap were an anchor keeping the slightest breeze from blowing her away.

Taking the initiative, Jayla placed the baggie into the gaping mouth of the purse and waited to be of use, however long that took. Minutes passed uneventfully as Jayla walked about the room, busying herself to keep the patient from feeling watched.

"I wasn't supposed to, you know, get pregnant," the woman said quietly, breaking the silence of the room and giving Jayla a surprise. "It wasn't supposed to happen."

Jayla walked forward toward the patient and took the seat next to her, waiting for her to speak again.

"I mean, who lies about getting a vasectomy?" she sniffled in disbelief. "He—he even had the icepack on for a week. Sitting in front of the TV, making me get him food, telling me to get the kids to pipe down, all because he was too sore to . . ." She closed her eyes and tightened as tears leaked out of the corners and ran down her colorless cheek. "And now I'm the one who . . ."

Jayla handed the woman a tissue, patiently waiting for her to continue, but she didn't. She would readjust in her seat and sigh, she would exhale painfully and suck in air as through a straw, but she would never open her mouth to speak closure into her story. Instead, after fifteen minutes of silence, the intercom notified the room of the arrival of her transportation. Jayla carefully helped the nameless woman to the car, making no eye contact with the driver.

CHAPTER 11

EVERYBODY'S GOT A BREAK ROOM

Throughout the morning, there were six additional women who passed into Jayla's care. Some more aware than others, some with snapshot stories to share. Others wanting as much solitude as possible, hating Jayla as much as they hated the position they found themselves in. The more to come in, the more Jayla patiently waited, striking a balance between lingering and listening, with a few animal crackers and a bottle of water in each hand.

There was a tan-skinned woman whose vomit splattered onto Jayla's shoes saying over and over, "I'm a good mother to the others. I'm a good mother to the others." A beautiful ebony patient who mentioned how she just saved her career through a smile laced with tears. A frenetic ghostly-white, heavily pierced, lesbian with red curly hair begging Jayla to believe she had sex with a man once and didn't think pregnancy was possible. A woman wearing layers of clothing punctuated with a long-sleeved shirt whispered a haunting phrase, "Now he can't hurt her too."

The more patients she saw, the more weighed down Jayla felt. She felt their pain, she caught their sorrow in a wastebasket. These women were lonely, unsure, and scared, just like she was. And like an inner-city confessional booth, Jayla absorbed their confessions, their brokenness, their open-ended lives. She stored them inside herself, not far from the secret she kept of her own. By the time her allotted lunch break came

around, Jayla was ready to disengage from the world to process everything she heard and saw and experienced that morning. *I can look for the
pills later*, she told herself, surprised by how fatigued she was feeling.

Walking to the break room to grab her lunch bag from the fridge,
she heard someone calling out from behind her.

"New Fran!" Hailey exclaimed, her scrubs making louder and louder
swooshing sounds the faster she tried to catch up.

Jayla turned, too mentally and emotionally drained to be flustered
by her new nickname. As soon as she did, she felt a toothpick arm link
through hers as Hailey's face glowed with a Cheshire Cat grin.

"Hi, friend," Hailey said and, contorting her smile into pouting lips,
added, "you promised you'd save me a seat!"

"Um, that is not how that happened," Jayla replied, partly frustrated,
partly exhausted. As much as Jayla's face in that moment was painted
with broad brushstrokes of pride, contempt, and judgment, on the
inside, she was wound up with a nervously excited electricity sparked
with the hint of a new friendship forming.

"It's okay, New Fran. We all make mistakes." Hailey winked as she
used the intertwined elbow lock to nudge Jayla forward. "First time
eating in the break room?"

"Yeah, it's my first day."

"Oh, you are in for a treat. A real treat," Hailey said as the two
reached the entrance to the break room. Then, unlinking their arms,
Hailey pushed the door open. "Ta da!"

Peering inside, Jayla saw two women sitting at different tables, one
facing away from the door and one toward the women as they entered.
The one facing away wore white scrubs over her spoon-shaped body,
her hips sagging over the seat. The other woman looked more around
Jayla's age, with dark blonde hair and an athletic build, picking the
onions off a cheeseburger dripping with grease.

"Come on," Hailey said as she walked toward the second woman's
table. Sitting, she said with excitement, "Hey, Nik, look who it is! It's
New Fran!"

At this, all eyes in the small break room turned to Jayla, who, though
smoothing the wrinkles out of her scrubs, couldn't smooth the cringed
expression from her face, as the others made nodding and waving ges-
tures to her.

"Keep your applause to a minimum, girls," Nik mused, "an absolute minimum."

Hailey grinned and bounded toward the fridge. "Which one is yours?" she asked Jayla as she scanned the community fridge. "Sad, lonely brown bag, or retro red lunchbox?"

"The brown bag," Jayla said as she took a seat at the table with Nik, giving in the same way a grain of sand gives into the oyster that swallows it. "My real name is Jayla," she added for the room to hear.

Nik nodded, distracted. "I'm Nikole, and all my life people have called me Nikole," she sighed, "until I met Hailey, who insists on Nik."

"Oh, you love it," Hailey said, sliding the brown bag across the tiny table as she resumed her seat.

"I'm Terri," said the spoon-shaped woman in white. Her Southern voice was more sugary than Jayla would have expected for this part of the world.

"Jayla."

"There, finally!" Nikole exclaimed as she flicked the last yellowed oval onto an oily, half onion covered napkin. "Barry Cheesey's Burgers suck at following directions—I said NO onions. I will definitely be giving them a zero star."

"I actually like Barry Cheesey's Burgers," Terri interjected.

Nikole shot a side-eye at Hailey and Jayla, before intentionally looking away as Hailey giggled.

"Oh, Terri," Hailey snickered, "you're so funny."

Jayla saw Terri's cheeks warm with crimson embarrassment. Then, with the corners of her mouth curling into a sly smile, Nikole peered over her burger at Jayla with expectancy. Intrinsically, Jayla understood this was her moment, a social crossroads, an invitation to friendship at the low price of someone else's welfare.

As the moon draws the tide to shore, Jayla's need for acceptance rose, reaching for validation through wormy flicks and rolls of her tongue. "Yeah—everybody knows that place is trash. It should be Barry Cheesey's Burgers Are a Bust."

Jayla looked at Nikole. Her words hadn't been overly clever or particularly truthful, but it was clear the sacrificial try was enough.

"Huh, time to get back on the clock already," Terri said as she stood from her seat and maneuver herself out of the break room.

Just then Jayla noticed Lynn walk up. "Jayla, just the girl I was hoping to see," Lynn said, entering the break room with a tall, scrawny man in tow. He wore a white lab coat over a black suit and had a long, bull snout of a nose that seemed to enter the room a full second before he did. As the pair came in, Jayla could see in her periphery Nikole and Hailey straightening in their seats.

"This," Lynn said, motioning to the gentleman behind her, "is Jacob Molech, our primary—ah—well—only doctor here on campus."

Jayla stood to her feet and smoothed over her scrubs. "Dr. Molech, it's a pleasure."

"Oh please, call me by my first name—Doc," Molech said to the laughter of everyone in the room, no one's laughter as loud as his own. He stuck his hand out for Jayla to shake.

Grabbing Dr. Molech's hand, Jayla was immediately overcome with its warmth, as if a hot constricting towel was gripping her rather than the slender extended fingers. His eyes were sleepless, red, and puffy, and sank into the deep purple rings above his cheeks.

"Oh, Jacob," Lynn said with a patently fake snort. "Jayla, I've been bragging to Dr. Molech all morning about the fantastic job you've been doing in our Recovery Room. You've been brilliant, absolutely brilliant at taking care of our patients."

"Brilliant," Nikole quipped.

"Absolutely," Hailey seconded, sarcastically.

"I'm just happy to be here, taking care of those girls," Jayla responded, managing to pull her hand away from the five-fingered furnace.

"Good answer. That's a good answer," the doctor said, pivoting from Jayla to the rest of the room. "We have our eye on you, young lady."

Jayla answered with a polite smile, everyone else in the room nodding in agreement.

"Er—what I mean to say is—we're not watching you because—you know—it's because you're doing a good job—it's not a race thing," Dr. Molech awkwardly continued.

"Right," Jayla said, fully aware of the fact she was the only non-white in the room. "I know what you mean."

"You can just ask anyone; I love black people. I have many, many black friends."

"That's good," Jayla affirmed, wondering why the doctor was digging himself into the very hole that hadn't existed before he tried to dig his way out.

"Heck, I even named my dog Barak because, when he gets going, he likes to ba-rack his little head off," Dr. Molech said with a laugh before repeating, "he likes to ba-rack his—like bark."

Lynn put her hand on Dr. Molech's shoulder, converting a dying laugh into a throat-clearing cough. "We can't forget about that noon consult of yours, Jacob," said Lynn, gently turning Dr. Molech toward the door.

"Yes, yes. Sorry for the intrusion, girls! I just love getting caught up chatting with you people. I could do it all day if you let me," the doctor said to the room before correcting himself, "Well, not you people—not—what I mean to say is . . ."

"Good afternoon, ladies," offered Lynn before the pair left the break room, leaving Jayla exchanging looks with Hailey and Nikole.

"What an idiot," Nikole said, assured no one was in earshot.

"I think he's sweet," said Hailey before siding with Nikole, "but definitely an idiot."

"What's up with his hands?" Jayla asked, still feeling a tingle in her fingers.

"Didn't you love how warm and cozy they are?" Hailey asked. "Makes me want to curl up and sleep in them."

"It's because they're always working. Molech is always here, working way past overtime, not that he complains. It would be one thing if we had two resident doctors, but he's it," Nikole added.

Jayla remembered the dark rings under his eyes and how his coat seemed less like a uniform and more like a robe in the way it hung around his black suit.

"Overworked and underpaid," Hailey agreed.

"You'd think with U.I. getting $500 million every year from the government, we'd be able to afford to pay people better around here," Nikole said, with a roll of the eye and a bite out of her burger.

"Preach!" said Hailey with a hand waving in the air.

"Five hundred million dollars?" Jayla asked.

"It's not all ours, silly. We all share it. All the licensed abortion—I mean reversal clinics," Hailey explained. "And it's not nearly as much as it sounds. The industry could lose a lot of that as surgical abortions are on the out since the ten-week abortion pill hit the market. We are distributing more of those pill packs than we do surgical abortions. It's good Molech's getting close to retirement. In five years, he could be out of a job anyway."

"Five hundred million dollars sounds like a lot to me," Jayla said, trying not to look at all interested in the ten-week abortion pill. "And that's every year you say?"

"Yeah, more or less. Hopefully, more next year," Nikole laughed. "And what did you think of Terri over there? There's certainly more than enough of her to go around."

Jayla wasn't quite sure how to respond, so she gobbled up her leftovers as Hailey and Nikole took turns filling Jayla in on what she needed to know about the other coworkers. "It's not gossip," Hailey explained as they all threw away their trash, "It's just being honest in the break room."

Jayla could not help but think to herself, *What kind of twenty-five-dollar-an-hour reality show have I gotten myself into this time?*

CHAPTER 12

A NEW FRIEND

Slightly queasy from scarfing down her lunch so quickly, Jayla took her time heading back to the Recovery Room, lamenting the missed opportunity to recharge. Allowing herself to get lost in the winding halls of Unplanned, Inc., she made mental notes of the building's layout, paying particular attention to the nooks and crannies where the prescription-only later-term abortion pills might be kept. Just in the process of meandering to her workstation, Jayla passed five examination rooms, three offices, and several custodial supply closets.

I bet it's in those closets, thought Jayla as she entered the Recovery Room. But when would she get to the closets? And what if they were locked? And what if someone saw her?

With fewer patients after lunch, the clock crawled slowly enough for Jayla to assemble a plan. She would wait until after her shift was over and walk confidently over to the first supply closet she saw. If anyone saw and stopped her, she would explain how she was trying to learn everything she could about where everything was in case there was an emergency. It wasn't the best plan, but it was a start.

After Jayla's shift ended, she immediately began rustling up her things. Her pulse climbed. *Confidence*, she said to herself as she approached the door, *own it, and no one will stop you.*

Jayla took a deep breath.

"Hey, New Friend!" Hailey said, stepping into the doorway.

Jayla froze, her earrings swaying from the momentum of her stop.

"See, I made sure to call you New Friend instead of New Fran," Hailey explained before leaning in and whispering loudly, "Nik secretly thinks you'll hate me forever if I keep calling you New Fran."

"It's not a secret. She will hate you," Nikole said from behind her smartphone, stopping by Hailey's side. "You about ready to leave?"

Jayla looked at the two of them incredulously. *Do they know? Why are they here?* Jayla tried to calm herself, knowing how fear can explode into a nightmare of paranoia.

"Yo, Jayla," Nikole said, looking up from her screen, "You ready to go?"

"Yeah," Jayla said before cautiously suggesting, "I was just going to grab something real quick. Y'all can go on without me."

"It's okay, we'll wait," responded Hailey.

Jayla's eyes pivoted between Hailey and Nikole. *Y'all serious?* she thought to herself. "Oh, you don't have to do that."

"Nikole and I walk each other out after work every day and since you're pretty much one of us now, we want you to join us! Don't we, Nik?"

"Thrilled," Nikole said, monotone.

"Plus, this way we'll be there to protect you in case any of those crazies are out there," Hailey added.

"Those crazies?" Jayla asked, and then remembered Amarika, decked in her blinding neon uniform.

"A bunch of conservative religious bigots and hypocrites who hate that we help women here and try their lame scare tactics on us," Nikole advised. "They have word-soaped our cars and thrown fake blood on us. They have even deflated our tires. Get yourself a ten-dollar tire inflator soon as you can. Hailey and me just like to look out for each other."

"Plus, the more of us there are, the harder it is to get spit on," Hailey added.

"Bet they didn't tell you that in your interview!" Nikole joked. "Hey, we going or what?"

Walking through the hallway at one another's side, Jayla listened as Nikole and Hailey took turns venting about their day. With each supply closet they passed, Jayla grew antsy, as if she were passing available lifeboats while pregnancy slowly scuttled her. This anxiety only rode harder on her nerves the more she thought about a possible run-in with Amarika, her short fuse slashed by the emotional toll of the day.

"Hey, girls," Jayla heard a syrupy Southern voice call out behind them.

"Oh, no," Nikole sighed up at the ceiling, quickening her pace. "Don't stop, don't stop, don't stop, don't stop."

"Girls?" Terri called again with a twinge of hopeful expectancy as if at any moment Jayla and the others would notice her and turn around.

Jayla felt Hailey's arm lock into hers as she began belting a peppy tune at the top of her lungs. A stanza or two in Nikole joined, and the two sang louder and louder until Terri's baying was drowned out. In the din of that singing, Jayla wondered what would greet her on the other side of the front entrance. Images of protesters with picket signs filled her mind, gnashing their teeth and throwing more than just hate-filled words. She fought to smooth over her scrubs with her free hand as the exit grew nearer.

Opening the door to the parking lot, Jayla nervously looked around, anticipating the worst, whatever form that took. But, aside from a few shoppers meandering around the complex, no one was there. There were no crowds, no protesters, and no Amarika.

"Whelp, have a good night!" Hailey said, breaking the bond, and walking off to her car.

"Yup," Nikole replied, walking the opposite direction with her eyes glued to her phone.

Wait! What about the protests? Were they just messing with me? Jayla wondered as she made the short walk to her Accord. But why would Hailey and Nikole lie? Was it a joke? To rile up the new kid at work? A cheap, easy laugh?

Pulling her car door open, Jayla plopped inside, feeling frustrated, betrayed, and belittled. Turning over her engine, she pulled out her earbuds and stared forward, and that's when something caught her eye. On top of her windshield, tucked into the wipers, a half sheet of paper wiggled and danced in the later afternoon breeze.

Leaving her car on, Jayla slowly stepped outside and tugged at the paper until it loosened into her hand. With one foot in the vehicle and one on the ground she turned the sheet over, instantly horrified. Printed was a 3-D color image of a fetus, the baby's wrinkled, contorted face stared at Jayla through closed eyes. At the top of the paper was written four simple words. "You Murdered Me Today." Jayla's breath caught and her knees began to buckle, her eyes following the script to the bottom of the page. "You Monsters Are Going to Hell."

CHAPTER 13

SHADOW YOU?

"Alright ladies, happy Fri-Yay!" Renee exclaimed to a room of whooping women at the start of the pregnancy center morning devotional.

But Jayla was adrift in her own mind, oblivious to anything else around her. Listening to soft music through concealed earbuds, she jostled her leg up and down, trying her best to distract herself from the message left on her windshield the day prior.

What at first began as shock to Jayla soon turned to anger and sadness, but the music in her earbuds could not drown out the accusations playing in her mind. *You Murdered Me Today,* she mockingly repeated to herself as she shook her head. *That's ridiculous. What a lie,* she thought with a smirk and then turned the music up louder, subconsciously unwilling to be left alone in the darkness and idleness of her mind where those four words might prey upon her.

"But that's a trend we're hoping to end as we get deeper into the month," Jayla heard Renee say over the music in her earbuds, wrapping up a long rambling about which Jayla had no clue. "That said, this morning, we have a special Faith Friday treat! Pastor Steve—from Friends Church, one of our biggest supporters, and our pastoral board liaison—has come in this morning with a special devotion for us. So, let's give a warm LifeLine Pregnancy Center welcome to Pastor Steve," Renee said, clapping her hands as the room enthusiastically applauded.

A middle-aged heavyset white man stepped to the front of the room with a Bible in one hand and a diet soda in the other. He wore a button-down shirt tucked into khaki pants and looked like he had been wearing brown loafers since the day he was born. "Thank you, Renee," he said in a deep voice. "It's so wonderful to be here with you all today and to give a lesson from God's Word. But before I do that, I have a question for you," he said, looking around the room. "Who here has held the most babies?"

The room instantly burst wide with simultaneous laughter and counting and rehashed stories. "Okay, okay," the pastor said, trying to corral his audience, "let me ask it this way. If you have held 100 babies, put your hand up."

Jayla looked around as the majority of the room put up their hands.

"My goodness," exclaimed the reverend to a stir of chuckles. "Let's say, 200."

Many hands remained raised high in the air.

"A thousand? One thousand babies?" Pastor Steve asked as he swirled the diet soda can around in his hand.

Who would want to do that? Jayla thought to herself as she watched all the hands in the room lower. Then she saw a single hand raised—Brittany!

A look of astonishment washed over the pastor's face as the gaggle of women emotionally thronged around her. "You've held over one thousand babies, ma'am?"

"Yes sir," Brittany said with pride. "Actually, it's closer to two thousand."

The room gasped. The number was so high Jayla had trouble processing.

"Two thou—" Pastor Steve began before pointing at Renee, "Somebody here had better get this wonderful woman a plaque and a day off, and STAT! Get on up here, girl!"

Brittany rose to a round of applause and received an awkward, but well-intended, hug from Steve.

Just like a church to reward a hypocrite, Jayla said to herself.

"Now, hopefully, those two thousand babies aren't all yours," Steve said, as laughter rippled through the audience.

"No sir. I got three babies here, and one more up in heaven."

The pastor looked at Brittany with genuine sympathy as the mood in the room shifted. "I know all your babies love you and are blessed to have you. And we're blessed to have you too."

As the room bowed their heads to pray, Jayla scanned her peers to see which ones had their eyes open. She wondered, could it have been one of them who placed that horrible note under the windshield of her car. *Probably not*, thinking to herself, *but I'll bet they know the person who did.*

As the morning meeting ended with prayer, the main request was for abortion-minded women to choose life and for those who had abortions to find hope and healing. The room gradually dispersed, with some coworkers heading to their stations as others lingered to thank the good pastor for his brief message. Jayla eyed Brittany still beaming with recognition, as she hummed and pranced around the edge of the room toward her station.

"Jayla?" a Southern voice twanged from behind her.

Jayla turned and saw Samantha in a set of paisley patterned teal scrubs, her blonde hair pulled back into a ponytail, revealing the darker roots underneath.

"You gotta tell me—are the rumors true?" Samantha asked.

"What rumors?" Jayla questioned, remembering with pristine accuracy the abstinence forms Renee had her sign. Her eyes shot over again to Brittany, feeling now with certainty the speculations over Jayla's pregnancy hadn't been contained.

"The rumors that you are going to be my new trainee!" Samantha beamed, pronouncing each syllable like the plucking of a banjo string. "Renee shared the big news with me yesterday!"

"Oh, yeah!" Jayla responded with relief. "I'm your new client advocate."

"Yay!" Samantha said, clapping her hands. "You know, just the other day I was thinking, *Samantha, now there is a girl who could really make a difference.*"

Jayla smiled. From what she could tell, Samantha had aged like a pressed rose, retaining the same girl-next-door beauty she had forty years ago. Between her peppy energy, Southern drawl, and endless rotation of homeschooler-inspired jean dresses, she looked like she had been bioengineered by the Moral Majority Shopping Club.

"Shall we?" Samantha asked.

"By the way, I hear a big pat on the back is in order," Samantha grinned as they walked the long hallway lined with Bible verses and pictures of new mothers playing with babies. "Going back to school? Now that's a big deal."

"Oh yeah, thanks," Jayla commented, doing her best to sound enthusiastic.

"I always wanted to go back to school, but Rick doesn't think I'd have the time."

"Rick?" Jayla asked.

"Rick, my husband. Yeah, he says he just can't see me going back. And, you know, I know he's right. Between all the softball games he's playing and all the housework I got to do, there's just no time."

"Makes sense," Jayla replied, shrugging her shoulders, "if that is what you really want to do."

"He tried talking me out of being here on account of how many hours I'm spending, but I just can't give it up," Samantha continued as they rounded the corner into the supply room. "I told him I could always volunteer during evening hours if he preferred. And don't you know that hushed him up pretty quick."

Jayla shook her head as she let out a quiet laugh. Then, going to the closet, Samantha grabbed five tissue boxes and a bottle of fragrance mist. "That should be—yup—we're good. Alrighty, let's go to the counseling rooms."

Jayla nodded and followed at Samantha's heels as she glided through the hall, spritzing the cinnamon mist every four steps and repositioning the vases of fake flowers whenever they were in reach. Then Samantha took a turn into a wing of the building Jayla only saw briefly on her first day tour.

Arriving at the first doorway, Jayla noticed a dark-stained wood sign with the words Hope Room hanging from a ribbon of burlap and lace. Entering the room, Samantha flipped the light switch and, rather than the overhead fluorescent Jayla was expecting, several table lamps around the room began to wash the walls with a warm and homey glow. The walls were two-toned, with a mint pastel green lower half and light tan upper half divided by a white chair rail. Against the wall rested a medium brown leather couch with a navy-blue tub accent chair to its right, the wooden end table conjoining them held a half-used box of tissues.

"This is real nice," Jayla said, impressed, absorbing every detail of the room, thinking to herself, *This would be a great place to take a nap.*

"That's sweet of you to say. There are still some finishing touches I'd like to add, but Ricky said this was all we could afford to do right now. Feels homey, right?"

"Wait, *you* did this?"

"Yup, me and some of the girls a few months back. We did this one and the two other counseling rooms. This one we called Hope, and the other two we named Faith and Love. I think they all look nice, but the greatest of them is definitely love," Samantha said with a twinkle in her eye, waiting for a laugh from Jayla. "Annnnd nobody's laughing— sorry—that's just a little Bible joke for you. Let's see. Can you replace that half-empty box of tissues with one of them new ones?"

"Yeah, sure," said Jayla, beginning to rip the top off the box. "And you paid for all this too?"

"We pitched in what we could. A lot of us ladies did. I wanted to do more, but Ricky put his foot down about it. We just wanted these girls to feel loved from the moment they came in, you know? They're going through so much. They're scared and alone. Many of them are the only ones who even want to keep their baby in the first place. I mean, can you imagine?"

Jayla paused and shook her head, her thoughts lingering on her own situation; nevertheless, she curled her lip corners to show acknowledgment.

"I know," Samantha continued, "And they're getting heat for it, and shame for it and—well—Renee feels the same as me. Knowing things are financially tight for the Center, a group of us pooled our money and remodeled these rooms." Samantha smiled, allowing a moment to admire the room for herself. "I just want these young girls to have one place in this world where they felt safe and loved. I think they deserve it, whatever the price tag."

Jayla could feel the authenticity in Samantha's words and passion. "Anything else we need to do in here?" Jayla finally asked.

"Well, I figure we'll restock all the tissues in the Faith and Love Rooms and put the half-used boxes in the storeroom for later. We don't waste a lot around here. We always try to reuse whatever we can when-ever we get a chance. Let's go unlock those front doors of answered prayers, and you'll shadow me for the day."

"Shadow you?" Jayla asked.

"Yeah, you know, stay at my hip, so you can get a feel for it. I'm a learn-as-you-go kinda person, so today you'll watch how I do things, and then next time you'll take the lead, and I'll be there to watch, and then you'll be on your own. And then one day, not too long from now, you'll be the one teaching some other wonderful lady how to be the best client advocate she can be. Sound good?"

"Sounds good," Jayla said with a smile, feeling comfortable for the first time since beginning to work there. And there in the pit of her soul, unexpectedly, something began to grow—a tiny root, a sapling of desire. A craving conceived in her heart for approval and achievement, to be recognized as both worthy and worthwhile. A longing Jayla long thought dead.

CHAPTER 14

UNDECIDED

Jayla tarried with Samantha in the Faith Room for twenty minutes after the center opened, watching as she rotated between spritzing air freshener and adjusting the tissue boxes on the corner table.

"Sam?" a female voice called from the hallway.

Finally, Jayla thought, pocketing the earbuds she secretly inserted into her ear after five minutes of listening to Samantha talk on and off to herself.

"In here!" Samantha yelled.

After a few sneaker creaks, a tall woman in black scrubs walked into the room, combing her dark red bangs out of her eyes with one hand as the other held a half-eaten carton of yogurt. Jayla recognized her as Darla, the only other regular client advocate at the center.

"I'm Darla," the redhead introduced herself.

I know, thought Jayla, also remembering meeting her husband by the dumpster. "I'm Jayla."

"How long has she been at this?" Darla asked Jayla, pointing at Samantha arranging tissues.

"About twenty minutes," Jayla replied.

"Oh, goodness, it's worse than I thought," Darla joked.

"You go on and laugh," Samantha said. "We both know the first impression a girl gets today will determine if she comes back for a second visit. It might look like I am arranging tissues, but I am spreading cheer and saving lives."

"I get it . . . Just wanted to let you know the first client of the day is here filling out her intake form, and I figured you would want to help her."

"Alright, Jayla, we're up. How we doing? Ready?" asked Samantha.

Jayla nodded and smoothed her scrubs as she stood, feeling anything but ready. Though she knew the burden of speaking would rest on Samantha's shoulders, Jayla still felt nervous.

"Alrighty then," Samantha winked as Jayla rose, the two of them walking silently to the entrance.

"Good morning, Mrs. Brittany. How are we doing today?" Samantha called gingerly. Jayla followed behind just far enough to hide her crossed arms and cross face from her mentor.

"Morning, Sam. Better than I deserve!" Brittany replied with a chuckle.

You got that right, Jayla thought.

"And good morning to you too, Miss Jayla," Brittany said with a smile.

Jayla allowed herself a grimaced grin before letting out a dry, "Thanks."

"You got an intake for any of our friends in the lobby?" Samantha asked.

"I do, honey, I sure do." Brittany opened a beige folder on the desk and pulled out the first form. "She's the one with the little princess running around her," she said, motioning to the back of the lobby.

"Alrighty, thanks, Mrs. B," Samantha said before turning around to Jayla, "You just stick behind me and we'll be alright," Samantha encouraged, pushing open the door to the foyer.

Over the last few weeks, Jayla stared out from her perch at the reception desk more times than she could count as Samantha and Darla strode through the lobby toward a patient with grace, poise, and sweetness. But now, walking two paces behind her experienced mentor, Jayla realized all she had previously taken for granted in their effortless demeanor. Behind Samantha, she felt mechanical and clunky as they approached a woman in the corner of the room.

Her hair was deep raven black and pulled into a messy bun. Around her neck hung an inexpensive gold necklace with a feather. In the seat next to her lay a purse, several grocery bags, and a backpack of coloring materials. A little girl played beside her—obviously her daughter if her hair was any indication.

"Eliana, let Momma sleep, baby. You wanna come up and play on Momma's phone?"

Late teens, Jayla thought, reverting to the mental guessing game she played as a receptionist.

"Good morning. You must be Bethany," Samantha said gently as the woman sat up and wiped her eyes. "I'm Samantha, one of the client advocates here, and the lovely lady behind me is Jayla, one of my associates."

"I'm Eliana," the little girl said as her mother released her.

"Well, hi there, Eliana, I'm Samantha. How are you today?"

"I'm three!" Eliana burst with excitement.

"Alright, Eliana," Bethany sighed tiredly as she began to collect her bags. "Can we go back now?"

"Yes," Samantha said. "If you're ready, I'd love for us to discuss your options in one of our private counseling rooms."

Eliana hummed and skipped while the women walked to the counseling room. Bethany fluctuated between yawning, rubbing her eyes, and checking the time. When they reached the Hope Room, Samantha held the door as Eliana ran in and careened onto the leather couch. Jayla, sizing up how well everyone would fit onto the couch, decided to stand in the corner and observe.

"Eliana, you want a lollipop?" Samantha asked. "If that's alright with your momma, of course."

"Please, Momma, please?"

"That's real nice, but I think you got enough energy for both of us as is," Bethany replied, sinking next to Eliana on the couch, setting her bags down with a plop.

"Alright," Samantha smiled, pulling a folding chair out from behind her for Jayla. Then, peering into the folder in her hands, asked, "So, honey, how are you feeling today?"

Bethany shrugged her shoulders as her body contoured into the sinking shape of the couch.

"I see on your intake form you'd like to take a free pregnancy test today?"

Bethany nodded with a yawn, glancing for a moment back at Jayla before looking back at Samantha, as if she were trying to anticipate which direction the rapid-fire condemnation and judgment would be coming from.

"That's no problem, no problem at all! But before we have you take that test, I want to confirm some information with you. When was the first day of your last menstrual period?"

"What's a period, Momma?" Eliana asked.

"About a month and a half ago," Bethany answered before pulling her phone out of her pocket. "Here you go, play one of your games, Eliana." As soon as her eyes hit the screen, Eliana became totally engrossed in the warm glow of her favorite drug.

"And was your last period normal?" Samantha continued down the questionnaire.

Bethany shrugged. "Yeah."

"Okay. Are you currently on any birth control?"

"Yes."

"And is this potential pregnancy the result of . . ." Samantha looked from Bethany to her daughter before spelling, "r-a-p-e?"

"No. Nothing like that."

"Great, and last question—if you are pregnant, are you considering abortion, parenting, adoption, or undecided."

"Undecided, at least, I'd like to think I'm undecided," Bethany said and then ran her fingers through Eliana's youthful hair. "I wanna say, you know—but it's just so hard . . ." Her lips contorted with a stifled yawn, as her sleep-deprived eyes became glassy.

"I definitely understand how you feel. It's an important decision," Samantha empathized. "Tell you what; you and I are going to step out into the hall where you will take one of our pregnancy tests and, depending on the result, I'd love for us to come back and discuss all your options. Sound good?"

"What about Eliana?" Bethany asked and then, looking at Jayla, "Can she stay in here with you?"

Jayla wanted to say yes, and knew she should, but she found herself just staring back at Bethany. For the entire visit up to this point she was a fly on the wall, a spectator. *Me? Kids aren't really my thing*, she thought to herself before engaging a response.

"Of course, she can!" Samantha answered on Jayla's behalf. "Jayla is great with children."

As Bethany and Samantha left the room, Jayla looked at the little girl playing on her mother's phone. *Why would someone have one of these?* Jayla wondered to herself, thinking of the effort needed just to get Eliana to exist in the room.

Someone had to buy this little girl clothes, someone had to buy food for her—and not just any food, but low processed, green, healthy food—and then cook it and serve it to her, only to watch her turn her nose up at the smell. Someone had to buy her diapers and change them, not to mention the wipes and baby cream or powder or ointment or whatever it was the baby needed. Jayla recalled one of her earliest memories as a child sitting on the toilet with a stomach virus. Her mom's latest boyfriend, stoned, mistakenly gave her chemical cleaning wipes instead of the kid-friendly flushable wipes her mom kept. She winced, remembering the stinging, the rash, and her mother's anger for stopping up the toilet. Something like that, stemming from an accident or not, stays with a child. A one-off moment—one moment of not giving your full attention, and they're wrecked for life.

Then there's the formula-buying and the shoe-tying and the teaching how to walk and talk and be a person. Not to mention the doctor's visits, and the worry, and the nightmares they have, and the headaches they give you, and the time and energy and focus it takes for the kid just to be well adjusted. *Why would someone ever want to have a kid?* Jayla thought and, directing her attention to her stomach, wondered, *Why would I?*

"Where did Momma go?" Eliana's small voice asked.

"She just left for a minute. She'll be right back," Jayla reassured.

Eliana nodded. "What's a period?"

Jayla held in a laugh. "What game are you playing?"

"It's called Animal Baby. Wanna sit with me?"

"No, I'm okay," Jayla declined as nicely as possible. "The game sounds fun, though."

Nodding for a second time, Eliana shimmied her body off the couch and walked over to Jayla, standing right beside her like they were old friends. Jayla saw cartoon puppies and kittens on the screen. She watched Eliana's diminutive fingers struggling to press the right buttons to change their clothes or give them a bath.

"Can you hold this for me?" Eliana asked, unable to grasp the over-sized screen without support.

Reluctantly, Jayla held the warm phone horizontally for the girl, eager for Bethany and Samantha to return. *How long does it take to pee on a plastic stick?* she thought.

A few minutes later, Jayla could hear Samantha and Bethany's voices growing louder from within the hall until the door swung open. Bethany was wiping her eyes and yawning.

"Come on, Eliana. We're leaving," Bethany said, double-checking the time as she began collecting their things. But Eliana didn't budge, engrossed in her game.

"Eliana!" Bethany reiterated as she snatched the phone out of Jayla's and Eliana's hands.

"But Momma, I just started painting kitty's nails!" Eliana protested and started to cry.

"Don't start. Don't start with this. Momma's got to work."

"I really would love for us to reschedule so we can talk about your options," Samantha said, handing Bethany her purse.

"Options?" Bethany exclaimed, distractedly trying to keep her phone out of Eliana's reach. "I don't have options. I have jobs. Too many of them."

"Momma . . ."

"I can't. I want to, but I just can't. I just—I'm so tired. I'm always so tired," Bethany said as her eyes became glassy, and she yawned once more.

"Momma, please, Momma!" Eliana whined.

"Fine! Fine. Here, you can play until we get to the car," Bethany resigned.

"I know this isn't the news you were wanting. And I know you don't have the time now to talk about it. But here, take this pamphlet; it has details about all your options and my phone number on it. And you can call that number, day or night, and I'll be there for you. Anything you need, you just call," Samantha emphasized.

Jayla watched Bethany apprehensively reach out for the sleek pages as Samantha held the other end for a moment until the women were looking eye to eye.

"You're a good mom, Bethany," Samantha said tenderly, sincerely, before letting go.

Bethany gave a bitter laugh in reply, looking at her kid and the five-inch electronic nanny holding her attention.

"I mean it. I know it's hard. But you're doing it. You're a good mom," Samantha said again.

And that's when, to Jayla's surprise, Bethany smiled. Not a great, big, room-filling-with-brightness kind of smile, but a better one. A bashful one that didn't believe Samantha's kind words but desperately wanted to believe them. A smile that stayed in the room long after Bethany and Eliana were gone.

CHAPTER 15

FIVE HUNDRED DOLLARS

"See, that wasn't so bad, was it?" Samantha elbowed Jayla as the afternoon shift ended at the pregnancy center. "I think you did just so great today. So, so great."

Jayla, in fact, had not done great. This was a reality of which she was very aware. And while she never enjoyed failure, there was something this time that particularly stung. A feeling she attributed to her newfound mentor.

It wasn't every day Jayla found someone worth striving hard for but Samantha brought out that side in her. She wanted Samantha to think well of her; she wanted her respect. She wanted to earn some small token of her approval. Sadly, to be handed an unearned compliment at the end of this shift was almost as bad as being outright worthless. After all, who needed to be coddled other than those who weren't good enough to cut it on their own? Jayla wanted no trophy for participating when, at best, she stammered over her words, was hesitant with her compassion, and relied far too heavily on her mentor for even the simplest tasks.

But still, Jayla smiled at Samantha as the two women worked side-by-side to disinfect the couch. So many women had been in that very spot earlier in the day they were all starting to blur. There was the pink-haired preteen whose grandmother brought her in, the mother who

87

came in with a double stroller full of kids and an extra strapped to her back, and the teacher who came in during her lunchtime at school and tried to grade papers as she awaited her results. Some of the women wanted pregnancy tests, and others wanted a follow-up ultrasound. Some came because they needed support and love and understanding. Others were repeats who came because of the great experience they had in their last visit. More than a few came because it was cheaper than buying their own pregnancy test.

There was joy and sorrow expressed on that couch when a woman received news of a healthy baby, and joy and sorrow with the news of no baby at all. And yet through it all, Samantha remained poised, sweet, and generous with her kindness and encouragement.

Still, with all Samantha did right, there was one thing she did in each visit that bothered Jayla. A statement that didn't seem to fit with the rest of what she understood about the pregnancy center's goals and values.

"Hey, Sam, can I ask you a question?"

"You sure can," Samantha replied, tossing her cleaning rag into the trash can.

"Each of the ladies who came in today, you asked them what they wanted to do with the baby—if they wanted to have it or not—and then, you told them about the abortion clinic in town. Why?" Jayla asked, concerned specifically about the occasions Unplanned, Inc. was referenced by name.

"Good question. For the record, they already know where the other services are. If I pretend I don't, then I look like I have a hidden agenda. It's up to each mother to decide what she wants to do with her baby."

Jayla stopped wiping down the couch, surprised by Samantha's answer.

"Don't give me that look! My agenda is not hidden," Samantha teased, seeing Jayla's face, "I mean, yeah, do I hope they all want to keep their baby? Of course. Do I think they should all keep the babies the Lord has blessed them with? Personally, yes. Listen, if a girl has the right to choose an abortion, she should also have the right to not choose abortion. But at the end of the day, that's not my call and that's not my job. My job is to be fully honest. I have nothing to hide, for right is on my side."

"But aren't we supposed to talk ladies out of getting an abortion?"

Samantha shook her head and laughed. "Lord have mercy—no! Who have you been talking to? We're not here to take the choice away from women. We want the women who come in here to experience as much help as we can give them so they can make an informed decision. It has to be their decision. You'll never see me or any of the other client advocates or ultrasound technicians trying to talk anyone out of anything. So please, when you have your own one-on-one meeting with one of our guests, please remember-remember-remember it is not your job to make a sales pitch. We don't love these women so they keep their babies. We love these women—period. We want to lift them to a place where they can make their own best decisions for life."

"Well, okay, then," Jayla chuckled through her teeth.

Samantha leaned in close to Jayla and whispered, "Not all client advocates tell the girls where they can get an abortion. They feel it violates their religious beliefs. I tell them where and how much it costs. Then I tell them it's like buying something on credit with a really high interest rate. You are paying for it the rest of your life. Every time you go a month, surprise, another bill pops up in your mailbox. Make a choice that does not come with a lifetime of regretted payments."

As Samantha spoke, Jayla heard the door to the hallway creak open and looked back to see Renee's head in the opening.

"And how did our newest client advocate do on her first day?" Renee asked, with an expectant gaze cast on Jayla.

"She was a natural. A real natural," Samantha answered. "I think with a few more sessions like today, she'll be ready to fly solo."

Jayla was appreciative of another unmerited compliment, but one look at Renee and the impressed look in her eyes, Jayla knew it was best to smile and keep any reservations to herself.

"That's great news! We had a feeling about you, Jayla," Renee said, "And good students are a reflection of good teachers, so thank you, Sam, for showing her the ropes today. Think I can steal Jayla away for a few minutes?"

"Sure! We're almost done here anyway," Samantha replied. "I'll go on and finish this up, Jayla. I hope you have a great weekend!"

Following Renee into her office, Jayla was unsure what this impromptu meeting was about. She hadn't been late to work. She hadn't been rude to Brittany, at least, not undeservingly rude. Samantha gave her a high recommendation on her first day on the new job. Everything, as far as she could tell, was on the up and up.

"Pardon the mess. You never quite get around to cleaning your office until you retire," Renee said as she took a seat behind her desk, her small frame making the chairback look extra-large.

Jayla sat, much less tense than the last time the two had a heart-to-heart, but still apprehensive of a reproach.

"How is school coming?" Renee asked.

"School—school . . .," Jayla pondered, trying to knit together the strands of the last web of lies she spun. "Going good, going good," she safely stated, her brain still not crisp on what bits of information might contradict prior confessions. "You know how it is, going back after being off it for so long."

"It's hard, that's for sure, right?"

"Mmmhmm," Jayla hummed.

"I hear business degrees there are tough."

"Tell me about it," Jayla said in agreement.

"Wait, it was business, wasn't it? Or was it nursing you said?"

"A bit of both," Jayla bluffed. "Nursing with a few business classes on the side—you know—to fall back on. I might want to start my own medical something or other someday."

"Ah. Well, as you know, something I've been really working to cultivate here since I took over is a feeling of family among our staffers. I want each employee to feel loved and connected. We're all part of a big family. All of us are a part of one another's lives."

Everybody in everybody's business, you mean.

"So, I hope you don't mind, but I shared with a few of our ladies here about you going back to school. I hope that's alright."

"Why wouldn't it be?" Jayla responded, hiding her frustration.

"Well, the thing is, like a big family, we all want to look out for each other and, well," Renee said before opening the drawer to her desk and pulling out a slip of paper. "Here."

Jayla sat up in her chair to reach for the rectangular sheet, extending as far as she could to make up for the lack of length on Renee's reach. It was a check. Jayla's eyes pinged to the dollar box, and her eyes got big.

"Five hundred dollars?" Jayla said in disbelief.

Renee was giddy with controlled excitement. "I know, I know, but some of the ladies and I were just thinking and talking about your situation and remembering how hard it was to work and go through college at the same time and, well, we wanted to give this to you. It's a small way to show you how proud of you we are. And even though this won't pay for a class or anything, we thought at the very least this might help cover the cost of books and some gas on your way to and from school. Whatever you might need."

"I don't know what to say," Jayla replied. "I can't take this."

"Oh, of course you can! And you don't need to say anything to anybody. All the ladies who contributed to this wanted to stay anonymous, so there's no one even to thank! You just do your best and make those grades, and we'll see if maybe later this semester we can do a little more for you."

Jayla sat there looking at the check, confliction burrowing into the pit of her stomach. "Thank you," she finally said as she stood to leave.

"We're in this together!" Renee cheered as Jayla opened the door.

With a closed mouth smile, she nodded at Renee and silently walked to her car. The drive home was likewise quiet. *Five hundred dollars*, she kept thinking to herself. *Free. Just like that—but I can't spend it—I mean—what kind of person would I be if I did? On the other hand, what kind of person would I be if I didn't?*

Walking up to her apartment, she passed neighbors in the hall complaining about their workweek and exaggerating big plans for the weekend. The smell of cheap cold beer and propane grills rose from the walkway below. The intoxicating pheromone of weekend freedom electrified the sky as the unbuttoned city awoke to greet the sunset.

Opening the pantry in her apartment, she saw her dinner menu limited to aging tuna in dented cans, stale instant mashed potatoes, or greasy dollar peanut butter slathered on hardening white bread. As she looked, she inhaled air drenched with smoked meats and seasoned rubs wafting from under the door; her stomach growled as the kings of barbecue joyfully received their burnt offerings. *Five hundred dollars*, she thought again to herself. *I could buy a lot of things with five hundred dollars.*

No! Jayla came to her senses. *It's not right. It's a lie—but—Renee is expecting this check to be cashed and, if it's not, then they'll know I lied for sure. Then I'd lose my job, and everyone at work would know I was a liar. I couldn't do that to Samantha. Not after how much she's said she believes in me. And I couldn't do that to myself, not after all the hard work I've put in there. I either cash the check and spend the money, or I don't and get fired.* Jayla reasoned, believing she was starting to see her situation more clearly. *But those ladies worked hard to get me that money. It would be selfish to spend it on me. What would I even spend it on? I don't need money for an abortion, not anymore, not since starting at Unplanned. I don't know, do I even want an abortion?*

I guess maybe I could just give the money away. But really, these ladies gave me the money to spend on me, for things I need like books or gas or whatever. It would probably be an even greater disservice to them if I didn't spend it on me, on things I need. That's what they want. Honestly, spending this money on me is kind of the only way to honor the heart of their gift. So what do I need? Jayla asked herself as she stared into her reflection in the microwave. *What do I need?*

CHAPTER 16

THE SANGER EXCHANGE

The next day Jayla was the first in line as soon as the banks opened. Then she strolled into the grocery store with five hundred dollars in hand and waltzed out with two shopping carts full of her favorite foods—so many items it took one of the store employees to help her load them into the car. And in one of the finest, most delightful moments Jayla could recall in years, she had the distinctly sweet pleasure of throwing out all the empty place-holding boxes playing house in her cabinet and replacing them with their full counterparts.

Then, with a little over two hundred dollars remaining, Jayla made the stop she had been most eager within the last few months to make. She stopped at her old hair salon. The same salon she hadn't visited since before the breakup, back when he used to pay for her. But, unlike those times, this time, she was free to be beautified however she pleased. There would be no one standing over her, controlling her, dictating how she could look. No one looking to purchase away the wants and decisions and freedom she was entitled to at the low price of a hairstyle.

Of course, part of her conceded she was there to look good, to boost her worth in the eyes of others. But this was more than a dye or cut or wash. This was more than a skin-deep treatment. This was recovering her ability to choose. This was becoming empowered again. This was cutting free from an emotionally abusive past with six-inch shears. This was emancipation long overdue.

Walking into the salon as she smoothed her blouse several times over, Jayla was hit with the blended perfume of warm blow-dried hair, shampoos, perm lotion, hot wax, and scented candles; nostalgic scents drudging up misplaced memories. With the entrance bell announcing her arrival, several stylists turned around to greet her, their typical welcome changing pitch upon recognition.

"Jayla? Oh, girl! Is that you?"

"Hey there, darlin'! How long has it been? You're looking good!"

"Well, well, look who's back in the old neighborhood!"

"Jayla, come here and have a seat. I'll take care of you! You just come on over," Aiysha, her old stylist, called out, her muscular arms patting the seat in front of her. Jayla was relieved to see Aiysha, who she had known since high school.

Making her way to the seat, Jayla smiled and waved and said countless how-do-you-dos to all the stylists and customers who recognized her.

"It's so good to see you, baby," Aiysha said with a strong embrace, her pineapple ponytail tickling Jayla's ears. "Have a seat, have a seat. I've missed you, girl!"

"Missed you too," Jayla said, sinking into the chair, allowing her body to uncoil.

"And how's that fine man of yours doing?" inserted Eloise, the stylist working next to Aiysha's station. "I hope you're keeping him on a short leash."

Suddenly, Jayla's stomach clenched and she ground her teeth. In her mind, she saw the face she was continually trying to block. The face that ushered so much heartache into her life. The last face she saw before the incident and the first face she saw after and never wished to see again.

"Shhh. No, Mmmhmmm," Aiysha whispered to Eloise. "They, uh . . ."

"Oh—sometimes you gotta cut them loose, huh, Jayla?" Eloise remarked, pivoting back to her client.

"Have you thought about what you want today?" Aiysha asked, drawing Jayla out of the mood she had begun to sink into.

"Yes. I want a side-swept pixie-cut," Jayla announced—words she had been waiting months to utter, and they felt so good coming out.

Aiysha studied Jayla with a questioning gaze. "Big change. You sure that's what you want?"

"I'm sure," said Jayla, adamantly. *A new hairstyle for a new me.*

"Well, alright then," Aiysha smiled, draping a well-worn paisley barber's gown over Jayla, immediately getting to work. "So, Jayla, where are you working at these days? Still at that old folk's home?"

"No, you know where I heard Jayla's at now? I heard she's at that woman's place, Unplanned, Inc. A friend of mine, Gianna from The Bricks, said she saw you walking out of there the other day arm in arm with the other employees," Eloise said.

Jayla could feel her cheeks warm as the safe haven of the salon didn't feel so safe anymore. Living a double life is harder than one thinks.

"Oh, yeah, Jayla? Is that where you're at now?" Aiysha asked.

Jayla took a moment to think, not wanting to land on any sort of definitive answer. Then, unable to come up with a suitable lie and with no distinguishable friend-of-a-friend of her coworkers in the room, Jayla creaked open her dry mouth. "Yeah, I'm working there now."

"Good for you, girl," Eloise exclaimed. "That's a great place to be."

"You've been there?" asked Aiysha.

"Once every few years. I'm more of a Plan-B girl myself. You know how it is. You're in the heat of passion, and he says he had a vasectomy, and then, about a month later, you realize he lied," Eloise said with the room behind her laughing in affirmation.

"You do what you gotta do, Jayla, but for me, I could never support that kind of place," Aiysha stated.

"Oh? And why is that?" asked Eloise.

"Okay, answer me this. Why does it always seem like abortion clinics are always in the ghetto?" retorted Aiysha. "I've never seen one in the suburbs. Why do you think that is?"

"Because you don't go to the suburbs?" Eloise replied.

"You don't see what I'm saying? Why's it always that these abortion clinics are rooted where poor minority people are?"

"Oh, so it's okay for other women to get abortions, but just not poor people, or African Americans? You think everyone else should get to choose but not them? They can't handle that?" Eloise responded. "Or is it black people in general who you feel can't decide that for themselves?"

"That's not what I mean, and you know that's not what I mean. Haven't you ever heard about the lady who started the whole abortion movement. White lady's name was Sanger. She was a eugenicist."

"A what?" asked Eloise.

"A eugenicist. It's someone who believes they can better humanity if they can control who populates and who doesn't. They believe if people with unwanted traits—like being disabled or poor or having an undesirable skin color, like maybe black. If these ladies don't have babies, or can't have babies, or have their babies aborted, then the world is better for it. Because then the favored white people don't have to worry about being outvoted. It's selective population control," Aiysha explained.

"And who made you the expert on eugenicists?" someone in the quickly quieting room asked.

"What do you think? I'm ignorant just because I work in a hair salon?" replied Aiysha.

"I don't know about all that," Eloise responded. "Sounds like a bunch of fake right-wing news. You been watching *Fox & Friends*?" The ladies all laughed.

"Oh, yeah? Then how come their centers removed Sanger's name from all their buildings?" Aiysha asked. Then, fishing her phone out of her pocket, she continued a few seconds later. "Here it is, the chair of the board is saying, and I quote: 'The removal of Margaret Sanger's name from our buildings is both a necessary and overdue step to reckon with our legacy and acknowledge our contributions to historical reproductive harm within communities of color . . . Margaret Sanger's concerns and advocacy for reproductive health have been clearly documented, but so too has her racist legacy.' End quote."

"I don't know," Eloise said after a beat of silence. "I still think the stuff they do is good. Just because a eugeni-whatever started it doesn't mean that's how they are today. They give free breast examinations and free birth control to the schoolgirls. You know a young girl ain't got a chance these days without that. I heard that over 40 percent of girls looking for abortions come from church-goin' families. Somethin' ain't right."

"I just can't support a system designed to keep us down, to kill our babies because they believe the world is better off without us. Entire generations of beautiful, healthy, strong black families eradicated, talked into murdering their own children, so tomorrow would be a little richer and whiter than today. I just can't. I can't support a system like that. I don't see how anyone who knows the truth could," Aiysha said, not making eye contact with Jayla, yet looking through her at the same time.

"Listen to me, girlfriend," a slim lady in a neighboring chair spoke up, "how many of our people died because they was afraid to take a Covid shot? Maybe that was all about controlling our population and destiny too? They knew we was afraid of that mess and either you just couldn't get it, or you was just too afraid to take it. I'm just sayin' somebody is doing something somewhere that we don't know about."

"Amens to that," rang out around the salon from everybody. Everybody but Jayla.

CHAPTER 17

LIE DETECTOR

Arriving back at the pregnancy center campus on Monday, Jayla felt and looked like a new woman. She adored everything about her new hairstyle from the way it swooped, to how much easier it was to keep up, to how much cooler her neck felt, to the way it's dark silky strands sometimes shone as raven's feather purple when the sun nicked it just right. Internally she was feeling better as well, having spent Sunday relaxing, cat-napping, and gorging herself on the bushels of groceries stocked in her apartment.

A few times, however, throughout the weekend, she replayed the conversation at the salon. Any twinge of nausea, any TV commercial featuring a family, and her mind would wander back to the predicament sprouting in her belly. Now though, quite unexpectedly, Jayla noticed the shock of her pregnancy had begun to wear off and with it the knee-jerk urgency to bring it to a resolution. Her panic was subsiding and her anxiety was procrastinating. The more she looked and felt like her usual self, the more fictional the situation became. With time it had become just another future, distant event that didn't affect her present day-to-day life, like a court date nine months from now, or a flight forty weeks away. She lost the forest of her pregnancy for the normalizing trees of everyday life, lulled to rest in the siren song of its shade.

Entering the LifeLine building, Jayla began to strut a little more like her old self. It wasn't just a resurrection; it was a reclamation. Not rushing in all at once, but with the steady rising gentleness of an orchestra tuning before a symphony takes flight. She thought, *Maybe the whole world just needs a new hairdo.*

"Ooo, honey, you are rocking it," came a familiar voice from beyond the reception desk. "New Jayla, who is this?"

Jayla smiled as her eyes fixed on Brittany. Just as quickly, the smile faded. "Thanks," she said, staring at the top of Brittany's head where a blue and gold African print head scarf stretched around her hairline, its oversized knot facing outward. "You too?"

"Thank you! I just got it over the weekend. I can't believe I've never owned one before."

"Yeah, hard to believe," Jayla responded while inwardly rolling her eyes, waiting for the inner door to unlatch.

"You have yourself a good…" was all Jayla heard Brittany say before the door opened, and she bolted, looking for Samantha.

"Sam?" Jayla called out down the counseling room hallway.

"In the Faith Room!" Samantha's voice shouted back.

As Jayla's footsteps approached the room, Samantha continued in conversation. "How was your weekend? I heard you and Renee had a nice little…oh my goodness, look at your hair!" she exclaimed as soon as Jayla came in view.

"It's great, right?" Jayla asked, modeling the new style for Samantha with a few poses.

"It's gorgeous! I just love it!"

"I do too!"

"Gosh, I feel like I'm looking at a completely new woman here!" Samantha exclaimed.

"Yup, yup."

"You're gonna have the boys on you like flies on molasses. I hope you have yourself a good boy-beating-bat because, girl, you're going to need one!"

"Boys—no—I don't—no. You were saying something about me and Renee?" Jayla asked, changing the topic.

"Just that you guys had a good talk before you left. Cover anything important?"

"Not really," Jayla replied, "mostly just talked about how the day went and how the school is going—my degree and all."

"That's good! Sounds like a good talk."

"Yeah . . ." Jayla trailed off as Samantha resumed rifling through a pile of paperwork. In all the excitement of her salon visit, Jayla hadn't considered how Renee and the women at the Center would perceive her new hairstyle, or the message it sent. *Hey, thanks for the free money! I know you said to use it on what I need, but instead, I got me this new hairdo. You like?* Jayla shot off in her mind. *What was I thinking?* "Yeah—my—uh—my neighbor is in that beauty school and she needed to practice on someone, so I got lucky," adding one more lie to the pile.

"What do you think? Ready for today?" Samantha asked.

"Yeah, I think I'm ready. I'm feeling a little better about it," Jayla answered, her confidence taking a dip.

"Feel up to taking the driver's seat?"

"Me? No, no, no, no," Jayla adamantly declined.

"Let me rephrase. What I meant to say was *I* feel like you're ready to take the driver's seat," Samantha said, "And I know what you're thinking, but I'll be right there in the room next to you! Anything you need, or if you start to panic and go off the rails, I'll be there to jump in. What's the worst that could happen?"

"That I panic and go off the rails." Jayla answered dryly.

"But just think about how great you're going to feel Samantha added, "I'll throw in a free lunch!"

Jayla chuckled, rebalancing the scales of doubt in favor of Samantha's request. "Alright, alright," she said. "What's the worst that can happen?"

As the morning progressed, Jayla heard that question ringing in her ears over and over again, each visit supplying its own pummeled answer worse than its predecessor. First, there was the session where she set a new record for the use of the phrase "menstrual period," then there were the lesbians who came in and she guessed wrong at which one was pregnant, and vying for first place was the visit where the pregnant woman's boyfriend kept awkwardly flirting with her and trying to get her cell number. "But what if I have more questions later tonight or something?" he kept insisting.

Now, sitting down to lunch in the break area with her face in her hands, she was feeling all that confidence beginning to drain, leaking through the pore of every imperfect decision.

"Hey, don't you feel better getting these first few under your belt? See, it wasn't that bad!" Samantha said, scooting the delivery Chinese food she bought them for lunch across the table.

Jayla looked up, trying to scowl, but unable to fully because of the self-aware grin on Samantha's face.

Samantha wiped her mouth with a napkin and said, "Jayla, part of me is saying, 'Samantha, you go on and keep this a surprise and don't say anything.'"

"Keep *what* a surprise?" Jayla asked, not sure if she could handle any more surprises.

"Okay, okay, all I can tell you is I guarantee your next guest coming in today will be a hit. That's all I can tell you."

Jayla dropped her spoon into her meal and stared at Samantha until she became uneasy.

"Alright, alright. All I can tell you is I've known this lady for a while and she's just the sweetest person ever and her coming in today may have been the reason I suggested you step up. Maybe. But there I've gone and said too much, and I just can't tell you anymore."

The lunch break was over too quickly for Jayla's liking. Taking a deep breath, the two women walked up to the reception area where Brittany was snacking on some sunflower seeds.

"Our friend, Terica, is here for you, Mrs. Sam," Brittany said as she handed a folder past Jayla.

"Actually, Jayla is going to be helping her today," Samantha replied.

"Well, excuse me! Here you go," Brittany redirected, passing the folder into Jayla's hands. "You'll love Terica. She's such a sweetheart."

I'm starting to think this is a setup, Jayla thought. Scanning the lobby to see who Terica was, her eyes stopped on a very pregnant woman in her early thirties with hickory skin and a tightly coiled orange-tipped afro. *You're definitely Terica*, Jayla said to herself, amassing enough resolve for another session. *Let's do this thing.*

"Sammy, I didn't know you had models in your entourage," Terica blurted before Jayla and Samantha made it halfway to her.

"I'm upgrading myself. It hit me one day, 'Samantha, if you can't be young, you had better just surround yourself with young, beautiful women. They'll keep you young and beautiful,'" Samantha answered, passing Jayla to give Terica a bear hug.

"It's working for you," Terica replied, patting Samantha at a distance because of her protruding stomach. "Ricky Rick still know what a good thing he's got with you?"

"Ricky Rick?" Samantha guffawed. "You know what he asked me over the weekend? We went to a friend's house, and they had the subtitles on for a movie we were watching. Rick turns to me and says 'Babe, how come their TV came with words and ours didn't?' I dang near for the rest of the film had to convince him their TV wasn't fancier than ours because it came with words on the bottom."

"I can't believe that man," Terica said, "and I can't believe today's the day! Seven months . . ."

"I know. It got here quick, didn't it, momma?" said Samantha.

"It sure did. It sure did. I don't know how I feel. Nervous or excited or—homicidal—or maybe hungry," Terica joked. "My feet are numb and my skin is always itchy."

"Why don't we go into one of our counseling rooms, Ms. Terica, to discuss your visit today more in private," Jayla interjected uncomfortably.

Once in the Hope counseling room, Jayla watched for twenty-five agonizing seconds as Terica tried to comfortably work her way down onto the couch. "So," she said as Terica caught her breath. "I see on your intake form you're here for an ultrasound?"

Terica nodded. "Yes, ma'am, I am."

"Oh, not just any old ultrasound!" Samantha added proudly. "Today is Terica's seven-month checkup. Close to five months ago today Terica made her decision to keep her child. And she's been attending our Mommy University Classes every week since!"

Mommy University? Jayla wondered to herself.

Samantha turned to Jayla, "That's what I call our new Bright Star online program, it's not the official name. It's my better one."

"And I have been taking my vitamins and not smoking," Terica added with enthusiasm.

"We're so proud of you," Samantha responded.

Terica spoke up, gently rubbing her belly, "Yeah, my boyfriend wanted me to get an abortion, but I know this wasn't just a blob of tissue. I went down to that Unplanned place to get a pregnancy test, but there were so many picketers outside I got scared. My sister told me there's another place down the road from where we stay, so I came here."

"That's great," remarked Jayla, feeling a bit like a third wheel. "So what was it that made you choose not to get an abortion?"

"Well, you know that ultrasound machine y'all got back there? Sammy here calls it the lie detector machine," Terica said in a conspiratorial tone that made Samantha laugh. "You see, all my life I had been told that a baby in your body is really just a blob of tissue, like a tumor or something. And then I got an ultrasound five months ago when I came in to see because I tested positive and all. Then all the sudden—*BAMM*—there is like a 3-D baby on the screen. I had been drinking some Mountain Dew that afternoon and that little baby girl swam all over in there. It's one thing to know what people say something is and another thing to see it yourself. Those little hands and little feet don't lie. Do you have any kids?"

"No, no kids for me," Jayla said, feeling the lie in her womb.

"Well, you come here if you get pregnant cause these people are for real," Terica encouraged. "Seeing that ultrasound will change your life."

"Oh! That reminds me. You come up with a name yet, momma?" Samantha asked, taking the attention off Jayla, for which she was relieved.

"No, I'm still thinking about it. I'm waiting for inspiration to strike," Terica answered.

"Well, inspiration better strike soon. From how you look I don't think you'll be making it two more months," Samantha said.

"From your lips to God's ears!" Terica laughed, waving a playful worshipping hand in the air.

Samantha chortled until she snorted. "If you don't mind, Terica, Miss Jayla here is going to join us for your ultrasound today?"

Jayla smiled through her discomfort as she pondered how best to reply. She feared that in watching the ultrasound monitor, she would somehow peer into her own stomach. She would see feet and eyes and fingers and ears. Jayla didn't want that. She could not afford to feel that, not yet anyway.

"No, no. Seven-month check-ups are special. I would only be in the way," Jayla deflected.

"I don't mind," Terica said. "This late into the pregnancy. I have no secrets left for anybody"

"Yeah, seriously, come with us!"

Jayla started to feel her quills come out. "Maybe next time. There is some behind-the-scenes stuff I need to take care of," her eyes roamed around the room in search of chores. "Like—emptying the wastebasket." she said, knowing how lame the excuse was even as the words left her mouth. "Next time, though."

"Well, okay, if you're sure." Samantha backed down.

"But I'll see you in here right after your ultrasound. I can't wait to hear how it goes," Jayla said. *I'm just not ready to see it.*

CHAPTER 18

BUT FOR MY DAUGHTER

A few weeks into her new positions, Jayla was finally beginning to feel at ease. At the pregnancy center, she learned all the terms and catchphrases from Samantha and could lead a patient through a full session with little to no help. The only difference was she never once mentioned the services of Unplanned as an alternative. During this time she looked up nursing facts to convince Renee of her fictitious degree track and watched Brittany sport more African headscarves in a fashion shift no one saw coming.

Likewise, at Unplanned, she settled into the tricky rhythm of tending to multiple patients at once. She perfected the art of holding a patient's hair while she vomited, kept the fridge full of apple juice and the cupboards stocked with animal crackers, and passed out baggies, sometimes both hands at a time. And best of all, her patients were so *out of it*, they never recognized her from the pregnancy center.

Some days she thought of herself as a comic book superhero, alter ego included. Other days she felt like a double agent, a spy who infiltrated the enemy's camp for an undercover mission. It was hard, emotionally exhausting work. But, as she had through so many other trials in her life, Jayla was adapting and evolving to become whatever she needed to be to overcome.

Equally unbelievable, Jayla got used to the morning sickness she was experiencing in the early hours of the day. She was shocked to find the combination of heightened food aversions and daily vomiting made her more slender than before she got pregnant. Between her pixie cut, counterintuitive weight loss, and her confidence slowly continuing to mount, Jayla was feeling better than ever. She relished her coworkers' comments that she had a certain glow about her, as ironic as they were.

Walking in at Unplanned a few minutes before her Thursday shift, Jayla was startled by the sound of a package dropping near the utility closet a few rooms to her left, followed by hushed cursing.

Moving closer, Jayla stumbled upon a peculiar sight. While the door to the utility closet was closed and locked, there was a dim fluorescent light cascading from beneath the doorway as wrappers rustled and crinkled from within. Jayla knocked quietly and pressed her ear up to the door. More cursing followed until the door swung open with a very disheveled Hailey standing there, panting, trying to look as if everything were normal.

"Hey there, New Fran!" she said, out of breath. "What's—what's up?" as if Jayla had just knocked on Hailey's condo door and interrupted her doing goat yoga.

"I thought we agreed to not call me that."

"What? New Fran?" Hailey coyly replied, sneakily maneuvering the closet door closed behind her.

Jayla knew something was going on. "Fess up now," she demanded.

"What?" Hailey asked petulantly. Jayla's chiseled countenance only hardened.

"Ugh—fine."

Hailey opened the closet door behind her and scurried in, motioning for Jayla to do the same. "Get in before Sham Jackson sees you!" she whisper-shouted as Jayla took a few cautious steps forward.

Inside Jayla saw fallen pill bottles strewn about the floor. A spice rack of very organized medical packets was in complete disarray.

"What are you up to?" Jayla asked as Hailey stooped to pick up the mess.

"I just thought the room could use some tidying up and then, silly me, I bumped into the rack of medicine. I'm such a klutz, you know, and—"

As she spoke Jayla saw a tiny shimmering corner of foil peeking out of Hailey's scrubs. Without asking, Jayla reached over and tugged it out. "What's this?" she asked.

Then, with the look of defiance and shame a child gets when they've been caught, Hailey confessed, "I came in here to get these—you know—the pills."

"The abortion pills?" Jayla asked.

"Well, just shout it out for our friends in the nose bleeds. Yes, abortion pills, Mother Theresa—Misoprostol and Mifepristone."

Jayla squinted, looking Hailey up and down. "Are you...?"

"No, no. Not me. Ha ha. I'm not stupid. I just, uh. I get them for people."

"For patients?"

"Well," she laughed nervously, "kind of. People I know who need the abortion pill but maybe can't afford them, or maybe are too embarrassed to come in here. God knows why? So I help them. We got an accidental double shipment last year, so it don't cost nobody nothing."

"How many did you get?"

Hailey pulled out the plastic container and counted. "Twelve of each," she said.

"How many times have you done this?"

"I don't know. A few. But I only ever take just a small amount so no one catches on. Nobody misses them."

Jayla nodded her head. Then, hearing a pair of heels clacking down the hallway, the girls quieted down,

"You know anyone who might could use one?" Hailey asked once the shadow passed from under the door.

"I might," Jayla answered warily.

Faster than she could react, Hailey tore two different pills out of their foil casing and plopped them into Jayla's palm. "Here you go," she said cheerfully. "You are now holding about a thousand dollars' worth of abortion pills in your hand. Go online to find out which one your friend should take first, and you're welcome."

"Find out what pill to take first?" Jayla questioned.

"Yeah, and here's the big secret. They are only supposed to be used up to ten weeks, but I know that we have given them to girls I knew were like fifteen weeks along. They still work. The FDA just hasn't given approval for that time yet."

"Thanks," Jayla replied, staring at the pills in her palm and the various forms they took. In one light they appeared almost as magic fairytale beans that could change the entire course of her future. In another light they were cyanide capsules capable of destroying two lives in one gulp, both mercy and mercury in a single glance.

"No worries! We're in this together! We *are* in this together, right?" Hailey asked, leveling her gaze. "You're going to be cool about this, right?"

"Yeah, you're good," Jayla mumbled.

"Yay! I knew we were destined to be great friends, New Fran. I just knew it. Our astrology says so."

Jayla looked up from her hand for the first time since receiving the pills. Hailey brushed past her and opened the door. She double-checked from side to side to ensure they could come out. "Don't forget," she said, "Jack, these are magic beans. Be careful."

Throughout her morning shift, Jayla felt the heaviness of those pills weighing in her pocket. Yes, *be careful*, she continued to hear as if she was trying to smuggle drugs through an international airport.

When her lunch break finally came, Jayla hurried out of the recovery room in search of something—anything—that could steal away her attention. She found that preoccupation standing in the lobby talking with Lynn. A six-foot-tall, muscular, not-too-bad-looking distraction. The same man she encountered the day of her interview.

"Those picketers are killing us. They are killing us in the press, and they get constant press," she overheard Lynn say in hushed aggravation, looking out the window. "There are women who are not being served because of these—idiots. I think it's all the work of that little LifeLine Pregnancy Center across town. They're a bunch of do-good-er, anti-feminist religious freaks. Don't they know God is dead—get on with it." As Lynn saw Jayla drawing closer, she straightened and changed her tone. "Tripp, I'm not sure if you've had the pleasure of meeting Jayla. She is our new recovery room manager."

Manager? thought Jayla as she smoothed her outfit. *That's a first.*

"So, you're New Fran?" the young man said with a smirk. Jayla cringed.

"New Fran? Oh, I love that. I absolutely love that, Tripp. New Fran. How clever," Lynn fawned.

"We've actually met," Jayla corrected. "On my first day. For my interview."

"That's right!" Tripp said. "I'm glad to see it worked out."

"Tripp comes from a long line of women's rights supporters. His father, Dr. Lionel Sage, actually teaches a whole course on women's lib at the University of Texas, way down in Austin. Now there is a town!" Lynn said to Jayla before pivoting her attention, "Again, do give Dr. Sage my best, won't you?"

"How could I give anything else, coming from you?" Tripp charmed.

Lynn giggled in a way Jayla never heard before, and never wanted to hear again. "Oh, Tripp, you . . ." she began before catching another sight of the picketers. "Ugh! You know, half of these religious fanatics believe condom usage is interfering with their God-ordained pregnancies, rapes, and incestuous behavior. Why are they not picketing their local liquor store? It seems like if they had any intelligence, they would start where the problem is starting and not in the middle of it. But that's religion," she fired off. "Think about it. The big box retailers and our favorite overnight prime truck already deliver more condoms, sperm-killing foam, and morning-after abortifacients products than Unplanned, Inc. and the private abortion providers put together! They have double standards—AHH!" Lynn threw up her hands and screamed, "GET OFF MY SIDEWALK!" walking as fast as stiletto heels and an fiery sense of justice could carry her.

Tripp laughed to himself. "Classic Lynn."

At the sound of the office phone ringing, Tripp excused himself and got back to his desk.

While half listening to the goings-on in and outside of the lobby, Jayla was fixated on the nurse practitioner next to her who was speaking to a client; Jayla strained to hear their conversation.

"So, take the first pill, the one marked with the green label when you get home, and then take the one with the red label twelve hours later, right?" the young woman asked. Her gold feather necklace bobbed with each unsure step she took. "It just——happens?"

"Well, like we discussed during your evaluation, the pill begins its work immediately, as soon as you take it, and the second pill makes the process complete. For half of the women who use it, the fetal material is expelled from their body within four to five hours of the second pill, but it can take up to a week for other women."

"A week? Because they've been scheduling me so much at both jobs—which is great, you know, because we need the money."

"I'd contact your employer and see if you can take a few days off. I can even have Dr. Molech write a note for you if you need it. If you can't, though, the best advice I can give is to take a few pads into work and to stay near the bathroom."

"Near the bathroom?" the patient asked as the game on her daughter's smartphone purred and cooed.

"Yes, so you can take care of it. So you can flush it down."

"Just flush it down," the mother repeated, stroking the hair of her daughter, becoming caught up in her thoughts as her fingers became entangled in her child's lush raven hair. "It's funny . . ." she said after a few moments to herself, her eyes still on the little girl beside her.

"What?"

"Eight months from now I could either be watching my Eliana holding a newborn baby sister or brother in her arms or in eight hours I could be watching it being sucked down the toilet."

The nurse practitioner and the mother stood silent as the rest of the lobby bustled around them, the nurse breaking the uncomfortable silence, "You do what is best for you."

Jayla kept her gaze on the woman whose hand refused to leave her daughter's hair.

CHAPTER 19

JUST THE PHONE

As Jayla sat inside LifeLine waiting for the Friday morning devotional to begin, she caught herself watching Pastor Steve add a few drops of coffee to his thermos full of artificial sweeteners and cream.

"Ooo, that's good," she overheard him say from across the room as ladies gradually sauntered in, forming a small line behind him. Averting her gaze so she didn't seem to be staring, Jayla felt the odd desire to get up and speak with the pastor, an impulse she never felt before. Growing up in The Bricks, Jayla never saw pastors as anything more than lower rung CEOs of a declining industry and sometimes outright charlatans. Attending church was a joke, a punchline at which she learned to laugh from her ma. "If pastors were for real, they would be coming down here for something more than personal visitation of a lost woman," Amarika once said, and the saying stuck. She attended a CEF Bible Club down her block for about eight weeks one summer, but her mother did not know. It was there she learned enough of the basics to answer the questions correctly on the spiritual portion of her LifeLine application. Something must have stuck. Unfortunately, no thriving churches ever made her neighborhood an ongoing target for their evangelism.

Yet now Jayla found her soul longing for someone, anyone, to speak wisdom to her. She quietly ached for someone to walk with her down this withering path. Someone without bias, or judgment, or anything to gain from her decision. At the same time, she knew to gain that person meant revealing certain things in her own life she was terrified to expose. Vulnerability, weakness, insecurity, fear, worry frightened her. The thought of stripping her heart and baring these emotions chaffed against Jayla's will and alerted every defense mechanism kept in her ample arsenal.

"Hey, there," Steve said kindly in passing to Jayla as he moseyed over to a group of coworkers waiting to speak with him.

"Morning," Jayla replied. For the time being she knew that was the extent of all she had to say.

"Well, hey, there," Darla greeted, sporting a giant water bottle in one hand. "Since Sam's out today, I was wondering if you could do me a favor?"

Sam's out today? Jayla pondered. "What's the favor?"

"My new diet has got my tummy in a bit of a rumble. Any way could you take the first patient of the day for me? Maybe the first few, you know, worst case?"

"I don't know . . ."

"If you help me today with this, and then next week, when I've adjusted a little more, I'll pick up some extra guests to give you a chance to get some extra break time. Maybe a long lunch, or maybe some extra study time for that degree you're getting?"

How does everyone know about that? "Sure," Jayla resigned, "sounds like a good trade."

"You're the best! Thank you!" Then Darla asked unexpectedly, "Which school was it again that you are going to?"

"Right here local, the community college," replied Jayla without hesitation, having memorized the lie thoroughly, but second-guessing herself.

"No way! What classes are you taking?"

"A mix of business and nursing—this and that. Sometimes it feels like I have so many classes I can't keep track of any of them."

"Do you know Judy McIntyre? Anybody who's anybody at ACC knows her."

"Judy—hmmm—yeah, that name sounds familiar."

"No. Way. Judy is my niece," bragged Darla. "What a small world!"

"Yeah, small world," replied Jayla, already looking for ways to pivot or backtrack as she felt her neckline tighten a bit.

"Have any classes together? I'm pretty sure she said she was a business major too."

"With Judy? No, no, I don't think so."

"Aww—well, I'll have to tell her to keep her eye out for you," Darla plotted excitingly. "Once you see her, you'll probably realize you've seen her around campus a lot. She's top of her class. Must run in the family."

"Must," Jayla agreed through a clenched jaw, trying to evaluate Darla. If she was suspicious at all, Jayla couldn't tell. "Well, I'm going to go and start prepping for our first patient."

"You're not staying for the devotional?"

"I just want to make sure everything is ready. Unless you want to help me prep later?" asked Jayla, banking on Darla's perceived dislike for additional work.

"If Renee asks, I'll cover for you!" Darla replied with a wink. "You can trust me."

Jayla stood, grateful to be out of the conversation. Then, walking toward the exit, she felt a grumble in her stomach that sent pangs of hunger sprawling across her abdomen. *How am I so hungry already?* she wondered, making a pit stop at the coffee area.

There she saw her eighty-year-old coworker, a lively lady with jet black hair. "It's Merridy, right?" Jayla asked. For an office of twenty people maximum, it was a silly question for anyone social to ask. Still, for Jayla, who rarely spoke to anyone outside her immediate need, it was necessary.

"That's right. Merridy. Merridy with a M," the woman said, sticking out her hand. Then, with a firm grip, added, "And I know you, Jayla, the new client advocate. I hear good things!"

Jayla smiled, liking the spunk of the little old woman. "How long have you been working here, Merridy?" she asked.

"Oh goodness, I started here when this place started twenty-three years ago, as the first director. Then we had Charlotte, then for one year Edith, and then about six years ago came Renee. What a go-getter she is."

Jayla was surprised. "You ran this place?" she inquired as she doused her coffee-flavored-water with sugar.

"I'm pretty sure it ran me more than I ran it, God's truth," Merridy chuckled. "But yes, you could say that. It was all new back then and we hardly knew what we were doing. We just wanted to save some lives and help some women, and we did. I think our total rescued baby count from abortion-minded mothers is over two thousand babies at this point."

"Why did you stop? Being in charge, I mean."

"Well, I went through a real struggle with my health, and although this place had been my life, being the leader wasn't the goal. It's always been about the life of the children and the healing of the women. So, I talked it over with my husband and decided I needed to leave the director position but not leave the center. I needed to rest a little more, and the director position offers little rest," Merridy mused as if even just the memory of that past exhaustion was wearing her thin.

"So what do you do now?" Jayla asked.

"Why, young lady, I'm the chief phone salesman!" Merridy answered self-importantly, yet with a humble smile. "Well, sales—woman."

"Wow! I didn't know we had one of those."

"Well," Merridy began, pausing with a sigh. "God's truth, we don't get a lot of phone calls anymore. Things have changed so much since the early years. The phone used to ring multiple times every day but now, between the morning-after pill and the ten-week pill, people are not afraid to take things into their own hands. That definitely lowers our call volume. Very low, and that grieves me. Nine times out of ten, when the phone does ring, it's a man on the other end shopping for the cheapest abortion services. I can talk to the young ladies, but the boyfriends are just looking for the quickest fix."

"That sounds rough," Jayla replied, seeing Merridy deflate.

"That's alright. It's all part of the role I play. You see, it's my job to get these ladies into the door to talk to a counselor person, like you, before they go and find an abortion provider," she said with a mischievous glint in her eye. "Sly as serpents and harmless as doves—that is my motto."

Jayla couldn't tell if she wanted to laugh or not, feeling her jaw gape a bit by Merridy's unconventional answer. "So what do you say to the girls who call?" she asked, intrigued.

"Well girls, or sometimes their boyfriend or husband, will call and ask about the cost of an abortion. And I give them an answer, but not always the answer they're expecting. Here, let me show you. Let's do a practice call, just you and me. Who knows, you may have to get the phone and help a girl get in here."

"Let's hope not." Jayla blurted, feeling uncomfortable with any type of role play.

"Okay, so you're calling. Ask me the question and answer me in your own words as I talk to you. 'Thank you for calling LifeLine Pregnancy Center, we are women helping women. How can I help you today?'"

"Ummm—uhhh," Jayla froze.

"Now is the part where you say I need an abortion," Merridy directed, feeding Jayla her line.

"I need . . ." Jayla began, feeling slimy and uncomfortable for repeating the words. Her mind going to the pills she had stored in the glove box of her car sitting in the parking lot.

"An abortion," Merridy quietly mouthed after Jayla stalled for too long.

"An abortion."

"And you want to know how much they cost?"

"Sure."

"Okay. First, I need to know how far along you are. How long has it been since your last cycle completed?"

"Ah, ah, two months," Jayla answered, shockingly close to the truth. The old woman's spunk was no longer amusing as her mining questions were accidentally unearthing reality.

"Okay, we would like to have you come in for pregnancy verification. Can we set up an appointment for a pregnancy test and a medical ultrasound? There is no charge, and all our services are completely confidential."

"I'm not sure I want an ultrasound. I don't really want to see—it," Jayla answered honestly. "I'd rather just have an abortion and get it over with." Then, jumping back into character, asked, "How much would that cost?"

"Cost, cost. There are different costs to an abortion. Really, it's not my place to say. But listen, honey, physically and emotionally, now that's the greater cost."

"What do you mean?"

"Well, physically, there can be heavy bleeding and cramping or infection. There is the damage to your cervix or your internal organs, not to mention the well-documented links between abortion and breast cancer. And, of course, this is only what you could experience physically, not to mention your baby, who would, of course, die. In rare cases, both the mother and baby die as a result of the abortion. It is rare, but it does happen. Only you know how good you are at avoiding Murphy's Law."

"But these physical effects are what? One in ten thousand abortions? They've been doing them long enough."

"It's one in a hundred for early abortions and one in fifty for later abortions," Merridy replied, holding up her invisible phone while looking Jayla squarely in the eyes. "Of course, the one doesn't know they're the one until they are."

"And emotionally?"

"If you came in for one of our counseling appointments, we could talk about all this in more detail."

"You have me on the phone now, I'm not ready to come in." Jayla replied with an earnestness that surprised even herself. "Tell me now."

"There is evidence that both physical health and emotional health decreases in women who have undergone an abortion. Guilt, depression, eating disorders, alcohol or drug abuse, not to mention flashbacks of the abortion. Suicidal thoughts can also manifest themselves after an abortion. And these emotional effects have been known to last for months to even decades in some cases."

Jayla was silent as she absorbed the information.

"So can you come in at three this afternoon? I'll have a private nurse waiting for you to answer any more questions you might have. We will even reimburse you for a taxi or Uber if you need one?"

"Sure. Sounds great," replied Jayla softly.

"Perfect. I know the perfect client advocate for you," Merridy said with a wink and hung up the phone. "Terrific, Jayla! Just terrific. If I didn't know any better, God's truth, I'd think you'd done this before."

CHAPTER 20

"I KNOW ABUSE
WHEN I SEE IT"

For close to thirty minutes, Jayla prepared the counseling rooms, hiding out more than cleaning and stocking. Channeling her inner Samantha, she restocked the hand sanitizer, spritzed a citrus air freshener, and fluffed the tissues until they looked picturesque. If there was anything to be done that could remotely distract her from the residue of the conversation she had with Merridy, she was willing to do it—twice.

By the time she came into the reception area, Brittany was already humming away with a few intake forms nestled nearby, sporting a creamy silk headscarf tightly wound around her brow.

"Morning," Jayla said before remembering, with Samantha's absence, she had no reason to keep up the pretense of caring.

"Good morning, honey," Brittany replied in between stanzas. "Some good devotional today, didn't you think?"

"Oh yeah, for sure," Jayla replied absentmindedly.

Brittany handed Jayla two folders. "So what did you think of the announcement about the Community Day? They appointed me to book the music. Did you have anyone you'd like to recommend? A band or DJ or anything? Right now, we're on the ground floor of the event, so we're open to any suggestions as long as they've got talent."

"No, I don't know anybody like that."

"Tell you the truth, I don't either, and that's the problem," Brittany chuckled. "If you think of anybody later, let me know. The only thing I ask is they're clean with their music. You know, no cursing or swearing or using the Lord's name in vain. And by all means, no music that makes anybody want to shake their backside."

There goes all the good music then, Jayla thought to herself as she opened the first intake folder. Then, seeing an opportunity for an easy jab, added, "I would have thought they would have picked someone . . ."

"Younger?" Brittany chortled, filling in the blank.

"Cooler," Jayla answered, wanting to say worse but satisfied the remark was small enough to not be reported.

To her surprise, Brittany laughed. "You're not wrong," she said, "but look at my competition. Comparatively, you're looking at the second coolest person here."

"Oh? Who's the first?" Jayla asked.

"You."

Lifting her eyes from the folder, Jayla stared back at Brittany, waiting for a punchline, but none came. *What just happened? Did she just turn that into a compliment?* she wondered. Unable to think of a good response, she returned her gaze to the intake form.

"Alexandria Clarke," Jayla muttered to herself before scanning the few women sitting in the lobby.

"She's the gal with the curly blonde hair and tank top," Brittany assisted, then began to hum a new tune as she typed "cool local good clean bands" into the search engine on her computer.

Walking toward Alexandria, Jayla was struck by the beauty of her tattoos painted across long thin arms and peeking between the holes in her jeans. Tiny splotches of paint collected around her cuticles, a small blue puzzle piece tattoo inked between her thumb and index finger.

Behind her sat a couple, a man with coffee in one hand and the other possessively strapped to the woman's thigh beside him. The woman, presumably his girlfriend, wore a long sweater and leggings and stared unblinkingly through the side window like a butterfly gazes at the world through a mason jar.

"Alexandria?" Jayla called from a few feet away.

"That's me," Alexandria answered, looking uncomfortable.

Must be her first time at a clinic, reasoned Jayla. "Hi, Mrs. Clarke, my name is Jayla, and I'm one of the client advocates here. If you're ready, I'd love for us to have a talk in one of our private counseling rooms."

"Actually, I think the woman behind me should go first," Alexandria said softly, her eyes subtly motioning to the couple. "I'm pretty sure they were here before me, anyway."

"Alright," Jayla replied, surprised, having never had a guest respond that way.

Turning her attention to the couple behind Alexandria, Jayla approached with a smile, flipping through the second intake form. "Evelyn?" she asked the long-sleeved woman.

Before the woman had a chance to speak, the man next to her responded. "We'll wait for the other one," he said before slurping some coffee.

"The other what?" Jayla asked.

"The other whatever-you-are," he answered, his hand pressing firmly on Evelyn's thigh.

"I'm the only client advocate here this morning," responded Jayla.

"Shoot fire," the man said sarcastically. "Does affirmative action run this place or something?"

"Excuse me?" Jayla replied, feeling her skin prickle with tension.

"Gerald," Evelyn interrupted.

Jayla could see the man's squeeze on Evelyn's leg tighten. "I think we'll wait for someone a little more, uh, qualified to help us."

"Sir, I can assure you I am highly qualified in this role and would be—"

"And I can assure you we will be fine to wait."

"Alright. That's fine. Another client advocate will be here later this afternoon. But she's black too," Jayla lied. "We all are. I think it's something in the water. Speaking of, how's that free coffee treating you, sir?"

Alexandria laughed quietly, making the situation even more uncomfortable.

"She thinks she's funny," the man said with a smile that felt even more menacing than his scowl. "Alright. We can go back with you."

"I'm sorry, sir, but we only allow the patient to come in the counseling session," Jayla said, not knowing if it was true, but not wanting to be anywhere close to a small private room with that man. "You are welcome to join her afterward for an ultrasound if one is required. It's HIPAA policy."

"HIPAA policy, huh?"

"Mmmm."

"Fine," the man said tersely, releasing Evelyn, the wrinkle from his handprint still visible in her jeans. Standing up, Evelyn pulled her sleeves down over her wrists.

"How long is this gonna take?" the man asked, reaching for his smartphone.

"It depends. The more qualified the client advocate, the longer the meeting. So it will probably be a really, really long meeting," Jayla quipped before assisting Evelyn. "Please follow me."

As they walked silently toward the interior door, Jayla couldn't shake the feeling that this woman needed her help more than her normal patients. The man's temper, his grip on Evelyn's thigh, her long sleeves on a warm day were all out of place. With all Jayla had experienced in her life, she could recognize evidence of abuse, and her instincts were screaming out. But, having never experienced a situation like this, what was the right next step?

I wish Samantha were here, Jayla thought as Brittany buzzed them inside. *What do I do?*

"Excuse me for one moment," Jayla smiled at Evelyn. Then, taking a few steps into the reception area while staying out of sight, she waved gently, getting Brittany's attention.

"Can you please have Renee meet me outside the Love Counseling Room?" Jayla asked calmly, which was at odds with the adrenaline steadily beginning to churn in her system.

"I think she's in a meeting with Pastor Steve," Brittany replied.

I don't care if she's in a meeting with God, Jayla thought. "Brittany. Please have Renee meet me outside the Love Counseling Room," she repeated commandingly.

Brittany looked at Evelyn and back at Jayla and lightly nodded her head before picking up her phone.

"Sorry about that," Jayla said as she returned to Evelyn. "This way."

"Everything okay?" Evelyn asked.

"Everything's great," Jayla lied.

"Okay. It's just that Gerald doesn't like me being away too long. He needs me too much."

"I understand," Jayla said as they rounded the corner, turning into the counseling area, where Renee stood just outside.

"Good morning, Renee," Jayla smiled before returning her attention to Evelyn. "We'll have our session in the Love Counseling Room. If you don't mind stepping in and making yourself comfortable, I'll be with you in a moment."

Evelyn nodded obediently. "You'll be in soon, won't you?"

"I sure will. Won't be but a minute," Jayla responded coolly. Then watching the door close, she looked at Renee with unconcealed concern.

"What's going on?" Renee asked.

Jayla stepped closer and began whispering quickly. "That woman in there, I'm pretty sure she's being abused. All the signs are there. I saw her, and I started thinking, you know, it's way too warm for those long sleeves. And this guy—Renee, you should have seen this guy. He's controlling and mean, not to mention racist, and I think he's abusing her."

Renee looked at Jayla soberly. "That's a very serious accusation, Jayla."

"I know."

"Did you see him physically assault her?" Renee asked.

"No."

"Emotionally or verbally assault her?"

"No."

"Did she complain about any abuse?"

"No, she didn't."

"Brittany was out there. What did she think?"

"Brittany doesn't know. She is too busy looking up bands that are cool but don't make people want to dance. But I know it, Renee. You gotta trust me on this. It's all there."

Renee studied Jayla's face, parsing out her words. "Give me the intake form."

Jayla passed Evelyn's folder to Renee. "What are you thinking?"

"I'll take over for this guest. You go ahead and help the next patient."

"But he's still out there," Jayla warned.

Renee nodded and pulled out her phone. "Brittany, have the next patient come inside for her visit and escort her to Jayla. I'm sending her back to you now," she said, then added to Jayla, "Make sure you hang back after this visit so we can debrief."

"Okay," Jayla replied. Then, turning to walk down the hall, Renee stopped her.

"You did the right thing," Renee said affirmingly, before opening the door to the counseling room.

That man won't know what's coming, Jayla thought to herself as she doubled back to the reception area. The nerves and tension of the moment mixed with the validation she got from Renee converted her jitters into a rabid excitement she found hard to suppress.

It wasn't long before Brittany and Alexandria came into view down the other end of the hallway. "There she is," Brittany said, relieved, "Jayla, I was just talking with Mrs. Clarke about you."

"Great," replied Jayla as she smoothed over her scrubs.

"Well, I will leave you two to it," Brittany said. "And thanks again for your band recommendations, sugar! You be sure to check us out at our Community Day."

"Okay, Alexandria, let's head to the Faith Room where we go over things in private," guided Jayla as she led the two of them back toward the counseling area.

"Were you able to talk to that girl?" Alexandria asked, looking around to see if anyone was in listening distance.

"I was, a little. Our director is in with her now," Jayla replied, reaching for the door handle.

"That guy was such a creep," Alexandria said bluntly. "What a sleazebag. Are you guys going to be able to help her?"

"I can't discuss another patient. I'm sorry," advised Jayla, wanting so badly to talk to someone about everything happening.

"But you guys have shelters you know about, places she could go, right? I mean, y'all are a Christian place, right? Isn't that what you do? You saw her, you could tell, right? The abuse?"

Jayla looked at Alexandria kindly, searching for a solid middle ground from which to respond. "I'm sorry. I can't discuss any other patient with you, but I can say we take abuse very seriously." Jayla did her best to let her eyes tell the woman they were working on it.

"Good. That's good. What a creep. Man, I hate guys like that," Alexandria said, choosing to sit in the oversized navy seat rather than the couch. "And then he pulled that race crap. Ugh! I just can't believe when people start with that, especially in the time we're living in. This isn't the 1950s."

Opening the intake folder in her lap, Jayla asked, "So, Alexandria, what brings you in today?"

"Well, I think I'm pregnant, but I want to be sure," Alexandria replied.

"Okay. When was the first day of your last menstrual period?"

"A little over three months ago."

"And was your last one normal?"

"Nothing's normal about having a period," Alexandria laughed, "but yeah. It was fine."

"Three months is a rather long time. Have you already taken a pregnancy test?" Jayla asked.

"No. Truth is, I'm scared to take one. I mean, don't get me wrong, I want to. I know I need to. But I was thinking maybe after it had been enough time, my period would come back."

"Enough time?"

"From the accident," replied Alexandria, beginning to pick at the paint on her fingers. "I didn't even notice not having my period the first month and the second month. I had heard that it's not uncommon when a lady is grieving for her body to, you know, stop. So I thought it would just come back when enough time had passed. But here we are. So . . ."

Jayla usually didn't dig deeper when it came to her patient's personal stories, but curiously she found herself putting down the intake form and going off-script. "What accident?"

"Oh, you know—everyone has a sob story—mine is nothing special," Alexandria replied, her eyes refusing to divert from her hand.

"Okay," Jayla said reassuringly. "There's no pressure to talk about it." Then, opening the intake form, continued where she left off. "Are you currently on any birth control?"

Alexandria sat in the oversized chair looking like a child in its high-raised arms, picking and flicking flecks of paint from her cuticles with such focus Jayla considered repeating the question. "My husband was in an accident," Alexandria began unexpectedly. "Two months and fourteen days ago."

"I'm sorry to hear that."

"We loved kids. Well, him more than me. We had been married for four years and had been trying to get pregnant. He had this idea in his head he would come back from deployment, and I would be there with a baby on my hip waiting for him, you know, like in all the return videos you see online. But we tried, and no baby, and he went on his first deployment, and I waited for him. Same thing after the second deployment."

"So sorry to hear that."

"Anyways he was getting ready for another deployment and he's wanting to make the night special—well, as special as a Marine can make it. And he orders food in and it's this real feast, you know, but before we start, he gets this look on his face and he tells me he'll be right back. And he won't tell me where he's going and he leaves and, while he's gone, I get real beautiful for him. I have the perfume on and the low-cut, high-skirt dress he likes and I light some candles and I wait for him for what seemed like a really long time. But sometimes that's how it was with Andy—he'd get talking with someone."

"And they say *we* do all the talking," Jayla said to lighten the mood.

"So I'm getting really hungry. I'm actually mad at him for taking so long, with all this food getting cold in front of me…" Alexandria said, choking on the words as they came out, picking and rubbing her hand more intensely. "And that's when the phone rings, and a man on the other end says to me, 'Hello, Mrs. Clarke? Your husband has been hit by a drunk driver,' and I remember thinking, *My God, two tours in Afghanistan and he comes out scratch-free, but a drunk driver has killed him?!* Come to find out he went to the supermarket to get me my favorite dessert. Can you believe that?"

Jayla watched as amazement, frustration, and crushing sorrow played across Alexandria's face. As Jayla reached for a box of tissues, Alexandria shook her head. "No, thanks, I'm fine."

"For your hand," Jayla advised, her gaze fixed on Alexandria's fingers, which had begun to bleed.

"Oh, thanks," Alexandria replied with surprise. Then, despite holding the tissue in her hand, she continued to watch as the blood slowly dried on her skin. "I still feel like I'm waiting for him, you know? Like he's just off on another deployment, and at any moment he'll just come right on through that door," she said, looking up to the entrance and pausing. "He won't though. He never will, and I just gotta be okay with that," Alexandria added dismissively as she wiped her hand clean. "And now, lo and behold, it looks like I might have that baby after all for him. And, truthfully, between you and me, I don't know if I'm happy about that or scared out of my mind."

Jayla nodded, wanting to comfort Alexandria but not fully knowing how. "I'm sorry."

"You're sorry, I'm sorry, the drunk driver is sorry, everybody is sorry. But, like I said, we all have our sob stories, mine just happens to be fresher than most other peoples."

Jayla didn't say anything for a while and Alexandria seemed to be content with that, up to a point. "So," she finally said, "are we finding out if there is a bun in this oven, or what?"

After ten minutes waiting for Alexandria's positive pregnancy results, Jayla found herself sitting outside the area she dreaded most at LifeLine—the ultrasound room. Sitting in the plush chairs waiting for their turn, Jayla was nervous as she felt something churning within her, unable to tell if it was her stomach or her womb giving her such unrest. She wasn't ready to see what was in Alexandria's womb because she didn't want to find out what was growing in her own body.

"Alexandria?" the ultrasound technician, Marta, asked. Then seeing Jayla, she added, "Hey sweetie, where's Sam today?"

Don't I wish I knew, Jayla thought to herself. "Having a long weekend."

"Oh, I hope she enjoys it. No one deserves it more. Are the two of you ready?"

"You go on in," Jayla said to Alexandria, seeing a way out. "We'll discuss your next steps after this appointment has been completed."

"Will you come in with me?" Alexandria asked sheepishly. "It's fine if you can't," she added, defensively. "It's just—I've got no one else right now. You know?"

It was then, looking at Alexandria, Jayla saw a reflection of herself. Scared but tough, hurt yet invincible, weathering worry under an utterly fearless exterior.

"I can be in there with you," Jayla said, by which she meant we can be in there for each other.

Alexandria smiled and walked into the dark room with Marta at her heels. Then, inhaling through her nose and exhaling out of her mouth, Jayla smoothed over her scrubs, taking the first step toward the plunge.

CHAPTER 21

BUY ONE, GET ONE FREE

"That thing looked like the Loch Ness Monster. Am I horrible for saying that?" Alexandria laughed as she and Jayla walked toward the front lobby.

"Girl, I couldn't tell what was its head and what was its butt," Jayla joked as the girls snickered together, conspiratorially. Allowing herself to access some emotions and not others, Jayla focused on the lightness she felt from having faced her fear.

"You must have seen about a million of those, huh?" asked Alexandria. "Does it ever get less weird?"

"Something like that," Jayla lied. "And no, it never gets less weird. So we will see you on the 27th of next month. Is that still a good date for you?"

"Yeah, that's fine," Alexandria said as she added an entry into her phone calendar, then added, "Would it be okay if I got your phone number? All this is so new to me—"

"Umm . . ." Jayla hesitated. Since getting out of her last relationship, Jayla had been resistant to pass out her phone number to anyone. She found herself much more guarded this side of the breakup, and for good reason.

"It's totally okay if you can't!"

"Yeah, no, sorry. We're not allowed to give our personal numbers to patients," Jayla advised convincingly, for the second untruth of their conversation. "But you can always call here anytime you have a question. And if you ask for Jayla, they'll patch you through to me."

"Okay, great. Thanks," Alexandria said, opening the door to the lobby. "I guess I'll start shopping? Or maybe I should wait until I know if I'm buying for blue or pink—who knows. I'm a mess," she laughed. "Thanks again for today. I hope your Jesus stuff keeps going strong, or whatever it is you Christians say to each other."

"Alright, you have a good day, Alexandria. Keep your Jesus hand strong," Jayla chuckled as the two women parted, catching a glimpse of Renee out of the corner of her eye and thinking, *I don't know what they say, either.*

"Keep your Jesus hand strong?" Renee asked, drawing closer to Jayla.

"You know, it's a new thing young Christians are saying to each other."

"Huh. I didn't know that," Renee said, mentally filing this new information. "Do you have a second to talk about what happened earlier?"

"Absolutely, of course, I've got to know," Jayla replied, following Renee into the hallway.

"Good morning, Ms. Renee," Brittany called out from the reception area as they passed. "Good morning, Brittany! Keep your Jesus hand strong!" Renee shouted back as Brittany's head cocked to one side in confusion.

"So, about your patient," Renee began once they reached the empty break area. "You did the right thing by getting me. I conducted the session and made sure to ask her some key questions along the way. 'How are things at home? Are you ever afraid of your partner? Are you concerned about the safety of you or your children?' And after I saw parallel bruising on her wrists, I said, 'When I see injuries like this, I wonder if someone possibly hurt you?'"

"And what did she say?" asked Jayla.

"She said nothing. She said she was fine, that everything at home was great, that her partner had a temper but who didn't, and said no one has been hurting her, but she is clumsy and sometimes runs into things."

"Like her boyfriend's fist!"

"Well, like I said, abuse is a big accusation for anyone to make, and we don't know all the facts of her story," Renee advised, "but I personally am inclined to agree with you. Many red flags were there—too many to ignore. So I'm really glad you got me."

"So what do we do now?" asked Jayla.

"Unfortunately, there's not much we can do. I'll file a report, and we'll do our due diligence with the police. I know a person to call. Unfortunately, beyond that, there's nothing we can do. At this point she isn't even alleging any abuse has taken place. We'll keep an eye on her if she ever comes back. We'll tell the police more, then, but that's about all that can be done."

"I hate that for her," Jayla said after a few moments of silence. "Sucks."

"I hate it too," Renee empathized. "You know, people think pro-life just means we're for babies getting to be born. But that's not all pro-life should be about. To be 'pro-life' is to be for all of life. And I don't want to fight for the right of a baby to be born into the world just to watch her get abused by the world a few years later. I'm not only for that baby being born—I'm for that baby for all her life. I'm for that mother to find a new life and a changed life."

"Yeah," Jayla replied, allowing Renee to stroke her shoulder in sympathy.

"By the way, good eye at spotting the potential for abuse there. Not all of our client advocates can see that so quickly, so kudos. I'm glad you've got such discernment."

"Thanks. By the way, where's Samantha? Darla said she's out today?"

"Her husband has a regional softball tournament, so she'll be out until Monday."

"Okay. Just making sure everything was okay."

For the rest of her shift Jayla walked briskly, spoke loudly, and worked with a fervency unmatched by her peers. To anyone watching, it seemed like she had found a new level of dedication to her job. But for Jayla this was all a show. It was an act to distract herself from what she wasn't yet ready to consider in the wake of Alexandria's ultrasound. Jayla was doing what she always did when she wasn't ready to process what was going on in her life—she held it in, damming up her emotions with distractions of every size until the right moment came for all of it to spew out of her.

That moment came after work when all the goodbyes had been said, all the patients had left, and her car was the last one left in the parking lot. There Jayla sat, car running, hands on the steering wheel, snapshots of the ultrasound running through her head. She could still hear Alexandria's gasp upon seeing the baby's small, round face replaying in her ears. "Oh, Andy," she whispered, thinking no one else was listening.

Sitting in the car now Jayla looked at her own fingers, polished and pristine, free from the press-on nails she had used to cover her own insecurities. Her gaze fixed, she saw in her mind's eye the ten small fingers and toes that came into focus on the ultrasound screen, each fitted with its own perfect tiny fingernail. Feeling her own heart begin to quicken its pace at the recollection, Jayla remembered listening to the baby's heartbeat, thumping and pulsing with sounds she would have expected from a submerged submarine. It was strange, and it was mesmerizing.

Jayla thought back of how she came out of character in the ultrasound room saying, "How big would it be if it was about two months old?" as the three ladies peered at the screen.

"Oh, this baby is older than that. I think we're looking at a little over three months," Marta started to reply before Jayla interrupted.

"But if it was only two months old—how big?"

Jayla remembered the confused look on Marta's face as she contemplated the answer. "Well, about a month ago, I'd say she'd be about the size of a raspberry. But she's progressing beautifully, dear."

"She?" Jayla remembered asking before Alexandria had the chance.

Marta laughed. "Don't you know, dear? All babies begin female."

And now, sitting in her car, Jayla put her hand over her own stomach, slowly, resistantly. *A girl*, she thought. No longer an it or a thing but a girl with a heartbeat like her own. With fingers and toes like her. The size of a raspberry.

Then, her eyes flitting to the glove box, she remarked, "The size of two pills." Part of her wished the window to what was growing inside her would have remained closed and locked and opaque so she could continue disconnecting herself from it. So she could compartmentalize it in her mind and distinguish it as just another unwanted organ, like her tonsils or appendix. That way it would have been all the easier to dispose of and never look back. She should put a stop to it right there, right then, leaving it impersonal, inhuman, inconvenient, and in the dark.

The other part, however, wanted to know more. Wanted to find out what exactly—or, more specifically who exactly—was being nurtured in her womb. The window was opened, why not peek a little further for a little longer? How could she know if she wanted to get rid of the baby or not if she didn't even know what it looked like?

"I think I'm gonna do it," Jayla said out loud, and then laughed at herself in disbelief, at the sheer craziness of hearing words come out of her mouth she swore she would never say.

No, no, no, if you do this, then you won't go back.

It won't go back to being an "it" after the ultrasound. You'll get attached. It will be a real person, with or without my consent.

Consent, there's that word. The word whose absence got you into this mess, Jayla thought. *You never wanted this. You never asked for this, and you're only here because someone didn't think your consent was worth anything. Just get rid of it. Get some closure. You have nothing to feel guilty about.*

But how awful was that lack of consent? Jayla's other instinct reminisced in agony. *I didn't consent and he hurt me—and now I want to take away consent from this baby and hurt it? I was innocent—what wrong has this baby done to me?*

"Seeing that ultrasound will change your life," Terica told her, and now Jayla was beginning to think she was right. *Okay,* Jayla firmly decided, *I'm going to do it.*

For a moment Jayla felt great. The brief mental victory Jayla won melted into a puddle of logistical uncertainty, her mind so full of questions it was starting to radiate with throbbing pain. *What am I doing wasting my Friday night like this?* she wondered, rubbing her temples. Then, as if jolted to her senses from that epiphany, Jayla declared out loud to her empty vehicle, "You know what? It's the weekend, and I deserve a break."

Driving wherever she wanted to go, free of responsibility or care, Jayla settled on the mall. She wanted to shop around a little first before going to the food court. She perused in and out of department store racks, up and down aisles of jeans and dresses and hats and purses. After twenty minutes lost in a shoe rack safari hunt, Jayla was surprised to hear someone calling out toward her. So surprised, in fact, she didn't immediately respond.

"New Fran, is that you? I told you that was her. New Fran, hey!" came a voice a few yards away.

Jayla looked up to see Hailey waving excitedly with one arm, blonde ponytail bobbing left to right as she dragged Nikole toward Jayla. Nikole remained engrossed in her phone, her feet shuffling offbeat beneath her. "Well, if it isn't everyone's favorite Fran!" Hailey greeted, going in for an unsolicited hug.

"Hey! What are you guys doing here?" Jayla asked, shocked.

"I am here as moral support for Nikole as she emotionally binges through the greatest hits of this capitalistic sweatshop. How about you?" Hailey asked.

"Just looking around. Long day at work."

"Oh yeah, I forgot you have a second job. Where at again?" Nikole asked.

Not wanting to discuss her employment with them, Jayla was relieved when Hailey looked at her and excitedly changed the subject. "We're about to try on some clothes. Wanna come with?"

"Umm, I was actually going to head to the food court soon."

"Perfect! Courting food is my favorite!" Hailey cheered, linking Jayla's arm in hers. "Now what should we try on first?"

After sizing Jayla up, Hailey grabbed several outfits off the rack and slung them over her arms, losing Nikole along the way. A few long lace blouses, some designer jeans, a yellow and black romper, two sundresses. "That should do nicely," Hailey said, finalizing some clothing options for herself.

"What are you doing with these?" Jayla asked.

"Me? They're for you, silly! Go on, let's see how they look."

"You want me to put on these clothes?"

"Yes! You put on clothes, we take pictures of you in clothes, your followers are mega-mega jealous. Capeesh?"

"No, I'm good," Jayla said, with none of this plan appealing to her.

"You are good—and you'll be even better with these pictures to post! Just imagine all the people looking at your account and seeing these and all the likes you're gonna get and all the people you'll inspire."

"I don't know . . ." Jayla replied.

"Oh, come on, grandma. You don't even have to spend any money. It's free to just take pictures. So come on!"

"Y'all are going to do it too?" inquired Jayla as Nikole strolled up to the conversation with an armful of clothes of her own.

"Yes, girl! All of us! It's an easy way to freshen up our posts—or our dating profiles. Right, Nikole?"

Nikole laughed, shaking her head.

"Ask her what app she's on," Hailey nudged Jayla.

"What app are you on?"

"Whichever ones Terri is on," Hailey answered before Nikole could speak.

With a perfect smile stretched ear to ear, Nikole pulled out her phone, scrolling and toggling until she lifted the screen for Jayla to see. There, before her, was a profile picture of Terri, wearing too much eye makeup, donning a black dress with a pearl necklace—the photo strategically tilted in the most flattering way, cropping out her bottom half.

"So, wait, you made a dating profile for Terri?" questioned Jayla, trying to fit together the pieces.

"I didn't make *one* dating profile. I made several. And it isn't for Terri. It's for her dates," advised Nikole with a devious glint in her eyes.

"What do you use them for?" asked Jayla.

"Whenever we get bored, we send little miss lonely heart a message from one of our accounts, and we crack open a bottle of wine, and we flirt with her and talk dirty to her—which is hilarious—and then we set up dates with her and, you know, stand her up," replied Hailey.

"Girls just wanna have fun," Nikole said with a giggle.

Hailey then shifted her heavy load of clothes and said, "Alright, ladies. Our modeling career awaits us!"

Jayla could feel her desire for acceptance pushing her into the changing station as the euphoria of being included, of having value, of being wanted cascaded into bursts of giggling. From the next stall over, Nikole began playing upbeat runway music from her phone. Coming out of the rooms the girls oooo'd and ahhhh'd at each other's ensemble. Group photos, single shots, and video selfies full of catwalk struts and duck lips and all manner of silliness. Growing up, Jayla never had any all-girl sleepovers but she imagined if she had, it would feel a little like this, and she was loving it.

"Do you mind keeping it down?" an employee eventually confronted them with a few bashful, frustrated customers huddled behind her.

A few minutes and an assistant manager later, the three ladies were on their way to the food court, laughing, purposely bumping into display cases as a grumbling mall cop followed them out.

Then the air became thick with the hodgepodge of food court smells, and Jayla's stomach let out an enormous, unbecoming growl. Nikole and Hailey looked at each other, and then all three of them laughed.

"I feel that," Nikole empathized. "If you ladies need me, I will be at Double Jack's Fry Shack stress-eating through some jalapeño chili cheese fries."

Hailey linked arms with Jayla again and said, "So, love, where shall we eat?" She then answered her own question: "Oh, I know! Taco Tim's!" she said, beginning to pull Jayla in that direction.

"I'm not really feeling tacos right now," Jayla replied, sensing the low likelihood of them having the kind of pickles she had been craving since that morning.

"Have you ever had them before? You're missing out. You have to get some!" Hailey insisted.

"Well—" Jayla began, then, seeing Hailey's oversized puppy-eyes begging expression, felt her need for approval overcome her lesser personal desires. "Alright. Taco Tim's it is."

Hailey cheered and skipped across the food court with Jayla lagging until they reached the short line of customers waiting to order. "Hmm," she said, patting her index finger against her chin, "what sounds good? You should totally get their number two meal. It's divine. You have to have it."

Jayla looked at the menu, trying to convince herself the number two meal sounded more appetizing than it did. "Tim's Wet Beany Burrito is really that good, huh?"

"So good. Get it. Get it."

Standing next in line to order, Jayla found herself asking for the Wet Beany Burrito combo with extra sour cream and a sweet tea to drink, hating the zero percentage of pickles in the meal.

Just as Jayla began to confirm her order and pay, Hailey stepped in, extending her smartphone to the attendant. "Actually, I have this buy-one-get-one-free coupon I'd like to use with her order. No tomatoes, extra onion, and in a to-go box."

Jayla was stunned, confused, speechless, and angry.

"What?" Hailey asked, seeing Jayla's soured expression. "You were going to buy it anyway."

"Okay. Your order comes to fifteen dollars and eighty-three cents," replied the teen at the cash register.

"I'll go get us a table with Nikole. Thanks, friend!" Hailey said, stepping out of the line and into the cafeteria.

As Jayla pulled out her credit card, she felt duped, stupid, and used. *I can't believe she just did that! Who does that to someone?* Then, in answer to her question, her mind flashed with an image of her ma.

Storming around the food court, a heavy red tray in each hand, Jayla searched for Nikole and Hailey. As soon as she got to their table, Jayla slammed the trays down, her unblinking eyes glaring at Hailey.

"Mucho gusto, New Fran!" Hailey smiled. Then, lifting the to-go box, added, "Ladies, I regret to inform you, but I gotta run. It's been fun! We have to do it again sometime. Bye!"

In a flash, Hailey was gone.

"Taco Tim's wasn't your idea, was it?" Nikole said laughing.

"Nope. What's so funny?" asked Jayla.

"She used a buy-one-get-one coupon, didn't she?"

"How did you know?"

Nikole raised her eyebrows in amusement. "She got that from me. Good one, right?" Nikole mused, "Sometimes I think she wants to be me when she grows up. But that's how it is most places I go, you know? Always copying me, trying to impress me or something. Sometimes I just want to tell these people, try being an individual for once—think for yourself."

"How long have y'all been friends?" asked Jayla.

"For as long as we've worked at the clinic together. Me two and a half years, her a little less."

"And what got you working there?"

"Wow, Nancy Drew, is this interview being recorded?" Nikole said, taking a sloppy, stringy bite of cheese fries. "Well, I started working there because I needed money and I wanted to move out on my own, and then I stayed for a boy, and now I'm there because I love the women who come in. Not in a sappy, teary-eyed, commercial kinda way, but for real. I really do love them. I hate seeing them so defeated and scared. I like being able to help restore balance to their lives and empower them and see them get the help they need."

"That's cool," acknowledged Jayla.

"How about you?" Nikole asked.

"Same as you. I like helping women."

"That's not true," Nikole stated matter-of-factly, staring Jayla in the eyes, mining for truth. "I can tell you're not a people-person. I think there's another reason you're there."

Jayla looked at Nikole and shook her head. "What do you mean?" she asked, wondering if there was any possible way of her knowing the truth, feeling less intimidation and more tentative caution.

"I think we both know," Nikole glared. "It's Tripp, isn't it."

Jayla let out a spontaneous bark of a laugh. "Tripp? You think I'm there for Tripp?"

"I saw the way you were looking at him the other day. I don't care either way, honestly. You can have him."

"I am not interested in Tripp," Jayla reassured.

"Oh yeah? Well, he's into you," Nikole advised with bitterness in her voice.

"Oh, he is, huh? And how do you know that?" Jayla asked, wiping the corners of her mouth with a napkin.

"Because he told me," Nikole said, picking up her phone. Then, showing Jayla the screen, waited for a reaction.

On the screen was a picture of Jayla from an hour ago. In the shot, she wore the short black and yellow romper Hailey picked out for her and was looking at the camera seductively, just like Nikole directed her to do at the time. *Jayla wanted me to send this*, said the text attached to the picture. *She wants to know if you want to see more.*

Jayla was furious. "Why would you send this!?" she asked, feeling her temper on the rise.

"Relax. He liked what he saw. I did you a favor," Nikole answered, shrugging off Jayla's intensity by reaching for another bite of fries.

With one swift motion Jayla knocked Nikole's tray to the ground, slapping the floor with a sloppy wet splat. The anger and disbelief at Nikole's presumption, the hurt of being played as a pawn for the second time that evening, the heartrending betrayal of thinking she was girl-time bonding when all the while she was being used, all culminated into a fiery rage. "You listen," Jayla said with controlled, annunciated words. "Don't you ever. Ever. Pull something like this again."

Nikole stared at Jayla from across the small table. On the outside Nikole looked cool and calm but, for a second, Jayla was sure she saw a look of terror flash across her unimpressed eyes.

"I need you to tell me you understand," Jayla advised, pushing her own tray out of the way. "Go on. Tell me."

Nikole sat back in her seat, crossing her arms, with an entertained smile. "I understand," she admitted.

"Good," Jayla said.

"But I want you to know something too," Nikole added, prompting Jayla to sit forward in her seat.

"I like you a whole lot more now than I did an hour ago. What do you say about some dessert?"

CHAPTER 22

PARALLEL LINES EVENTUALLY MEET

Four days later Jayla sat in her car in the remaining minutes of her lunch break watching big drops of rain as they fell onto her windshield, steadily water-logging the protestors outside Unplanned, Inc. Their megaphones were drowned out by steady drumming of water, their homemade poster board signs becoming soggy and droopy as picketers fumbled for their umbrellas.

"I give it ten minutes before they scatter," Jayla barked, taking a bite out of her Reuben sandwich.

"This bunch? No. They're in it to win it," Nikole replied before cramming a fist full of salt and vinegar potato chips into her mouth.

Since Friday night Nikole and Jayla spent more time together than Jayla previously thought possible. Jayla asked, "Who do you think will be the first one to ask to use our bathroom? They do that just to bother us knowing when you take government funding you have to have a public restroom. Then they leave their little pamphlets taped to the backside of the stall doors."

Nikole scanned the small crowd. "There," she said. "Red shirt, white hair. She won't last."

"Nah. To the right of yours, three umbrellas over. White shirt lady, getting soaked, looks a little like a baby elephant," Jayla said, having realized the meaner comments, tastier gossip, and more entertaining conversation kept Nikole engaged and off her phone.

"Looks like it's about time for us to get back to work," Jayla advised, looking at the analog dashboard clock and then, flitting her eyes over to Nikole, found her with her smartphone up to her ear. "Everything okay?"

"Shhhh," Nikole chastised. Then, changing her tone, spoke into the phone with a cartoonishly thick Southern twang, "Hello? Yes. We need an ambulance now. Right now. It's an emergency. Oh, please hurry. Yes. Yes, I'll hold . . ."

Jayla looked at Nikole grinning. "What are you doing?"

"You mess with us, we mess right back," she winked. Then, changing her accent again, hyperventilated into her phone, "Yes, I'm still here. My church and I were protesting outside the Unplanned Incorporated when it started to rain, and my friend slipped and hit her head on the concrete ledge. There's so much blood. She's got on a white shirt, sopping wet, lots of blood, you'll see her . . . My name? Hailey . . . Mmmhmmm."

At the use of Hailey's name, Jayla became slack-jawed, but Nikole only shrugged and, after giving the address to the operator, shouted, "Thank you, thank you. Help is coming!" As soon as she hung up the phone, a huge mischievous smile spread across Nikole's face. "And *now* we can go inside."

"Nikole, they know what number that call came from!" Jayla exclaimed.

"It's a pay-by-the-minute phone, get them for fifteen bucks at any convenience store. It's how we do all the prank calls. Nikole here wasn't born yesterday."

Dodging raindrops as they ran toward the entrance, Jayla and Nikole heard the megaphones faintly through the storm. "Pro Life! Pro Love! Pro Life! Pro Love!" Looking through the glass window of the lobby, Jayla could see Lynn and a few other employees watching, dry and warm, as the rain and the mini mob continued to drive potential patients away.

The closer they jogged to the front door, the more visible the signs became until Jayla was able to read a few before cautiously bounding into the lobby of Unplanned, Inc. Love Them Both: Defend Life, Pray to End Abortion, Protect All Life, We Love Your Child, and as always, Overturn Roe!

"Viva la women's rights!" Nikole yelled at the crowd before going inside, riling up the small crowd outside, invigorating them to chant all the louder. As she went inside, Nikole grinned, raising and lowering her eyebrows.

"Those people make me sick," Lynn muttered. "Defend Life, ha! How can you say you defend life while trouncing, absolutely trouncing, women's rights." Then, as if realizing for the first time a congregation of employees had gathered around her, she said, "Alright. Show's over. Go find something to clean. I'm not paying you to hold up the walls."

With her coworkers clearing out and Nikole out of sight, Jayla walked over to Lynn, watching the woman in red as she held up her side of a homemade banner.

"Enjoying the circus? Bring any peanuts?" Lynn asked Jayla as they stood watching out the window. "Bunch of elephants rolling around in the rain. Down in Texas the pro-choice regime has started picketing their beloved pregnancy centers, giving them a taste of their own medicine." Then she let out a string of expletives.

"Are these the same people who put all that stuff on our windshields?" Jayla inquired, finding it hard to reconcile the love and life-promoting signs outside with the weekly written accusations neatly placed under her wipers calling her a monster, a murderer, headed to hell. One of them keyed Terri's car last week. At that moment Jayla wondered if they keyed the car or if Nikole and Hailey set Terri up again for another disappointment.

"It might be a different group, but they're all the same people. Angry. Women-hating. Progress-fearing. Uncompromising idiots. I don't get them."

"What don't you get?" asked Jayla.

"These people and their inability to prioritize anything. Their logical inconsistencies. Their backwater, hypocritical soapboxing. They hate abortion, spend millions to stop it, but they sure won't fund adoptions. They protest abortions, but they won't promote birth control. They hate what they consider to be the problem, but they refuse to love any of society's solutions. It's like hating car accident fatalities but also hating drivers ed and the use of seatbelts. It doesn't make sense. I'll tell you one thing, Jayla, the Bible Belt does not have any condoms in the pockets of the pants it holds up. You talk about hypocrites—last August, the son of Mr. Moral Majority got caught messin' with his pool boy and his wife, together! It's all moral malarkey. This is why I could never believe in God. If that is the behind-the-scenes look at religion, I will stay with my heathen friends." Then she let out another string of her favorite filthy descriptions.

Lynn stopped as red and white flashing lights shone through the half-steamed window. "What happened? Who called an ambulance? We better not get sued for one of these ninety-year-old Bible thumpers falling in the rain!"

As if on cue, coworkers from every part of the building began funneling in to watch the spectacle, each offering their own commentary and theory as EMS workers rushed to the scene. Lynn draped her designer rain jacket over her shoulders, preparing to see for herself what was going on. As soon as Lynn's dry heels hit the wet sidewalk, the volume in the lobby swelled tenfold.

"Serves them right. If anyone deserves to get hurt, it's those Bible thumpers," a coworker on the periphery asserted. "Anyone recording this?"

"What did I tell you? Here they come faster than you can say lawsuit, lawsuit, lawsuit," Jayla distinguished Shamice Jackson's croon above the crowd before feeling a not-so-gentle nudge to her right. Turning her gaze she saw a smiling, self-satisfied Nikole staring out the window beside her.

Jayla watched as two soaked EMS workers approached the soggy, heavyset woman clad in white like zookeepers nearing a cornered tiger. With their hands up and a gurney outstretched, the paramedics closed in on the woman with an exchange of muffled words as the protesting group around her stumbled backward, looking at each other in confusion.

Just then, something caught Jayla's eye. Through the downpour, Jayla saw a pair of neon yellow vests reflecting the orange light of the ambulance beacon. Jayla could feel the hard stare of one of those figures whose countenance was so encircled with smoke it seemed like a hellish halo snarled around their face. The slanted gate, the hardened weathered silhouette, in an instant, Jayla knew it was Amarika.

"Jayla? Leaving already? You're gonna miss the best part!" Nikole said as Jayla's feet began moving her backward into the crowd.

"Yeah, I gotta go," Jayla excused, turning her body away from the glass, smoothing over her scrubs. She felt exposed, suddenly, and shamed, morphing to vulnerable and defensive and withdrawn all at once. Having seen Amarika outside, she simply wanted her shift to be over.

Jayla heard a sound that caught her attention. It was muffled and pulsing, higher-pitched and heaving. Following the noise, Jayla listened as she moved through the hallway until the faint whimpering became louder. It wasn't long before Jayla found herself in the ultrasound wing of the building with her ear pressed to a purple steel door listening to someone on the other side blubbering.

Slowly Jayla opened the door to find Terri with her back to the door, her shoulders shaking with stifled cries as she sat hugging the edge of the examination seat. Jayla waited a few moments and considered walking out of the room before anyone noticed, but Terri turned as if sensing someone behind her.

"Oh, my," Terri blushed, startled, as she began wiping tears from her eyes with obvious embarrassment. "Jayla, I . . ." she stuttered as her mascara ran like black ink down her wet cheeks.

"I'm sorry," Jayla said, regretting not being a few seconds faster to leave. "I'll leave you alone."

"No, no. I'm sorry. It's okay. Really, you can stay," encouraged Terri in her sweet Southern voice as she reached for a box of tissues. "It's just, there's just a lot going on—I'm sure you don't want to hear about it," Terri began before continuing without pause. "Men are just the worst," she declared, emphasizing her point by blowing her nose.

"That's the truth."

"I haven't had the best luck with dating—not in person, anyway. And I was told this whole online dating thing would be better, but it seems men have found a new way to stomp on a woman's heart. I mean, is there really something that's just so wrong with me?" Terri asked, each tear a new and different hurt being exposed.

The doorway was only an arm's length away, but Jayla silently accepted the reality that she was stuck. Sitting on the rolling stool next to Terri, Jayla looked around the room at the various posters and diagrams and waited for enough time to pass so she could leave.

"You've been here long enough, you know me. Am I really that awful?"

"No," replied Jayla, noticing Terri's eyes were locked on her own, the woman's eyes streaked like a peppermint candy.

"What is it? What is it about me? I mean, if I just knew what it was, I would change it, you know? What is it that makes these men like me until they get to know me? They—they—they message me, and they flirt with me, and they want to get to know me, and each time—each time I tell myself not to get my hopes up. Each time I tell myself, 'You know what happened last time, be smart about this.' But we get to talking, and it just feels so good to connect with someone, you know? Because I'm not like you, Jayla. I wish I was—I mean, you've made more friends here in the last few months than I have in. . . .Truth is, I don't have two friends to rub together. You've seen the way they look at me, how they treat me here. And I just get to feeling so lonely, you know? So I start talking to these guys, and they really seem sweet, and they really seem like they see me, you know? ME. And it's ugh. It's . . ." Terri looked away from Jayla as she grasped for the word.

"Intoxicating," Jayla said.

Terri's face lit up. "That's it. Intoxicating," she said, looking at Jayla now as if she were the only person in the world who understood or could relate to her. This stare of desperation was painful for Jayla to hold because of the guilt she felt inside. The guilt over knowing that behind Terri's tears was the mocking from Nikole and Hailey. Her sorrow, their sport—her real pain, their imaginary accounts.

"And I look at these guys—these funny, handsome, smart guys— and think how could he see anything in me? And then, like he hears me through the screen, he loses interest in me. He doesn't show up to the date. He deactivates his account. He realizes what I've known all along—there's nothing in me worth pursuing. I'm ugly and I'm fat and I'm used goods and there are so many other prettier women, smarter women, why waste his time on me."

"I don't know about all that," Jayla comforted as if her sympathy were somehow a form of absolution from any involvement she may have had behind the scenes. "I think it says more about the guy than it does about you. These guys don't sound like they were worth your time anyway."

"If it were one guy, I'd say yeah. If it were two, I would agree, maybe. But if everyone takes a sip of the milk and says it's rotten, it's rotten and it's not anyone's fault but the cow. And do you wanna know something?" Terri asked with a sad smirk, "I'm not even the one who signed me up for these stupid accounts, it's my momma and daddy. But they're the ones always going, 'Terri, when are you gonna get married? Terri, you're not going to catch a husband dressed like that. Terri, when are you going to give me some grandkids? Terri, we're not getting any younger.' And they're the ones standing over my shoulder telling me which ones they like best, and they're the ones who ask for pictures when I'm out on these dates no one but me shows up for. So I sit there, and I take pictures of myself smiling while my heart is breaking and I take pictures of the fancy restaurant and those nice meals, and then I cry as I eat and eat, and I eat. And my parents are like, 'He seemed like such a nice young man. What did you do this time, Terri? Why don't they ever stick around, Terri? It's as if you like being alone.'"

Jayla watched Terri as she dabbed her eyes with the corner of a tissue. Jayla imagined her driving alone from work with all the freedom of an unattached woman but none of the fun. She pictured Terri on the long commute back to an empty house, or sitting by herself in a movie theater, or dining at a restaurant at a table set for one. She saw Terri checking and refreshing her dating app again and again. Jayla pictured her cycling endlessly between dieting and depression and overeating on spiteful bites of fleeting happiness.

And then she thought of her own life, which sadly wasn't much different. Long ago, Jayla made the decision to distance herself away from toxic people in her life, pushing out the good with the bad under the guise of self-protection. There was no one waiting for her at home either, no one meaningful to join her at a restaurant, not anymore. Despite how things appeared to Terri, Jayla had no real relationships in her life she could rely on when things got bad. And who did she have in her life to share her life-altering news with? No one. Who would be there to help her with this baby when the time came? Nobody. In that way, she and Terri were alike. They had no one to keep their secrets. No one to betray their secrets. Somehow these two women, who looked so different, viewed the world so differently, spoke and acted so differently, were in the same room at the same time in the same terminal of life.

That's when Jayla realized it wasn't by some accident she and Terri were sharing this moment now; this was her chance. This was her opportunity to get the ultrasound she wanted. Here she was with an ultrasound technician who had no friends to blab to and who would feel so special to be included in Jayla's life and the possibility of friendship that she would hold onto this secret until her dying breath.

Jayla scooted closer to Terri, close enough to feel the warmth. Then, with a measured hushed tone and a quickened pulse, Jayla smoothed over her scrubs and began to speak. "I know how you feel Terri, and it means a lot to me that you would share with me."

"You do?" Terri asked, surprised.

Jayla nodded her head somberly. "I want you to know I'm the type of friend who would never share anything you tell me with other people."

Terri became reflexively teary-eyed again. "Thank you, Jayla. I appreciate that."

"If I had something to share with you, would you also promise to keep it just between the two of us?" Jayla probed.

"Of course," Terri replied with a serious, dedicated tone.

"Terri, I want to tell you something I haven't told anyone before."

By this point, Terri was bending forward on the edge of her seat, as if she had been preparing for this moment since girlhood with the backlogged intensity of a hundred missed slumber parties.

"I am—" Jayla hesitated. *Just say it, just say it.* "I am—pregnant." The last word tumbled out of her mouth like a boulder.

Terri's jaw dropped as she gave Jayla a once-over. "No . . ." she said.

"Yup," Jayla repeated, feeling her shoulders lighten a bit, her posture less hunched than it was under the weight of untold truth. "I am pregnant."

"What?! Oh my goodness—how exciting! Congratulations, girl! Do you have any names? Was it planned?"

"Thanks, and definitely not planned," Jayla replied, each celebratory sentiment landing like an uppercut on her psyche. "Truth is—I'm not sure if I want to keep it."

Terri straightened in her seat as she swiftly changed gears, grabbing Jayla's hand. "You poor thing. You poor, poor thing," she cooed as if she wasn't sure how to respond but saw this done in a few of the romantic comedies she watched alone. "I know just what you mean."

I highly doubt that, Jayla remarked to herself. "I was wondering—would you be able to help me with something?"

"Me?" Terri wondered aloud, a bit shocked. "Yeah, sure. Of course! Anything."

"Could you—would you—" Jayla smoothed over her blouse before uneasily continuing. "Is there any way you could give me an ultrasound?"

"You mean you haven't had one yet?"

"No."

"How far along do you think you are? Because it could be the difference in the kind of ultra—"

"Around three months," interrupted Jayla.

Terri nodded. "Lock the door," she said intensely, grabbing a pair of latex gloves, white powder pollinating the air between them. "Why don't you come have a seat."

Jayla sat in the examination chair as Terri cut off the lights. "Now I need you to lift up your scrubs so your stomach is showing," Terri advised. Following directions, Jayla uncovered her midsection, instantly feeling the typical nerves she got when exposing any part of her body to another person's eyes. "Oh, I see. You do have a bit of a belly. Look at that," commented Terri as Jayla situated herself in the chair, feeling even more insecure.

Jayla watched as Terri rolled a tube in her hands, allowing the friction to warm up the gel inside.

"Excited?" Terri asked to fill the silence. Jayla nodded but inside felt a mixture of nervous, anxious, excited, worried, hesitant, wanting to call the whole thing off, and wishing it was already over at the same time.

"Okay, here comes the gel," Terri said as she squeezed the tube, which made a gurgling noise as the cool goo splattered onto Jayla's stomach, making her flinch a bit. "And here we go," Terri announced, pressing the probe to Jayla's abdomen. Jayla immediately closed her eyes and gripped the bottom of the seat where Teri couldn't see, hating the unexpected feeling of her control being lost. *I want this to be over. I want this to be over*, she thought, feeling helpless and distressed, her mind going back to the moment of lost control three months ago that launched her into this mess.

"Okay, I'm seeing a little something," said Terri, prompting Jayla to open her eyes. Looking at the monitor to her right, she expected to see the same type of image she was privy to at LifeLine when accompanying Alexandria in her ultrasound visit. But this monitor wasn't four-dimensional, and there was no forty-inch television on the ceiling showing the client the child. This screen wasn't clear or incredibly discernable. Instead, in a black-and-white setting on an undersized monitor, Jayla saw a little peanut-shaped body appear in between fluctuating waves of gyrating concentric rings.

"Is that it?" Jayla asked, underwhelmed and confused.

"That's it," Terri replied as she circled around the fetus for alternate angles.

Jayla stared ahead, trying to project personhood onto the blob she saw on the screen. *Maybe when we check the chambers of the heart I'll feel different—or maybe when I see the fingers and the toes—or maybe even when I see the peach fuzz on the body or the tiny nails that are coming in. Maybe then I'll feel differently*, Jayla said to herself. But as she was in mid-thought, Terri flipped on the lights.

"Here are some tissues. I know it can be kind of icky having all that gel on you," Terri said compassionately as she extended the same box of tissues to Jayla she used not twenty minutes prior.

"We're done?" Jayla queried, feeling the visit had been cut off prematurely.

"That's right. So what do you think you want to do? Want me to get you scheduled with Dr. Molech sometime soon? Oh, wait. Duh! You want to keep this more hush-hush, right?"

"But what about counting the fingers and toes? What about making sure the heart is okay?" asked Jayla.

"Do places normally do that?" Terri asked in authentic innocence.

"Yeah. And like they give you a picture of the fetus."

"Oh . . . umm, well, we don't do that here. We just see if there is a fetus. The more a client sees a fetus, the less likely they are of continuing to the final abortive procedure. We've not had paper for that printer since the day it came in here."

Jayla grabbed a fistful of tissues and began to wipe off her stomach. "So this is what all your visits in here are like?"

"For the most part, yeah."

"Are all the ultrasound screens in all the Unplanned operations this small?"

"I think so. They should be all the same. Why?" asked Terri.

"It just seemed so—I don't know. You would think with the millions and millions of dollars we get from the government we would be able to afford some nicer screens is all."

"I get that," Terri said, reaching out her hand to take Jayla's tissue. "I guess we use that money for more important stuff."

"But isn't it important for the ladies to come in here to see their baby?"

"You did see the fetus, though. Remember?" Terri answered. "We are only doing pre-abortion ultrasounds, nobody's in this room 'cause they want to have a baby."

Jayla pulled her scrubs back over her stomach. A small residue of the gel stuck to her shirt as she got situated as if a large slug had warmed itself on top of her abdomen. On the one hand, she knew Terri was right—she saw inside her womb. But on the other hand, Jayla felt misled and a bit disillusioned, as the expectation was so much more than the reality of what she got.

At LifeLine, seeing the ultrasound with the best technology available was like seeing a sunrise in person with all its hues and nuances and splendor. At LifeLine you could hear the heartbeat of the child. They gave you a large printout of the child in your womb. But seeing this ultrasound just now was like someone taking a black and white picture of an orange and yellow sunset. The gray took all emotion and vibrancy and beauty out until it became meaningless. *Why wouldn't they want women to see their babies in the best way possible, in full view, so they could make the best decision?* Jayla asked herself. *Why would they want to make it so hard for these fetuses to look human?*

"So what do you think you want to do about the baby?" Terri asked.

Jayla took a deep breath and shrugged. She wasn't sure what she wanted to do.

"It's a hard choice," Terri responded softly. "Believe me, I know . . ." Then, taking a seat on the bench next to the entryway, she continued. "You know, I don't tell a lot of people this—but since you let me into your secret—" Terri paused. "I was actually pregnant once . . ."

Jayla was speechless, partly at the unsolicited information and partly out of the shock that anyone would be with Terri long enough to get her pregnant.

"I decided not to have the baby," Terri said in answer to an unasked question. "Sometimes I think about that . . ."

"What happened?" Jayla asked.

"My daddy had this friend who had a son, and they always talked about wanting to set us up together. This was a long time ago, and I was a lot thinner then," Terri said, looking down at her own body sheepishly. "They finally convinced us to go out on a date, and things were going well—like really well—and I was surprised. We really hit it off. And after dinner he invites me back to his place for some drinks. And of course, I know what that means—every woman knows what that means. But he's cute, and I like him, and I was a little buzzed anyway, and I was ready, you know? I had decided I was going to sleep with him—but then we get to his apartment, and he gives me something to drink to loosen up. And that's when, I don't know, this feeling—this bad feeling starts to come over me, and I get really sleepy. And he offers to help me lie down in his bed. I can still see his carpet in his bedroom—his dirty, stringy, orange carpet in my mind, and I remember thinking how ugly it was. And that's the last thing I remember about that night. The next thing I know, it's a few hours later, and he's mad at me and rough with me and is telling me I need to get out of his house. And I can feel my clothes—" Terri said, feeling her scrubs as if reliving the moment. "My clothes are put on all funny and they don't feel right, and I feel sore down . . . and I ask him what happened and the more questions I ask, the angrier he gets until he gets me out the door. And then a few weeks later I miss my period."

At this point, Terri's eyes moistened. "And what I don't understand is he didn't have to do it like he did. I would have given myself to him, but he took it from me instead. He stole it from me. And then my parents—my daddy is so mad at me because now his friend's son doesn't want anything to do with me, and he's asking me what I did to ruin it all, and everyone is blaming me!"

"Did they know?" Jayla asked, feeling an unanticipated deep empathy for her.

"No. Of course not. I didn't want to tell them what happened. I didn't want to tell anyone what happened because as soon as I told someone, it became real. So I had the baby taken care of, and now, all these years later, he has a family of four, and my parents show me the Christmas cards of them every year laughing, smiling. He still sends them Christmas cards after all that, do you believe it? And, meanwhile, I eat and eat until I can feel my pain go away," Terri mourned, her chest caving into deep, heaving sobs. "I've become—this."

Then something happened Jayla never expected. She felt a warm, streaky tear fall from her eye and melt its way down her cheek. Whether pregnancy hormones or unspoken identifiability with her own story, Jayla wasn't sure, but an unshakable sadness gripped her and wouldn't let go.

Jayla looked over at Terri and—rather than consoling her or putting a quiet hand on her shoulder—she quickly wiped the tear away, gritted her teeth, and stiffened the muscles in her face into a dignified expression. It was one thing for someone like Terri to admit what happened to her, but it was another for Jayla, who was strong and independent, to show signs of cracking. She wasn't a weak woman and refused to play the part. Instead, she glanced at the clock, passed the tissues, and waited for an opportune time to exit, not wanting to be associated in the least with the kind of trauma and frailty and self-pity on display before her now. She waited, watching tears roll down Terri's cheeks, patronizing her with a hard stare as if she were looking at the embodiment of disappointment from the other side of a glass window.

CHAPTER 23

POSITIVE THINKING

As Jayla tidied up the Hope Room at LifeLine the next day, flashes of the image on the black-and-white monitor and of Terri's tears came back to her mind during quiet moments of the morning. Inside her swirled an emotive cocktail of helplessness and confusion, blended with the bitters of self-loathing.

The more Jayla cleaned and ruminated, the more physically and emotionally exhausted she became until she needed to sit. There, stargazing at the perforations in the ceiling panels, she finally allowed herself to admit the personal progress she made over the past few months was receding. In her numbness and reinforced persona of independence and strength, she told herself if she could fix herself up once, she could do it again whenever she felt like it. She could project herself as proud and self-sustaining even if she didn't fully feel that way on the inside. *After all,* Jayla told herself, *if others believed she was enough on her own, maybe soon she would believe it too.*

"Buenos dias, Jayla," Renee greeted from the doorway, "you haven't seen Brittany pass by this way, have you?"

"No," Jayla replied, shaking her head as she quickly reached over to dust off the corner table lampshade from her seated position.

"I was hoping to catch her before our morning devotional," Renee said, looking at her watch. "Would you please tell her I'm looking for her if she passes this way?"

"Okay, I can do that," Jayla confirmed reluctantly, not wanting to do any favors for Brittany. Since that moment in Renee's office, Jayla viewed every word and act of Brittany's as an affront to her character. Each micro-quirk and mannerism intensified and exaggerated Jayla's dislike, until her very presence was noxious.

"Great! Thank you! You're a lifesaver," Renee enthused as she cantered out of view. Then, retracing her steps, she came back into the doorway and surveyed the room. "You're really getting good at this," Renee said proudly, taking in all Jayla's hard work. "Samantha was right. Keep up the great work!"

Jayla smiled but didn't say anything, savoring the compliment under an indifferent exterior. Renee's heels receded down the corridor, then Samantha's light footsteps approached. Jayla soon heard her sugary Southern voice stopping every few paces to greet someone new and ask them about their weekend plans. It always amazed Jayla how Samantha could muster enough energy to authentically care about each person she spoke with.

Samantha entered the room, balancing three warmed-over cold brew coffees, the whipped dollop on top now resembling a white flattened toupee. "You get a coffee, you get a coffee, you get a coffee! Nothing says weekend like a frozen cappuccino," Samantha beamed as she passed the sweating cup over to Jayla. "They're supposed to be colder but, you know me. I got tied up in the hall longer than I meant to. I hope it's still okay."

"Mmmhmm, thank you!" Jayla nodded as she slurped the whipped cream off the melted coffee.

"Aren't they fantastic! If Jesus were to come back right now, instead of turning water into wine, He would turn water into iced cappuccinos, and they would taste like this. Am I right?"

Jayla laughed between sips. "Who's the third one for?"

"It's for Terica! She's coming in today for her last appointment! Seems like only yesterday she was coming in for the first time," Samantha reminisced before reaching for Jayla's arm. "So I have good news, and I have better news," Samantha began, which only intensified Jayla's suspicion. "The good news is you have been doing a super great, really good job being a client advocate. You're such a natural with the girls who come in here, and all I ever hear are positive things after your sessions are over."

"Okay . . ." said Jayla, waiting for the other shoe to drop.

"So because of that, I have some news—today is going to be your last day with me. Starting Monday, you'll be on your own!" Samantha announced with an over-the-top smile and jazz hands. "Yay, right! The baby bird has become the mama bird and is leaving the nest."

"On my own? What if I don't want to be on my own yet?" Jayla objected, her stomach tumbling.

"Why not? It's okay to be nervous or worried," Samantha comforted. "Jayla, you're so good at this job; you're a natural! And Renee and I feel like you're ready to take that next big step. And, if you think about it, this way we can help even more of our girls because we can divide and conquer. This is a good thing! Now you won't have my old bones slowing you down," Samantha joked, but Jayla wasn't in the mood. "And there may be other reasons to celebrate. You never know what's around the corner," added Samantha ambiguously.

"What's around the corner?" asked Jayla.

"Oh, nothing," Samantha said, stirring her straw around blocks of melting coffee chunks. "I'm just saying something might be, might not be, but—might be. You know?"

"What don't I know, Sam?"

"Nothing—I shouldn't have even said anything at all in the first place. All I'm saying is you should be at the devotional this morning."

"Sam . . ."

"What! You should be at it—we all should be at it. Think about this. There's a lot to learn, and Jesus wants us all to be there. You should be there too," Samantha said before loudly slurping her drink.

Jayla stared at Samantha. Finally, unable to endure the atmosphere any longer, Samantha relented, her face wincing. "If I tell you, do you *promise* to act surprised?"

Jayla stared expectantly, not promising anything, letting the silence mount in her favor.

"I overheard Renee talking with some people and you were brought up. She was saying how impressed she was with you and how she'd noticed a real change and then said something to the effect of, '*If she keeps this up, it won't be long until she's Employee of the Month,'* and then I walked in because I couldn't help myself. I told them you were every bit as wonderful as they thought you might be, and then they asked me how long I had been listening to their conversation."

Jayla was amused, both at Samantha's unwavering honesty and at the quaint nature of the recognition itself. Still, if she was honest, this was precisely the kind of tangible affirmation she needed to prove the progress she was making was real and worth holding onto. With this award, Jayla would have proven to herself and everyone watching that she had what it takes—despite all the trauma and abuse.

"Well, say something," Samantha said as she squirmed.

"I won't say a word," Jayla smiled, taking another sip of the diluted drink.

"And you're okay with doing this alone beginning next week?"

"Yeah—I can manage," replied Jayla, deciding how unbecoming it was for an employee of the month to still be driving around with training wheels.

"Wonderful! I'll be just in the next room if you need anything."

"Yeah, Sam, I got it. I'll be fine!"

Samantha looked at Jayla with eyes leaking pride onto her cheeks. "I feel like a proud mama right now," she said, her face sweet and a little sad. "You're already doing much better than I did when I started. I remember just sitting in the parking lot mentally going over all the procedures and protocols and rules. I didn't want to come inside. I knew—I just knew I was going to screw up. Rick was practically placing bets that I was going to be coming home early in tears. He had a lot going on back then, though. Stuff with his dad, I totally got where he was coming from, but still . . ."

"You were worried you'd get in trouble?" asked Jayla.

"At work? Oh yeah. That's an understatement. I was worried I was going to say the wrong thing or do the wrong thing, and some young girl who was already on the fence about keeping her baby was going to get an abortion on account of me, you know? We have the power in these ladies' lives over life and death, which is just crazy and overwhelming to think about. The fact that we wear scrubs amplifies our connection as someone with greater medical wisdom."

"So what made you get out of the car?"

"Well," Samantha began but then paused and pursed her lips, her eyes welling. "I saw this girl in my side mirror—sitting in her car looking like she was just a breath away from leaving. Like the smallest breeze would frighten her off. She looked so scared," Samantha halted again. "And I knew I had to go in—I I had to be in here for her so whenever she was ready, however long it took, I would be here to hug her and hear her stories and give her my strength and love her the way she should be loved. The way Jesus loved her." Samantha smiled as she dabbed her eyes. "Loving these girls. That was what got me out of the car," she summarized and then, to Jayla's surprise, asked, "What about you?"

"What about me?"

"What's your reason? What gets you out of the car in the morning? It's silly, but I don't know if I've ever really asked."

"Yeah, you know. Exactly what you said," Jayla replied, "it's about the girls." She shifted her body on the couch as she felt her stomach gurgle.

"Right! And not just about the girls we can see. Did you know worldwide, way more girls get aborted than boys. Renee had charts showing there are over twenty-three million fewer girls in the world today because of sex-selection abortions. Twenty-three million. That's the thing that's so crazy warped about this whole pro-choice thing, isn't it? Women keep believing the lie that abortions are empowering women. But who is it getting aborted? Mostly girls! Are women today stronger for aborting the women of tomorrow? Being pro-choice doesn't empower us—that's a lie men told us, and we believed it, and we keep believing it," Samantha trailed off as a faraway look passed over her eyes. Jayla wasn't sure, but it seemed as if Samantha was seeing the ghost embodied of all the times she willingly believed untruths from the men in her life, perhaps her own husband.

"It's like . . ." Samantha continued slowly, thoughtfully, "Only two kinds of beings in the history of the world have ever been able to do that, uh, God *and women*. We create within us these images of God. And that's a power—we bring life into the world! Men can't do that—it's *our* gift. It is *our* unique strength. And when we abort our babies, it's like we're stripping ourselves of this unbelievable, God-given, God-like ability we have been given."

Samantha's passion, her desire to see women properly vitalized took Jayla back to her pre-friendship food court talk with Nikole all those weeks ago. "I love the women who come in," Nikole said. "I like being able to help restore balance to their lives and empower them and see them get the help they need." How was it, Jayla wondered, the same desire could lead these two women in her lives to such wildly different answers and outcomes. Who was right? And was there a *right* a person could be, especially when it came to a body that wasn't their own?

"I hear all the time that being pro-choice will give us strength," Samantha continued, "but it robs us of our strength. We're told it will make us equal, but anyone can take a life. That's not special, men have been specializing in that for thousands of years. What's special is not the ability to take a life but the ability to create a life, and that's unique only to women. I'm so tired of being told by the media I can only be a feminist if I am congruently pro-choice! How can you say you're *for* women while working *against* them? How can you call yourself a feminist when you're supporting something that takes away your unique feminine strength and is the number one killer of girls around the world? That's like saying the only way to be pro-lung is to be pro-smoking. And I'm thinking, 'Is no one else seeing this?' But you see it, right? Don't you, Jayla?"

Before Jayla could answer, there was a rapping on the door. Darla peeked her head in and announced the devotional was about to start.

Samantha switched gears and responded, "Come on, girls, we had better get a move on. I just wouldn't know what to do if all the best seats were already taken."

"I'll be there in a minute," Jayla said. She wanted to do a quick search on her phone about all the gas bubbles and stomach flexes she had been feeling recently. Could it be the baby moving inside her?

"Okay, remember, they can't give out the award without you in there," Samantha whispered and winked. Then she bounded into the hallway, chatting with coworkers as she went.

Jayla remained in her chair, scrolling for any tips. The good news was, based on how far along Jayla thought she was, the stomach issues were nothing to be concerned with. But increasingly, it was becoming more difficult for her to ignore the reality of her condition. Somewhere deep down, Jayla knew the longer her pregnancy remained suppressed, the harder it would be to make a final decision.

Jayla walked toward the mirror hanging on the wall of the counseling room and took a look at herself. Her eyes loitered around her stomach, fighting the urge to place a hand on her womb with a well-timed smoothing out of her scrubs. She could hear the women fraternizing with one another from all the way down the hall, sounding more like a bingo rally than a work meeting. Then, taking a deep breath, she made her way to the devotional with the lure of a longed-for prize of recognition.

CHAPTER 24

AWARDS ARE MADE FOR WINNING

Entering the common room for the devotional, Jayla scanned the aisles for a free chair, with all the poise and confidence of a queen searching for her throne. It would be easier to walk up to get her award from the front row, she reasoned to herself, cutting down the commute to the center of everyone's attention. Jayla was surprised to find someone sitting in the front row—someone new.

For a moment, Jayla mistook the stranger for Brittany. Brittany and this girl had the same round face and body type. But this girl was much younger and dressed in what appeared to be a school uniform—a white collared shirt with a stretched-out neckline semi-tucked into a navy-blue skirt. She sported knee-high socks with silver smiley faces on them.

Now I know where I DON'T want to sit, Jayla sighed to herself, rocking her weight back to her hind leg, before catching sight of the employee of the month plaque sitting face-down on the seat next to Renee. For a second, Jayla imagined what the award would look like with her name and face on it, calling to mind the row of prior recipients' pictures hanging along the wall of the break room.

Walking back through the crowd, Jayla found a seat in the rear of the room as Renee began to open the assembly. "Good morning, everyone! Another week—do you believe it?" she asked to a mixed reception of groans and chuckles. "First, I want to tell you all that you have done a marvelous job this past week making our guests feel welcome and at home. And that's why I encourage your goals to be so big," Renee continued. "If you're not occasionally failing to meet your goals, you're not stretching yourself far enough. And speaking of stretching yourself . . ."

"That's my cue," Pastor Steve loudly whispered to the young lady sitting next to him. Then, counterbalancing the plaque in his left hand with a diet cola in his right, he moseyed to the front and Jayla straightened up in her chair, noticing several other women around the room doing the same.

"It's time to announce this month's employee of the month!" Renee continued. "This employee has really gone above and beyond this month."

I'd agree with that, thought Jayla to herself.

"She has taken on new responsibility and set some big goals for herself, and she's been doing it with such a work ethic that is just top notch."

Why, thank you, Jayla thought, harkening back to Renee's comments to her less than an hour before.

"Making a significant impact to women inside our ministry and out in the community, you know her as Miss Positive Attitude herself—"

Jayla scooted to the edge of her chair, ready to pounce.

"It's . . ."

She watched the plaque in Steve's hands as he flipped it over, revealing the employee's photo inside.

"Brittany!" Renee exclaimed, the name binding Jayla to where she sat on the cusp of her chair. Her eyes panned from the award to the young woman on the front row who was jumping up and down as she cheered, "That's my momma!" It wasn't long before a few of Brittany's friends stood to their feet as the new employee of the month seemed just as frozen as Jayla, although Jayla wasn't sure if it was genuine surprise or half-decent showmanship, milking the most out of her win.

Then, as she scanned the crowd, she saw the only face not absorbed with Brittany's win—Samantha's face, which wore a stunned, contrite expression. Jayla quietly and inconspicuously got out of her seat in the back row and hurried to the bathroom, locking the door behind her.

There, twisting the dual faucet handles on full, she sank to the floor, wanting to yell and cry and throw something and throw up, all at the same time.

"Stupid," Jayla mustered out, kicking the wicker wastebasket, not entirely sure if she was referring to the award or to herself. *It doesn't even matter*, she reconciled to herself. *It's not a big deal.* But deep down, she knew that wasn't true. This was supposed to have been *her* moment. The moment when she proved to everyone watching she was worth something, she was somebody. A moment proving she mattered. That she was more than just the sum of the people who had hurt her.

It doesn't matter, Jayla shook her head, tapping it in intervals against the tile wall behind her. *It's not enough. It will never be enough. All this change, all this hell I put myself through, and for what? It doesn't matter what I do. No one sees the change. What's even the point?*

She played and replayed her conversation with Samantha in her mind, scouring for hints of being misled or lied to. It was then, tasting the salt on her lips from the tears rolling down her cheeks, she locked her jaw in place and willed herself off the floor.

"Had enough?" she asked with a tone as soft as cyanide, a venomous voice burned as it passed her lips. Amarika's voice in her head. Then, staring into the mirror, she repeated to herself as she dampened paper towels and scrubbed her cheeks with disdain. "Tears for the weak, and the weak for tears," she muttered. "You're pathetic. You stupid, ugly thing. Weak. Needy," she spoke in staccato strokes as her face stung with each wipe. Then, throwing the used towels on top of the overturned trashcan, she straightened out and smoothed over the creases and ruffles on her scrubs, inhaling and exhaling with slow, controlled breaths.

"You don't need them," she reminded herself, making eye contact with the strong, self-sufficient woman in the mirror. Moving back and forth from vocalization to internalization she thought, *They need you. This whole place would fall apart if you weren't here.* "But they would never admit that!" *Not to you. That's why you'll never get that award. They can't give it to someone who won't play by their stupid rules, who won't bow to their system. That's why you didn't get it. That's why she did. She'll get on her knees, but you won't. She'll give in, but you won't.* "You're too strong for that. You're too strong for them." *They don't own you—they need you. You don't need them, and don't you forget it.*

Before Jayla got both feet out of the bathroom, she heard the sound of scattering footsteps. As she stepped out, she locked eyes with Renee who began to charge in her direction. "Jayla! I was afraid I missed you," she said. "Exciting morning, right? Listen, I was wondering if you could do me a huge favor."

Jayla crossed her arms defensively, hoping the favor had nothing to do with Brittany but fearing the worst.

"As you know, Brittany is our employee of the month and, as part of her celebration, we're taking her out for breakfast with her daughter, Nia. While we're out, I was wondering if there was any way you might be willing to cover her shift back at your old post in reception? No one knows how to fill her shoes in there like you do."

"I can't. Sorry. Samantha told me this morning I'm going to start seeing patients on my own and I'm sure she needs me—"

"Well, actually, Samantha gave us the green light! Let's make it next Monday that you're officially on your own. So, you're okay to cover reception until we get back?" Renee asked.

Jayla gave a single nod, restraining the molten fury peeking through her cracking impassive façade.

"Wonderful! Thanks again, Jayla. Keep up the great work! You never know—it could be *your* name we call up next as employee of the month!"

Jayla gave her a forced, grimaced grin.

"Oh, and by the way," Renee added, "don't forget—we will be needing your receipts from this semester." Then, perceiving the blank look on Jayla's face, elaborated, "The receipts—for your books. I know you're juggling a lot but try to get those in soon. It will help us register how much we should contribute next term! We really do need to catch up sometime. I'd love to hear how things are going. Who knows, if this big community event Brittany is planning is the smash we're hoping it is, we might actually have enough capital to start a scholarship! Wouldn't that be something!" said Renee, allowing herself to dream aloud before walking away.

Furious and aching, Jayla picked her emotions off the floor and carried them with her into the reception area, where Brittany had already set everything up for the opening of business. *Employee of the month*, Jayla growled under her breath as she looked for little ways to undermine Brittany's efforts. Jayla just knew Brittany thought better of herself than anyone else. Brittany obviously wanted to make others look bad so she could look better, even by wearing an African headscarf each day made her blacker than Jayla. Someone needed to bring her back down to reality, and Jayla was up for the challenge.

Just then the phone rang, startling Jayla. She answered, "Hello, LifeLine, we are women helping women, how may I help you?"

"Yes, good morning, is Brittany there?" asked a man on the other end of the line.

"May I ask who's calling?" probed Jayla, the wheels of her mind turning.

"Yeah, this is Teddy Riddleson, the band manager for Ichthys. I need to talk to Brittany, but if she's not in now, can you just tell her to give me a call back later?"

"No, no, she's here. Hold on one moment," replied Jayla before putting the call on mute. She could feel her pulse in her neck as she stared at the red-lit resume call button on the cordless phone, wondering how far she should go into this ruse. She measured the likelihood of getting caught and weighed the risk against the euphoria of Brittany finally getting what was coming for her. With steady fingers she un-muted the call, "This is Brittany," she answered in a slightly lower voice.

"Brittany, Tom here from Ichthys. How are you doing? Everyone okay? The kids okay?"

"Yeah, mmmhmm, everyone is good, thanks. What's up, Tom?" asked Jayla, keeping an eye on the door behind her.

"So, good news and bad news. The good news is we received your check in the mail, and the band is really excited to perform at the community event you guys have going on. Really great cause, you know. The bad news is there's a typo. You spelled the band's name *Ichthus* when it's spelled *Ichthys* with a *y* instead of a *u*. It happens all the time. I wish we'd changed the name years ago—it would save me this same headache I get over and over again! But we can't cash the check until we get it fixed."

"Oh, sorry about that, Tom," replied Jayla, half of her brain telling her she hadn't gone so far as to not turn back, the other half telling the reasonable side to shut up.

"So, what do you think? Can you get a new check cut soon? If not, no worries, we can just pick it up from you at the gig."

"Well, the thing is—we actually *don't need* you to perform anymore," Jayla lied, throwing herself into the deep end.

"If it's a matter of getting the checks to us in time, like I said, we can always—"

"No, sorry, we actually decided to go a different direction for the event. But if something changes, we'll let you know."

There was a pause on the other line, then Tom finally said, "I understand. All the best with everything! Would have loved to have been there to support you all. And, just so you know, if you do reach back out later on, I can't promise we'll still be available on the dates you'll need."

As his words lingered, Jayla caught a glimpse through the front window of Brittany and her daughter climbing into Renee's van with Pastor Steve in tow. They were smiling and laughing as they closed the door.

"I understand," Jayla finalized before disconnecting the call, wielding the cordless phone in her hand like a knife poised at Brittany's back. Jayla watched as the van left the parking lot on its way to what should have been her own hard-earned breakfast celebration.

CHAPTER 25

THE PROBLEM WITH SECRETS

While it had been several days since she was passed over at the certainly rigged employee of the month celebration, Jayla was still bothered, though she told herself otherwise. And now, sitting in the empty Recovery Room at Unplanned, scrolling through the internet for textbook titles and prices to scrawl down on a handmade receipt, she allowed her thoughts again to ferment in the toxins of past injustices.

"Ugh! This bra!" she said, readjusting herself for the fourth time since arriving at her shift that morning, finding herself extra sore and tender to the touch.

"You know," Jayla heard a male voice from the doorway say, startling her, "I always wondered what it was you did in here." It was Tripp, a breakfast burrito in hand, leaning against the door in a casual and possessive manner.

"You don't happen to have an extra one of those with smoked sausage, do you?" Jayla inquired, half joking, half hoping.

"No, I don't get that stuff. I'm vegetarian. Even just the thought of killing something with a face . . ." Tripp paused, repulsed. Then, looking around added, "Slow day for abortions, huh?"

"Yeah. Are those protestors still outside in the rain?" inquired Jayla, her eyes reverting back to her phone screen.

"Wouldn't be slow if they weren't," Tripp replied with a smirk.

"Do you think if we started 'the wave' in here, they'd finish it out there?" she heard Nikole speculate from around the corner, immediately recognizing her sarcastic tone.

"I have a beach ball in the trunk," Hailey chimed in. "Crank up the music, turn this thing into a free love parking lot music festival. We laugh. We cry. We share our stories. Everyone becomes best friends. By tonight we would all be smoking weed in a drum circle."

I guess Hailey's back in Nikole's good graces for the moment, thought Jayla, less than enthusiastic to be reintegrating Hailey into her friend circle.

"Beach balls are the best," added a third voice. Jayla saw Terri standing with Nikole and Hailey as they munched on toffee popcorn, looking from a distance out the large lobby window.

"Beach balls *are* the best," Nikole mocked subtly in a way that made Terri's face beam with misperceived acceptance.

"Well, hey, there Jayla," Hailey said with a big smile. "Why, you're just positively glowing this morning."

"Thanks. Anything happening with the protestors so far?" Jayla asked.

"Not yet. It's too early still," replied Nikole. "I think they're a new batch, from the looks of it."

"I wonder how many Jesus points they get for being here?" Hailey speculated.

"It's not Jesus points. It is Heaven bucks! How many times do I have to tell you," chided Terri. "You are getting three weeks in purgatory for getting it wrong again."

"Oh, here we go, more recruits," Nikole pointed out to the distance as a dark blue sedan pulled into the parking lot. "Where do they find these people?"

Jayla watched as the vehicle stopped at the threshold of the crowd. A girl, a few years younger than Jayla, sat in the backseat, her eyes wide, panic-stricken.

"That's not a protestor," Terri said. "I think she's here for us."

The longer the car sat idle, the more protestors began to converge around it, like white blood cells attacking a perceived threat. From between the shuffling bodies, Jayla could see the driver of the vehicle look to the girl in the backseat for payment for the trip, but it seemed she was frozen with fear.

"Why doesn't she come in?" Hailey asked.

"She can't," Jayla replied as her own pulse started to race. The protestors began to press their posters to the glass of the vehicle and chant "Let your baby live" and "Murderers go to hell!"

"Someone should help her," Terri said, looking around for confirmation. "Right? Someone needs to do something. Should we get Lynn?"

Jayla moved closer to the window in front of her, catching glimpses of the young woman inside the car. Although she didn't recognize her, Jayla knew her still. She knew the fear and grief she carried. She knew the hours or days it took for her to come to this decision. She knew the shame and the numbness that followed. She could see the girl but not without seeing her through the reflection of herself in the glass.

"I'll go get Lynn," said Nikole, but it was too late; Jayla was already walking to the entrance area.

"Where are you going?" asked Hailey, but Jayla didn't reply. Instead, she veered to the reception desk and grabbed the lost and found box. Rummaging inside, she grabbed a couple umbrellas and a scarf as the war cry of the protestors outside resounded louder throughout the parking lot. Huffing her way to the automatic door, she wrapped the scarf around her face, covering her mouth and nose as the fight-or-flight adrenaline made her hands shake. She popped open one umbrella and then the other, and—before anyone could join her or stop her—she headed into the fray, holding the outstretched umbrellas as shields on her left and right flank.

"Move!" Jayla yelled at the mob as she approached the vehicle. With her eyes locked onto the girl inside, she advanced until the shouting of the crowd swarmed around her. Pushing, swatting, shouting, furor—she made her way to the car door. Positioning her body as a barrier against the girl inside, Jayla prodded the mass back enough for the young woman to exit. The girl nested in the nylon cocoon as the two shuffled forward in the deafening crowd, each tiny step feeling like a great leap.

"Get back! Get back!" Jayla heard Lynn shrill as they inched closer to the Unplanned, Inc. building. "If you want hell, I'll show you hell! You are not allowed to circle the cars. You know it."

The crowd was now at their backs as Lynn swooped in, putting her arm around the girl, as the three of them reached the safe harbor of the sidewalk. Jayla looked around the reception area. She was shocked to see all the employees huddled together, staring at her as though she had just parted the Red Sea. Tripp was smiling, Nikole was recording with her phone, Terri looked like she wanted to clap but was waiting for someone else to start—even Dr. Molech was there standing with others, impressed.

"You poor thing. You poor, poor thing. Come have a seat," Lynn soothed in an unnaturally nurturing tone before again barking orders to the spectators in uniform. "Hailey, go and get us some of the snacks we keep in the recovery area. Shamice, bring us some tissues. Oh, you poor thing. Come, let's sit down and let you catch your breath. My name is Lynn. I am the general manager here. Whatever you need—anything you need—you come straight to me, got it? You poor thing. Everyone else, back to work! We all have a job to do!"

Then Lynn barked an order: "Hailey, call the police right now and tell them the protesters are violating the distance rule again. These are not the martyr type. They will back down when the police show up. Cowards!"

As the small crowd began to disperse, Nikole could hardly veil her excitement as she pranced up to Jayla. "Umm—what just happened?" she exclaimed in a whisper. "Who ARE you and what have you done with Jayla? You're like a hero!"

Jayla laughed, exhaling the last bit of adrenaline from her system as she realized the scarf was still partly wound around her head. Unmummifying herself, she didn't feel like a hero.

"Seriously! That was amazing! We're going to get like a million views!"

"Wait! You're going to post that?" Jayla asked as the short-lived euphoria of her good deed began to peel away.

"No, I live-streamed it! We already have like a thousand views," Nikole replied before refreshing the internet browser on her smartphone. "No—*thirteen hundred!*"

"You can't post that," answered Jayla, trying to control the damage already well beyond her capabilities. "Take it down."

"What? You can't even tell it's you! Here—watch," Nikole said, slipping her phone into Jayla's hands. The footage was wobbly from the start as Nikole ran to the glass window, slipping on expletives along the way. From the angle she was filming, you could only see the back of Jayla's head between the outstretched umbrellas. Jayla turned up the audio to hear Nikole and Hailey and Terri shouting half-phrases of disbelief and cheering and calling all their coworkers out to watch the show. The video was much shorter than how the event felt in real time to Jayla. After only eighty-seven seconds, the clip ended. Jayla swiped her finger across the screen and rewatched the video just to be sure, but it seemed like Nikole was right—between the scarf and umbrellas and a miraculous absence of anyone saying her name, there was no way to tell this was Jayla. She felt her limbs loosen again as her body expelled a sigh of relief.

"I don't know if you can see it on there, but Lynn only ran out to you when she saw I was recording," Nikole said with a grin. "Here, watch," she said as she manipulated the timeline. In the shot, Jayla could see Lynn staring bewildered out the window before making eye contact with the lens of the iPhone. It only took a second for an idea to spark as Lynn's demeanor changed and she courageously exclaimed, "Don't worry! I'm coming!"

Nikole paused the video and zoomed into Lynn's ferocious face. But the more she stared at the frozen frame, the more Jayla saw something she hadn't seen before. She double-tapped the screen to magnify the image even more and then turned her attention to the wall of protestors standing outside. There, embedded in the thick of the hornets' nest, was a woman with red hair who stood holding a clear cup full of mushy green confetti chunks in one hand and a sign in the other that read *Babies Are People Too*. It was Darla!

Jayla turned her back to the glass, her head swimming, wondering if she had been spotted. *Stupid, stupid. I just had to go out there*, she chastised herself. "I'm going to go back to the Recovery Room," Jayla announced as she began walking away. *It's okay. Just chill. It's fine. She didn't see you. You were covered. Just wait it out in the back until they're gone*, she coached herself.

"Wait—you're leaving? This thing is going viral!" challenged Nikole. Then, catching up with Jayla, said, "Okay, okay. I have an idea. Let's go get some brunch together, you and me."

"No thanks," Jayla replied, feeling safer the deeper into the building she hid herself.

"Then I'm coming with you to wherever you're going," Nikole declared. "We have to see how many views this gets! Besides, no one is here, and you'd be really bored without me."

Reaching the Recovery Room, Nikole grabbed an organic apple juice out of the refrigerator. She made herself comfortable, sprawling out on a recliner. "We are at— 9,803 views!"

"That's great," replied Jayla unenthusiastically as she grabbed a juice for herself.

"Want me to tag you in it?" Nikole asked before remembering, "Oh, right, right—you don't want people to know it's you. Why is that again? This thing could get you famous! You could be the patron saint of reproductive clinics around the country."

"Pass," Jayla said as she took a seat across from Nikole.

"We could start selling key chains with your picture on it. *All hail the un-virgin Mother Jayla.*"

Jayla chuckled and took a sip of her drink before noticing Nikole staring at her. "What? You want a miracle?"

"Oh, nothing. Just 'Mother Jayla' has a kinda nice ring to it, don't you think? Just rolls off the tongue," Nikole said mockingly. "Just—just tell me one thing. Why, why of *all people*, would you tell Terri before you would tell *me*?"

"Tell Terri *what*?" asked Jayla before what should have been obvious clicked into place. *Tell me you didn't, Terri. Tell me you didn't.*

"Girl, I know you're . . ." Nikole started before pointing to her own stomach and whistling. "I just always thought you would come to me first before you told anyone else."

Steadily Jayla's anger began to rise, especially as she replayed the conversation between the four women from earlier that morning.

"Terri told us everything," Nikole continued. "It's actually kinda sad—she thinks we're friends now. I almost feel bad for her, but I don't because she can't keep secrets, and who wants a friend they can't trust. I can keep secrets—you'd know that if you told me yourself. You can tell me anything."

"Us. You said *us*; who is 'us' exactly?"

"Us includes me, Hailey, and Terri. So how far along are you anyways?"

Jayla was silent as she weighed whether or not to divulge any more information, inwardly kicking herself for being so weak and foolish to have trusted Terri and not wanting to make the same mistake again with someone else.

"I mean you've told everyone else—might as well tell me."

"Like three months," Jayla sighed.

"Three months? Scandalous! That's the whole time I've known you! It's like our friendship is based on a lie!" Nikole exaggerated. "Do you know who the daddy is?"

Jayla's dead-eyed glare bored a hole into Nikole. "Okay, okay, wow—just asking—and he wants you to keep it?"

"Nikole, just *drop* it, okay?"

"Why are you mad at me? You're the one who didn't tell me in the first place! I should be the one mad at you!" Nikole defended. "Do I know the guy?"

"Trust me, you don't."

"If I don't know him then what's the harm in telling me who it is?"

Jayla's mind flashed with images of her ex-boyfriend. "We worked together at my last job," she said as she sighed.

"The nursing home?"

Jayla nodded.

Nikole filed away that bit of information and said, "Oh, look at that—cell service in here sucks. Still says we have nine thousand views," she reasoned before knocking over the rest of her apple juice onto the floor. "Whoopsies. What a mess. I would help, but I gotta go."

Finally alone, Jayla scrunched down into her chair and stared at the clock on the wall. *What a day—and it's not even ten*, she thought as she began processing the events of the morning. *How could I have been so stupid?* Jayla groaned, not knowing if she referred to almost getting caught by Darla or trusted Terri with her secret or both. *Do you practice being stupid, or does it come naturally?* She asked herself the same question she heard over and over again as a child.

As she waited for her lunch break to come, Jayla helped what few patients entered the clinic. She enjoyed the distraction found from her own problems in helping the women in her care.

"He better not leave me now," her last patient before lunch slurred, "not after all I've been through." She looked to be in her mid-twenties with wavy golden hair pulled back in a bun and wore an oversized baseball jersey, the fabric of which she rubbed through her fingers like a wishing stone. "He couldn't leave me now, right?" she asked Jayla as if they were the most intimate friends unburdening themselves over brunch, the anesthesia lowering her inhibitions. "I know he was with *her* first, but he's with *me* now—and she would never do this for him. Never. Ever."

"Jayla, the patient's ride is here," Tripp's voice called over the intercom.

"Oh, he's here now. Great! Fantastic! Just in time for nothing," the woman rambled sarcastically as Jayla helped her into the wheelchair to cart her to the main entrance. "He missed the whole show, and do you know where he was? Was he at work? Hmm? No. Softball practice," the woman grumbled as Jayla wheeled her through the hall. "Is it softball season? Nope. I hope it's clear I'm not the one he's having an affair with. Mmm no, no, no. He's cheating on both of us with softball."

As they rounded the corner into the lobby, Jayla saw a mustached man in sweaty red sportswear and a gold chain with a matching softball medallion dangling off his gritty neck.

"And there he is, folks! The one, the only, Mr. Fredrick, himself. My knight in shining armor. Here when I need him, gone when I, well—when I—the woman in the wheelchair trailed off.

"Hey there, sweetheart," the man said in a raspy Southern accent, "I sure hope you haven't been botherin' this nice lady here."

Before Jayla could say anything, the woman in the wheelchair tugged at the man's sleeve. "Snack? Where's my snack? You said you'd bring me one."

The man smiled with labored patience as he reached in his pocket, pulling out a can of dip and a convenience store packet of peanuts.

"Peanuts? Peanuts!" the woman replied. "I come here to have an abortion—for *you*—and you can't even bring me a veggie snack like I ask? I didn't ask for the moon, Ricky. Just something healthy *for once*."

"Since when are peanuts not vegetables?" the man defended, but rather than show any anger, he smiled all the more at Jayla. "I can take it from here," he said. "Thanks darlin'."

As the couple exited the building, Jayla couldn't shake the feeling of déjà vu. She knew she hadn't met the man, yet something about him and their conversation stuck in Jayla's mind. "Has he been here before?" she asked Tripp, who was standing behind the reception counter.

He shook his head. "Not that I can remember, at least not while I've been here. Why don't you check the logbook? Remember, we have to make a copy of everyone's driver's license before they can check anyone out. Unplanned can't afford to have just anyone picking them up and litigatin' later. Why you so interested?"

"No reason," she replied. Then, glancing at the check-out log, she suddenly realized why he seemed so familiar. The man's name was Goodall. *Rick Goodall. Hmmmm, that's interesting . . .*

CHAPTER 26

LETTERS

Given a full weekend for the video to go viral, the LifeLine Pregnancy Center was all a buzz. "Did you see it?" Jayla overheard Darla's upraised voice from across the Lifeline parking lot as small gusts of her souring well-being escaped the front door each time it opened. "Did you notice anything strange about it? Anything—I don't know—*odd*? Look closer. Mmmhmm—that's right—it's *me*. And do you think anyone asked *me* before they took my video? Before they posted it for the whole world to see?!"

Since arriving home at her apartment on Thursday afternoon, Jayla watched from behind the shielded anonymity of her smartphone as her unplanned stunt at Unplanned continued to skyrocket in popularity. Now, walking into work Monday morning, it seemed like she was entering some odd living art performance for which she had been preparing herself for all weekend.

"Good morning, sunshine; it's good to have you back," Brittany welcomed as Jayla entered the building. As she spoke, her hands worked like an automated assembly line, unboxing brightly colored sheets of paper and organizing them into perfectly symmetrical stacks. "I wouldn't go in there if I were you," Brittany advised as Jayla neared the interior entrance beside the reception area.

"Why's that?" Jayla asked.

"I don't know if you've noticed, but Darla is on a bit of a warpath this morning over some video that came out. She's upset about being in it, other folks are upset about hearing about it, Renee is upset about her being in it."

Inside the hallway Jayla could see Darla angrily rambling to Samantha. The latter looked like she was the hostage of a scorned woman wildly shooting off at the mouth. Seeing Samantha made Jayla's stomach drop, intensifying the nausea she had been fighting off that morning. One part of her wanted more than anything to tell her what she saw during her last shift at Unplanned, and yet, the other part of her knew she couldn't say a word. She couldn't share what she knew without sharing where she was when she first learned about it, and that wouldn't end well for anyone. It was because of this struggle Jayla called out of work on Friday, anxiously anticipating this moment over which she had forfeited many hours of sleep. And now that she was there—now that Samantha was within view—dread gripped her and wouldn't let go.

"Would you like to help me make some flyers for our Community Day rally coming up?" Brittany suggested. "I sure could use the help!"

"Okay," Jayla agreed reluctantly.

At Brittany's direction, Jayla grabbed a ream of bright orange paper and slowly made her way over to the copier, feeding the sheets as apathetically as possible. She looked at the flyer design, which was undoubtedly Brittany's handiwork. It featured a jumbled collage of crosses, babies, a smiley-faced drum set, and lightning bolt graphics. It looked like something a twelve-year-old made as a class project. '*Community Day!*' it read in big, bold letters on the top, '*Featuring the hit band Ichthus!*' Jayla smirked as she readjusted her bra, imagining the future look on Brittany's face when she realized no band was coming.

Jayla imagined Brittany on the day of the event—first excited and anxious, then growing in nervousness the later the day got without the band being there, and then shock and sorrow and confusion as she watched more and more people leave the failed festival until, finally, she was the only one there. And, for a moment, Jayla felt sorry for Brittany.

Pushing that thought down, Jayla turned her attention again to the flyer design. '*Come join us for a time of music, celebration, and fun! All donations are going to the LifeLine Pregnancy Center!*' But then came a phrase Jayla didn't expect: '*Re-Elect Charlie Crix! Crix It to Fix It!*'"

"Hey, why is this on here—this part about re-electing Charlie Crix? Is this going to be a political thing?" inquired Jayla.

"Not really," Brittany replied, before correcting herself. "Well, I guess everything is political in a way, isn't it? I just wanted to put it on there to remind people to vote for the good guy, is all. He is going to try and make an appearance there, but we don't know for sure."

"The *good guy?* You think Crix is a good guy?"

"Why? You don't like him?" chortled Brittany.

Jayla shrugged. She didn't know much about Charlie Crix or his politics; she just remembered him from the newspaper headlines a year earlier regarding an alleged inappropriate relationship with a staffer.

"In my book, if you're running for office, and you're pro-life, you're a good guy. It don't matter what you did in the past. I'm about saving babies," Brittany reasoned. "Plus, have you heard about that abortion ban he's wanting to do? It's a Godsend."

"Abortion ban?" Jayla repeated, concerned and oblivious.

Brittany's face lit up with excitement. "Governor Crix is promising to pass a six-week abortion ban. Isn't that great?"

"Like no one can get an abortion in the state for six weeks?" replied Jayla.

"No, if someone is pregnant and she wants to get an abortion, she'll only have six weeks from the time of conception to do it. After six weeks, it's banned—she has *to keep her baby!* Or go out of the state. But think about how many lives could be saved by that. He's calling it the Lifebeat Six Bill."

Jayla counted the number of weeks she of her pregnant and felt a panic start to come on, realizing she was well past the time allotted within the ban. While any given day, she was on a different side of the fence about whether or not to keep her pregnancy going, the gift of time allowed her to mull over her options. An opportunity she didn't think to consider was now a luxury that could one day soon be stripped from her. Getting pregnant wasn't her decision. Her ability to make that decision had been stolen from her, and she would not allow someone else to steal this from her too. In aborting her right to time, she felt as if they were forcing her hand to abort the fetus. "How soon until the ban starts?" she asked.

"Not soon enough! You know how politics can be. He'll have to get different people to sign off on it before it can become law, which could take a while. But the first thing we have to do is get Governor Crix re-elected! If we can't do that, we can't get this bill passed! This is step one," she said as she held up one of the flyers with conviction. Brittany leaned in as if to share a big secret, "He's an Independent, but he used to be a Republican. Everybody says it was so more of the conflicted side would vote for him, but he's really just a regular Republican, so you know you can trust him."

"He is deceiving the people, so we know we can *trust* him? Did I get that right?"

"Well, no, he's like—"

Before Jayla could respond, she heard the chirping of the bell on the front door, alerting the reception area to a visitor's presence. An African American woman with a braided updo and a yellow-striped bag walked up to the counter where Jayla and Brittany stood in the middle of their discussion. "Good morning, ladies. Having a blessed day?"

"Every day I wake up breathing is a blessed day!" replied Brittany as Jayla just smiled, feeling as if she were listening to code talkers.

"Good, good. I didn't know if you could do something for me," the woman began, pulling a form out of her bag. "I'm from Alive Church, and our pastor recently did a sermon on adoption, and some people in our congregation were moved to want to adopt. A sign-up sheet went around our Sunday school classes, and, anyway, this is the list of people who are interested in adoption. I'm going around the different places, the Christian bookstores, coffee shops, laundromats, and over here to the pregnancy center to see if we can post it," she said, showing the paper to Jayla and Brittany, pointing to different columns. "It's their names and addresses and contact information. Would you mind if I left this somewhere women can see it? Maybe tape it to the door?"

"Honey, it's so wonderful what y'all are doing, and I love the heart behind this, so I'll tell you what I'll do," affirmed Brittany, "I'll hold onto this form, and I'll show it to our director and, if she says we can share it, we'll share it. How's that sound?"

"Great! Sounds great. Thank you!" the woman applauded, passing the form to Brittany. Then, with a second ringing of the bell, she was off to another location.

"Wow—there are a lot of names on that list," Jayla commented, surprised.

"Yeah. A lot of people in the world want to adopt; too bad we can't use this," Brittany said as she folded the paper into quarters.

"Didn't you just say you'd ask Renee if we can post it?"

"I already know what Renee is going to say! It's nice what these people want to do, but we're not allowed to share private adoption ads. Our covenant or code of conduct says we are not supposed to push or coerce a woman toward adoption in any way. Too many things could go wrong. We could even be found liable if abuse or something happened to a child. So it's best to just get rid of it," Brittany reasoned, passing the folded note to Jayla. "Speaking of—would you mind taking out the trash?"

Jayla glanced at the empty boxes and tape and crumpled pieces of paper littering the ground, then eyeballed Brittany, who was the last person at work she would ever want to take orders from. "I was going to head out to the dumpster anyway to toss something," Jayla replied. "Might as well take a few more things," she said, putting the folded note into her back pocket.

Lugging the deconstructed boxes outside, Jayla was glad to have a few moments to herself.

"Mornin', miss," came a voice from the back lot of the pawnshop.

Not these guys again, thought Jayla, knowing the second she looked up she would see two smokestacks of men in full uniformed regalia. This time there was only one—the lanky one was missing. "Good morning."

"Need help with those boxes?" the stout pawnshop worker asked.

"No, I got it, thanks," Jayla replied, hoping this was the last time she would be unlucky enough to be found alone with either of these men. Something about them put her on edge.

"You women seen that video they shot across town last week? The one at that abortion clinic?" the man asked between drags from his unfiltered cigarette. "Y'all been talking about what to do about it?"

The jitters Jayla felt intensified as she replayed that last phrase through her mind. "What to *do about it?*" she asked.

"My buddy Clem is hoppin' mad. His wife was there protesting and them murderers got video of her. And that girl, they're calling her the

Abortion Angel—" the man said with disgust. "Clem says she is an 'Abortion *Demon*'! So, so, what are y'all gonna do? You gonna put out your own video or somethin'?"

"I don't think so—but that's a good idea. I'll pass that along to our boss," Jayla encouraged, being as agreeable as she needed to be to leave.

"Y'all figure it out and figure it out quick! We can't let those baby killers win."

Baby killers. That short phrase struck Jayla between the ribs, and it replayed on a loop as she walked around the corner and toward the entrance of the pregnancy center. But rather than holding onto the accusation, Jayla smoothed it out of her system as she ran her hand over the front of her scrubs, feeling a bit more of a bump than usual. *Abortion Angel*, she smiled to herself defiantly. *Never been accused of being an angel before.*

When Jayla came back into the building, she was met by Brittany and Renee doting over the Community Day flyers. "Fantastic job," Renee fawned as Brittany's demeanor became bashful. "Beautiful work. You should be proud," she complimented, then redirecting her gaze at Jayla, added, "You both should be!"

"This was all Brittany," stated Jayla, not wanting to get any credit for the awful design on the flyers.

"She told me how you've been helping her this morning!" Renee responded. "I think that shows just so much team spirit," Renee continued as she approached Jayla. "I'm not sure if you'd be up for it, but our abortion support group has been working on a project, and I think they would be over the moon thrilled if you helped them with it."

"We have an abortion support group?" Jayla wondered aloud.

"Oh, yes. Most pregnancy resource centers do, or at least offer it when needed. People make the mistake of thinking abortion is just a physical action, but it's not. It has mental, emotional—even spiritual—ramifications. Many women think, *Okay, if I get an abortion, my problem is solved*—and in one sense, that is true, they have been able to resolve that particular side of the issue in their life through abortion. But now, they enter a new phase of enduring a whole new set of problems, arguably worse than the first. Our support groups are for the women who have made their decision and wish they had done things differently. It is led by some of our volunteers who had their own abortions and want to help love others as they weather the worst part of the storm, the backside. We even have some of the people who were almost aborted by their mothers joining us. It's open to everyone—we don't discriminate who does and does not need support."

"And they've been doing a group project or something?" asked Jayla, deflecting and despising the sermonizing tendency of Renee.

"No, not quite. Each person in the group was asked to write a letter. I think it would be nice if we made a presentation out of the letters and put them on the community board to be an encouragement to our volunteers and the guests who come here. Just be creative."

This wasn't a project Jayla particularly wanted to volunteer for. Still, if it bought her more time away from Samantha, she was happy to devote every minute of her shift to its completion. "Of course, I'll help," Jayla replied, to Renee's elation.

"Great! You can use my office. I won't be using it today, and I really want this to be a surprise for everyone."

Jayla followed Renee through the hallway to her office, where Renee pulled out a box of letters. She placed it on the desk in front of Jayla, followed by a giant corkboard and a container of craft material. "Here you go! Take your time with it—we really want it to look nice," she advised Jayla, "And remember, *it's our secret!*"

Jayla nodded, turning the term *remember* over and over in her head as if there were something she had forgotten. "Hey!" she blurted, pulling a slip out of her front pocket, catching Renee's attention before she left the room. "What do you want me to do with this receipt?" she asked.

"What's it for?" asked Renee.

"It's for the books—the ones for school. The lady I bought them from was out of ink, so it's handwritten. I told her that would be fine," Jayla explained, trying as nonchalantly as possible to put out whatever future fires might come.

"Great! You can leave it on my desk when you're through. I'll let you know if we have any questions," said Renee, as she hurried off to her next task.

Alone in Renee's office, Jayla lazily brushed her hand over the letters inside, each handwritten. As slowly and precisely as she could, Jayla decorated the board, giving it a beautiful border, before pinning up the letters one at a time. By the time she was done, the panel looked immaculate with each piece in place, with only one problem: there was still far too much time left to her shift. Unwilling to admit defeat and having a low battery on her smartphone, Jayla found herself staring at the wall of letters.. Reluctantly she trained her eyes on the first few letters she pinned to the board and began to read:

Dear You,

I'm not sure what to say. This is my first time ever trying to write to you although I've imagined a lot what you might tell me if I hadn't done what I did. You have every reason to hate me. I haven't slept without nightmares since it happened 3 years ago. It's like I'm stuck in the moments leading up to and right after my abortion. My husband says I talk in my sleep, commenting on things that don't make sense to him—wouldn't make sense to anyone not in the room that day.

I just wanted you to know that I'm sorry for what I did. I was young and I thought it was the right thing to do. That's no excuse, but you wouldn't want to be around me anyways. But I think about you every day.
If there is a heaven like Marta at the pregnancy center says, I hope I get to meet you in it, if God can forgive me. I hope one day I can forgive myself for what I did, and that you'll forgive me too. Will you forgive me?

Signed,

Me

Dear You,

I was 17 when I found out you were inside of me. I was afraid if I told my boyfriend he would leave me, so I told my parents instead. My dad told me to either have you aborted or to leave the house. It still feels like it happened yesterday. I was a mess. I was way too much of a mess to make the appointment, so my mom had to. We drove to the clinic and back in silence and she didn't talk to me for the rest of the night. A few days later I was crying in my room about what happened, and she came in yelling and screaming at me and telling me to forget that it ever happened and to never bring it up again.

Two years later I got pregnant again and I was too afraid to tell my parents until I was 5 months along. When I finally had to tell them because I started to show, they offered to pay for me to get another abortion, but I said no. You now have a ten-month-old little sister named Julietta Jade, and I really wish she could meet you. My parents are actually thrilled to be grandparents which, I'll admit, surprised me after they tried to have Julietta aborted 4 months before she was born. I know now they would have grown to love you too. All our family photos we've taken are beautiful, but I can't help but feel a hole in our family. I'm so sorry.

Me

Dear You,

I wish the abortion never happened. As soon as I went in for my first appointment, I knew I didn't want to get it, so I left. My boyfriend said I chickened out. He wanted me to call to book it again, but I knew I didn't want to. I was so scared and I was only 8 weeks along, and he said you weren't even a person yet so we made a second appointment at a different clinic. They took me in and got me on the table and the nurse was putting the IV in me and all those heart monitor things and wires and I knew I didn't want to go through with it. So I said, "No! stop! I don't want it!" but the nurse said I was just afraid. I started to cry. She said once she gave me the drug to make me sleep, I'd start to relax and when I woke up it all would be taken care of, but I said, "No! let me go! I don't want to!" But the nurse said, "No—you already paid for this, and we've already started. This is just your nerves talking." She gave me the medicine and the next thing I remember I was unpregnant sitting in a recovery room with six other girls and I was holding an apple juice and vomiting and I kept saying "stop!" even though the abortion had already happened—like if I said it enough I could go back and stop it from ever happening. I remember when my boyfriend came to pick me up, I was wearing these black stretchy shorts and I still had that yellow antiseptic paint stuff all over my legs that they put on me, and he didn't want me in the car because he thought I might ruin his seats and I just kept saying "stop." We broke up a week later.

Today would have been your first birthday. I miss you.

Me

CHAPTER 27

LIFE'S A JOURNEY, NOT A DESTINATION

Jayla regretted reading those three letters, but not enough to stop her from consuming the others until the end of her shift. She was drawn in by them and repulsed at the same time. Deep into the night she thought about the women who authored them and replayed their stories, wondering how many initial drafts they attempted. She pictured them staring at the blank paper in front of them, weighing what to censor or share, having to relive every moment. She wondered how they would feel seeing their private letters on display or how she would feel if her own secrets were shared on the community board for all to gawk at.

Arriving for her shift at LifeLine the following Wednesday, Jayla was repulsed to see her crafted letter board hung with pride.

"Jayla! Hey!" came a sweet Southern voice as Samantha jogged up to her.

"Hey, girl!" Samantha smiled as she came in for a big hug. "I've missed you! When you flew the nest, I knew I wouldn't see you as much, but *weepin-willows,* how have you been? What's new with you?"

Jayla opened her mouth but before she could say a word, Darla inserted herself into the conversation. "Well, I'll tell you what's new with me," she began, "you know that video I told you about? Well, I've talked to my husband about it, and we've come to a decision. We're going to sue," said Darla matter-of-factly.

"Sue? Who's there to sue?" asked Samantha, exchanging baffled glances with Jayla.

"All of them!" declared Darla. "The clinic, the person who shot the video—that self-proclaimed *Abortion Angel* fanatic—we're going to sue the whole lot of them."

"Oh really? For what? Weren't you the one on *their* property? Isn't that trespassing? What lawyer in their right mind would take on a case like that?" Samantha stated to Darla's dismay.

"I can't believe you just said that. After all I've been through. They've made me a public spectacle!" Darla asserted loudly, drawing the attention of all the staff in the hallway.

"They may have posted the video, but you seem to be doing the spectacle part all on your own," Samantha replied.

With a grunt, Darla stormed off, her red hair forcefully swinging to the beat of her tyrannical stomps.

"Life is too short," Samantha sighed, turning her attention back to Jayla. "You know, one day that girl is going to have a real trial, and she won't know what to do. If you sweat the small stuff, how can you deal with the big stuff? Oh well. That's enough soapboxing from me. What do you got going on today?"

Jayla shook her head. "I don't know. Normal stuff. Why?"

"Do you remember Terica?"

Jayla racked her memory. "The really, really pregnant one?"

"That's her," Samantha laughed. "She already came in for her last monthly check-in. The poor thing is supposed to be on bed rest, but she's gotten a little stir crazy being cooped up like that, so she's coming in a few minutes to check out the baby boutique. I figured, if you were free, you could join us?"

Baby boutique? Jayla pondered, unfamiliar with that term. "I should probably be getting the rooms ready."

"You can if you want, but I'd love it if you joined us!"

"Yeah, alright," Jayla said, "I guess I could help. Just let me know when she gets here."

Thirty minutes later, when Terica arrived, no one had to get Jayla. She could hear Terica's protests and bellows from the moment she entered the building. "Sammy? Sammy! Get me a plunger, or a crowbar, or a piñata stick 'cause I am getting this thing out *today!*" Terica declared as Jayla entered the room.

"Soon, momma. It's going to happen soon," Samantha soothed as she lightly rubbed Terica's lower back.

"I feel like one of them Thanksgiving parade balloons. People got to clear the street for me to walk past!" Terica exclaimed.

"Here, Terica, you follow us to the new mothers support area, and we'll get you a place to sit and a snack," Samantha negotiated.

When they arrived at the room that doubled as their conference area, Jayla volunteered to get the refreshments as Samantha provided Terica with two folding chairs, one for her to sit on, and one for her feet.

By the time Jayla walked over with a few cellophane packages of chips and peanut butter crackers, Terica had lost her appetite. "I can't tell if I'm hungry or full or up or down anymore," she explained. "Sorry, Layla."

"That's alright," Jayla said, resisting the urge to correct her name.

"Can we go to the mommy supply room, or whatever you all are call'n it now? The last time I was in there, I saw a little pajama set with these sweet little yellow ducks on the feet. I thought that would be just the most cutest thing for me to get my baby girl. Think it's still in there?"

"Won't hurt to check!" Samantha replied, taking the handful of treats. "And we'll take these for the road."

Samantha walked over to a door at the other end of the room next to a poster of three crosses on a hill with the expression, *'When you're at a crossroad, look to the cross.'* The other women joined her as she flipped on the overhead lights and opened the doors revealing a hidden oasis so well maintained and beautified it seemed they entered a portal to a different reality. There were car seats and strollers against a pink wall, bassinets and bouncy seats against a blue wall, with shelf after shelf of diapers and baby clothes and formula. There was also an area related to a mother's self-care with items like candles, packs of coffee inside colorful mugs, and even a few water foot massagers. Jayla was amazed something as young and fresh and exciting as this could exist within such a dilapidated building conference room.

"I give you—drum roll, please—the combination mothers supply baby boutique and conference room," Samantha said cheerfully.

"This place is— wow!" said Jayla as she snooped around, finding new things everywhere she looked.

"It's for all the mommas who come to our Mommy University as a reward for finishing each class. Once the session is done, they get to come in here and take their pick of something they earned for studying!" Samantha proudly said. "It's proof of the promise we're making to them."

"What promise?" asked Jayla.

"The promise that we're here for them! Here to help! When young mommas come into our program, we don't just tell her to keep her baby. We come alongside her and partner with her. We connect them with all the social services the state offers. The thing is, there's help out there for almost anyone if you know where to go for it. We set ourselves up as a clearinghouse for finding help for each lady who comes through our door. Then we try to connect each momma with a church in their area to partner with them for the rest of their life. We do everything we can for them as they get started. But it is their personal faith and a local church that brings a lifetime of partnership. We want to set them up for success. That's our promise, and we do everything we can to keep that promise."

"Mmmhmm, you sure do," agreed Terica as she dug around for the pajamas she wanted.

"So, you help them, so they'll convert? That's what you get out of it?" asked Jayla, the concept of free, no-strings-attached altruism was as foreign a concept to her as a nurturing mother.

"Nobody has to say yes or be a part of it. We're not in it to *convert* someone, and we don't make someone pray or say they are Christian before we help them. That's not what we're about. What I've seen over the years is tons of these women never had a good momma to raise them, and it's hard for them to do for their baby what they've never seen or experienced someone do for them. All we want to do is journey with them, come alongside them, try to inspire them, and teach them the parenting skills they need. We want to give them all the love they can handle. If they choose to get partnered with a church for even more help, great! But if not, we might be sad for them, but we won't love them any less."

"That's pretty cool you help the moms like that," replied Jayla, resisting the urge to apply what she was hearing to her own situation.

"It's not just for the mom! Think about it. We transform their lives, well—scratch that—*God* transforms their lives through what we do. Them being transformed often impacts their entire family, which reaches out and transforms their neighborhood. And the next thing you know, we're changing our communities!"

"Found it!" Terica exclaimed, holding the duck pajama onesie in the air like a trophy.

After two bathroom breaks and three more laps around the boutique, Terica was satisfied enough to leave. As the women sauntered down the hall together, Jayla felt Terica grab her hand as well as Samantha's. "You know, nobody's ever done for me what you all have been doing for me. I won't forget it," Terica said, looking Jayla in the eye. "And I won't forget you, Layla."

Jayla gladly smiled and allowed her hand to be squeezed as she helped Terica navigate the hallway. When they finally reached the lobby, Jayla was surprised to see Alexandria waiting for her check-up, her bare arms covered with splotches of paint. Of all the guests she ever helped, the only one who made an impression on her was Alexandria, though it was hard for Jayla to believe enough time had already passed for a follow-up appointment.

"Alexandria C., Alexandria?" Darla called from the reception desk with a clipboard in her hand.

As Alexandria stood, Jayla intercepted her. "It's okay, Darla. I'll take her," she said, receiving an enthusiastic smile and wave from the young mother.

"I guess when you can pick and choose what hours you work, you can pick and choose what patients you want to see," snipped Darla, who left the clipboard on the front counter before sulking away.

"Don't mind her," reassured Jayla, "it's so good to see you!"

"It's so good to see *you*! You said to be here on the 27th, so here I am," Alexandria said.

Jayla smiled and noticed again the small blue puzzle piece tattoo inked between her thumb and index finger. "Why is it every time I see you, you're covered in paint?"

"Well, if by 'every time' you mean this time and last time, it's because I've been painting," Alexandria answered, joining Jayla as she picked up her intake form on the reception counter.

"One of my friends recommended art therapy after Andy—and, I don't know, it just stuck."

"You any good at it?"

"No," Alexandria snorted, "but I can't drink and I can't smoke, but I can paint the bejeebers out of a blank canvas."

"That's good," Jayla replied as the two ladies made their way to the Hope Room. Skimming over her intake form quickly, she noticed the word *ultrasound* circled as the reason for the appointment. "You want another ultrasound? Didn't we do that last time we were together?" Jayla asked, remembering in detail the terror she felt the first time they ventured into that room.

"Yeah, we did, and I know it's probably too soon for another scan, but my in-laws are really excited and want a picture, and I didn't get one last time."

"They're excited for the baby, that's great!" said Jayla, trying to keep the conversation as light as possible.

"It is. I wasn't sure I wanted to tell them, or even how they'd react, but when I asked like a hypothetical '*Hey, if I'm pregnant, is that a good thing or bad thing*,' they got really excited. Silvia, my mother-in-law, cried and said it was like they were getting Andy back. They're pumped, Louis is pumped, everyone gets what they want. And they are helping with some expenses. So, bonus nachos!"

"Louis?"

"My brother-in-law," explained Alexandria.

"Oh wow, you got yourself a whole support system," observed Jayla, realizing how different their situations were from one another despite feeling a natural kinship.

"It's no glossy magazine cover perfect family thing, but we get along. I disagree with what they're doing with Louis. Still, I can't really say anything about it because I'm not going to do anything to change it," Alexandria said then, seeing Jayla's confusion, explained, "Louis has Down Syndrome and Autism. He's a little older than me, but mentally, he's like a five-year-old. He's the sweetest thing. And currently, my in-laws have him living at a nursing home. He's the youngest person there by like forty years."

"Which nursing home?" Jayla asked, wondering if it was Heritage Park.

"Brighter Days off Anderson Road. It's a nice place and all, and the people take care of him, and I guess he doesn't know enough to be miserable there, but it just sucks, you know? He's lonely, and anytime we come to visit him, he like inflates, you know? He just gets this huge, big smile, and his whole face just lights up, and then when it's time to go, it's like he's been unplugged. Like he only lives for the moments we're there to visit him. And my in-laws don't go nearly enough. Like, maybe once a month. Maybe. Andy and I used to go a lot when he was back from his tours. I still try to visit him twice a week, and I think he should be living somewhere else that's better for him, but unless I'm willing to take him home and care for him, my in-laws don't want to hear about it."

"I'm sorry," Jayla sympathized.

"That's why I have this," Alexandria said, extending her blue puzzle piece tattoo. "He really is just the sweetest thing. When I told him, or rather when my in-laws told him, I was going to have a baby Louis," Alexandria stopped and giggled as if she were seeing it again in her head, "Louis jumped up and down, saying, '*Imma be a big bruder! Imma be a big bruder!*' and, I mean, what heartless person would try to tell him otherwise. Silvia did try, but I think it's fine. He's excited. Everyone is," she said somberly.

"I think Marta would be free for an ultrasound. That shouldn't be a problem," Jayla encouraged.

"Wanna head down there now?"

With the door closed behind them and Alexandria's tank top pulled up to her bra, Marta maneuvered the probe over her gelled-up stomach. "Now, where is that little dear?" asked Marta, scanning the monitor. "Ah, there we are. Hello, little one. And how are we today?"

The baby on the screen was much clearer to see than the month before and much larger in size.

"How big is it now?" asked Alexandria.

"She's the size of an apple, dear. And look!" Marta said as she hovered over a particular area of the womb. "She's sucking her thumb!"

Alexandria looked happy and peaceful. "And I can get some images to take back with me?" she asked, but Marta remained quiet. "Is that okay, Marta?" she asked again, looking from the technician to Jayla to the screen ahead. "I can just use my phone, if—"

"One second, dear," Marta replied, clacking the keys of her computer and enhancing the image on the monitor. Then, after a pronounced silence, Marta asked, "Dear, did you go in for a CVS?"

"A CV—no—what's that? Was I supposed to?" asked Alexandria.

"A chorionic villus sampling. Something your OBGYN should have done for you? It would have been around the ten-week mark?"

"No. No one said I needed to do that. Actually, at ten weeks, I didn't even know I was pregnant Why? Is something wrong?"

Marta pointed her finger at the middle of the screen. "This is the baby's spine and—not to cause any alarm or worry—but I may see some spinal abnormalities. But I'm not a doctor. I really can't say any more than that, dear. I just share what I can see on the screen, but it all will just be speculation until you get a CVS done."

"And I can do that here?" asked Alexandria with concern in her voice.

"Everything is okay, dear. Everything is okay. I didn't mean to worry you. I was just talking out loud."

"You tell me there's something wrong with the baby, but you won't tell me what it is, and I'm just supposed to be *not worried?*"

"You're okay. The best thing we can do is calm down and go to the OBGYN and get the CVS done. That's all we can do," Marta said, trying to deescalate Alexandria's building emotion. "Do you still want that picture?"

"No, I don't want anything. Get this thing off me," Alexandria said as she pushed the probe from off her stomach. "I'm done. I'm leaving. Where's the stupid box of tissues to get this junk off me?"

Jayla looked at Marta, who seemed frazzled, hurt, and apologetic. "Marta, can you give us a few minutes?" she asked.

As Marta left the room, Alexandria wiped the goop off her belly, cursing under her breath. In her eyes, Jayla saw behind the anger the same panic and fear she knew too well. "I'm really sorry for today," Jayla offered,

"I'm sorry too. I'm sorry I came here," replied Alexandria, pulling her shirt down. "I don't have enough to do without more errands and tests and doctors. It's not enough that my husband just died? And what am I supposed to tell my in-laws? '*Sorry, looks like something's wrong with your precious little Andy Jr.*'" she said, looking up with closed eyes and tight lips as tears dripped down her cheeks and into her neckline.

"I know this is the last thing you needed, but—" Jayla began and then paused as Samantha's words from earlier that day came to mind. *All we want to do is journey with them and give them all the love they can handle.* Jayla looked around for a pen and found one next to Marta's keyboard. Then, feeling her pockets for a scrap piece of paper, she reached into her back pocket and found the list of adoption families Brittany gave her earlier in the week. Finding a blank corner, Jayla ripped the paper and jotted something down.

"But what?" asked Alexandria who was picking the paint off her arms, causing her skin to redden.

"I want to journey with you through this. So here," Jayla said, passing Alexandria her handwritten note. "This is my phone number. You can call me or message me and, I—I'll help when I can, how I can."

"You said last time you weren't supposed to give this out?"

"I know I did, but I think this is okay," replied Jayla. "Just don't give it out to nobody."

"Okay. Thanks," said Alexandria, her tone hollow.

"I'm serious. You call me or message me. Okay? And don't you come back here without one of those ugly paintings you like so much," Jayla smirked, easing the pressure in the room.

Alexandria nodded and gave a semi-smile before leaving the room. Rather than catching up with her, Jayla decided to give her some space, so she loitered in the ultrasound room for a few minutes more before rising to leave. The adoption sheet in her hand, Jayla walked over to the trash container and popped open its metallic lid. Then, her hand hovering, she hesitated and put the list back into her pocket. "Journey with them and give them all the love they can handle," she whispered. "Maybe . . . maybe . . ."

CHAPTER 28

MEETING MYRTLE

Late Thursday afternoon at U.I., Jayla and the staff were counting down the minutes before closing time when suddenly a woman's deep voice from behind the group, croaked, "Good evening," causing them to startle. The late-hour visitor appeared to be in her mid-sixties with fraying short blonde hair and a white button-up shirt. "I'm sorry, have I come too late? Are you still open?"

Hailey, Nikole, Tripp, and Jayla exchanged glances before Lynn spoke up. "Yes, of course, we're open. Everyone, back to your stations!"

"Is she here for an abortion?" Hailey whispered loudly to Nikole.

The older woman chuckled. "No, no, my name is Myrtle, I'm here to sign up for volunteer work," she explained in a baritone voice; Hailey was visibly surprised the guest could hear her comment.

Then the woman turned to Jayla and studied her as she might examine a coupon to see if it was still in date. "Why you're her, aren't you?" she queried. "The one from that video? My husband and I saw a clip of it on the news program last night. All our church friends are talking about it. I must say, I have you to thank for coming here tonight. That clip has inspired me to do more volunteer work here for the community—and I know I'm not the only one."

"No, that wasn't me," responded Jayla, committed to keeping as publicly unconnected with the video as possible.

"No, it wasn't," confirmed Lynn, "but you might recognize me. I was in the video. My name is Lynn, and I am the general manager here."

"Oh yes!" the woman exclaimed with the clasp of her hands. "You're the one who came out to help. I do remember you! Thank you for all you did for that poor girl."

"Oh, it's my responsibility to make sure everyone is taken care of here. It's more than a job—it's a pleasure," assured Lynn. "And might I say how refreshing it is to have someone from a religious background wanting to join us on this side of the fight."

"There are a bunch of us," insisted the woman, her voice booming with sincerity. "Not every religious person is with this group of radical evangelicals, or whatever they are these days. Everyone knows if a baby dies before it's born, it's pure and sinless before God and goes to heaven. Our pastor explained that as mankind gets older, we commit the sins that could send us to hell. Wouldn't it be better for these poor ethnic children to go straight to heaven rather than be raised in the slums, live in drug dens until they go to prison and maybe then go to hell?" she smiled eerily, in a way that gave Jayla the creeps.

"Well, it sure is nice you're here," replied Lynn uneasily. "Follow me to the office for a brief interview. The rest of you all, back to work. We still have a few minutes left on the clock!"

"Kinda cool she came to volunteer because of you, Jayla," Tripp said.

"It wasn't because of Jayla. It was because of the *video*," Nikole clarified. "And I filmed it, and I posted it, so it's actually because of *me*." Her irritation was evident as she stomped away, with her shadow, Hailey, close behind.

There was a long silence in the lobby. "Well, that was awkward," Jayla remarked, her hushed voice filling the room. She and Tripp small-talked the last moments of their shifts until she looked at the clock and casually said, "Work's done, time is up!" Making a beeline for the door, she called back, "Have a good night!" as she walked toward her car. Sticking her key into the driver's side door to unlock it, she noticed something stuck under the windshield wiper. *Not this again*, she lamented, preparing herself for whatever derogatory, offensive note some spineless camouflaged protestor left behind. *I shouldn't even look*, she told herself as she flipped over the page.

Her eyes looked at the image on the other side. At first, it didn't seem real to her, like something from a movie or done with practical effects or photo manipulation. But there was so much blood in the picture she knew it had to be fake; she pleaded with herself for to be fake. *This can't be real*, she thought. There was no way that baby's torso was really separated from its arms, from its legs. It wasn't possible for the baby's face to be that twisted, that writhing, in that much agony. It was too small. There was too much blood. It couldn't be real. *God, please don't let this be real*, she begged.

As soon as Jayla's mind registered what she was looking at, she dropped the paper. She vomited, orange-yellow slime splattering on her shoes. Her hands began to shake as she leaned against her car. The smell of her sickness was making her doubly queasy, so she put her trembling fingers under her nose to block the stench, but too little too late. She vomited for a second time, down the front of her scrubs, acidity burning her throat.

Despite the way she looked, Jayla walked back up to the office, knowing she was too rattled physically and emotionally to drive, trying in vain to smooth out the front of her sullied shirt. "Oh my god! What happened to you?" Tripp asked, alarmed, horrified as Jayla re-entered the lobby.

"The—there was . . ." Jayla tried to speak but shook her head and spit.

"Wait here," he said as he sprinted toward the break room.

"Oh, my! Jayla? What the . . . ?" Lynn exclaimed as she entered the foyer with Myrtle.

"You look like you need to sit down," the new volunteer encouraged.

"You can have a seat. Just try not to drip anywhere," said Lynn who obviously was more worried about the lobby.

Jayla walked over to one of the chairs in the waiting area as Tripp came with a bottle of water and a handful of paper towels. "Here," he said. Jayla took the paper towels and wiped her face and chest off as best she could.

"Alright, listen up!" Lynn barked everyone to attention. "Jayla, come with me to my office. Myrtle, go home. Thanks for coming. Everyone else can go too. Shift's over."

A few moments later, Jayla followed behind Lynn to the office. "Those low-down, inbred, savage, sons of..." she said as she led Jayla through the door. "Don't sit down yet," Lynn blurted, reaching for the roll of paper towels in Jayla's hand. Sheet after sheet, she layered the seat of a chair. "There. No, please sit, you poor thing." Jayla obeyed—she was too weak to do otherwise.

"I really can't believe them. This is a new low. And you know why, don't you? It's because of our video. They've seen me and you in action and how we protect women, and now they think they can scare us. Well, not today. Not today, not ever. Right?"

Jayla nodded, her head swirling as her blood sugar dropped, wanting badly to be home. "Do you have a candy bar or something I could eat?"

Lynn reached into her desk and handed over chocolate pretzels and a fruit nut bar without pausing to take a breath. "You're right I'm right! And you know why they hate us so much, don't you? Because we know their secrets! We know the dirty little things they don't want anyone to know, and they *hate* that we know it. Like how we know 40 percent of their precious pastors' wives have had an abortion during their college or seminary years. That's right—religious seminary. And does that make them more empathetic to our women? Does that make them step down from their pulpits and cross the picket line and tell everyone how we've helped *them*? Maybe if Christians actually forgave one another, they would be able to talk about it with their congregations. But they can't, so they won't. God forbid they actually relate to someone in the audience going through a struggle! Statistics don't lie, Jayla. Thirty-nine percent of the girls who come through our doors go to church somewhere."

"That's a lot of church folk," Jayla admitted.

"You know what these *Christians* do, don't you? I'm sure you've heard it on the news. They burned down an abortion doctor's office and then tried to kill the doctor. Do you remember that? Or how about the fact these so-called pro-life charlatans have committed eleven murders, twenty-six attempted murders, forty-two bombings, over 100 arsons, and over 600 Anthrax threats? And they say they're *pro-life!* Ha! Are they pro-life over the doctors and staff at our clinics? Are they pro-life regarding the women who come in here? That's what drives me absolutely crazy! If you're going to call yourself pro-life, you have to be pro-the-life to everyone. Period. That's the bare minimum. You can argue that it's more than that, but it cannot be less. Don't just say you care about the baby. Prove you care about the baby by how you love its mother. Am I right?" Lynn said in exasperation.

By the time Lynn's rant was over, and both snacks had been eaten, Jayla was feeling mostly back to normal. "Thanks for— everything—I think I'm gonna go home," Jayla said, standing from her chair.

"You do that. And remember, no good deed goes unrewarded. What I did in helping that young woman last week during the video has started to stir up some great movement around here for women's rights. You were a big part of that. I know it, and Dr. Molech knows it. That won't go overlooked," Lynn acknowledged in the closest thing to a compliment Jayla had ever gotten from her.

Following the droplets of hurl to the lobby, Jayla was surprised to see Hailey still in the building.

"Hey, I heard you tossed your cookies. How you feeling, champ?"

"I just want a shower. I want to go home," Jayla replied as she walked out of the building.

"Right, of course," Hailey said, following Jayla to the parking lot. "Listen, I know this was a crappy way to end the day, and Nikole was thinking—well, Nikole and I were thinking—if you'd want to join us tomorrow night? We're going to a party. Wanna come and just get your mind off things? Girls-night-out style?"

"I don't really feel like partying, to be honest."

"It's not tonight! It's tomorrow! And it could be a lot of fun! What do you say? Please? Please, please, please?" she said with a pouting lower lip and fluttering eyelashes.

"Okay," Jayla agreed against her better judgment. "Okay, I'll come."

"Great! Yay! We'll pick you up!" Hailey applauded. "Try to wear something not so throw up-y. Just kidding! Girls just wanna have fun! And this might be the last time you can have fun until your big day, right girl?"

CHAPTER 29

NOT SO FUN CITY

Hailey's leased Chevy Cruze zigged and zagged in and out of Friday night traffic. Music blasting, bass thumping, Nikole and Hailey sang loudly to songs on their special *girlz night* playlist. By the time they arrived at Jayla's apartment, Nikole was already tipsy from her multiple airplane bottles of liquor in her purse. "The trick to a good party," she explained, "is to arrive drunk and leave sober. It's just like clubbing. You can't get drunk in the club 'cause you'll realize how much you're spending on drinks, and it will ruin your fun! That's why we have elected you the D.D."

So THIS is why they wanted me, they needed a sober driver 'cause they know I can't drink, Jayla thought to herself. While sometimes watching intoxicated people do dumb things could be fun, it always felt like being on the outside of an inside joke and paled in comparison to a night spent eating bacon and pickles and watching reality television.

"Where are we going?" Jayla yelled, competing with the volume of the throbbing speakers, as they made their way through the city.

"I can't tell you, it would ruin the fun!" laughed Hailey. "Just keep following the GPS. It knows the way."

Jayla stared out the window for a few more turns, each one bringing her back closer to her past—The Bricks—the rundown apartment complex where she grew up; every road a neurological pathway in her mind full of fighting, abuse, partying, sex, brokenness, and remorse. On the corner was the bus stop where, at six years old, she waited for

205

Amarika from the time school let out until nearly midnight because she forgot to tell Jayla she picked up an extra shift, and Jayla was too scared to walk home alone. "Someone could have taken your house keys!" Amarika reprimanded. "Just think what they could have stolen."

"Hailey, where is this party at anyway?" Jayla asked, hoping they were just taking a shortcut.

"I already told you," Hailey sang to the tune to the song blaring through the speakers. "We're going to *Fun City*! No boys allowed!"

"Well, maybe one or two boys," chimed Nikole, drinking another miniature bottle of vodka.

"Blackout, here we come!" Hailey cheered as Jayla followed the GPS, turning the vehicle toward the single place Jayla never wanted to see again. Pulling into the complex, Jayla slammed on the brakes. The gas-saving computer shut the engine off. Jayla looked out the window, hearing the sound of laughing, music, shouting, and chaos.

"Before I forget," Hailey said as she pulled something out of her handbag. "Here is one for me, and one for you, and one for you," she continued handing each woman a small pill which Jayla recognized as the same kind Hailey previously gave her the day Jayla caught her stealing them out of the Unplanned, Inc. pantry. "Why birth control tonight when you can *day after* tomorrow? Oh wait, Jayla—duh, you don't need one! Lucky ducky. I am so wasted already. This is going to be great."

Jayla stared straight ahead thinking, *What I have gotten myself into?*

Hailey and Nikole got out of the vehicle while Jayla refused to move. There under the lamp posts, as Nikole and Hailey took selfies and critiqued the other's makeup, Jayla recognized the evening for what it was—a babysitting mission. The *Girls' Night Out* idea was a ruse. They didn't care about her, or how she was feeling or if this would be any fun for her. Nikole and Hailey just wanted someone sober to keep them from falling over, and to pin their hair back if they got sick, and to hold their hand until it was time to tuck them in, back in their safe homes, miles away from their tourist visit where they went slumming in poverty hell.

"I'm not going in," Jayla said, but Nikole and Hailey were too deep into their own conversation to hear her.

"Oops—just got a text from those guys. We meet them on the third floor!" Hailey confirmed before making air horn noises with her mouth.

"I'm not coming with you!" Jayla repeated firmly, loud enough for the other women to hear her.

"But, but—you're going to drive us home? What about sisters over drifters?" Hailey said, confused. "I can't drive this thing back drunk. It's a lease!"

"Yeah, Jayla, it's a lease. Don't be so selfish," Nikole attested with irritation.

Without another word of discussion, Jayla got out of the car and began walking, unsure where she was going but positive she wouldn't stay there.

"Don't leave us!" Hailey called out after her.

"Hey! Hey!" Nikole yelled, "Don't forget I know who you are, *Little Miss Angel!* You want me to tell the world? Huh? Jayla? You want me to tell the whole—Hey! Come back or . . ." her voice trailed off the farther Jayla walked down the block.—

The sounds of bottles clanking and sirens and loud televisions surrounded her. Overhead, streetlights glitched and strobed as she stepped over and around the minefield of fast-food boxes, broken glass, and used syringes. In her pocket, she could feel her phone vibrating, but she ignored it. *I'm not coming back*, she replied to the incessant ringing. *Find your own way home.*

After three blocks of walking, Jayla noticed out of the corner of her eye a low-riding burgundy El Camino pulling up slowly next to her, keeping pace with her strides, its engine revving to get her attention. As the window rolled down, loud music and smoke rose into the air beside her as Jayla hardened her exterior.

"Need a lift?" the male driver asked, but Jayla was unresponsive and stoic on the outside, fluttery and ready to run on the inside. "Where you going? Maybe I'm going there too?" he asked again. But Jayla didn't say a word or look in his direction. She kept her head steady and her feet moving forward, unchanged as if the man were invisible. After all, he was nothing more to her than a night-roaming bloodsucker wanting to sink his needle into her.

With a string of derogatory expletives, the car sped off, and Jayla was able to let out the air pent up in her lungs. And that's when she saw another vehicle approaching her slowly from the other side of the road, reducing speed the closer it came. *Not this again*, she groaned as the driver lowered their window.

"Jay? Jay, that you?" asked a weathered, leathery voice. Jayla knew without so much as a glance who the driver of the car was, and she wasn't interested in a ride from her.

"*Jay—it's Ma*," the voice said. "Jay!"

"I know who it is," Jayla replied as she smoothed over the front of her blouse, instantly wishing she hadn't spoken up.

"If you know who it is, then what you waitin' for?" Amarika inquired, stopping the car. "Go on and get in."

"I like walking."

"Oh, you like walking, huh?" Amarika laughed out a sound similar to a rattlesnake's tail shaking. "Maybe you right. Nice night for a midnight stroll," Amarika teased.

Exhausted, Jayla sighed and walked over to the passenger side of the car, letting herself inside. As she buckled her seatbelt, Amarika snickered and stared at her, the vehicle still in the park.

"Well?" Jayla asked, annoyed.

"Just waitin' to find out where we going, where you stay," Amarika said in a mocking patient tone.

"Oh," Jayla thought for a moment and gave her the name of the apartment complex adjacent to her own, not wanting Amarika to stop by her actual residence on future unsolicited visits.

For several minutes they rode in silence, the same funk soul music playing quietly that provided the soundtrack for the majority of Jayla's memories.

"Work going good?" Amarika asked, and Jayla wordlessly nodded her head. "They give you a raise yet?"

Feeling her pocket vibrating again, Jayla pulled out her phone. She saw three venomous text messages from Nikole and six missed calls from an unknown number. *I'm not falling for that*, Jayla said to herself as she pictured Nikole and Hailey huddled around a phone they borrowed, hoping Jayla would change her mind.

"They give you any discounts anywhere?" Amarika inquired. "If you was smart you would have gotten a job with some perks or free food or something. You could have shared that with me. How are you going to share what you do with people? I don't need no abortion. I'm always looking for some good food, though. When folk around the neighborhood ask, you know what I tell people you do? I tell them you work in poverty management."

"Because you don't like that I work there? Is it really *that* embarrassing for you?" Jayla growled.

"It's not that. It's because that's what you really do. That's what the clinic does. You make sure there ain't too many poor people around. Don't get me wrong. It's a good thing! Nobody likes too many poor people. Rich people don't like it, and you better believe poor folk don't neither."

"That's not what we do. We provide a service. We help women," Jayla disagreed.

"Hey, if you're gonna be there, be proud of what you do. You know what I say? Better to be dead than to be poor," Amarika asserted to Jayla's surprise.

"You really think that?" Jayla asked after a long pause. "You'd rather be dead right now than poor?"

"Absolutely. Absolutely. There's nothing worse in the world than being poor," Amarika declared, then, skimming a look at Jayla, added, "I thought you would have figured that out by now, you of all people."

"You know what I think? If you're poor, you can maybe one day get rich. There's hope to it. There's possibility. If you're dead, you can't ever one day be alive again. It's the end. Just darkness, nothing, no chances."

"But think about all the bad stuff those babies miss by not being born. Think of all that me and you would have been saved from, Jay, and tell me you wouldn't pick that."

Jayla was pensive, speechless as she began reflecting on the lowest, most cruel parts of her life —the abandonment, the physical and verbal and mental abuse, the multiple rapes and addictions, the tears and aggression, and loneliness and scars. *No one deserves that*, she said to herself. But then she remembered the image from her windshield, and her stomach tensed. *But no one deserves that either.*

Sitting silently, Jayla listened to a tune playing softly in the background that triggered a childhood memory. She remembered this song playing in her apartment as she danced to it, giggling, twirling around and around pretending to be a ballerina before a sold-out audience of her two stuffed animals, both tattered from love and adventures together. She remembered the first time she ever had a slice of cheese pizza and the strings of gooey cheese stretching out and wobbled down her chin as she took a bite. She remembered her first friend Daisey and how they spent all summer together and squealed every time someone asked if they were sisters and how, when Daisey lost her first tooth, Jayla wiggled the same tooth in her mouth all night long until it twisted out. She remembered when their neighbor Ms. Colliers had a dog with new puppies and how magical it was to hold one for the first time, and how special she felt when one of the litter sat with her and only her and fell asleep in her lap.

"Yeah, you miss a lot of bad not being born," Jayla agreed, "but you miss a lot of good too. And I guess if being born is only for those guaranteed to have perfect lives, no one should be born. Everyone's life is hard at some part. And, yeah, some lives are harder than others, but I think if you give people the choice to keep living or to die right now, they'd pick life—rich or poor."

"Well, you *would* think that, wouldn't you," Amarika dismissed. "You're too young. That's your problem. I shielded you from too much pain. You wait and live a little longer, and you'll see I'm right," she said as they pulled into the address Jayla gave her. "You'll see. Ma is always right."

CHAPTER 30

UNANSWERED CALL

Jayla's weekend was an endless rotation of online shopping for clothing with more stretch, binge-watching reality television, sleeping on anything with a cushion, and craving avocados on all things edible. She also kept her *Abortion Angel* video pulled up on her smartphone so she could refresh it multiple times an hour, waiting to see if Nikole would make good on her threat to expose her and wondering how tense things would be when she arrived back to work. To her surprise, the revelatory post never came, and the weekend passed, but the sense of unfinished business mounted and led to a subtle sense of dread carried into Tuesday morning's commute.

Stepping foot inside Unplanned for her shift felt like something was coming around the corner as Nikole's vindictive personality demanded it for Jayla's disobedience. The question wasn't *if* retribution would come, but when and how.

"Good morning, Jayla," Nikole smiled icily as Jayla entered the Recovery Room, waiting for her in the dark. "Have a nice weekend?"

"It was alright, you?" Jayla asked with similar cheerfulness. "I see you made it home?"

"We had fun. Wish you could have joined us."

"I noticed over the weekend you didn't post anything on the video," Jayla remarked casually as she put her avocado-themed lunch in the fridge next to the apple juice.

"Why would I do that?" asked Nikole. "It's *my* video, it's *my* views, and that would only get *you* more attention."

"So, are we okay then?" probed Jayla, knowing regardless the verbal answer, they weren't, but hoping to gauge how bad things were between them. *If she says 'no,' then it's going to be mild. If she says 'yes, we're good,' then it will be worse*, reasoned Jayla.

"It's all water under the bridge," Nikole grinned. "But you might want to check on Hailey. I know her little feelings got hurt."

"Okay. Where is she?"

"She's in the break room. Here, I'll go with you," Nikole offered.

With no words exchanged, Jayla and Nikole walked to the break room, the halls were eerily quiet. Approaching the room, Jayla noticed the door was closed, which was unusual for first thing in the morning. *Is this girl gonna stab me or something?* Jayla questioned, exaggerating the suspense of the moment.

"After you," encouraged Nikole with an extended, courteous arm.

Jayla grabbed the handle and swung the door open, wondering what was on the other side.

"*SURPRISE!*" the room full of Jayla's colleagues exclaimed to her as she walked in. Startled, puzzled, Jayla glanced around, her eyes pinging from one excited coworker to another. There were pink balloons all over the walls, and pink polka-dotted party hats on everyone's head. On the table was some kind of cake in the shape of a diaper. On the wall behind the crowd hung a banner that read, "*It's a Girl!*"

"Congratulations, Jayla! We are so excited for you! Woohoo!" beamed Hailey as she popped a confetti cannon.

"Wonderful news! Absolutely wonderful news!" Lynn agreed as she came over for a stiff hug from Jayla. "I can just see the headlines now— *Baby Born at Abortion Clinic!*"

Jayla felt numb and nauseous and wanted to run away or bash the cake over Nikole's head. The room around her seemed to be tilting like she was living in some artificial reality.

"Great news, Jayla!" Shamice toasted with a glass of pink lemonade.

"I didn't even know!" exclaimed Tripp. "This is such big news! You must be thrilled! But for the official record, listen up everyone," clapping his hands, "this is a new day, you don't have to have the gender reveal until the child decides what gender they will be." Tripp laughed as if this was the funniest thing that had ever been said before.

"I know what you're thinking, and it wasn't me," Terri insisted. "It was Nikole and Hailey. They spent all day yesterday in here getting everything set up!"

"Who wants cake?" Nikole asked the room as she began to pass out plates, accepting people's adulations with phrases like, "Oh, it's not about me, it's about Jayla," and, "She's a friend, and this is what good friends do for each other."

As cake and pink lemonade was being passed around and music began to play from Terri's phone, Dr. Molech stepped forward and took Jayla's hand into his own. His long, warm fingers wrapped around her clammy hands like a five-pronged radiator. "We're all so happy for you. Have we a name for the baby yet?"

Jayla shook her head, unable to speak.

"It'll come. It'll come. You can always name the baby after me if you want." Dr. Molech paused for the punch line. "Name her *Doc!* Oh, I'm kidding. Listen, I wanted to get you something to celebrate," he said as he passed a white gift bag into her open hand. "It was last minute, mind you, but the missus and I went out and found some of our favorite Black Lives Matter type movies and got them for you. Some really entertaining films in there. Many of our favorite evenings we've spent popping popcorn and having a good cry watching them. We hope you enjoy them too."

"Thanks," Jayla replied flatly, thinking, *Thanks for always being somehow inappropriate no matter what you say.* But she was feeling too foggy and out of sorts to react any other way.

"Well, I really must be going. The abortions can't start without me!" he joked and then looked at Jayla's stomach. "Goodbye, little one! Be seeing you soon!"

"Jacob is right, everyone. The day is about to begin, and women will be here soon! Grab your cake, and let's go to our stations!" Lynn advised as the room began to clear until only Jayla, Nikole, Hailey, and Terri remained.

"Aww, mommy-to-be doesn't look happy," Hailey frowned. "I know what can cheer her up—*Tada!* A sash!" Hailey answered, pulling out a pink ribbon with silvery glitter lettering that read *World's Best Mommy!* She bounded over to Jayla. "Who's a good momma?" she asked patronizingly, opening the sash and lifting it over Jayla's head.

Suddenly Jayla smacked the sash out of Hailey's hand, startling her more than wounding her.

"Hey!" Hailey shrieked, frightened, as the ribbon fell to the ground.

"Don't you touch me," Jayla hissed with controlled rage.

"Why, Jayla, how could you? After all we've done for you?" Nikole asked as she licked her fork.

"I think I'm going to—" Terri said as she began to walk out of the room.

"Sit down, Terri," Jayla ordered, and Terri listened, her eyes glued to the ground. "You all think this is funny?" Jayla asked the room, nostrils flaring. "This—this…"

"Is a game," Nikole said, inserting her own ending to Jayla's sentence. "It's all just a game. You got us, we got you."

"This isn't tag—this is my life," Jayla seethed.

"You mean you didn't want the baby shower?" asked Terri innocently.

"Shut up, Terri," Nikole snapped. "You left us, Jayla. I warned you not to leave us, but you didn't listen. Bad things happen when you don't listen."

"I didn't listen, huh?" asked Jayla, her eyes the color of brimstone. "I listened enough. Like the time I listened to you and sash girl over there talk about your interest in Terri's love life."

Nikole glanced at Hailey and then at Terri before glaring at Jayla. "Watch it," she warned.

"What? I thought you liked games?" Jayla taunted, too hyped to back down.

"What is she talking about?" Terri asked Nikole with glistening eyes. "What's going on?"

"Hey, Terri, you know how all those *perfect* guys you meet online never show up for any of your dates? All those times you were stood up by *Mr. Right*, and you cried and cried because who could ever want you? Well, guess what? All those perfect profile matches are right here in this room," announced Jayla, revving up for the big reveal.

"I don't understand," Terri cried.

"*Tada!*" Jayla exclaimed, arms outstretched. "It's been Nikole and Hailey the whole time!"

"No! What? How?" Terri asked through her tears, her eyes pinging around the room pleading for answers. Nikole's face was purple, icing still on her lips; Hailey looked like a petulant child who just got caught in mischief by their parents.

"They found out what dating websites you were on and created fake profiles to message you. They used pictures from the internet and told you everything they knew you wanted to hear. Then they would plan dates just to stand you up. They loved it. Thought it was hilarious."

"That's not true! They're my friends," Terri exclaimed, looking to her companions for support or another explanation, but neither Nikole nor Hailey could look her in the eye.

Terri ran out of the room past Jayla, knocking the diaper cake to the floor as she went. Now it was just the three former friends in the room as the balloons on the wall began to deflate.

"Way to ruin a good party," Hailey managed to say as she left the break room in a huff, her favorite plaything having been taken away.

"You know, you're right. I get why you like games so much," Jayla mused, victorious. "And this one just ended. Now clean up my baby shower and wipe that stupid cake off your face," she said before turning to leave.

Jayla roamed the halls to the Recovery Room. Soon she would benefit by distractions, surrounded by women as alone and hurting as she was. But for the time being, she was isolated with her thoughts. She replayed the baby shower in her mind over and over again, seeing the faces of her colleagues in mid-celebration. She felt the heat of Dr. Molech's hands, smelled the richness of the buttercream icing, watched as a thousand different shades of confetti fell through the air dusting her shoes. She saw Terri's crushed face and finally allowed herself in the solitude of the room to really feel the heartache of the morning. Jayla's secret was shared and her privacy shattered. Who now knew and who they passed the news onto was beyond her scope of control.

Midway through Jayla replaying the last half hour, she got a call from an unknown number. No longer caring what was on the other end, Jayla impulsively answered.

"Hello, Jayla—? Is that you? It's Alexandria."

Jayla was shaken back to reality. "Oh hi, Alexandria. Are you okay?"

"No, I'm not okay," Alexandria replied in frustration. "And I haven't been. I tried contacting you Friday night—several times. I really needed someone to talk to. You said you would be there. I'm kind of in a confusing place, ya know?"

Jayla suddenly remembered all the unknown calls from the awful "girls' night out" and she berated herself for letting yet another person down. "I'm so sorry—yeah, that night was kind of a disaster. What is going on?"

"I'm so messed up. I'm torn between keeping this baby—it's all I have left of Andy—and getting rid of it. I'm petrified to care for a special needs child, especially all by myself," Alexandria said between sobs.

Jayla didn't know how to counsel her, but she tried to think of what Samantha would do. So she said the only thing she could think of: "Alexandria, I don't know why bad things happen to good people. Sometimes everything just sucks and nothing is fair. But maybe it's not a coincidence that you have this baby growing inside you. Maybe the universe is trying to tell you something."

And before Alexandria could reply, Jayla thought, *Yeah, maybe I need to listen to the universe too.*

CHAPTER 31

TIME IS ON THEIR SIDE

The following Thursday morning, Jayla sat in her car behind 13 Madeleine Street, the never-used-but-for-emergencies back entrance to Unplanned, Inc. She stared at the same folded form she had been considering since her last encounter with Alexandria. Her finger traced the ridges that rose and fell across its face, her eyes examining name after name of couples wanting to adopt.

What am I going to do? Jayla asked herself, knowing the time for making an ultimate decision about her own pregnancy was coming.

I could reach out and meet them and hear what they have to say. No, that's stupid. What would I even tell them? Hi, my name is Jayla. Do you want my baby? Jayla snickered to herself and then straightened up in her seat. She could reach out with a concise, straightforward message and see what response would come. If no one was interested—great, she had her answer. Jayla knew raising this baby wasn't an option for her. If no one wanted the baby, she would just have the abortion and go on with her life; but if someone *was* interested, then what?

What do I have to lose? Jayla queried before she unfurled the sheet and pulled out her phone.

She looked at the first name on the list. *Meyer and Kensie DuVall, that sounds wealthy. Okay DuValls*, she thought, *the ball's in your court.*

And before she could stop herself, she opened her email app and created a short message.

Hello, my name is Jayla. I heard you're interested in adoption. Would you maybe want to have my baby? Thanks. – Jayla

Closing her eyes, she held her breath and tapped the screen. In an instant, the debate was over, as a swooshing sound proved the deed was done. Now all she could do was wait.

Getting out of the car, Jayla told herself she did the reasonable thing, but in all reality, she wasn't sure. She entered the building, immediately hearing Nikole and Hailey loudly giggling and gossiping like usual, their critical comments audible up and down the hall from the break room.

"These flyers are *freakin' hilarious!*" she heard Hailey sneer. "I especially like these lightning bolts. How 1985! Maybe we should go to watch the circus."

"You couldn't pay me to go," Nikole stated. "That concert is going to be a big flaming bag of dog droppings."

"How many trees were killed in the making of this rally? Don't they know about digital social media?" Hailey derided.

"Right, a bunch of climate change deniers too," Nikole added as Jayla rounded the corner away from the bluster in the break room and toward her workstation, grateful the banter would soon be at an end.

With her mind focused on the conversation happening several rooms away, Jayla was too distracted to notice the figure standing in front of her. "Woah!" she jumped, alarmed. It was Tripp looking less than his usual excitable self.

"Umm, Jayla," Tripp greeted with concern in his voice. "Lynn is looking for you, Hailey too. She said I should get you both."

The short walk to Lynn's office felt like a mile as both women walked on either side of Tripp who acted as a buffer.

"Thank you, Tripp. You can leave us now," Lynn said once Jayla and Hailey took their seats. Lynn was standing beside her desk chair, arms folded, a large latte sitting unattended nearby as her high heels tapped with the steady pulse of a metronome. "I'm going to get right to it, ladies. Jayla, yesterday afternoon Hailey came in here to share with me something she found quite distressing. Quite distressing."

Jayla looked over at Hailey, who was acting bashful and nervous; a vulnerable, regretful look smeared across her face.

"Hailey brought to my attention that, on several occasions, she has seen you stealing various prescriptions out of our medical closet. Upon the conclusion of our conversation, I investigated things for myself and, just as she said, there are many packets and pill bottles either tampered with or unaccounted for."

Jayla could feel her blood pressure rising and knew she had to speak up. "Lynn—"

"Please don't interrupt," Lynn objected, her eyes harsh and determined. "When I asked Hailey why she hadn't mentioned anything before now, she said it was because of your friendship and how she had tried to counsel you one-on-one about your pilfering, hoping she could help you control your impulses, but once she saw you were beyond her help, she came to me."

"I'm sorry, Jayla," Hailey whispered with coaxed tears filling her eyes. "I didn't want it to come to this. I'm just trying to help."

"Hailey, please," Lynn shushed before continuing. "Everyone knows stealing is not only a crime against the State, but grounds for termination from our organization. And that's why it gives me no pleasure to say—"

"Lynn, wait!" Jayla interrupted, desperate for the truth to come out.

"Hailey, *you're fired*," Lynn stated.

Jayla saw Hailey's jaw drop open as bewilderment and astonishment came over her. "What?" she shrieked. "But she—she—"

"She is innocent," Lynn advised. "I don't know if you're aware, Hailey, but we're a multimillion-dollar organization. And, while multimillion-dollar organizations may not always have the *time* to check the footage from their surveillance system, they still have those surveillance systems for reference."

"I—I—but—but . . ." Hailey stammered, pointing her fingers at Jayla and exploding upward out of her chair.

This is the best day of my life, thought Jayla, thoroughly enjoying her front-row seat.

"I saw you, Hailey. I saw you over and over again enter the medical closets and take what you wanted. I have enough evidence that should

I choose to prosecute you for workplace theft, I could. But I won't. At least not unless you make a scene. So, here are your options—pack your things and never come within five hundred yards of this place again or prepare yourself for prosecution. Which is it to be?"

Hailey glared at Jayla, her eyes bulging and the vein in her forehead protruding through her perfectly moisturized skin.

With a banshee growl, Hailey stomped across the room and threw open the door in full tantrum display.

"Oh, and Hailey," Lynn added as Hailey exited, "I remind you that the confidentiality agreement you signed at the time of your employment legally forbids you from taking any of this matter, or anything related to our work, to social media—even under a bogus name—yes, I heard about that too. Do you understand that fully?"

Jayla stifled a laugh as Lynn sat for the first time, massaging her temples and groaning. "What a headache. This is the last thing we need. Now we're down two employees when we need all-hands-on-deck."

"Two employees?" probed Jayla, hoping Nikole was also on the chopping block.

"I got a voicemail from Terri over the weekend saying that she quit," Lynn answered. "So, if you know anyone interested in applying, we need at minimum eight additional employees, preferably with competency high enough not to try and steal from our organization. We'll have ladies banging down the door soon, and I'd like a fully trained staff to meet them."

"What makes you so sure we're going to be that busy?" asked Jayla, trying to redirect her mind away from any guilt over Terri's leaving.

"Haven't you noticed the uptick already?" Lynn replied with a tone of surprise at Jayla's lack of observation. "All this talk in the news about the Supreme Court reviewing the *Roe* decision or the Lifebeat Six legislation every conservative is touting has driven up the number of girls we've seen—and it hasn't even happened yet! Fear is a great motivator. Add fear of pregnancy to fear of losing choice and you get rash decisions. Once it does take effect, we'll have tons of panicked girls in here. A whole parking lot full. That's why we need to get on the ball now before the ball of girls rolls us over, whatever the decision. You look confused?" queried Lynn as a perplexed look canvassed Jayla's face.

"It's just— I thought a six-week abortion ban would *lower* the number of people coming for an abortion. Isn't that why they're doing it?"

"Are you kidding me? The only thing hurting us is the Haileys of the world, who want to pass out abortion pills like they're trying to earn a Girl Scout pharmaceutical merit badge, cutting us out of the picture entirely. Believe me, this bill is a godsend. It's practically going to do our job for us! Listen to me—time is on the side of the fetus—always has been, always will be. The stats tell us the longer a fetus is in the womb, the longer women have to think and listen to their Darwinian mommy instincts and picture a happy, thriving, not-at-all-realistic life for the baby—*blah, blah, blah*—no offense," Lynn said as she quickly made eye contact with Jayla's stomach. "The longer the fetus remains alive, the longer a mom has to be guilted and shamed by her religious friends and family. When you make a woman rush to make a decision, her stress goes up, she panics, boom. She's in our lobby before that beautiful six-week timer goes off."

"But that's only if Crix gets elected," Jayla clarified.

"I hope he DOES get elected! I'm planning on voting for him," Lynn said with an arched eyebrow as she took a long sip of her latte. "But really, who planted the seed on the decision for the six-week baby age? Laugh out loud! Our own government-funded ultrasound technicians. We've got this covered either way. Most girls don't know they are pregnant until week five. Yep, give 'em only seven days to decide, and they will freak out getting to our doors. Here is the wild thing, that conservative Florida governor guy is doing more for the pro-lifers by leaving the fifteen-week ban than any of his party cronies. He might be the only smart one. Heck—he might be a for-real pro-lifer? But he will cave to the pressure eventually as there is a lot of money riding on the pro-lifer political table."

"You're kidding—" Jayla said, surprised at Lynn's take.

"I'm not looking at the colors red and blue. I'm looking at the numbers. Just the mere possibility of this bill being introduced has caused reproductive clinics like ours in many neighboring states to be rushed for abortions. It's already a huge win. Just imagine the good it would do if it passed."

"I bet if Crix knew all this, he wouldn't try to pass that bill anymore. Can you picture his face when this all backfires on him? " Jayla said chuckling.

"Don't be so sure about that," Lynn bantered as she took another prolonged sip of coffee. "Think about it. This bill gets him votes from both thoughtless Republicans, conservative Independents, pro-life Democrats—and there are some, and maybe from scheming Democrats like myself. *He's not pushing this bill to stop abortions—he's doing it to get re-elected.* Deep down, he doesn't want abortions to go away. No politician does. Not really."

"I don't get it; that's like all they talk about."

Lynn looked at the open door of her office and then squinted at Jayla as if she were about to share the secret of the universe. "Okay. If you had to guess, how many votes do you think Republicans get over the abortion issue each election? Thirty percent. Thirty percent of people automatically vote red on this issue without even considering the other factors. *Gotta stop them Dems from killin' all our babies!*" Lynn chuffed satirically. "What happens if this issue gets resolved? The Republicans lose those automatic 30 percent of the votes, and they can't let that happen. So do the Democrats. Same thing. This is the best distractor ever. It will never go away. Each party needs those guaranteed votes to stay in power. So what do they do? They stall and promise to change things, but the only change that happens is slow and non-effective in the grand scheme of things because they know if abortion really goes away, they've all lost all their lemmings who only vote their party because of this single issue."

"So Crix doesn't really want the heartbeat bill to stop anything?"

"Nah—he needs the votes too much. They all do. But it's not just about the votes—many Republicans don't want abortion to go away because, I hate to say it, but you and I both know it's true, the top demographic to get abortions are poor people and people of color. Not all, but lots. No judgment on them. Suppose tomorrow America wakes up to find abortion isn't an option anymore. What happens then? I'll tell you what happens. These poor babies are born to poor families, which means welfare and WIC costs go up like crazy, which means government assistance goes up astronomically, and that bankrupts the country. Check and mate. Some economists estimate, if abortion was ended, each household in America would owe increased taxes of a thousand dollars *every month*. Can the average family afford to see twelve thousand fewer dollars in their income this year to pay for a child a mother didn't want? Listen, Jayla, babies matter—but bucks matter more."

"I had not thought of that," Jayla weighed in, trying to keep up with this obscure line of reasoning.

"And, if you had to guess, which way do you think the poor community that gets the majority of abortions in this quote-unquote 'great country of ours' likes to vote? Red or blue? If abortion stops and the poor Democrat-voting mom has a poor Democrat-voting baby, then the conservatives have legislated themselves out of enough red-voting people."

"No freakin' way!" Jayla blurted as if she experienced an apparition.

"A little fun fact for you. It's estimated that if only *60 percent* of aborted babies had lived, there would be at least *fifty million more Democrats than Republicans in America*, and it wouldn't be long until we were a two-party system made up of Democrats and Liberal Independents. Even left to itself, the pro-choice world will poverty-birth itself out of business." Lynn was on fire.

"I never thought of it like this," Jayla commented.

Lynn leaned back in her oversized leather chair and folded her hands. "So, short story long—no, I don't think Crix really knows what he wants other than to be re-elected. Neither he nor his conservative clones in Washington have ever passed any real abortion-ending legislation, even during George W's term, when his so-called pro-life party controlled both the House and Senate. To them, the more dead Democrats, the merrier, whether inside the womb or not. Follow the money, Jayla, when any politician has everyone focused on one hand, you can bet they are doing something sneaky with the other. And I mean that for all the parties."

"That is unbelievable—you're so right."

"And while I despise these wife-beating, third-grade-educated cousin-marrying conservatives more than I hate seeing a great latte go to waste, you have to kind of respect the manipulative fundraising genius of the conservative conventions on this issue. So, that's why I'm not really worried about *this*," Lynn said, holding up a neon green poster for the LifeLine Pregnancy Center's Community Day.

"What's that?" Jayla asked, putting as much distance between herself and her other job as possible.

"This? It's one of four posters I found this morning on our front window as I was coming in. Can you believe the gall? I was tempted to leave it up, though. *Re-Elect Charlie Crix! Crix It to Fix It!*" Lynn read with a cackling enthusiasm, "Oh, they are so gullible. Did legislation take care of alcohol? No. Drugs? No. But by golly-gosh-jeepers, it will solve abortion! *The third time's the charm—I just know it.* Meanwhile, they're re-electing the guy who's going to be sending droves of women into our clinic, and secure for us more grants from the federal government, deepen women's reproductive rights across the nation and beyond, and get me a promotion while they're at it. What do you think? Should I send a bouquet of roses to their event? I would offer champagne, but rumor is Christians only drink behind locked doors or on cruises. They will be drinking when they all lose their liability insurance in the next few months."

After a few more minutes of Lynn's impromptu education session, Jayla was released to her station for the first time since she arrived for her shift. Walking down the hall, she tried to process the overwhelming morning. The shock of being accused of theft, the exhilaration of Hailey being fired, the remorse of Terri quitting, the mind-bending rollercoaster of political information Lynn doused on her added to her overall pregnancy fogginess to make the morning feel somewhat unreal.

Out of nowhere Nikole appeared in the doorway of the Recovery Room. "*You got Hailey fired?!*" she shrieked.

"Hailey got herself fired. I was just in the room," Jayla replied calmly, unthreatened, attempting to figure out how to pass Nikole to get into the room.

"You think you're real cute, huh?" Nikole asked forcefully, extending her arms so Jayla couldn't get past. "Just so you know, you didn't beat me. There will *always* be more Haileys that come to work here. But there's only one me—so don't you think for *one second* this game between us is over because it *isn't*. Not by a long shot."

"Didn't beat you. Check. Game not over. Also, check. Can I get in my room now?" Jayla asked unfazed, almost playfully.

"Jayla," the intercom called out. "You have a visitor in the reception area."

A smile swept across Nikole's face as she re-postured her body and crossed her arms. "Well, well, I wonder who that could be?"

"Probably not Hailey," Jayla quipped. Turning to leave she watched Nikole's smirk dissolve into a frustrated scowl.

This is the least worked workday I've ever had, Jayla thought to herself as she made her way to the foyer. *I could get used to this,* she chuckled to herself before halting in her tracks, stone sober.

There at the front desk chatting to Tripp was a man with short dark-brown hair and a long stubble beard with a blue box in his hands. The outline of his back looked like an upside-down triangle from underneath his shirt that bore the crest for Heritage Park Nursing Home at chest level. He was handsome, he was charming, and he was the man who raped her and whose baby she was now carrying.

Jayla's stomach turned, and she felt sick. She wanted to leave, to slip out the back door and never come back to work—not now, not after it became unsafe—but that's when he made eye contact with her. A large smile whipped across his face as he turned his broad shoulders in her direction. "There you are, gorgeous!"

Jayla attempted to smooth over her shirt as he swaggered over to her, but she couldn't remove her hands from protectively clenching the sides of her shirt. "What are you doing here?" she muttered, her eyes frantically looking around the lobby to assure herself they were not alone enough where he could hurt her.

"I'm just bringing my favorite person in the world some of her favorite donuts," he replied.

Jayla stood frozen. "How did you find me?"

"Your friend Nikole stopped by the nursing home the other day looking for you. She said she was worried about you and asked if anyone knew you. I told her I did. Then she asked me if I could help her and point her to—" he paused as his forehead creased, "the father of your baby."

Jayla was silent. She imagined in the long sleepless hours of the night what it would be like to run into him again, what kind of conversation they would have, and how it would play out. Sometimes she pictured herself berating him for how he treated her. Other times she smashed his windshield or kneed him in the groin. Still, whatever she did, she was always characterized by strength, resilience, and confidence. But now, standing toe to toe with him, as she breathed in his nauseating cologne and stood under the suffocating weight of his shadow, she regressed into the woman she became under his control.

"So—it's true?" he asked, stroking the hairs on his chin.

"Go away," Jayla meekly directed with as much defiance as she could manage.

"Listen—I just want you to know it's okay," he said, putting his bear paw on her shoulder. "I forgive you."

"You forgive me?" Jayla repeated, pushing his hand off her like the net she perceived it as.

"Nikole told me everything, baby. She told me you were sorry for everything you did and that you wanted to come back to me, but you didn't know how. She said this whole pregnancy thing was too hard for you to do on your own. But you don't have to. Not anymore," he advised, reaching for her hand.

Jayla instinctively folded her arms as a look of agitation flashed on his face. "I—have to go," she said, looking everywhere but in his eyes.

"Okay. I get it. You're working," he replied softly, recommitting himself to the role of the compassionate, wounded lover. "I should probably go too. But I'll come back, and we'll finish this conversation sometime one on one," he advised, placing the blue box of donuts on an empty nearby seat. "I really like the new look, by the way. Who knew scrubs could look that good on you! I wonder if they look even better *off* you," he winked as a thousand-watt smile radiated from cheek to cheek. "Be seeing you."

After fist-bumping Tripp, he left the way he came, and Jayla could see his silver Mercedes speeding out of the parking lot and out of sight. Blood rushed back into Jayla's brain as oxygen flooded her lungs.

"What a cool dude," Tripp commented. "So that's your—"

Jayla was already halfway to the employee bathroom, lips quivering, eyes watering. Closing the stall door behind her, she leaned against the wall and wept. A million different thoughts raced around her mind, things she should have said, ways she should have conducted herself. *I gotta get out of here. I can't be here when he comes again. What if he comes tonight? I can't believe Nikole would do this to me. I can't believe he found me. You're so stupid! Why didn't you say anything to him! No wonder people walk all over you. Oh God, don't let him come back tonight.*

Through her sobs, she could feel her phone vibrating in the pocket of her pants, and panic spilled over her. *Please tell me she didn't give him my number too*, she begged as she pulled her phone out with trembling hands. But it wasn't a text message or a missed phone call. Instead, it was an email, the short response of which read:

Hey Jayla! This is such an answer to prayer! Yes, Meyer and I would love to meet and talk. When would be good for you? - Kensie DuVall

CHAPTER 32

MAC N' CHEESE

Jayla sat alone at a booth for four in the food court of the mall, her knees bobbing up and down as she waited for the DuValls to show up. She scanned from couple to couple, anxious to distinguish Meyer and Kensie from the throng of Saturday afternoon shoppers.

Pulling out her phone, Jayla re-read the exchange of messages between her and Kensie over the last few days. For the sixth time she studied the description of what the couple would be wearing as she smoothed over the maroon blouse she indicated she would have on. *Come on, come on*, she mentally repeated, both wanting the meeting to be over and dreading its beginning.

"I'm Governor Charles Crix, and I approved this message," the television announced as yet another campaign advertisement commenced on screen. Jayla turned to see images of Governor Crix walking hand in hand with his family through a park, each member looking tanner and more photogenic than the last. His wife and teenage daughter were the spitting images of the other with their identical blonde hair, designer dresses, and pearl earnings. The only apparent difference between the women was a medium-sized dark mole above the daughter's lip. High-def clips of the jovial family hugging, laughing, and skipping stones together across a lake were contrasted with footage of Crix's opponent who, in black-and-white footage, was put on trial as an antisocial, workaholic loner who never spent time with his loved ones. "Governor Crix: Pro-Family, Pro-Life, Pro-People, Pro-gress starts here," the narrator concluded. "*Crix It to Fix It!*"

Where was that family of yours when you were cheating with your secretary? Jayla scoffed to herself.

Looking away from the TV, Jayla saw a white man and woman out of the corner of her eye studying her. The man had a buzz cut and red flannel shirt, while the woman wore a black shirt with white pants and touted an ornate purse with a gold chain. It seemed to Jayla they shared the same thought, as the man turned and whispered something into the woman's ear.

"Kensie? Meyer?" inquired Jayla, feeling more awkward the longer they evaluated her.

Kensie grinned, extending a hand to Jayla. "Hi! Yes! You must be Jayla?"

Jayla nodded and shook her hand, and then reached for Meyer's hand. "It's so nice to meet you in person," Meyer said as the couple sat across from Jayla, both smiling at her while exchanging looks of uncertainty with each other.

"So . . ." Jayla said, initiating an interruption to the silence.

"So—" Kensie echoed, "thank you again so much for coming out all this way and meeting us. It's so kind."

"Yeah, so kind, for sure," echoed Meyer.

"Have you already eaten?" Kensie asked, reaching for her purse.

"No, but I'm fine. Not really hungry," Jayla answered as the conversation again lulled.

"And how far along are you?" Kensie asked.

"A little over four months."

"Do you—is—umm . . ." Meyer leaned forward in his chair as he opened and closed his mouth several times in hesitation before speaking. "You're very light-skinned; uh, is the father of the baby the same? Is he black, or mixed? Uh, I don't know how to say it, uh, a person of color as well?"

"What difference does that make?" replied Jayla defensively, offended by the question.

Kensie grabbed Meyer's hand, hushing him. "I think what Meyer is trying to ask is—are you expecting the baby to be—well, how dark exactly do you think the baby's skin will be?" She probed in the most politically correct way she could manage, then, seeing the affronted look on Jayla's face, winced, and continued, "Oh gosh, I know that must sound like just such an awful question—and it's not a racist thing, I promise! We love all people of all colors. White, black—purple—it's just that, when it comes to adoption, we didn't know you were—and we just think that—well, if the baby is *darker*, wouldn't it be better if an African American couple adopted the baby?"

"I don't think the baby will care one way or another," Jayla retorted.

"Right," Kensie agreed momentarily as she and Meyer exchanged glances, "it's just that, you know, there are things with an African American baby you need to know that's different than for white babies— like how to do their hair—and things like that."

"Don't they have videos online about that?" asked Jayla.

As Kensie searched for words, Meyer picked up the thorny baton and continued, "Being a white couple, we don't want people to get the wrong impression and think we think we know how to raise a black baby better than black parents would. Or that we're out to make a statement or be some kind of *white saviors* or something. We think—and I'm sure you'd agree—black parents are just as good parents as white parents, and a different couple would probably know all the best ways to make your baby feel, you know—normal. We're just trying to think through what would be best for the baby, that's all."

"I don't get it—so, are you wanting to adopt or not?" Jayla quizzed, confused and feeling politely passed over like a warm dish of ham salad.

"We just think there's a family out there that could better meet the needs of your baby than us, that's all," Kensie smiled warmly. "And if you'd like, I'm sure Meyer would agree, we could give you something to tide you over until then?" she said, pulling back out her purse.

Jayla sat back in her chair and crossed her arms, her hands tucked away from receiving any handouts. "So you'd rather me get an abortion?"

"God, no!" Meyer declared.

"No! By all means, no!" Kensie shook her head adamantly, dropping several twenty-dollar bills onto the table.

"So then why don't you adopt the baby?" Jayla petitioned. "Didn't your church talk about this? Isn't that why you're here? You want to adopt a baby, and I have a baby that needs adopting. You can't be against abortion and not be for adoption, can you? Being a different skin color or living someplace different or whatever, the baby won't care one way or another. Just be a safe place for them—that's all. Good parents are good parents, right? No matter what color they are—white, black, or purple."

Again, Kensie and Meyer looked at each other, trying to read the other's mind. "Here, I have an idea," Kensie finally said, "Why don't we take your picture and show it around the church and see if there's another family who might be interested? That way, everybody wins! Let me just—"

Before Kensie could pull out her smartphone, Jayla was gone, swirled into the hive of customers buzzing around the food court. Within minutes she was entering the parking lot, approaching her vehicle with disbelief, feeling patronized, deceived, hopeless, and numb. *I guess that's that*, she told herself on the long drive back to her apartment complex. *I tried my best. I gave them a chance*, she said to herself, tightening her grip on the steering wheel. *For a second there—I really thought— but I guess not.*

There was no way she could take care of this baby alone, and she refused to spend more time being rejected as the problem inside her would quickly grow too large to abort. *As soon as I get back home, I'll make the call*, she resolved. *As soon as I get inside.*

Walking up the staircase to her apartment, she couldn't stand to think about one more moment with the baby inside her, one more moment of lying to the baby with empty promises of birth and life and a future. Waiting any longer would be cruel. *I guess Ma really was right*, she admitted. *Maybe it really is better this way.*

Unlocking the door, Jayla pulled her phone into her view, so preoccupied with the task at hand she hadn't noticed the figure following in her footsteps or the silver Mercedes parked outside. With one foot across the threshold, she felt a shove from behind and stumbled forward, her phone knocked out of her grasp. Turning around, Jayla saw the man she hated blocking the doorway, an entirely different look on his face than what she saw the last time they met.

"Help!" Jayla yelled, panicking. "Help me!"

"Are you out of your mind?" he asked, slamming the door behind him so hard it ricocheted open again as Jayla dove for the phone at his feet. Swiftly kicking it out of sight under the sofa, he repeated, "What do you think you're doing? I just want to talk!"

Dodging backward away from his reach, Jayla grabbed a nearby lamp, ripping it out of the socket; she began swinging it wildly, slamming it against his neck and shoulder. The bulb broke against his skin as he pulled the lamp out of her grasp, tossing it to the side like a matchstick.

The kitchen! she thought, knowing better than to go toe to toe with him. *If I can't get out, get a knife!* But as she turned, she felt the back of her head painfully yank, causing her to shriek, as he pulled her by the hair, ripping it by the roots.

"What is wrong with you!" he yelled, throwing her into the corner of her television, which jabbed into Jayla's side like a dull screwdriver. As he inched closer to her, Jayla reared her hand back and dug her nails into his face, down his cheek, narrowly missing his eyes.

Preparing for a kick and aiming at his kneecap Jayla cocked her leg back just to receive the man's clenched fist against her jaw, causing her to fall to the ground. "Picking up where we left off, I see," he observed with a chuckle, flexing his hand as his knuckles crackled. Then added, "You still move pretty fast for being so fat now."

"How did you find me?" Jayla panted through a busted lip, looking for something low to the ground she could grab and throw at him.

"See, that's where you mess up. I've always known where you've been. And I'll always know where you will be." He glowered at her and pointed to her stomach. "Both of you."

Out of nowhere, a female voice called from the doorway. "Jayla? Is that you?" she heard, the voice sounding to Jayla's ears like a Southern angel.

"Who are you?" the man demanded, closing the gap between Jayla and the exit, blocking the view into the apartment with his body mass. As he spoke, Jayla looked around the room trying to decide what could be used as a makeshift weapon.

"Who am I? I'm Mrs. Glock, buddy. Mrs. Glock 42 to be exact," the woman said as Jayla watched the man take a few steps back with his hands out to his side.

"Jay, you know this crazy lady?" he asked.

Jayla looked up, able at last to get a glimpse at the woman in the doorway. It was Samantha, with one hand in her purse and a snarl that would make the devil run.

"Know me? I live here," Samantha corrected, stepping inside as the man kept a seven-foot distance from her.

The man studied Samantha and then turned his attention to Jayla. "Nah," he said, "I don't buy it. Not her. Not you."

"The only thing you'll be buying is a new TV for the one you just broke," Samantha threatened. Then dipping her other hand into her purse, she pulled out some pieces of paper and threw them onto the floor. They were shooting range targets with solid black figures on them, each with holes in the chest and head in tight groupings. "That is if you don't buy yourself a casket first," she added, one hand still in her purse, aiming it at his midsection.

Scowling at Jayla, the man brushed the cloudy pieces of glass off his ruffled polyester shirt. "Okay," he relented with amusement, "okay, be seeing you, Jay," he said as he approached the exit.

"You see her again and that will be the last thing you see, *buddy*," Samantha warned with steel in her voice as the man walked out the door, wiping the blood from his face with his sleeve.

Samantha quickly closed the door and locked it before coming over to Jayla, stepping over the patch of dark hair that had been torn out of the back of her scalp. As she stooped to console her friend, Jayla turned her face away, ashamed of the situation and conscious of her appearance. "Let me take a look at you," Samantha said gently, but Jayla pulled away even more.

"Just get out," Jayla said, embarrassed, trembling, and anxious, her head swimming in pain. "I don't need you! I don't need your help!" she shrieked, pushing Samantha away as she allowed her hair to fall in her face, somewhat masking her appearance.

"Okay, well, I'm calling the cops," Samantha replied, whipping her phone out of her purse.

"No! His brother is a cop," Jayla insisted. "Just leave me alone. It's none of your business. It will just make it worse."

Jayla watched as Samantha hesitatingly stood and took a few steps toward the front door. Pausing again for a few moments, she turned back around and walked past Jayla into the kitchen. The sound of drawers opening and rustling could be heard, then Samantha reemerged with a roll of paper towels in one hand and a glass of water in the other.

Without any words exchanged, Samantha placed the cup next to Jayla and began to get to work cleaning the warzone the front room had been turned into. She picked up the hair and broken pieces of bulb, set the lamp back in its place, and threw away all the paper targets, allowing Jayla time to eventually collect herself. When Jayla moved to the couch, Samantha brought her the glass of water and laid a paper towel filled with ice cubes next to her, then continued to tidy up. And when the mess was cleared and Jayla was too numb to interact, Samantha took a seat on the floor and quietly stayed, waiting to be of assistance.

"Why are you still sitting here?" Jayla asked, breaking the long silence.

"I want to be here in case that man comes back. I don't want you to be alone," Samantha replied.

"Why? What do you care?" Jayla asked, but there was no response. Then, after a few more minutes, she asked another question. "What are you doing here? How did you find me?"

"I heard someone calling out for help, so I came. I didn't know it was you until I got here," Samantha answered.

"What? Are you Superwoman or something? You heard me from all the way across town?"

"No—Renee thought it would be a good idea if we went out to pass out invites to the event next week. Thought we should start in the neighborhoods of everyone who works with us in case follow-up was needed. I volunteered to start here, at your apartment complex."

"That's some luck," Jayla said bitterly, trying to take a drink of water with the least amount of pain.

"I don't think it's luck. I think it's God wanting me to be here. To help you."

"If God wanted to help me, He wouldn't have let any of this happen," Jayla replied, but again there was no response from Samantha. "So what, you got a gun in there or something?"

"Me? No, I don't carry a gun," Samantha answered.

"What about all the posters and stuff?"

"The shooting range targets? Those are Ricky's. He gave them to me last week and asked me to hold on to his good ones and take them home. I forgot they were there until—you know."

"So you totally just bluffed earlier?" Jayla asked, surprised and impressed.

"Yeah, I guess I did," Samantha laughed.

"What would you have done if he didn't believe you?"

"He almost didn't! I don't know what I would do. Maybe poke my car keys in his eye or something?"

Jayla chuckled, making her lip split all over again. "Poke your keys—"

"In his eye. I know! I'm just glad he believed me," Samantha said. Then, seeing how it made Jayla laugh, continued, "You know, I don't know what makes this come to mind, but I remember there was this guy in high school I was dating, and things were getting kind of serious—well as serious as high school romances get—and when things ended, I took it kinda not in the most healthy way. Well anyways, one day one of my girlfriends got his keys from out of his book bag, and we took them back to my house, and we made this mega-huge pan of mac n' cheese, which was his favorite dish. Then we took this giant plastic storage bag and filled it up halfway and then put his keys in there and then filled it up the rest of the way."

"What?" Jayla snickered. "And you gave it to him like that?"

"Oh no. I wasn't going to let him off the hook that easy. I put that sucker in my daddy's outdoor chest freezer that he used for deer and stuff and we froze the mess out of it. The next day I gave it to him. It was—amazing," Samantha reminisced, her face glowing. "It was just so glorious. Because you can't microwave it because it has the keys in it, so you just have to let it thaw. Me and my girlfriends called it *mac n' keys*."

"Mac n' keys?" Jayla laughed, making her bruised side resonate with pain, but she didn't mind.

"That's right. Good ol' mac n' keys."

"You're a trip, Sam," Jayla said, repositioning her body on the couch and pressing the icepack to her lips. "Sounds like I would have liked you in high school."

"Yeah, I was something else back then," Samantha sighed. "That was a lifetime ago. I mean, you've practically been born and lived all the way up till now in the time I've been out of school—which, don't agree with me, or you'll make me feel old."

"Is that where you met Rick? High school?" Jayla asked, the thought of his affair never far from her mind in Samantha's presence.

"You kidding me? If I had met Rick back then, I don't think I would have given him a second thought. Younger me and Rick wouldn't have lasted long, I'm afraid. I'd have mac n' key'd him by now."

"So, why are you with him?" asked Jayla, realizing soon after the words left her mouth how nonsensical it was for her to ask Samantha such a question since she could still feel in her face the fist of her last boyfriend. "Sorry, I don't mean to—"

"No, no. It's a fair question," Samantha exhaled sharply. "I think, well, it's a bit of a long story. Umm—you sure you're up for this? So, well, like I said, when I was young, I was this wild, spirited thing, and I loved the feeling of just being— just—un-tethered. You know? Nothing holding me down, no one holding me back. My favorite thing was to jump into my car and roll the windows down and pick a place on the map I'd never been to, and just drive. Music up, a bag full of snacks— absolutely free. I was like the wind, going where I wanted—however I wanted, not stopping for nobody, and I think that's one reason the boys liked me. Boys always like what they can't have; have you noticed that? The more they try and can't have you, the more they want you, and I think that's how it was for me. I would go on dates and enjoyed the attention and really enjoyed all the free food. But only one or two ever got serious for me—the mac n' keys boy I was tellin' you about being one of them. And when I got to college, it was Fitz."

"Fitz?"

"Fitz, with no r. Before Fitz, I had gone on dates with a lot of boys, but he was the first *man* I went out with if you know what I mean," Samantha continued. "He was a few years older than me and just had this air to him—this, I don't know, tall, handsome, would drive me out in the middle of nowhere for us to get out a blanket and he would play this beautiful acoustic guitar, and we'd just watch the stars, and then do a lot more than just watch the stars. I don't know if I would say I loved him, but I sure was infatuated with him. Maybe he was to me what I had been to all those boys in high school—this raw, uncatchable force. And then, one day I was late for my period and, sure enough, I was pregnant. Me—this free-spirited, go-with-the-flow, can't-tie-me-down girl. I didn't want it—and Lord knows Fitz didn't want to be a daddy, not back then, not in his prime. And so, he told me to do what I already knew I wanted to do, and he gave me the money to do it, and, yeah, without a second thought, I went and got an abortion."

Jayla's eyes widened as she tried to contain her shock. She would have *never* thought, of all people, Samantha had abortion. "Then what happened?"

"Then—I started to take a dive. Whether I wanted it to or not, getting that abortion changed me. I wasn't that un-tethered, wind-chasing girl anymore. I guess, yeah, from the abortion forward, I wouldn't be a girl again. I was a woman now, and I didn't know it at the time, but I had this kind of PTSD. And because I hadn't told any-body about the pregnancy or the abortion, I didn't feel like I had anyone to talk to about this stuff. All my friends still saw me as the kind of person I always had been, and they expected me to still be that person. So I started drinking a lot. Like a lot, a lot. Of course, by this time, Fitz was long out of the picture. And the worse I felt, the more I'd drink, and the more I'd drink, the more I'd sleep around, and the more I'd sleep around, the worse I'd feel. This cycle—this unending cycle—just consumed my life. And then I had a new set of friends who liked the new me because my old set didn't like who I had become. Lord, I didn't like who I had become. And out of that new set of friends, I met a new guy, a guy who was great and fun and treated me good—better than I thought I deserved, and three months after we graduated, we tied the knot."

"This was Rick?" asked Jayla.

"This was *not* Rick," Samantha corrected. "This was Lukas. Lukas Montgomery. And I was now Mrs. Samantha Montgomery, devoted wife by day and functional alcoholic by night. And I mean, I put the *fun* in *functional alcoholic*, if you know what I mean. And by then, it'd been—what? Six, maybe seven years since the abortion? And we're now settling into our mid-twenties, and we start wanting a baby. So, miracle of miracles, I stopped drinking alcohol, which nearly killed me. I mean when you have been drunk for seven years straight, it is tough. And we started trying. And we tried, and we tried, and nothing was happening. And I remember thinking how strange it was. With Fitz, the pregnancy was so accidental and effortless, but with this. . . . Finally, we see the doctor, and he tells us the news. I can't have babies anymore. Before, I could, but now I'm sterile."

As Samantha stopped for a breath, Jayla gasped, "What happened?"

"I don't know. Apparently, something during the abortion went wrong, and now, I just can't have kids. Not many women know that it's a possibility—I know I didn't—and I don't know if that would have changed my mind back then, but now, sitting in that doctor's office, looking at all the scans and paperwork and the look on Lucas's face—the guilt I felt. Guilt added to shame, added to PSTD, added to, you name it. And when we got home, I dove right into a whole bottle of whisky and didn't come back up for air until four months after our divorce."

For the second time in this confessional, Jayla was shocked. *An abortion, a divorce, alcoholism—who ARE you?* Invested in the story and grateful to be distracted from the mess of her own life. And maybe to have found someone else as broken as she felt.

"Before I knew it, I was back in the spiral I got sucked into during college. Then one day around Christmas time, I went out for lunch, already buzzed. And who do I see? Lo and behold, there is Fitz, dressed in this cheesy white turtleneck, holding a baby. And next to him is a woman—a gorgeous, younger woman—holding a toddler, and they're all matching and perfect, like they had just come out from making their annual Christmas cards or something. And, I mean, I just hit rock bottom right then and there. There he was with his beautiful, picturesque family, and there I was, divorced and drunk and alone and sterile. So I got back in my car and found myself doing something I never in a million years would have imagined. I started to pray. I don't really know why I did and it wasn't some polished prayer, either. I just said, *God, if You're real, then stop me.*"

"Stop you?" asked Jayla.

"Stop me from continuing down this path I was on. I didn't know what would happen to me or where I would end up, but I knew I wasn't going anywhere good. And that was it. That was the prayer from start to finish."

"And He stopped you?"

"Uh-huh. Before I even got to the stoplight, someone T-boned my vehicle. I was in the hospital for a week with some cracked ribs and a broken leg that got infected. But—it's the best thing that could have happened to me." Seeing Jaya roll her eyes, Samantha declared, "Honest truth. Those days in the hospital gave me time to get sober and get perspective on things and to reach out and ask for help. And I think that was the hardest part of it all, you know, I think if I had to go back and relive over and over again either the car accident or the asking for help part, I'd pick the accident. It's just—there's just something about asking for help can be just—so. . . ." Samantha sighed.

"Yeah," Jayla agreed, her head throbbing as she lay on the couch.

Samantha looked around the room at the shadows and stains of the mess she just cleaned. By the time her eyes reached Jayla's, they were filled with the kind of hurt and empathy that left Jayla feeling uncomfortable with a sneaking sense of what was soon to come. The phrase that always followed moments like this. The question former teachers would ask after a similar expression washed over them. Eight loaded words.

"Is there anything you want to talk about?" Samantha asked sweetly, sheepishly, fulfilling Jayla's premonition.

"About what?" she replied dismissively. There was nothing she had to share Samantha really wanted to hear. She didn't want to hear about how Marcus was a bad man in a very long list of evil men revolving in and out of her life. Samantha may have *thought* she wanted to know— but she didn't. Not really. In Jayla's experience, nobody ever wanted to stick around to wade knee-deep in the graphic details of the physical, sexual, verbal, and emotional abuse she had endured. What they wanted was to feel virtuous in their offer to help so they could sleep better at night. People liked the idea of a fixer-upper at a distance, but few had the stomach or stamina to endure the darker stuff. In her life, she only experienced one couple who was any different, but she effectively pushed them away many years ago.

And now Samantha will say if I ever want to talk about it, she'll be there to help, and that will be the end of that, Jayla anticipated.

Instead, Jayla watched as Samantha's eyes softened and empathy pursed on her lips, a lump of grief lodging in her throat. "When I first found out I couldn't get pregnant, do you know what the worst part was? It wasn't that I was sterile, which, believe me, was terrible. It wasn't even the guilt or the voice in the back of my head telling me again and again how this was all my fault and how I deserved what was happening. The *worst part* was feeling like I was completely and utterly alone. That no one was with me or could help me, or even wanted to help me for that matter. And there was this belief, this understanding, I had accepted inside of me that this was all there was, and life would always be like this," Samantha looked squarely at Jayla and continued, "So, I'm going to tell you something I wish someone back then had told me." She paused and, scooting closer, took in a deep breath. "You are not alone. And you don't have to be alone. And things won't always be like this. And you deserve better."

"Alright," Jayla replied, automatically downplaying and minimizing Samantha's words into nothing more than a lackluster pep talk.

"Jayla," Samantha said, placing a hand on the couch beside Jayla, "You're not alone."

Jayla rolled her eyes, "I know. You said that already."

"You're not alone, and I'm here for you, I know I don't know your situation, but I promise things won't always be like this, and you do not—*do not*—deserve this."

"I know," Jayla replied, furrowing her brow in aggravation. *Good Lord—just give it a rest*, she thought.

"Okay—I just—I want to make sure you know I'm here for you," Samantha reiterated. "I want to be in your corner. So just tell me what to do, and I'll do it. You say *jump*, and I'll ask *how high*, you know? Anything you need."

"Anything?" Jayla asked, looking for a way to bring the motivational speech to an end.

"Absolutely. Anything at all," Samantha replied, perking up.

"Can you—make sure to take the trash out when you leave?"

Samantha sighed, smiling with her lips but not with her eyes. "You got it, sure thing."

"And maybe get me a new door while you're at it?" Jayla offered, wanting to lighten the mood.

Samantha chuckled and replied, "I could have Ricky stop by here to add a few more locks to the door. Maybe even another deadbolt? He's a good handyman."

"No, it's fine," Jayla declined quickly. "So explain that to me," Jayla inquired. "How did you get from seeing Fitz and getting into a crash to getting together with Rick?"

"Oh! Um, yeah, that's a good question. Well, okay, so I prayed to God, and then He let me get into the crash, and then I went to the hospital."

"Right," Jayla said, reminding herself how prayer leads to car crashes.

"After I got out of the hospital, a friend asked me to go with them to this twelve-step alcohol dependency group called *Celebrate Recovery* that met in a church close by. That group really changed my life. God used it to just turn me around and bring me to Himself. And, one day, some of the people in the group invited me to join them on Sunday for church, and so I went and, wouldn't you know, Rick was there—clean-cut and looking sharp in his Sunday finest. Of course, I didn't know at the time he was only going because church attendance was required to play in the church softball league," Samantha derided. "But still here was this nice, employed, reliable, church-going guy who was interested in me, even though I was this broken mess trying to get back on track. And I felt like I could be relaxed around him and he was okay with me not being okay all the time. He had this way of making me laugh in ways I hadn't in a long time—sometimes on purpose and sometimes not. And at the age I was back then, most men I met were in a hurry to settle down and start a family, but not Ricky. He never pressured me to rush our relationship, even though neither of us was getting any younger. And when I told him I couldn't have children, he was actually relieved. He didn't want kids, which I guess is a little ironic. I wanted them but couldn't have them; he didn't want them but could have them just fine. Well, I assume he can? Who knows?"

Oh, he can, alright, Jayla thought. "Why didn't he want them?"

"Uh, I don't think there's a good answer. Probably life is just simpler without them, I guess. No one to stand in the way of his softball league. I even told him once if we adopted a boy, that would probably be a great way to bond—playing sports together, going on the road, and all that. But he didn't go for it."

Adopt? Samantha wanted to adopt? Jayla's eyes widened. "And that wasn't a deal-breaker for you? Him not wanting to adopt kids?"

"That would be pretty hypocritical of me, wouldn't it? If he was able to accept me not being able to have children, I had to be able to accept him not wanting them. I guess that's marriage—the art of compromising."

"How about now? Is adoption still something you're interested in?" Jayla pressed. Samantha seemed loving enough and stable enough to make a good mother to any kid, especially Jayla's. The way she helped the girls at the pregnancy center, the way she took care of things around the apartment today, and the protectiveness, compassion, and consideration she conveyed over the last few months surely demonstrated it.

"Well, I mean, yeah, but it's not in the cards."

"Because of Rick?"

"Yes, but unless Rick has a change of heart, it's just not going to happen," Samantha said, looking confused as to why this was such a sudden topic of interest.

What if Rick wasn't in the picture? How long would Samantha stay with him if she knew what he had been up to? Jayla wondered to herself. "That's a shame. I think you'd make a good mom."

Samantha basked in the kindness of the compliment. "That's sweet of you to say. I think you'd be a good mom too, one day."

"Thanks," Jayla forced a small smile, knowing Samantha meant the words in a nice way.

"Well, I'll go ahead and take that trash out now," Samantha replied, as she stood and brushed herself off.

"And Sam," Jayla added, "please don't tell anyone at work about this."

"Not to worry," Samantha nodded and made a motion of zipping her lips shut. "I wasn't even here."

CHAPTER 33

COMMUNITY DAY
OR BUST

The following week at the center Jayla was at Samantha's side, making herself a student of her habits, watching her interactions with others, and paying special interest in how she reacted to setbacks or moments of frustration. The word that kept coming to Jayla's mind as she drove home Friday afternoon was *consistent*. Consistently, Samantha was compassionate, approachable, and genuine. Consistently, she gave the right measure of tenderness and tough love. Regardless the age, race, or gender—whether having twenty minutes to spare or just a few seconds—Samantha was her best self. If there was anyone Jayla was going to ask to take care of her baby, it was going to be Samantha. The question now was when to ask, how to approach the subject, and—trickiest of all—how to navigate the biggest obstacle to Samantha agreeing to take Jayla's baby: Ricky.

Jayla began stepping away from her obligations at Unplanned. Tapping into her untouched sick time and vacation time, she requested as many dates off from work as possible, using her maternity leave and its predelivery option to her advantage, sidestepping Lynn's prying calls, while maneuvering steadily to a well-timed exit. Jayla began thinking through what it might look like to increase her shifts at LifeLine to make ends meet before having the baby or possibly updating her résumé for employment elsewhere.

245

The sound of her phone ringing woke Jayla early the following Saturday morning. She was surprised to see it was Renee. *Why is she calling me on my day off?* With the loss of half her income on the horizon, she knew she better answer it to stay in Renee's good graces until another opportunity came along and she could get out from under her thumb.

"Hey, Renee," Jayla said, milking her grogginess. "You okay?"

"Jayla? Yeah, hey. Listen," Renee huffed, anxiety in her voice, "I know you were planning on coming later with everyone else, but I need you to come right away to Bicentennial Park. We're having a bit of an emergency and need all-hands-on-deck."

Bicentennial Park? Jayla ruminated before realizing what day it was. "Right! The Park!" she spouted, the lightbulb turning on in her mind. This was the big day—Community Day.

"So I'll see you soon then, yes?"

"Of course! I'll be right over," Jayla replied, covering the smile that relaxed onto her face. *This is it*, she thought to herself. *Payback time.*

But she suddenly felt a sinking feeling in the pit of her stomach. It seemed the more time she spent around Samantha, the more she saw Brittany ecstatic about her special project, and the greater the temptation grew for Jayla to second-guess herself and what she did. "With this," she overheard Brittany confide to a coworker earlier in the week, "I really feel like I'm starting to step into the person God has made me to be." With statements like this, Jayla couldn't help but feel less excited about her plan than when she first set it in motion.

When she finally pulled into the lot belonging to Bicentennial Park, Jayla discovered the Community Day decorations in complete disarray, with boxes unopened, and Pastor Steve talking to himself, scurrying around a small crooked makeshift stage area covered in cables. Their rented pavilion showcased dangling streamers and sagging balloons giving an all-around impression a large quinceañera was not cleaned up from the night before. As she got deeper into the havoc, she overheard Renee calling orders into her phone like a military radio operator as Brittany labored alone to set up tables, her shoulders gyrating with the impact of quiet sobs.

"Si, si, I'll call you back, està bien?" Renee announced into her phone as soon she spotted Jayla. "Thank goodness. Jayla, I need you to help Brittany get some tables set up, and once you finish that, please start putting up the signs to help people find their way over here."

"Did something happen?" Jayla asked, expecting to find chaos but not of disaster movie proportions.

Renee sighed. "It's just been one thing after another. First, Brittany's youngest came down with a bad fever late Thursday night, and now several of them have it, and two churches called me this morning saying they needed to cancel because of a mix-up in scheduling, and to top it all off some miscommunication happened with the band, and now they're not coming. So, nothing has been set up, and no entertainment is coming, and whoever *is* coming will be here in—" Renee paused to check the time on her phone, "a little less than two hours. But Darla's on her way, and she's bringing help, and Marta and the girls are picking up some last-minute things for us, so we should be good. I think we'll be good. Yeah—all good."

"So what happened with the band?" Jayla probed, the gravity of her role in it was beginning to weigh on her conscience.

"I don't know. Brittany called them an hour ago when they were late for their setup, and they said they thought we wanted to cancel or something? I don't know. That's all I was able to get out of Brittany. In all honesty, she shouldn't be here right now what with all going on in her family but try telling her that." Renee paused, crooking her jaw pensively. "There was something I was going to ask you—" she began. "Oh, well. Too much on my brain, I guess. You just help with those tables and then see what else needs doing. Darla and her husband should be here soon. Oh, and don't forget the sign stuff too, you know, when you have time. You're the best."

Within seconds Renee was back on her phone, trying to throttle the event full-speed reverse out of the pit it had careened into. The closer Jayla got to Brittany, the more she could overhear her talking to herself as she tugged at the legs of a folding table positioned next to an open cardboard box, while her white headscarf glistened in the sun.

"I did—I know I did," Brittany said under her breath, "Flyers? Yes. Handouts? Yes. Contact Pastor Steve for a sound system? Check. Food prep? All done. Schedule the band? Yes. Absolutely. Double yes. I know I did. *Don't tell me I didn't,*" she ranted to the table, aggressively flipping it over onto its wobbly legs. Then, as she forcefully straightened the table out, the left side of its unlocked legs gave way, banging loudly onto the ground. Unaware anyone was watching, Brittany flexed her hands at her side and softly asked Jesus for strength. Then in sheer frustration, she kicked over the folding table and yelped in frustration. Placing her hands on her headscarf, she sniveled to herself, "*I did everything right.*"

Jayla absorbed the moment, but the longer she watched, the more she realized she experienced this exact situation before, many times, only playing the role opposite the victor. Her mind circled back to scenes from her childhood where she would say or do something wrong, and Amarika would grin spitefully. Too many times that look of dominating, ridiculing glee soured her stomach and made her want to run away, or turn back time, or become invisible. Too many times she was humiliated and mocked by the same person who sabotaged her and caused her to fail. And now here was Jayla's moment to do the same thing to Brittany, the same thing she swore no one would ever do to her again.-

Just then, as if she sensed someone behind her, Brittany spun, her eyes wet and red. "I was just—just getting set up," she sniffed. "How long have you been standing there?"

"Just got here," replied Jayla. "Renee said you needed some help?"

"Everything's just falling apart. Maybe you could help me with the table?" Brittany offered. Slowly, with reluctance, Jayla made her way over to the table and helped set it up properly. Then, seeing it was sturdy, Brittany plopped the cardboard box on top and started pulling out handfuls of large red pin-on button badges featuring the governor's face and the phrase *Crix It to Fix It.*

Jayla groaned. "Why are we putting these things out?"

"Haven't you heard about the Heartbeat Bill?" asked Brittany in a surprised tone. "It's the bill that's going to finally put a stop to abortions! Governor Crix said he would do that even before the Supreme Court leak, so you know he means business. He would have already done it if it were not for those liberals."

"Yeah, I've heard of it," Jayla answered ominously, "but I don't think it's going to help."

"It sure can't hurt! Just think of the snowball it will cause. Even if, worst-case scenario, *Roe* stays in effect, if we pass a six-week abortion ban bill, and Texas does too, certainly Florida will follow and then the other states are bound to follow our lead. Then, one state at a time, as more and more conservatives are elected, abortions in America start to go the way of the dodo bird. I mean, can you imagine it—abortions outlawed within our lifetime?" Brittany said, caught up in the splendor of possibilities as she emptied another handful of buttons on the table.

"That's naive. Abortions won't stop," Jayla corrected, partially because of her recent conversation with Lynn and partially because she was still in the mood for an argument. "People will always find a way to have them. Take away abortions in one state, and people will just go to another to have them. I'm betting California's governor would provide the planes and buses to bring them there."

"Okay, so the plan isn't perfect, but at least it's a start," conceded Brittany. "With how fast these abortion pills are being sold over the internet, we need something on our side, and we need it fast. The pills, Jayla, that's the future. And the U.S. Post Office is the big delivery agent. That burns my candle. My tax dollars have propped them up for years."

"I'm not sure I follow."

"The abortion pill is rapidly becoming the leader in the number of abortions. In a lot of places in America, you need to have a parent or guardian's approval before getting an abortion at a place like Unplanned, Inc., right? But online, who's checking that? You'll have twelve-year-olds ordering abortion pills with zero accountability, or big sisters buying it for their little sisters or Lord knows what else. We're just around the corner from seeing abortion pills in colorful retail packaging sold in all the major drug store chains. We will be seeing TV commercials for it. I'm telling you."

"I imagine you are right."

"That's why we need to get legislation to start mounting in our favor, because do you know what? Society tells these kids, *Take the pill, and you'll be okay. Just flush whatever comes out of you (and don't look at it).* But they don't know what comes next. Because, heaven forbid, they see in their toilet more than just a blob of tissue. But every now and again, the *waste*—that's what they call it—the waste won't flush. And now what are you gonna do? That's the thing about these abortion pills. You don't know how large the baby is because you don't know how old they are because you never had to see anyone to do any kind of examination.

Or, worse yet, we've been told about doctors at abortion clinics who will tell a girl she's only so far along when she's really farther along, so it goes easier on her conscience. Then later they take the abortion pill, but now they're staring in the toilet at a dead baby that won't flush."

"Oh, pray tell me that doesn't really happen," Jayla said, feeling nauseous, muzzling her imagination.

"Yes, why just this past week, I got a phone call from a girl in that very situation! She was struggling with PTSD from it. We got her set up with a counselor we work with. Someone real good, who I really think is going to help her start her recovery. And we're starting to plan a memorial service for her baby," replied Brittany as she continued placing badges on the tabletop.

"You do that for people?" Jayla asked, stunned. "The memorial service, I mean?"

"There isn't anything we won't do for a mom who asks," Brittany asserted. "Help me with the signs, sugar?"

As the two women went from task to task, Jayla's desire to belittle or tease Brittany began to wane. The sun was inching higher and higher into the sky, incinerating the air around Jayla, causing her to feel over-heated as sweat bathed her neckline. Finding a seat on a nearby bench, Jayla rubbed her aching lower back as Brittany left to grab some cold waters from a nearby cooler.

"Starting to come together now, huh?" Brittany asked, taking a swig of her drink. "Lordy, lordy. It sure is hot today," she exclaimed as she patted the side of her headscarf to relieve an itch, the sweat from her scalp badly blotching through the fabric. "It's a good day to be in a pool."

"Or in some air conditioning," Jayla agreed. "Hot day to be wearing one of those," she remarked.

"What? This?" Brittany inquired, pointing at her head covering. "You know I got to represent, especially today of all days."

"Represent? Who do you think you're representing with that?"

"*Us,*" Brittany replied. "*Our people.* Africa, baby."

"*Africa,*" Jayla snickered, "I was born twenty minutes from here. Never been to Africa in my life."

"You haven't been noticing me wearing this around the office the last few months?"

"Oh, I've noticed."

"And didn't you ever wonder why I started wearing them?" Brittany asked, pausing for Jayla to answer. Then, in the lack of Jayla's response, she continued, "My oldest daughter, Nia, had to do this project for her school. Some kind of contest to see how far back you could trace your family tree. So she's all in. She's figuring out our family tree and, sugar, she is going deep—I mean deep into this thing. *Great Uncle Al came from Chattanooga. Nanny was born in Kingsport. Oh, what do you know, we're related to so-and-so!* Our living room started looking like one of those conspiracy theory maps. You know with the red yarn, and the pictures taped to the wall? I felt like I was living in a true crime series. And at first, I was just mildly interested in what she was finding, but the deeper she got, the more I was too. And she's wholehearted into this thing and really wants to win and comes and asks her daddy and me if we could do some kind of online ancestry thing where they take our DNA and blah, blah, blah, before we know it, we find out everything about our family past all at once—even going back to Nigeria and Scotland, of all places," Brittany chuckled.

"Scotland?" asked Jayla, slightly intrigued.

"That's right," Brittany nodded. "From the minute I saw it on the report, I knew what had happened," Brittany said, looking down at her shoes as Jayla's interest rose. "My ancestors were taken from Nigeria against their will and forced to come to this country as slaves. The only one that makes any sense, is that somewhere along the way a great-great-grandma of mine was sexually assaulted by a plantation owner or by somebody in his family. And because of that unwanted—*rape*—that's how me and my family are here today. And it just got me thinking about my past and our future, and how I'm so, so glad I'm here doing what I'm doing with the pregnancy center."

"Wait," interrupted Jayla, who followed until that last statement. "I—why—how do those two connect?"

"Because of the work we're doing to save lives!" Brittany exclaimed. "It makes me proud."

"No, no, that doesn't make sense. If *anything*, you should have switched teams and become more pro-choice. I mean, if your grandma was *raped* by somebody," Jayla started, feeling the weight of the term *rape* as it came out of her lips, "why wouldn't you have wanted her to have the choice to have an abortion? Wouldn't you have wanted her to have rights?"

"But then I wouldn't be here. My family wouldn't be here . . .. Besides that, the one doesn't undo the other," Brittany contended. "Having an abortion wouldn't have undone the rape. Having an abortion wouldn't have hurt that plantation owner in the least. The only ones it would have hurt were my great- great-grandma—who hadn't done anything wrong—and the baby inside of her—who didn't do anything wrong either. Killing someone innocent doesn't hurt another person who's guilty. It's like as Christians, we are to love the sinner and hate the sin."

Jayla began to feel irritated—perhaps it was too close to her own circumstances. "Oh, so it's a *sin* now?" Jayla interjected, starting to steam. "Having rights is a *sin*?"

"I'm for life. I'm *pro-life*, for *all* life," Brittany continued. "But if we can't defend the weakest people in society, what hope do the rest of us got? At some point any of us—a people group, a nationality, a religion, whatever—could be considered uncomfortable for society, or unconscionable to the mainstream, or deplorable to the powerful. Then what happens? Do we abort a people group? My people have been aborted for years, and I am putting my protest on display!"

Jayla staggered slightly at her compelling argument, not expecting this kind of intellectual thought to come from Brittany.

"I want justice, don't you? I want social action. I want systematic abuse to end, just like you, right? Even though my family came here as slaves, I want to believe we can live today as equals with everyone on the same level. But how can we expect rape to stop, or oppression to stop, or for people like us in America to have any hope of social justice if we can't give it to the least defensible, weakest members of our society—the unborn baby? Who is weaker? Who is smaller? Who matters least and is most easily thrown away? If we can't get justice for them, at the bottom, we can't get it for the rest of us. Remember what Dr. King said, 'Injustice anywhere is a threat to justice everywhere.' Did you know his daughter goes around the country speaking against abortion?"

"No, I didn't."

"So if we can't value them little babies, who can we value? If we can't protect them, who can we protect? They're the starting point. Back then, people used to say black people only counted as three-fifths of a person. A less than not-quite-human. And that's exactly what people are trying to say now about those babies in the womb! How can somebody who says they are *for* social equality among different races, at the same time be *against* the social equality of the unborn with the born? How can I fight the oppression of one while endorsing the oppression of the other? A house divided against itself is gonna fall, Jayla. You of all people should get this."

"Me, of *all people*?!" Jayla rebutted emphatically, the association of her skin color a distant second to the reflexive thoughts springing up over her own rape and pregnancy. She could feel herself growing impatient and irritated the longer Brittany ran her monologue. The decision to play nice and the reasons behind it were evaporating now in the sun's grip. Jayla was beginning to feel agitated. "You know what I think?" she said, "I think that head wrap is too tight. I think it's cutting off the circulation to your brain."

"What am I saying that's so crazy? I want social reform with every ounce of my body. Let it to start here, let it start in me. But before I can say black lives matter, I first have to say little black lives matter. And as a Christian, I have to say all lives matter. Either all life is equal or not. So I put on my uniform, wear my headscarf, and endure the weird looks because I remember who I'm fighting for and what I'm trying to achieve."

Before Jayla could counter with a snarky comment, Renee appeared. "Hey, ladies! Things are looking great!" Renee exclaimed. "And look what Marta brought," she said as she proudly unfurled the teal T-shirts in her hand, holding them up by the shoulders. *PC Community Day!* the shirts read in large white lettering. "Amazing, right?"

"Wow! So great!" Jayla feigned praise.

"I had better get back to things," muttered Brittany.

"Aww, don't worry, Brit. Things are coming together! You're doing so great, and the event is really shaping up," encouraged Renee as Brittany stood from the bench, slinging the teal shirt over her shoulder. "Oh! And—get this—on top of everything, some of our biggest financial supporters have already shown up. I overheard some of them say they've invited some other potential sponsors to come too! The event is already a success—and it hasn't even started!"

"I'm not sure if you're still helping Brittany with setting up, but there's someone I'd really . . ." Renee began as the ringing of the phone in her hand interrupted her train of thought. "I'd really like . . ." she repeated, peaking at the screen. "I'm so sorry. I have to take this."

"Take your time," Jayla replied as she shut her eyes and stretched out on the searing bench, covering her face with the spare shirt Renee gave her to shade from the burning sun.

"Hey, did you see the two protests?" Jayla involuntarily overheard one woman say to another in a conversation that evidentially had been going on in the background since Brittany began her monologue. "Two protests, both on main roads getting here."

"Uh, no. I took some side roads getting in," replied the second.

Peeling the shirt off her face, Jayla squinted to see who dared interrupt her rest. To her left, she saw two women around her age, one with short brown hair in a thick strap tank with a camera hung on her neck, the other with rolled-up sleeves and a pull-through Mohawk braid snapping pictures on her phone.

"I love a good protest!" the camerawoman exclaimed. "Who knows, it could be fun! Agua Fria Street is only a five-dollar Uber from here, and it's gonna be slammed with people. Just imagine the great shots we could get. Plus, they're all right next to the Brewery."

At this, Jayla's attention perked up. "What was that about Agua Fria Street?" she asked loudly, knowing it was her fastest route home.

"There's two going on," the camerawoman explained. "It's actually kinda funny. First, when news of your Community Day event got out, a bunch of pro-abortion sheeple at the Community College heard about it and decided to protest, you know, with the whole Supreme Court thing up in the air students are hot."

"Sheeple?" Jayla asked.

"Sheep people. Lemmings. Unquestioning followers. They don't think for themselves," the woman with the Mohawk braid clarified. "Do you mind if I take your picture? For the pregnancy center social media page? I think it would be nice to showcase that some other college people are here."

"No, I don't want my picture taken," Jayla declined adamantly.

"I can crop out your head or blur your face if you'd like!" the braid woman insisted. "See—" she said, walking closer to Jayla and showing her a photo taken earlier.

"Oh good!" Renee applauded as she reentered the conversation, the sound of crisp, dry grass crunching under her footsteps. "I'm so glad you both have been able to connect face to face." Jayla and the woman with the phone exchanged confused glances as Renee debriefed: "Adalyn, this is Jayla, the one I've been telling you about. Our PC student at Community College. And Jayla, this is Adalyn, Darla's niece."

"Oh!" Adalyn blurted, "You're Jayla! I've heard so much about you."

"Same!" Jayla agreed, inwardly scanning her mental database for any information on Darla's niece. "You go to school around here too, right?"

"Yes," Adalyn shared, "don't we have the same major? I think that's what my aunt told me?"

"Yeah, I'm doing the Nursing Program," replied Jayla as the ladies began making an informal circle around her.

"Which one? The Nursing Assistant Certificate, or the Nursing, A.A.S., or the Practical Nursing Certificate?" Adalyn asked.

"The first one," clarified Jayla as sweat began trickling down her neck.

"I thought you were getting the Practical Nursing Certificate?" Renee probed. "Wasn't that what you told me?"

"Yeah, that's the one I meant. Wasn't that the first one?" Jayla feigned a laugh. "I'm doing the Practical Nursing Certificate, I already have my CNA license."

"Crazy! That's the same one as me. I don't remember seeing you around, though. Are you in the group chat?" Adalyn inquired as she scoured the messages on her phone.

"I was, but I left," Jayla fibbed. "I kept getting distracted during my shifts at the pregnancy center, and I really wanted to give my best to the ladies there, you know?"

"Ice waters, anyone?" a fifth voice chimed. It was Darla carrying two bottles in each hand. Her hair was pulled up in a ponytail, and she was wearing a red shirt with large white lettering that read *Abortion = Abhor + Sin.*

"Darla, you are just too thoughtful!" Renee complimented, taking a couple bottles, and offering them to the other ladies before she opened one for herself. "I hope you kept the receipt for those. I definitely want you to get paid back!" Then a stunned look swept over her face as if something had finally clicked into place. "Receipts! That's what I wanted to talk to you about!" Renee said to Jayla, relieved to have finally introduced the topic.

"Yeah, I left them on your desk, remember?" Jayla replied, hoping the conversation would end there.

"You did, but the receipts are handwritten. Were you not able to get a printed version?"

"No, the guy at the bookstore said the printer was down," Jayla answered, taking a swallow of water.

"What bookstore did you go to?" Adalyn inquired, to Jayla's instant irritation.

"The one on campus," Jayla replied.

"That's weird. They always just email me the receipts," Adalyn said, then, after scrolling in her phone for a moment, presented a digital receipt to the audience. "See?"

"Adalyn is such a good student," Darla piped up. "It's amazing to me how she's able to do so well in school with all the new volunteer work she's taken on with doing the PC social media, especially when she's not getting paid for it."

"So, they didn't send you one of these?" Adalyn asked again.

Jayla wiped her forehead as a sweaty residue from her foundation smeared in her hand. "No, maybe the person behind the counter didn't know about it. I think they were new. I don't know. It was my first time going there."

"Okay, well next time you purchase books, we need you to get a digital or printed copy," Renee replied.

"You're so lucky to have that scholarship, Jayla," Darla congratulated in an accusatory tone. "How are your grades this semester? Are they all A's like Adalyn?"

"Aunt Darla!" Adalyn drawled, embarrassed.

"What? I can't be proud of my niece!" Darla replied with a defensive laugh.

Jayla could see Renee weighing the comment in her mind before opening her mouth. "That's a great point, Darla. Jayla, I'll need your grades as soon as possible so we can get the ball rolling on renewing the scholarship for next semester. Good grades are like engagement rings; they're made for showing off!"

"Darla, honey, can we talk in private?" Renee said, pulling Darla off to the side to remind her of the need to keep everyone's shirts from being offensive, and telling her where she could get her own Community Day shirt, pronto.

CHAPTER 34

SPICY POTATO CHIPS

Dirt clods and dried grass crunched under Jayla's feet as she made her way from the grungy, suffocating public bathroom to the parking lot. With her car in sight, Jayla's mind fantasized about how amazing it would soon feel to have air conditioning blasting on her skin. She was considering how best to utilize her time in relaxation now that her volunteer time was complete when she saw Samantha stepping out of the passenger side of a white Toyota Highlander.

"All I'm saying, Rick, is that if I ask for a Christian radio station, you put on a Christian radio station," Samantha said to the driver as she fixed her purse. "Is that so much to ask?"

"Terica didn't mind, did you darlin'?" Ricky asked the back seat as he opened his car door.

"Besides, everybody knows that country music *is* Christian music. Lots of songs say Jesus and God in 'em."

"You're unbelievable," Samantha replied. Ricky pulled a pack of cigarettes out of his pocket, the golden softball pendant hanging from his necklace catching the sunlight as he swiveled.

"Don't you even *think* about smoking here," Samantha warned.

Rick raised his hands in the air like he had been busted by a sheriff's deputy as the car rocked back and forth with Terica's weight shifting out of her seat. "I wouldn't even think of it," he said, stuffing the pack into his back pocket.

Just the sight of Ricky made Jayla nauseous as her mind retrieved the images of the last time she saw him, with a woman who wasn't his wife, right after her abortion procedure.

Landing on her feet with her legs bowed out, Terica moaned. "How are we feeling, momma?" asked Samantha, stabilizing her friend.

"Like I'm going to be pregnant forever," Terica replied. "Like I want to cry and punch someone in the face and . . . Is that Jayla?"

Jayla strained a smile as all eyes turned to her. "Hey, guys."

"Hey, girl!" Samantha replied. "How's the event going so far? Looks like a great turnout!"

"How many chairs they got?" Terica interjected before Jayla could speak.

"It's *going*—" Jayla answered, "lots of people showed up, so that's good, and there are some benches but they're pretty uncomfortable, unless you're desperate."

"That's just like a man," Terica shook her head as she waddled up to Jayla, Samantha by her side. "Plan an event and not think ahead."

"So you're the great and powerful Jayla Sam's always talking about?" Ricky quizzed.

"Oh, I'm sorry! I forgot you two don't know each other," Samantha apologized. "Jayla, this is my husband Rick, and Rick, this is Jayla."

We know each other alright, Jayla thought to herself as Samantha acquainted the pair.

Ricky stuck out his hand for a handshake. "Mighty good to meet you, Jayla."

Preferring to get stung by a horde of hornets over making contact with Rick's reptilian skin, Jayla stuck her hands in her pockets and grimaced. "Sorry, they're dirty from all the setup," she explained.

"So where are these benches at?" asked Terica, her hands massaging her lower back.

"Over there," Jayla pointed, looking everywhere but at Rick. "Remind me, girl, when are you due?"

"Not soon enough," Terica groaned. "I keep going to the hospital thinkin' I'm havin' the baby, but it's all these stupid Braxton Hacks contractions."

"It's Braxton *Hicks*," Samantha gently corrected.

"That baby's not gonna come out until you have a name for it," Ricky jested as Samantha playfully gave him a push.

"Terica will find a name for the baby when the time is right," Samantha defended. "She's just waiting for inspiration to strike."

"I'll know the baby's name when I see her," Terica stated and then paused as if she had just noticed something. "What kind of food they got over there?"

"Burgers and hotdogs, I think, and some desserts," Jayla replied.

"Lead the way, girl!" Terica exclaimed.

"Could you grab me some banana pudding, if they have any?" Rick asked his wife as he scratched his stomach.

"You're not coming?" Samantha asked, surprised.

"I figure I'd give you two some girl time while I unpack the car," Rick rasped as Samantha arched an eyebrow. "What? I told you I wasn't gonna smoke. The cigarettes are staying in my pocket."

"Jayla, you keep an eye on this one," Samantha said sternly, then winked. "Come on, momma. We got us some desserts to try."

As soon as the women were out of range, Jayla started again for her car but stopped a few steps later as Rick pulled out the pack of cigarettes from his back pocket and drew one to his mouth.

"Sam said not to do that," Jayla stated with disgust.

"What my wife meant was not to smoke around any pregnant women," Ricky said, looking from side to side. "I don't see any pregnant women here. Do you?"

"Whatever," Jayla replied. Then, taking a few more steps, couldn't help herself from adding, "You should learn to respect Sam enough to listen to her."

"I listen good; it's the doin' part I struggle with," Rick said with Southern charm as he blew a gray puff into the air.

Jayla shook her head in revulsion, continuing to walk to her car when she was halted by the distinct sound of a FaceTime call. Surprised, Jayla looked down and saw it was from Lynn. Not thinking of her surroundings, she touched accept on the phone.

Without even a hello, Lynn started rambling. "I figured I had to see your face for myself to know you are alive—you haven't been to work in several days. What is going on? Is everything alright with your pregnancy?"

"Yes, um—everything is fine—just been feeling a little under the weather," Jayla replied, feeling worried Lynn would notice her location at the park.

"Well, oh okay—hope you're ready to get back to work soon. We are really hurtin'. Pregnant or not, I need you to step up and take on more responsibilities and—say—looks like you must be feeling 'up and about,' outside enjoying the sunny day."

Jayla thought of anything to get off this very loud and public phone call. "Oh yes, absolutely. Just getting fresh air—so yeah, I'll see you soon. Gotta go, my battery is dying." With that, Jayla disconnected the call and turned to find Ricky, exaggerated in his efforts not to look her direction.

"How much of that did you hear?" inquired Jayla, wondering how big a mess she needed to clean up.

"I may have heard a little bit of this, a little bit of that," Rick blabbered, sneaking a peek at Jayla's stomach.

So he knows everything, Jayla confirmed as she tried to gauge what level of collateral damage would come from this explosive news going into such unreliable hands as Ricky's.

"What did Sam say when you told her?" Rick asked. Then, when Jayla hesitated a fraction of a second too long, he searched her face and *tsked* before taking another drag off his cigarette. "Shoowee. She doesn't know, huh?"

"She knows," Jayla stated matter-of-factly. "She was the first person I told."

"Oh really?" The corner of Ricky's dark mustache lifted in a grin. "And how did that go over?"

"You know, Sam loves babies. She's thrilled," Jayla answered in punctuated sentences. Seeing she wasn't quite convincing, she decided to throw him a curveball. "She actually said she wanted to help me get the baby adopted, maybe even adopt the baby herself."

Rick choked on the smoke in his lungs and stared with watery eyes at Jayla. "She wants to adopt *your baby*?" he restated. "Bull crap."

"What's so hard to believe about that? She has always wanted a baby."

"There's no way she'd even think about doing that without talking to me first, and she hasn't talked to me," rationalized Ricky. "She knows better than that."

"She knows you'd say no! She said she wanted to wait for the right moment to talk to you about it. And, from the sound of it, I guess she hasn't."

Rick squinted as he used the butt of his cigarette like an ashy, crumbling extension of his index finger. "Samantha—my Samantha—wants to adopt your baby, and she wants to do it so badly that not once has she mentioned it or hinted at it at all. Zip. Nothing. Anything about that sound suspicious to you?"

"Do you always tell everything to your wife?" Jayla retorted.

"Something this big? You bet I would," Rick replied, clueless as to what cards Jayla was holding to her chest.

"I happen to know that you *don't* tell everything to Samantha; and if you don't want her to know what I know, then you'll let her adopt my baby like she wants to," Jayla stated as the words clumsily came out of her mouth.

"Come again?" Rick inquired, baffled.

"I know about little miss *Goldie Locks*," Jayla advised, double-checking that the parking lot still had people coming and going nearby.

"I don't know what you're talking about," Rick said as he flicked his finished cigarette into the dirt.

"Yeah, you do. I know all about her and the affair you're having with her," Jayla disclosed before deciding to up the ante. "*And* I know about what you made softball girl get downtown."

The look on Rick's face morphed from perplexed to a stunned intensity before a relaxed calm prompted the crowsfeet around his eyes to roost into relaxation. "Oh, that?" he said, acting unfazed as he dug a pouch of dip out of his pocket and smacked it with his finger. "I already told Sam. We've already worked through it."

"No, you didn't," Jayla replied, replaying the interaction she witnessed earlier that morning. "When?"

"Few weeks ago," Rick answered, sticking the wad of dip into his bottom lip. "She was hurt, obviously, but, you know, she's a forgiving person and, yeah. I promised I wouldn't do it again. So we're good now."

"So you won't mind if I ask her about it?" Jayla challenged as she pointed behind Rick to a slowly approaching Samantha and Terica, moving at a turtle's pace.

Rick, whose lips were already puckered to spit, accidentally let out a mouthful of dip onto his shirt as he turned to look. Wiping the goo from his shirt as he muttered a few curse words, he tried to regain his formerly projected composure. "I—I don't think that's a good idea. Especially not with Terica around. Don't want to rip off old bandages, gotta let sleeping dogs lie, that sort of thing."

"Rick, you are lying."

Ricky's immediate look of belligerence broke against Jayla's iron stare until a solemn, dour expression settled in its place. "If you know about all that stuff that's happened, and you know Sam, then you know news of something like that would kill her. One hundred percent kill her," he urged with a frankness that lacked remorse. "If you're a real friend, you won't tell her—you can't tell her. It would ruin her. And, on top of all that, it would ruin what she does helping these ladies at the center. I mean, that's her whole life! Do you really think Renee or anybody else would want her working there after finding out something like that? She would lose *everything*," Ricky stated as he snapped his fingers. "Just like *that*. And it would be all your fault."

"*My* fault!" Jayla repeated with shock.

"Your fault because *you* would be the one who pulled down this whole thing on her head. And she would never forgive you. And she'd never want your baby if you did that," Rick declared, looking over his shoulder to check on how close Terica and Samantha were.

"You know what I think?" replied Jayla. "I think you're scared. And you should be. Because Samantha is a lot stronger than you think. And she'd be better off without you, and I think you know that," she said, then, searching his eyes, continued. "*But*—let her adopt my baby and don't be a jerk about it, and my mouth is closed, and you can figure out your own way to break things off with Goldie Locks; but this adoption is happening with or without you."

Rick fell silent as the crunching sound of Terica and Samantha's footsteps became audible. Jayla could see the women were just a few yards away now, both balancing multiple paper plates and water bottles in their hands.

"I swear I got acid reflux just by looking at those bags of chips," Jayla overheard Terica say.

"Then why'd you get some?" Samantha asked, pausing every few steps to keep in step with her friend.

"Because they're spicy! Spicy food helps you have a baby," Terica replied with a crunch. "Everybody knows that, Sammy."

"Oh, babe!" Samantha lamented to Rick as the pair reentered Jayla and Rick's conversational sphere. "Look at you! I told you not to use that stuff.

"You told me not to smoke," Rick deflected. "And this ain't smoke, is it?"

Samantha rolled her eyes. "Smoke would be easier to clean up," she said, extending her trove of plates to Jayla. "Can you hold these for a sec? I got extra cookies in case you wanted any."

Turning back to Rick she said, "Now, hold still," pulling a napkin from the fold of her arm and wiping at the tar stain.

"Well, how do you like that," Rick complained for sympathy as Samantha wet her napkin with water and began a fresh scrubbing. "First, I get in trouble for not smoking, and then she says it would have been better if I did. I can't win!"

"You'll win when you stop dipping and smoking," Samantha reasoned as the wet spot on Rick's shirt had grown twice as large. Then, reaching back to take the plates from Jayla, Samantha continued, "It looks like you two found something to talk about. Hopefully he wasn't boring you with all that softball talk."

"I'll have you know, Jayla loves talking softball, as does everyone I talk softball with," Rick argued.

"Oh really, Jayla," Samantha said. "You've never mentioned softball to me! Do you play? Or were you just being nice to Ricky?"

"I've seen a few games," Jayla answered, then, thinking it over for a moment, continued. "There was this one game I saw a while ago where a man got in trouble for his bat."

"His bat?" probed Samantha as she glanced over to her husband, an encyclopedia on the subject. "How so? Was it corked or something?"

"Yeah. A corked bat," Jayla answered. "His bat got him in real trouble." she said, looking at Rick to see if he would pick up on her coded terms.

"Well, that sounds like cheating?" Samantha asked.

"I hate cheaters," Jayla said, turning her gaze to Rick, who stared back at her unamused. "That's exactly what it was. And the player just kept swinging his corked bat, thinking he'd never get caught, until one day he did. I could be wrong, but I think he was even kicked off his team for that."

"Don't get Rick started on cheaters," Samantha told Jayla as she patted her husband with her free hand. "He's like a bloodhound out there on the field. And if anything seems to be even the teeniest bit suspicious, he's the first one to say something. Aren't you, babe?"

Jayla smugly took a bite of cookie and glared at Rick, whose mustache wasn't large enough to conceal the terror of the tightrope Jayla put him on. "Cheaters, yeah," he agreed, nodding to his wife with an unsure smile. "But I think we need to remember that, at the end of the day, these players are just regular guys trying to do what they think is right, and they get it wrong like we all do from time to time. But you gotta give some of these guys second chances."

"Second chances? Rick, are you feeling okay?" Samantha said, snorting in disbelief.

"Yeah, well, it's just, you know, it's not just the cheaters who get penalized. The whole team does," Rick explained, returning Jayla's stare. "Lots of innocent players who ain't never done nothing wrong get hurt from it. So, yeah, maybe I'm just getting soft in my old age. But being kicked off the team. I don't know, seems a bit harsh."

"Aww," Samantha cooed, leaning her head against her husband's chest. "I sure married a good one."

Jayla tried to mask a look of disgust while a pained, glum smile crawled through Ricky's lips. "I mean, isn't that what the whole church thing is about?" he proceeded, "forgiving others like—"

"Jesus, help me!" Terica exclaimed, surprising the group, nearly causing Jayla to choke on her last bite of cookie. Terica pressed one of her hands into her lower back and the other on her stomach, a look of anguish spread across her face. "I think," she winced, "I think it's happening!"

"What? The baby! Now?" Samantha shrieked.

Terica nodded; her eyes squinted. "These ain't no Braxton Hacks!"

"Okay, okay," Samantha processed. Then, looking at Ricky, extended her hands, "Keys!"

"Is she gonna have her baby in our car?" Rick blurted, hesitating. "I mean, is her water gonna break in there? Who's gonna clean that up?"

"Rick! Keys!" Samantha insisted a second time, emphatically wiggling her hands.

"We can take my car," Jayla offered, spotting this as her chance to get alone with Samantha. "I'm just right over there."

Jayla began walking toward her vehicle with Terica slowly following behind. "Lord, I knew I shouldn't have ate those spicy chips!"

Then, as if abruptly realizing Jayla being unsupervised with Samantha could pose a larger problem, Rick hollered after them and jangled his keys. "No, it's okay! I'll drive you!" But by then, Jayla was already unlocking the passenger side door for Terica.

"I'll text you," Samantha called out to her husband as she climbed into the backseat. Then, with three car doors slamming, Jayla's Honda Accord sped out of the dirt parking lot, consuming Rick in a cloud of dust.

CHAPTER 35

THE BOYFRIEND

Threading through backstreets and side roads to avoid any potential blockage by protestors, Jayla raced to Watson Women's Hospital with Samantha repeating soft encouragements from the back seat along the way. To her relief, the ride was nothing like what she came to expect from movies. There was no dramatic breaking of water in the car, or breach baby, or comedic sequence of errors. There was just Terica pleading, blaming, and crying into her phone to her boyfriend.

"You better be here before the baby comes!" Terica proclaimed into her phone before abruptly hanging up, as the large tan maternity building came into view.

"You're doing a great job, Momma. See, we're almost there," Sam comforted as the vehicle pulled underneath the large columned overhang to the hospital.

"I'll find you inside," Jayla advised as Samantha helped Terica out of the passenger seat. "You can do this!" she encouraged, joining Samantha in her cheering, wondering if a push from behind would help or topple the pregnant lady.

As Samantha and Terica toddled inside Watkins, Jayla found a place to park and negotiated the various bends and elevators to the birthing area. Heading straight to the reception desk, she asked the attendant, "My friend was just brought in here. First name is Terica," Jayla said, realizing she didn't know the last name. "Very pregnant. With a blonde lady."

"Oh, the one with Sam? That lovely lady was just taken back," he advised. "Sam is in the waiting room if you'd like to join her."

"You know Sam?" asked Jayla, pleasantly surprised.

"Do I know Sam?" he laughed. "Girl, she's in here more than I am. More than most of us, really."

Jayla smiled and thanked the man before walking over to Samantha, who was sitting along the back row of the mostly empty waiting area.

"Hey," Jayla whispered, taking a seat next to Sam, who had been checking messages on her phone.

"Oh, hey! You just missed Terica. They came and took her back to the birthing suite not five minutes ago.," Samantha said. "I figure her boyfriend will arrive very—"

A loud thud from the entrance of the ward interrupted Samantha, captivating the attention of both women. Looking toward the automatic doors Jayla saw a thin white man, holding a broken bouquet of roses and rushing to the reception desk, his shoes sliding and squeaking on the tile floor.

Suddenly in Jayla's mind it clicked who he was. "That's the boyfriend?" she speculated as the man rushed to the double doors of the birthing unit, pulling hard at the door handles in frustration, before spotting and pressing a green button to the side that electronically released the lock and slowly sprung the doors open.

"That's the boyfriend," Samantha confirmed as the man vanished from sight, softly calling Terica's name down the hallway. "He really is a big sweetheart once you get to know him," she considerately insisted. "Believe it or not, when she first told him she was pregnant, he told her he wanted her to get an abortion. Even put the money in her handbag to do it—but now, I think he's more excited for the baby than she is. The way he's stuck around, how he's been a big support to Terica these last few months even tagging along once or twice to Mommy University—he's really proven himself. He's gonna make for a great daddy. I know it."

How Samantha could remember so many people and the small, intimate details of their lives was beyond Jayla. If she was honest with herself, it wasn't for a lack of brain power that she didn't remember, but for a lack of desire. She just didn't care enough to devote her mind on people who were such an insignificant, though recurring part of her life. They weren't family members. They weren't friends. Knowing them, remembering their stories, wouldn't help improve her life condition. And yet, here was Samantha, a storehouse of information about the boyfriend of a client from a job she could just as easily stick in a manila folder and leave behind at work. But her level of care dictated that she remember. The tidbits she shared came from the overflow of a heart dedicated to loving and Jayla bet that, for every one detail shared, there was an iceberg of emotions and memories and details hidden away in her heart. It wasn't that Samantha had a bigger memory than Jayla, it was that she somehow had a bigger heart.

"How do you do it, Sam?" Jayla marveled.

"Do what?"

"You know—care about so many people. Terica, Renee, Rick, the patients at the center, the volunteers, Brittany, Darla—me—how do you do it? Why do you do it?"

Samantha cocked her head and shrugged her shoulders and inhaled deeply. "I just think that's what being a Jesus-follower is all about. In the Bible there's this part of where Jesus says He came so we could have life, and so our life would be more abundant. More abundant meaning to the full, to the top, overflowing. And if that's what Jesus has come to do, and I'm trying to be like Him, then that's what I'm trying to do. Help people have a more abundant life—and that means caring for people. I feel like people try to overcomplicate it, but really following Jesus is loving whoever is in front of you, no matter who it is. I think that's something a lot of pro-life people get so wrong, because when you say you're pro-life what you're really meaning is you're for the life of the baby. And, sure, that's the start. But what if we were *pro* the life of the baby *and pro* the life of the mom? And what if we were for the life of the baby past their birth and through their entire life? That's why I don't want to be called *pro-life*. I want to be pro-*abundant* life. The baby's life, the mother's life, the family's life, from the first ultrasound to the autopsy."

Not knowing what to say, Jayla resumed her rock-like exterior and started clapping her hands slowly with an impressed look on her face, prompting a few of the other visitors in the waiting room to peek over their magazines or phone screens. "Well okay then. Get it, Samantha!"

Samantha blushed at the attention. "Basically, I just act loving toward a person. There's a reason for everyone to be loved, even if it's just the fact they were made in the image of the God I love."

Jayla thought for a moment, teetering on the edge of the next question queued on her lips. "Have you found something to love about me?" she finally worked up enough courage to ask, hating herself the moment the words came out of her mouth. "I'm sorry. You don't have to answer that."

Samantha looked at Jayla with such compassion and fervency. "Of course I have! You are strong, resilient. You are protective and will speak your mind, even if there are consequences. You're smart and, when you apply yourself, are really good at what you do, and you pick up on new things quickly. And you're loyal. And I think you're a real blessing too all of us at the resource center. Especially me."

"No one has ever called me a blessing before." Jayla laughed ruefully to herself, puncturing the prolonged silence. In her mind she added Samantha's assessment of her with the formula she gave on cultivating care. If Samantha was ever going to agree to adopt Jayla's baby—if she was ever going to apply her whole heart to this pregnancy—Jayla had to open to her in a way that was petrifying to consider. And Jayla knew, in this case, the benefit of divulging long-kept secrets of herself far outweighed the risk. If ever there were a person who displayed worthiness of seeing her scars, someone who was already looking for and seeing the best in her, it was Samantha. If the seed of this adoption had any hope of growing, it had to be planted in the naked, honest soil of this moment.

"Amarika never called me that—that's for sure." Jayla said quietly, lining up the first domino she knew would lead to her whole external armor being toppled. Mentally she braced to expose herself, not entirely sure the way things would play out.

"Who's Amarika?" asked Samantha.

"My mom. Or, the woman who was supposed to be my mom," Jayla shared introspectively. "I was on my own even when I was in the same house as her—she was always working. Never at home. And whenever she worked, it always seemed to be on the opposite schedule as whatever boyfriend was living with us at the time. Maybe she didn't want to see them. I don't know. I know she kept these boyfriends around to help with the rent, help with me. The last one I really remember her having was this bald man named Byron. He was always taking showers and would leave the door open when it was just me and him at home. I was only ten years old. He told me to keep secret what he did to me—especially from Amarika. I would stay out playing with friends or just wander around—anything to avoid being alone with that man. I had this best friend back then named Daisey. She was the closest thing to a sister I ever had and I remember asking her if her stepdad ever touched her like that. I thought she was lying when she said no. Do you believe that? To me it was a normal part of life as regular as going to school or getting groceries.

"One night I came home thinking Amarika was supposed to be back, but she wasn't there. It was just Byron, sitting in a chair, smiling at me. He told me Amarika called saying she was taking an extra shift and wouldn't be back for three more hours. The next three hours—he wouldn't let me leave the house. Three hours of hell . . ." Jayla's voice trailed off.

"From then on he couldn't stand the sight of me. He told me it was all my fault for what happened. It was like he was disgusted with himself but he was taking it out on me. I couldn't believe it but, somehow, life became twice as bad as it was before. And then this cycle started, this sick, *sick* cycle."

"How long did that go on for?" Samantha asked delicately.

"Close to two years. Life became so unbearable that finally I told Amarika about what had been happening, thinking things couldn't get worse. It was a mess. A huge blow-up. I told her either Byron would leave or I would leave, but one of us had to go. I was twelve then and I wasn't going to put up with it anymore. And so Amarika had to decide who would stay and who would leave—this child-raping monster of a man, or her daughter. She chose him."

"Oh, Jayla," Samantha whispered, her voice cracking. "I'm so sorry. Where did you go? Do you mind sharing?"

"Wherever I could, you know? But there was this teacher I had in fourth grade before Byron moved in. Her name was Mrs. Neidringhouse and she and I were really close. And one day, out of the blue, by luck, I ran into her outside a grocery store. She and her husband let me stay with them and they said I could stay there until I was ready to leave.

And one night turned into two, turned into a week, then a year, and for the first time I had a home—a *real* home. Over time I started calling them my auntie and uncle." Jayla stopped and, for the first time in her story, looked Samantha in the eye. "That's who you remind me of," she said, as if a long-considered mystery had just been solved. "You're like Mrs. Neidringhouse."

Samantha smiled softly and wiped away a tear as she reached for Jayla's hand. Jayla, however, didn't reciprocate, knowing there was more to the story to share. "But then," she continued, "years later, I met a man who seemed like a good man, like my uncle, who promised me we could make a home for our own. He was handsome, funny, strong, and, at first, kind. Too kind. And I knew it seemed too good to be true. And slowly I started making excuses for him, I guess, the same way Amarika made excuses for all her boyfriends when the mask came off. *He's just having a bad day. I just shouldn't have said anything. He's just really stressed right now. Once he's gotten enough sleep, or had enough sex, or gotten enough time out of the house, things will go back to the way they were.* His name was Marcus. He's the man you saved me from—the one who broke into my apartment a few weeks ago," Jayla stated then thoughtfully, matter-of-factly, continued, "I say all that to say Marcus was just another Byron. Abusive. Manipulative. And he's the reason I'm . . ." she hesitated knowing that what she shared next would change the dynamic of their relationship forever. "The reason I'm pregnant right now."

Samantha's mouth fell open as she leaned back in her chair. "*You're pregnant?*" she asked in disbelief, chancing a look at Jayla's stomach.

"After we broke up for the last time, he asked to meet me to talk things over but, instead, he . . ." she stopped, realizing this was the first time she publicly shared the abuse Marcus inflicted on her. "He—raped me. And now I have his baby inside me."

"How long ago was that?" Samantha asked, the wheels in her mind turning.

"About five months ago."

"But—" Samantha shook her head. "You were working at the Center then . . ." she stated as disbelief and heartache pained her face, tears welling up in her eyes. "How could I have not known something was wrong? Oh my—there you were, sitting in our meetings, right next to me, passing me in the halls, and I—" Samantha said, blaming herself. "I wasn't there for you *at all*. All your hurt. And here I am going on and on about being *pro-abundant life* when you're here and you're hurting and I haven't been there for you at all. I'm so, so sorry," Samantha's mouth sealed, her throat pulsing as she tried to keep herself composed.

"You can be here for me now," Jayla said, going so far as to take Samantha by the hand.

Samantha looked down at their hands clasped, her empathy heightened. "Of course!" she mouthed, wiping her cheeks. "Whatever you need. For you, for the baby. Count me in. I want to help."

"Okay—here's what I need," Jayla began, looking squarely at her friend. "I need you—to keep this baby for me."

Samantha's eyes flashed with confusion. "*Keep the baby for you?*"

Jayla nodded, squeezing Samantha's hand. "I want you—I *need* you to adopt this baby, otherwise . . ." Jayla stopped herself. "I just, I just can't."

Samantha let go of Jayla's hand. "Jayla—I—I . . . that's a really big—I mean, that's a *huge* ask," she flinched, her eyes pinging back and forth as if she were playing out the scenario in her head.

"Sam, I can't do this. I need you," Jayla reiterated. "You have to do this for me. There's no one else I trust with this. It has to be you."

The whooshing buzz of the automatic doors to the ward opening rippled through the stillness and tenderness of the moment, frazzling Jayla, prompting her eyes to chase the source of the sound. To her dismay it was Renee, dressed in teal and scanning the room for familiar faces.

Jayla quickly turned back to Samantha who was lost in consideration. "Don't say anything about this," she demanded. "Promise. Not to anyone."

Samantha looked at Jayla and then at Renee who by now had spotted the couple and was making her way over to them at the back of the waiting room. "Okay," Samantha agreed, wiping her eyes with her fingers, erasing signs of their conversation.

"Sam, thank you for your message," Renee greeted, "I came as fast as I could. The event just ended. And how is the mother doing? Is the baby already here?"

"Not yet," Samantha advised, "but probably soon. That poor girl was ready to pop."

Suddenly the doors of the birthing unit opened and Terica's boy-friend stepped out with a thick expression of joy slathered on his face. "The baby has been born!" he exclaimed, searching faces in the small crowd for Samantha as he spoke. "It's a girl!"

Sam congratulated him with a big hug as Jayla and Renee joined them in a celebration Then, pulling away, Sam asked, "Do we have a name?"

The man's smile couldn't be contained. "*Samjay*. Terica took one look at her and knew. Samjay Angel Washington. She said it's a combination of Sammy and—"

"Jayla," Sam interrupted, looking at a stunned Jayla and giving her a side hug squeeze.

"She said she could never have done this without you both," the boyfriend explained as a range of emotions cascaded through Jayla's mind. "You want to come see her?"

Samantha's gaze fell on Jayla. "Only one visitor is allowed in at a time. *You* go," she said to Jayla. "After you're done, I'll come in."

Reluctantly, a dumbstruck Jayla stepped forward, entering the double doors to the birthing unit with trepidation and uncertainty. "She named it after me?" Jayla softly asked.

"Are you Jayla?" the boyfriend queried back and Jayla gave a single nod. "Then, yeah. She did—said she couldn't have done this without you and Sammy."

Three doors into the hall Terica's boyfriend stopped and creaked the door open. "There's someone here who wants to see you," he calmly spoke into the room before making way for Jayla to pass through.

Jayla locked eyes with Terica who was laying propped up with several pillows, her bed at an angle. Her clothes from the event had been exchanged for a blue hospital gown. There was sweat on her forehead and she looked absolutely exhausted as the monitor next to her registered her heart rate and blood pressure with occasional beeps. There, nestled in her arms, bundled in a white blanket with blue and pink stripes, was a baby smaller than any Jayla had ever seen in person. Her nose was squished down and her eyes were swollen and squinted. On the top of her head was a little white beanie and, rather than crying, she cooed and rooted around Terica's arm.

"She's—" Jayla began, not sure how to put into words what she felt. "Beautiful." Then, with a slight grin, asked, "You named her after me?"

"I didn't think *Spicy Chips Washington* had the same ring to it," Terica smiled tiredly. "Wanna hold her?"

Jayla's heart began to race as the boyfriend, picking up on Terica's cue, began to lift the baby. "Watch the neck, watch the neck!" she cautioned her boyfriend who readjusted his hold to better support the baby's little neck. Then, as if she were the most valuable and fragile treasure in the world, he placed the baby in Jayla's care. "Meet Samjay."

The baby was lighter than Jayla imagined, the blanket she was in was warm and soft against her bare arm. *Cradle the neck*, she coached herself as she carefully supported the baby's head; the baby's small body wriggling for maximum comfort. There was this smell about the baby, this indefinable smell, Jayla breathed in as the baby gurgled and yawned. She could feel her tiny arms and legs moving, her back arching, her elbows pressing outward in the wrapping around her. Through the swaddling of the blanket she could feel the baby's little hand and petite fingers as a look of complete peace passed over the baby's face.

"Hi, Samjay," Jayla whispered, risking a smile. "You *are* beautiful."

"Kinda makes you want one of your own, doesn't it?" Terica asked, situating the pillows behind her.

"Kinda." Jayla replied as she fought to keep her heart to herself.

CHAPTER 36

ALMOST BY THE BOOK

Jayla stared at herself in the mirror the following Friday before work, her work scrubs lifted to her bra. She frowned at her distended stomach as it stuck out past her waistline, as a dark vertical line was becoming very visible down her abdomen. It was a miracle she was able to hide the pregnancy for so long, but she knew her days of successful concealment were numbered. She pondered how she would break the news to Renee. Even if she explained the forced nature of her pregnancy, it was still possible she could be fired for lying several months before when Renee asked if she was pregnant. These considerations weighed heavily on Jayla as long put-off worry mounted.

Thankfully, Samantha was true to her word and hadn't gossiped about the pregnancy or anything about Jayla's past. Jayla was sure the more time passed, Samantha would come around to the idea of adoption. Late at night, when sleep was stolen from her, she allowed herself to imagine her child, an extension of herself, being raised full-time by a new generation of Mrs. Neidringhouse. How wildly different their upbringing would be. What fewer scars that baby would carry. There were even times over the past week when Jayla eased an uncertain hand onto her stomach or permitted thoughts of holding Terica's baby to enter her mind, blaming her hormones on any emerging sentimentality.

But, whatever the case, it seemed everything surrounding the pregnancy was increasing—the swelling in her feet and ankles, the size of her belly, and, if she could admit it, the affection blossoming toward the baby in her womb; no longer an *it* but a *her.*

Entering the LifeLine parking lot, Jayla was surprised to find more cars than usual. Pulling open the door to the entryway, Jayla noticed every volunteer and coworker, including those not scheduled for Fridays, mingling, laughing, in a state of euphoric celebration. Praise and worship music played in the background as Darla handed out small clear plastic cups filled with a light, bubbly beverage.

"What's going on?" Jayla asked Marta and some female volunteers who were lounging and cackling together in the guest waiting area.

"Jayla!" Samantha exclaimed as she pranced over, extending a cup to her. "Don't worry, I know what you're thinking, but it's non-alcoholic fizzy grape juice."

"Did I miss something?" Jayla queried Samantha, sniffing the sparkling drink.

"Just that the Supreme Court finally did something *right*!" Marta chirped as the front door opened and Pastor Steve walked in. The room hooted and applauded as he lifted his hands sporting those infamous Richard Nixon victory fingers.

"We have been praying for this day!" Pastor Steve declared as more volunteers, hearing the sound of his voice, entered the waiting area from the counseling rooms. "Mark this day, June 24, 2022, as the day we won the war! Praise God for answered prayers." The small crowd cheered as some of the older women who had been a part of the struggle for decades shed tears of hope rewarded.

"So—what does that mean?" Jayla asked Samantha, not realizing until this moment how much she took the ruling for granted or how little she expected it to ever be overturned.

"It means each state gets to decide its own rules about abortion," Samantha answered loudly, her voice trying to hurdle over the volume of the room. "And thus, some states will now outlaw abortions completely." Unlike her colleagues, Jayla was far from thrilled with the news. The decision not to get an abortion was still fresh, and the thought of having her right to change her mind taken from her made her sick, or scared, or both.

"Does that mean the six-week abortion ban will happen for sure now?" Jayla asked, leaning into Samantha to filter out any unsolicited opinions from around the room.

"It means, if Governor Crix gets re-elected, he could make it a *zero-week* abortion ban, and I know this is a man who would do it," Samantha said joyfully, her high emotions blinding her to how Jayla might be feeling. "He just announced he'll be having a live interview tonight to talk about his plans, so we should know more then, but can you *imagine* it? We could be an abortion-less state?"

"I bet Jane Roe is rolling in her grave," Jayla overheard Darla joke, triumphantly sipping on her faux champagne.

"Hold on, Darla, you didn't hear?" a different woman disagreed. "She became a pro-life Christian later in life and never did end up having that abortion. Someone told me she was actually fighting for the court to overturn her case when she passed away. I'd think she'd be ecstatic right now!"

"All I know is it's about time," one of the women behind Jayla bleated. "It's *past* time. You're a drunk driver who kills a pregnant woman's baby, and you go to jail. You're a sober doctor and perform abortions, and you get money. Where's the justice?" she asked, then raising her glass in the air proudly exclaimed, "*Today is justice!*"

"History is being made!" Brittany proclaimed from the other side of the room as Jayla felt her phone vibrating in her pocket again. Looking at the screen, it was a text from *Unplanned Lynn: Call me 911 ASAP!*

Jayla felt a squall in her stomach and knew today of all days, she needed to respond to Lynn's urgent message. Zigzagging through the crowded area, Jayla entered an empty counseling room and closed the door behind her to block out the festivities. Holding her phone up to her ear, she prepared herself to deal with her other boss.

"Jayla, thank goodness you called me back," Lynn answered, distressed. "Have you heard what that spineless jaded jury-rigged court did? If Ruth Ginsburg was alive, this never would have happened."

"Yeah, for sure," Jayla replied.

"It's a mess. What an absolute miscarriage of justice," Lynn decried, cursing every other word. "These states with abortion ban trigger laws have kicked in, and women are running scared. I know you've been sick recently because of the baby and everything, but listen, I need you to come in today. Women are already beating our door down, and with Nikole out—"

"Nikole is out?" Jayla questioned for clarity, as those three little words were a massive game changer to her willingness to work.

"Yeah, she's on this cruise thing. Worst timing imaginable," Lynn bemoaned as Jayla's mind processed the news. "It's a perfect storm, really. Women are already lining up even though we don't open for another hour, and Dr. Molech is beside himself. It's his wife's birthday today, and they made these reservations, and Tripp has called out sick on top of that. Women are panicking—absolutely panicking. I think anyone supportive of women's rights—the rights of anyone, for that matter—is panicking right now. What's that sound?" she asked as a loud chorus of "Amazing Grace" resounded through the hallway, Pastor Steve's voice standing out above the rest.

"It's nothing. Just some neighbors," Jayla lied. "Yeah, of course. Let me see what I can do, and I'll be there if I can."

"Hurry," Lynn implored before disconnecting the call, the sound of pounding glass in the background.

Jayla smoothed over the front of her scrubs. While she knew asking Renee for the day off would be difficult to rationalize if the women outside Unplanned were feeling at all similar to how she was at the moment, Jayla somehow believed she needed to be there for them, which outweighed any risk in her request. She made her way to Renee's office.

Jayla gave two quick knocks, then entered, greeting her with "Hey, Renee?"

"Just two minutes, stay right there, almost done," Renee advised, her attention remaining glued to the screen as she read over her document. Then, turning around with a pensive smile, she welcomed Jayla and offered her a seat as a fresh wave of ruckus drenched the room. "Quite the happening out there, isn't it?"

"Yeah. People are going crazy," Jayla agreed. "Why aren't you out there with them?"

"Emails never take a day off," Renee replied, taking a small sip of juice. "I'll give them a few more minutes, and then we'll get set up for the day."

Jayla could tell it was more than that. "You don't seem as happy as the rest of them out there." Jayla remarked, still wondering how she would broach the subject of time off.

"No, no. I am. I'm just celebrating in my own way," Renee said, her tone more reserved and apprehensive than congratulatory.

"You think it's a bad thing what happened?" Jayla asked, curious about the stark contrast between LifeLine's sullen head and the rest of its overjoyed body.

"Not bad, not exactly," Renee began. "It's just, now we think we've won, but this isn't the end of a fight. This is just the end of a single early round. There is good to come from this ruling, *a lot of good*, don't get me wrong. But there's a lot of not-good to follow. The people who passed this bill are an almost invisible force, while we are the brick-and-mortar services. We need to prepare for all hell to break loose on us. I just pray we are ready."

Jayla nodded in agreement, thinking of all the women waiting for her at Unplanned Inc. "Yeah."

"If anything, things will only get more divisive now. For years many have said this issue would be the next Civil War, and we are about to find out," Renee predicted. "The reds and blues of this county will only get more divided. Some states will ban abortions, which seems like a win, but other states will become even more encouraging of them. Some liberal states are already saying they're willing to cover the expenses of anyone traveling there to get an abortion. But I've yet to hear of any conservative states offering to cover the cost of an adoption for anyone looking for alternatives. And of course, this doesn't even touch on abortion pills being sent through the mail—which was already on the rise—and which will only skyrocket further after today. Now, more than ever, desperate women will turn to an unregulated medication they don't understand. We must temper our celebration and prepare. You can bet your bottom dollar today the other side is meeting, rallying, raising money, working on ways to make this ruling useless. I wouldn't be surprised if there was a line of women in front of Unplanned this morning."

"I'll bet you're right," Jayla said, knowing full well she was. "I was just wond—"

"You ever feel like your trapped in the middle?" Renee interrupted. "Between the pro-life *crazies* and the pro-choice *crazies* representing neither of our sides. Then you have the churches that are not really pro-life between the churches that will get all involved in holding signs on a street once a year riling up the enemies but won't darken the streets of the neighborhoods during the year when the real work of saving children could happen. And then I have my own board who makes me keep a LifeLine sign, the largest branding on our building, that by its name keeps abortion-minded girls from walking in. And all because they are afraid of losing the support of a wealthy long-time donor," Renee vented. "Jayla, do you ever feel caught in the middle?"

You have no idea how caught in the middle I feel, Jayla thought. "I was just wondering," Jayla began, "I'm not feeling all that great," she said, defaulting to her old standby excuse. "And, since so many people are here, I didn't know if there was someone to maybe cover for me?"

"Oh, I'm so sorry to hear that," Renee consoled as she considered the request. "Umm, yeah. That's fine. Sadly, I think it will be a slow day here anyway." Then, massaging the bridge of her nose, painfully admitted, "If it's in a woman's heart to kill her baby, she's going to do it, law or not. I just pray we're still around in a few months to pick up the broken pieces."

Without saying goodbye to anyone, Jayla slipped quietly out the front door. By the time she reached Unplanned, she had to park across the street, as the complex parking lot overflowed with vehicles. As she approached the entrance of the building, she saw a wide array of women spanning every bracket of society. There were black and white women, wealthy and on welfare, teens and middle-aged, some alone, others waiting in line with their mothers. Confusion, anger, fear, speculation, and disbelief enveloped the crowd as fresh-faced Unplanned employees Jayla hadn't yet met passed out tissues to women who were openly crying.

"They haven't banned abortions—only *safe* abortions," Jayla overheard one girl say, "We've gone back fifty years of progress."

"First they take away abortions, then they take away *all* of women's rights," stated a mother of a young teenager waiting in line for an abortion. "Half the country just blacklisted us."

"Now is our time to fight. Today there are no protesters outside our doors, no picketers, no bomb threats, and no bullhorns. These do-gooders think they have won. While they celebrate, we will have the biggest day for women's freedom ever!" shouted another of the younger Unplanned employees. "The Supreme Court fired the second shot heard around the world!"

Positioned on the other side of the front doors stood Lynn, a mother of exiles, who personally welcomed the tempest-tossed women as they entered. "Mark this day as another day America has done great injustice to women. Another great injustice," she comforted before spotting Jayla through the throng. Then, politely stepping away from her conversation, she approached Jayla with a look of protective ferocity. "I'm so glad you're here. Can you believe this? Dr. Molech is moving as fast as he can. There are already four patients in the recovery room waiting for you. Not all of them will need to come to you, of course, but just so you know, for those who do, we've reduced the length of recovery time so we can get the maximum number of women in and out today. Just do what you do, one patient at a time, and try not to get overwhelmed. It's got to be a real team effort today," she advised, then, surveying the group, took a deep breath through her nostrils. "I was made for today. This is my purpose."

A steady hailstorm of patients descended on Jayla in the recovery room that day. Some reflected past her as they quietly mended and left. Some were ice-cold nuisances Jayla couldn't seem to do anything right by. She wanted so badly to make the worst day of their lives more tolerable and tried, in both little ways and large, to take Samantha's advice of loving the person who was in front of her, but the triage was overwhelming. As the day wore on, these women's faces slowly blurred together into a homogenous heap of pain.

By the end of her shift, Jayla was in tatters, exhausted physically and emotionally. She could feel massive swelling in her feet and ankles as her feet pressed against the confines of her shoe. Her back was sore, her mind was spilling over, and at her core, she felt punished for trying to do good. All she wanted to do now was retreat to her home and sleep the weekend away between bouts of compulsive DoorDash orders.

"Jayla! Wait," Lynn called out as Jayla hobbled over to the front doors to leave, the waiting room now eerily quiet. "I just wanted to thank you again for coming in today," she said, crossing the lobby. "You really are the best at what you do. Absolutely the best, and we've really been missing you."

"Thanks," Jayla breathed, overheated and parched, seven feet from freedom.

"Listen," Lynn continued, speaking softer the closer she came. "I know it's been a long day for you, for all of us. But—there's one last patient coming in today. Tonight, rather. And we really need your help with this one."

Jayla didn't know if she wanted to cry or punch Lynn in the throat at the mention of extra hours. "I—just—can't," she said, each word an elephant to get out of her mouth.

"I know. I know. But this last girl—she's different. She's coming in at the request of one of our *biggest* donors, well, not really a donor, but let's just say a silent influencer. It's best that you don't even know who, but it's really important we get this one done right. Better than right. Perfect."

"Lynn, I'm tired, my feet hurt, my *hair* even hurts."

"You think any of us want to stay for this one? Dr. Molech had to be talked off a ledge because it is his wife's birthday, and he had the whole night planned. But, despite that, he's choosing to help because he *gets* how important this is. And, really, you're the only one I trust to help with it. You and me, we have history. I need you," Lynn expressed, then, with groveling sincerity, insisted, "We need *the Abortion Angel.*"

"Come on, Lynn. Don't do that." Jayla rolled her eyes.

"You know why you came in today? Do you? For the same reason I did. Because we *care* about these women. Who do they have if we don't show up?" Lynn exhorted like a Fortune 500 motivational speaker.

"Listen, I think I did all the Good Samaritan work I can for today. I'm exhausted," Jayla declined.

"Okay, okay," Lynn acquiesced, re-strategizing. "There's a bonus. A big bonus for helping out with this last patient." Seeing she had piqued Jayla's interest, Lynn took the liberty to continue. "They want this thing done tonight. I can have $2,500 deposited directly into your account before you come back to the lobby after it's all done. *And* I'll buy your dinner tonight if you stay."

Jayla thought about it for a moment, *$2,500?* "What time tonight?"

"Eight. Our—*friend*—wants to make sure no one else is here when it happens," Lynn advised. Then, in a very serious tone, she added, "Needless to say, *discretion* is *key* for this evening—so—you in?"

"It's a good bonus," Jayla admitted reluctantly.

"You know that's a *very* generous bonus," Lynn grinned. "And I will be here to help of course. I started in the recovery room fifteen years ago. I know my way around that room."

"Alright. I'll do it. But I'm gonna sit down until I do it," Jayla begrudgingly agreed.

Around seven-thirty at night, Jayla woke from an accidental nap to the sound of Dr. Moloch walking up.

"Good morning, sleepyhead," he said, rolling up the sleeves of his white button-up coat with his large fingers. "What a day. I've never seen anything like it."

"Is it time?" Jayla speculated as she stretched out, her lower back protesting.

"No, no. We have a few minutes still. But I wanted to have a quick conversation with you regarding the procedure for this particular client. Can we talk in my office upstairs?"

"We have an upstairs?" Jayla asked, groggily, her breath smelling like garlic and peanuts from the takeout dinner.

Dr. Molech chuckled. "Do we have an upstairs? My dear, have you seen the building from the outside?"

"Can we just talk down here?" Jayla counter-offered, fighting odd feelings of embarrassment.

He quickly checked the halls, before agreeing and walking over to a seat. "Jayla, how much has Lynn told you about the procedure tonight?"

Jayla shrugged. "Not much. I'm just waiting in here until it's done, and then I will take care of whoever it is, just like I would anyone else. She did mention not to say anything about it to anyone. That it's something special for, ah, shall we say like a business partner, a very social and political influencer."

"It's a special interest person's daughter, yes. But you won't be in here. You'll be with me in the operating room," Dr. Molech corrected. Then, seeing the surprise on Jayla's face, asked, "Lynn didn't tell you?"

"No, I mean," Jayla stammered, "I've never participated in the actual abortion procedure before."

"*Pregnancy Reversal*," Dr. Molech rephrased, "That sounds so much nicer than that old *abortion* word, doesn't it? It's all in the wording, Jayla.

Listen, you'll be fine. You've cared for patients before, yes? You've put together puzzles before, yes? From what I hear, you have a very good bedside manner with the young ladies who come in here. Besides, it's not like you'll be in there alone. I'll be right there with you. Just another Friday night," he said before catching himself and playfully putting a finger over his lips. "Oops. Don't tell the missus that. We don't want Jezze thinking I've forgotten her birthday, now do we."

"What do I do?" asked Jayla.

"Follow my lead, and we'll be just fine," Dr. Molech advised. "There's no bloodwork needed, no physical, no check-up for sexually transmitted infections. It's bare bones. Very simple. The sponsor wants her in and out as quickly as possible. Otherwise, Jezze would have never let me stay. She's at home now, probably staring at her birthday cake, dogs in her lap, counting the seconds until I can come home. She is very possessive." Then he laughed heartily.

Jayla soaked in the new information, silently evaluating if the change of responsibility was large enough for her to reconsider.

"Okay," Jayla agreed, still unsure she was making the right decision.

Following Dr. Molech down the hall, Jayla entered a white room where, predominantly at its center, stood an examination table complete with stirrups. To the left of the examination table was a small white desk with a black computer console, a large video monitor, and an attached transducer. "These I assume you recognize," the doctor said, turning to Jayla with an expectant look.

"For ultrasounds," Jayla replied, recognizing the machine from her visit with Terica several months ago.

"Good. Very good," Dr. Molech affirmed. "I've been told our patient this evening is just over twenty weeks along, in the early stages of her second trimester. So, we will be performing a *D&E* procedure."

"*D and E*?" Jayla asked. Her eyes strayed to a stainless-steel table to the right of the examination bed on which lay a white cloth with some medical tools she recognized from watching her favorite good doctor television shows. Among those were cotton balls, gels, gauze, small white cups of medication, swabs, a suction tube, and two full syringes. But for every two items she recognized, there was one she had never seen used in action. First, there was a metal tool that looked like a large bottle opener with a flat, sloped top; next to it were what looked like seven metal bendy straws. Adjacent to these was a large clamp, about thirteen inches long, with a two-inch head and rows of sharp, jagged teeth. Beside that was an instrument that looked like a pair of pliers and two tools that looked like they came from a dental catalog for picking out plaque. On the opposite side of the table was stationed a drip stand with a full intravenous bag, line, and pump, along with the most unexplainable item of all—an empty freestanding metal tray.

"A dilatation and evacuation," Dr. Molech explained. "It's what we do when a patient is this far along. While some say the abortion pills could still work at this place on the girl's calendar, it is not recommended as the baby's head—sorry, I mean the fetal cranium is too large. The client would totally freak out. So, the *D&E* is a common procedure. On average, we do five or six a day here. But, nevertheless, we must still be alert and attentive."

Jayla nodded. "And what are these used for?" she asked, pointing at the unfamiliar bits of equipment.

"Those—" he began, as a boisterous ringtone resonated through the air. "Pardon me," taking his phone out of his pocket and holding it to his ear. "Yes, Lynn," he answered. "Yes, already? My, oh, my. Okay then, we'll come out to you," he replied before disconnecting the call. "They're here," he informed Jayla. "Don't forget. You follow my lead, and before you know it, it'll all be over, and we'll be eating birthday cake. Well, I will."

Jayla and Dr. Molech backtracked through the recovery area until they reached the doors usually letting people out. Looking out the security window, Jayla could see a black SUV and two large men standing next to it. Opening the side door, one man watched the parking lot as Lynn and the other man carefully guided a teenager, all of what looked to be seventeen or so years old. She had long, blonde hair and looked beautiful despite her face quivering with fright and insecurity. Her eyes were puffy, and above her lips sat a medium-sized mole. For a moment Jayla thought she recognized the young woman.

"Good evening," Dr. Molech greeted the visitors, as he unlocked and opened the door. "What a pleasure it is to be serving you this evening."

Lynn's phone ringer interrupted the eerie silence of the transition, bringing the men to high alert. Lynn apologized, left the group and walked down the hall, purposefully limiting her conversation volume.

The young woman didn't say anything but offered a dampened, tight-lipped smile, wringing her hands nervously and grasping at the bottom corners of her shirt, as her eyes darted from the doctor to Jayla.

"Please, come inside," Dr. Molech encouraged as the men entered the building behind the girl. "Gentlemen, make yourself comfortable in here. Miss Crix, grab Jayla's arm and follow me into the next room. You are going to be fine."

Miss Crix? Jayla repeated to herself before getting hit with a lightning bolt of realization. She knew where she recognized the beautiful teenager from—the gosh-awful governor election ads plaguing her TV every commercial break for the past three months. Jayla chastised herself for being so blind. It was all clicking together now. *Mister Six-Week Abortion Ban Bill*, she scoffed to herself, careful to keep her face stoic and without judgment.

Before long, Jayla, Dr. Molech, and their young patient were in the operation room. Miss Crix, now changed and lying on the examination bed with her feet in the stirrups, quivered in the cold sterile room.

"There, there, Miss Crix," Dr. Molech soothed as Jayla began attaching the IV line. "Nothing to worry about."

"Is it going to hurt?" she asked, looking first at Jayla and then at Dr. Molech for reassurance.

"Not at all. In a moment, we will administer a general anesthetic. Swallow these pills, lay back, and imagine you're sleeping, and when you wake up, it will all be over. There will be some—minor—discomfort after you wake up, but my colleague here is going to take marvelous care of you," Dr. Molech comforted.

Within a few minutes, the nervous girl was asleep, her hands finally at rest by her side, her legs spread outward. Jayla watched as Dr. Molech removed something from the young woman's vagina and discarded it into a red-lidded trashcan. "The cervix is looking great. That's good. Well done for keeping the Laminaria in," he said to the sleeping girl, then, feeling Jayla's eyes on him, asked, "So, Jayla, how do you like to celebrate your birthday?"

"My birthday?" Jayla repeated, still thinking about the unknown word *Laminaria*. Dr. Molech placed the large metal bottle opener device into the patient's vagina, opening it widely.

"Yes," Dr. Molech confirmed, getting up from his squeaky rolling stool and walking over to the ultrasound machine. "You're, what? Mid-twenties? Do you celebrate by going to a nice meal? Or throwing a shindig at your home?"

"I never really—uh—do you need me to help you?" Jayla asked, feeling underutilized as Dr. Molech busied himself around the room like a conductor playing every instrument in the band. "Don't we need to get Lynn in here?"

"I'm fine, thank you," he assured, placing some gel on the ultrasound transducer and pressing it against the sleeping girl's exposed stomach. "I'm sorry, it's just faster if I do this part myself. For many years I had no assistant for these sorts of things and . . ." he paused as images of the woman's womb began appearing on screen. "There we go." On the screen appeared a small baby about the size of Jayla's hand. "Hello there," Dr. Molech said to the screen before turning to Jayla. "Okay, now, if you can hold this here, we can get started."

Jayla reached over taking the transducer out of his hand, making sure to keep it in the same spot. Dr. Molech, plopped down on his stool, rolled over to his place between the woman's legs and began utilizing the metal bendy straws from the table.

"What are those?" Jayla asked.

"These are dilators," explained Dr. Molech. "The Laminaria did its job, but now we need the cervix as open as possible. If the cervix isn't open enough, it's possible we could perforate or lacerate it. Or even the uterus, for that matter. And then you get even more lawsuits, and eventually the insurance cancels you. It's quite important we do this one by the books. Seriously, if you knew what I pay in malpractice insurance, you would be glad you work in recovery. Those insurance companies rape you."

"Oh, wow," Jayla swallowed, shocked at the term *lawsuit,* but uncomfortable with the flippant way he used the term *rape.* "But I mean, that's not going to happen, right? This is safe?"

"Safe? Yes. But every operation has its risks. If we're not careful, we could damage the bladder, or the patient could begin to hemorrhage,"

Dr. Molech warned, then, changing his tone, added, "*But* that's why we're doing it by the books! No music. No distractions. No guesswork. By the books. On the other hand, tonight, we also have a great safety net. This young lady would never be allowed to go public with any of this."

Placing a suction tube deep inside the sleeping beauty, Dr. Molech flipped a switch as an electric whirring sound filled the room. Pale yellow amniotic fluid passed through the tube, as Dr. Molech checked the ultrasound monitor to verify his progress. "So, do you like big parties? Small parties?"

"I don't know," Jayla reckoned, keeping a tight watch on the procedure and patient, wondering if her medical partner was doing the same. "I never really celebrate birthdays."

"A minimalist! I love it. I didn't know any more of those existed in your generation," exclaimed Dr. Molech, as the amniotic fluid stopped flowing. "My Jezze is quite the opposite. The missus is a maximalist in every sense of the word. I imagine every penny of tonight's after-hours bonus will be spent trying in vain to make this evening back up to her. Alas, all the money in the world can't buy you back your birthday. Can you hand me the forceps please, my dear?"

Jayla looked at the doctor and then at the table of medical equipment, mostly sure she knew what tool he was referring to but shy at the thought of embarrassing herself again. *Where is Lynn?* she thought to herself again.

"Wait—wait—far more important you stay there. I'll grab them," Dr. Molech deduced, rolling his stool over to the spread of instruments and selecting the long clamp ending with rows of sharp teeth. "Alrighty. Now it's time for the big show. Jayla, make sure you don't lose the fetus on the screen."

Jayla nodded and turned her attention to the ultrasound as the sound of squeaking wheels echoed through the room. On the screen, she saw the baby, smaller than little Samjay but similar in every other way. In hues of purple and pink, she watched the monitor as the baby placed her hand to her mouth and gently began to suck her thumb. She looked at peace; she looked at home. *Twenty weeks along,* Jayla thought to herself, wondering how many weeks along her own baby would be if she took the time to do the math.

Then, onto the screen emerged the forceps, the mass of their jaws approaching the baby's leg. Jayla's pulse quickened as the horrific reality of what was about to happen settled in. In an instant, the forceps clamped onto the leg, and with a quick twist and pull of the sharp metal ridges, the baby's leg was ripped apart from her body.

Jayla wanted to throw up. She wanted to run away or force herself to wake up from this nightmare. She felt the floor begin to swim under her. Her hands became cold and she had trouble keeping the transducer steady, ruining the image on the screen. She turned to Dr. Molech just in time to see him pull out the small, bloody leg from the patient's vagina and place it on the empty table next to him. "Jayla, the ultrasound!" he reprimanded sternly, his bark fierce enough to pull her out of her shock.

Jayla screamed silently, *Get in here, Lynn! You said you would be here!*

Maneuvering the transducer slowly around the patient's stomach, Jayla watched the screen as the baby slowly reappeared, her face in agony as she let out a silent scream. Over the next few minutes, Jayla watched as the baby was torn to pieces. First, the legs, white and meaty, then the entrails. The petite heart and lungs came out next, followed by the spine, one broken bit at a time. Then came the supple arms with hands attached, ten perfect fingernails adorning ten perfect fingers. Each clumsy shred coming out dripping red.

The more Jayla watched, the more a dual-opposing reality emerged inside of her. As her emotions became numbed, her senses heightened. There was this smell about the baby, this indefinable smell that Jayla breathed in as the fleshy amputated pieces of the baby lay on the tray. A smell so odious, so disgusting, it made Jayla want to quit breathing altogether. The lump of baby parts on the table grew, looking less like a blob of tissue and more like a child's baby doll ripped apart by rabid bulldogs. "Almost over," Dr. Molech said soothingly, as he scooted over to the tray of surgical instruments and replaced his forceps with the tool that resembled a pair of pliers. Jayla watched the screen as the doctor carefully positioned the pliers around the baby's head, the only part of her body still in the womb. "*Watch the head, watch the head,*" he coached himself. Then, with a crunch, the pliers crushed the head, contorting it to a more manageable size as runny white brain matter trickled out of the woman's cervix. Jayla watched as he dabbed away the fluid carefully with cotton balls and grabbed the dental-looking instrument. Scraping out one skull piece at a time, Dr. Molech carefully emptied the womb, gradually removing the rest of the placenta until, at last, he meticulously suctioned out the evacuated womb.

"There we go," Dr. Molech concluded, placing the last ruddy surgical tool on the table before exhaling and wiping his brow with his arm. "What did I say? Painless." Then, rising from his stool, he came over to the ultrasound screen and leaned in. "Great. Looks great. We got it all. Piece of cake." Then, with a look of shock and disappointment, lamented, "Candles! I forgot the candles! I can't believe myself." Then, taking off his gloves and pulling out his phone, said, "I need to step out to make a phone call. You go ahead and finish up without me."

"Finish up?" Jayla asked, her words slow and shaky. "What's left to do?"

"Why, the puzzle, of course," Dr. Molech informed, seemingly astonished at the stupidity of Jayla's question before remembering her inexperience. "You must put the fetus back together—reassemble it on this tray, like a puzzle."

"Back—together?" Jayla mouthed, appalled at the notion of the despicable request.

"To make sure we didn't miss anything," Dr. Molech explained. "We must leave no stone unturned, my dear. Anything left inside and, well, it is bad news for all three of us." And with that, he walked out of the room, leaving Jayla alone with a sleeping patient and the ghastliest jigsaw puzzle imaginable.

Jayla slowly, unwillingly, made her way over to the remains and gagged. No sooner had she reluctantly raised her gloved hands than she recoiled with a shudder. *You have to do this*, she told herself, *just think of it like a puzzle, like Molech said.*

Moving closer to the table of blood-speckled medical tools, Jayla lifted the forceps, flexing them in her grasp like tongs. Then, taking a deep breath, she reminded herself, *It's already happened. The worst has already happened. I can do this.*

Quickly, before she could talk herself out of it, Jayla began assembling the remains, one dainty body part at a time—her leg severed at the thigh, the right half of her torso, her small hands, first left then right, then a small thumb still outstretched for self-soothing. As she reassembled the severed head, she could still distinguish the eyes, squinting and small, and the scrunched-up nose and mouth, frozen in agony as the baby experienced its first and final sensation of pain.

With the puzzle pieces complete, Jayla took a step back for perspective to make sure everything was in its place when the door to the operating room opened and Dr. Molech sauntered inside.

"Great news! Jezze was able to find a spare set of candles. Crisis averted," he said jovially before glancing down at the tray. "Oh, you've finished! Excellent. Let's have a look."

Dr. Molech stretched out a long finger and, without making contact with the body, ticked off each part in its place, his demeanor electric with excitement over the evening ahead. Then, finishing up the inspection with a nod of approval, said, "This is great work, Jayla! I can see a career in this for you if you ever have an interest. Now go ahead and toss it in the trash, and I'll start the process of waking up Sleeping-Beauty."

Jayla stared at the doctor. *Toss it in the trash.*

Not realizing this was more of an existential response, Dr. Molech replied, "The receptacle with the biohazard label. Right over there," pointing a long finger toward the trashcan. "Same one I used earlier."

Jayla slowly lifted the tray, which unhooked easily from its base, and walked the dead baby girl's remains to the trash can. Then, with somewhat pensive body mechanics, she twisted her wrist and watched the pieces of life tumble into the bin.

"Now what do I do?" Jayla asked, discarding her own gloves as the wastebasket tomb slowly closed tightly.

"Disinfectants are by the sink. Go ahead and clean up," Dr. Molech instructed. Then, pivoting away from his patient, he reached inside a drawer, pulled out a white washcloth, and tossed it in Jayla's direction.

"Things need to be wiped down before the patient wakes up," Dr. Molech urged.

Numb, Jayla despondently did as she was told until she polished the stainless-steel so well she could see her reflection.

"Good, Jayla. Very good. You put my work to shame," Dr. Molech encouraged. "Now, in just a moment, the patient will be waking. She'll be groggy, to say the least. I'm not fully positive, but I believe her gentleman friends outside want her back in the vehicle as soon as possible. So, that being said," the doctor paused, framing his words, "is it possible, instead of moving her to the recovery room, we skip that formality and wheel her straight out to the car?"

"No! No, we can't do that," Jayla disapproved, speaking through a stupor. "She needs time to rest. To heal."

"I know—I know. I hear what you are saying, and you're not wrong. But these men, they have their own way they expect things to be done."

"We aren't moving her," Jayla snapped back, her subdued emotions spilling over into a protective furor over the needy patient. "She needs, at minimum, a half hour of recovery."

Dr. Molech was stunned speechless. He looked at his watch and then at the door to the operating room, peering so intently it was as if he could see the two large men waiting expectantly on the other side. "But, my wife's birthday."

"And it will still be her birthday when you get home later tonight. Now I need for you to get me some apple juice and a box of animal crackers from the recovery room and bring them back after you've explained to the men outside that they'll have to wait."

"But what do I tell them?" he asked sheepishly.

"Tell them the truth—that we need to monitor her to make sure there are no complications to the procedure," Jayla protested. "That's part of the whole reason why we have a recovery room to begin with. Or would you rather you were the abortion doctor that accidentally killed the governor's daughter? We're doing this thing *by the book*, remember?"

CHAPTER 37

ONE MUST DIE FOR
THE MANY

Jayla crossed the empty parking lot to her car like a zombie, the adrenaline and distraction of helping someone else in need having passed. She sat speechless, motionless in the driver's seat, looking through her windshield into the void of the night. There was no energy for thoughts or remorse, no bandwidth for processing or grieving. There was only an all-pervading numbness pumping from her heart to the rest of her body.

Then, in the quiet stillness of the car, a single vibration from her phone resounded in her ears. Barely having the motivation to breathe, let alone move, Jayla read her screen. It was a notification from her bank that a $2,500 deposit from Unplanned, Inc. had just been received in her account. *That's not enough*, Jayla thought wearily. Then, breathing in through her nose and out through her mouth, Jayla rallied the energy to smooth over the front of her shirt and turn over the ignition.

The next forty-eight hours began a sleepless relapse of non-stop entertainment binging and retail therapy. The buzz of acquiring flattering new clothes and the superficial happiness of having her hair and nails flawlessly sculpted and colored helped numb her mind to the deed. Any whispered reminder of the pregnancy reversal she participated in ushered in a new round of delivered take-out and online shopping, each element of amusement supplying a fresh layer of plaster over her con-science as she coped the only way she knew how.

By the time Monday morning came, Jayla had spent over half of her bonus, which she swore would be the last money she ever received from Unplanned. Despite feeling physically tired and mentally hun-gover from continual overstimulation, Jayla was full of eagerness on her drive to LifeLine Pregnancy Center. She oozed with excitement to get back to focusing her attention on helping needy women, which had been so effective in distracting her the previous Friday night. She rea-soned that, if anything, this whole experience would only serve to make her that much more caring, more devoted to the women who arrived at the doorstep of the center. She would simply busy herself throughout the day with her patients. She would self-medicate throughout the evening with easy-to-reach diversions. But no sooner had Jayla pulled into the parking lot than she realized her plan had fallen apart before it ever had a chance to get started.

The windows of the center had been smashed; glass glistened beneath each rock-sized hole. There was trash thrown on the lawn, as if someone had rummaged through the dumpster and emptied its con-tents, causing a fermenting rotten smell to stick to the grass. On the front doors, a large can of red paint had been emptied, making it look like blood was pouring out of the building. And on the wall, the words *Jane Says Revenge* was spray-painted in black.

Jayla watched as Pastor Steve and her coworkers surveyed the dam-age. While some women chatted or investigated the full extent of the situation, some picked up garbage while others cried. The memory of the *Roe No More* celebration three days prior was now in sharp contrast to the scene of such unanticipated fear and sorrow. The shot was heard with repugnant red enamel. Had the next Civil War begun?

"Leave it! Drop it, ladies," Renee called out, rounding the corner of the building with her phone up to her ear. Samantha followed closely behind her taking pictures. "I'm on the phone with the police department now. We need everything left just like this until they arrive. Thank you." Then, redirecting her attention to her phone, asked, "What? No. *No, me estás escuchando.* That's not what I'm saying. I was—hello? Hello, can you hear me?" she paused, then circled back to the other side of the building.

Jayla walked up to Samantha, who was beginning to photograph the fractured windows. "Sam, what in the world happened here?"

"Oh, hey," Samantha replied as she turned toward Jayla. Unlike the typically upbeat, feisty friend Jayla had come to expect, this Samantha was stressed and disheveled. "I don't know. Renee called me first thing this morning and told me to come quickly. I just—I would never in a million years expect anything like this to happen to us. Ever."

Jayla nodded as both women looked at the battered building before them. "What do you think *Jane Says Revenge* means?"

As Jayla spoke, a black truck sped into the parking lot and screeched to a halt. Out stepped Darla from the passenger side, a hand over her mouth. Her tall toothpick of a husband jumped out of the driver's side and slammed the door, startling the already unsettled women.

"Good lord almighty," Clem yelled as he took in the sight. "When you said Renee said it was bad, I didn't know you meant *this* bad. Why aren't the police here already?" Clem asked as his wife leaned into his shoulder and began to cry. "Isn't this what we pay them for?"

As Clem railed and Darla howled, Samantha turned back to Jayla. "Your question. They're a militant, extremist, pro-abortion rights group. I didn't know we had one in the area, but I guess—"

Renee emerged back into view as Clem continued to shout his frustrations.

"Not now, Clem," Renee dismissed as she walked briskly to her car.

"I told you—we need to be ready when this kind of stuff happens! I told you that months ago, back when only a few centers were hit. They need to know we mean business, that they can't get away with this kinda thing!" Clem yelled back, approaching to intercept Renee, leaving Darla behind. "We have to do something! I've got paint too! An eye for an eye—"

"What do you want us to do, Clem? Huh?" challenged Renee, shaking her head. "You don't know what you're talking about, okay? I've called the police. They're on their way. That's what we have to do. Wait for them to get here. And until then, I have an insurance report to file, and we have several women we need to contact to cancel their appointments. None of that gets done by me rehashing the need for a security program we can't afford anyway. So if you want to do something? How about you start by moving your truck so the police can come in. Alright?"

Clem's face was as red as the paint on the door, his embarrassment not simply due to being reprimanded in public but for being berated by a woman in front of a group of women. "Yeah, well . . ." he stammered, looking around for his next target and finding it in Pastor Steve. "And where do you get off with all your *turn-the-other-cheek* mumbo jumbo now? This—this is as much on you as anyone else." Then, with all eyes watching him, Darla's husband walked back over to his truck, fuming. "Someone needs to do something!" he yelled, throwing open the door and jumping inside. He reversed his truck full throttle and raced off into the distance, leaving Darla in just as much disbelief as the rest of the volunteers.

"So what do we do?" asked one of the women who had been picking up trash. "Are we open today?"

"The best thing for you all to do is to go home," Renee reluctantly advised. "Go home, and I'll let you all know the plan soon. Until then, just—pray. Pray for the girls that they'll still get support while we're closed. Pray for wisdom for me, for the board, as we figure out our next steps. And pray for the people who did this, that God would change their hearts."

"Should we come back tomorrow?" one of the older volunteers asked.

"I think, probably, we'll at least be closed for the rest of the week," Renee answered. Her statement was met with gasps as her team became even more disheartened. "So thank you for coming in today, and I'm so sorry this happened, but go home. I'll get this sorted out."

"But then it's like *they* win," someone objected as other women began to walk dejectedly to their cars. Pastor Steve's head hung low.

Jayla watched as Darla fidgeted, mascara running down her cheeks; her ride was gone and, along with it, her safe space. Then, realizing how awful having the whole day to herself would be, Jayla turned back around to Samantha who was scrolling through the images of the vandalism and deleting blurry pictures. "So do you want to go get some breakfast?"

"I'm not all that hungry, to be honest. And plus, I promised Renee I'd stay. Brittany and her family are on a road trip to Georgia, doing a family tree project for Nia's school or something, and since she'd usually step in with this sort of thing, I figured I'd help how I could. I'll be calling the women who had appointments today. Then, after that, I'll probably start calling some window repair places. I don't know. That seems like the right order to do things. But you're welcome to help if you want?" Then, focusing on Jayla, undistracted for the first time that morning, commented, "Wow—that's a really nice look! You're practically glowing," she complimented.

Jayla had forgotten about her new hair, nails, and makeup, which seemed somewhat inappropriate as she stood in the shadow of their defaced workplace. "Thanks," Jayla replied, "and thanks for the offer, but I think I'll pass."

"Okay. You make sure to keep off your feet," Samantha said, glancing down at Jayla's stomach before looking around a second time to see if anyone was watching, concealing a smile.

"By the way, I need to talk with you about, uh, the conversation we never finished."

"Oh, yeah? Everything okay?" Jayla questioned, sincerely hoping Samantha wasn't going to turn down the adoption, especially now that she couldn't bear the thought of going through with an abortion.

"Yeah! Yeah. All good. Rick and I finally got the chance to sit down this weekend and talk. There are some things you and I need to catch up on," Sam informed, trying hard to appear nonchalant as her lightheartedness momentarily returned.

"Okay, so—is it good news or bad?"

Samantha playfully shrugged her shoulders. "I guess you'll just have to find out. Oh! Also, just a heads-up, you'll be getting a package in the mail. Don't open it until we talk. Okay?"

"Okay," Jayla replied, wishing to hear a concrete affirmation from her friend and the peace of mind that would follow. "Well, it looks like my week just freed up."

Driving away from LifeLine, Jayla felt restless, her ability to control her thoughts diminishing the more fatigued she felt. Images of the baby from Friday night started coming to the surface, growing in graphic detail with each unwanted emergence. Jayla aimlessly drove until she pulled into a parking space and turned off her car. She looked around her surroundings to find out where she was, and immediately the blood went cold in her veins. Her subconscious had brought her back to The Bricks, to the same apartment where she was raised, the same one she hadn't seen since she was abandoned all those years ago.

Suddenly, something within Jayla gave way, and the tears she dammed with the distractions broke loose. Alone with her conscience, in the solitude of her car, she wept. Jayla wept for both what she did and for what she hadn't been strong enough to do. She wept for the baby she discarded and for the young mother who would have gladly kept her. She lamented living in a world where tragedies like rape, coercion, abuse, and abortion were realities. She wept for her Auntie Neidringhouse and for never having told her goodbye. She wept for the loss of her childhood in the apartment overlooking her breakdown. Even after her eyes ran dry, she heaved and mourned until every bit of grief was expelled.

I can't go back to U.I., Jayla promised herself. *I won't. I quit.*

Before she could reason herself out of her decision, Jayla picked up her phone and called Lynn's personal number.

"Jayla, you must be a mind reader," Lynn answered. "I was just about to call you."

"We need to talk, Lynn."

"My sentiment exactly. Right now, we're slammed, as you can imagine. So why don't you come by today after work? There's something we need to discuss."

Jayla rubbed her bloodshot, puffy eyes, unwilling to return to Unplanned, Inc. "No, let's just talk now."

"Tonight," Lynn insisted. "Call me when you get here." She hung up with no goodbye.

Jayla sighed. *Tonight, I'll end this tonight.*

Arriving at the Unplanned building a little before closing time, Jayla stepped out of her vehicle and walked toward the dastardly place for the last time. Knocking on the front doors, she waited for Lynn, smoothing over her outfit while taking deep, steady breaths.

"Jayla," Lynn greeted, carrying a beige folder. "I thought I said to call me?"

"Oh, I'm sorry, I forgot," Jayla apologized, wondering why she was feeling so nervous.

"Thanks again for coming in on short notice," Lynn remarked as they walked toward her office. "Just a few things from Friday I forgot to discuss."

Then, rather than making a right down the hall as Jayla anticipated, Lynn stopped at an unassuming gray door that, when opened, revealed a long, narrow set of stairs to an upper level. *So, there IS a second floor*, Jayla laughed to herself, recalling Dr. Molech's shock at her spatial cluelessness.

"We'll be talking in Dr. Molech's private office. It's bigger than mine," Lynn intimated with marked annoyance.

Jayla gazed up at the staircase, too slender for the pair to ascend shoulder to shoulder. "Who all is coming tonight?" probed Jayla, preparing herself for any surprise guests.

"Just the three of us. It's the same conversation we all need to have," Lynn assured, holding the door open with her free hand. "After you."

Jayla squeezed upward on the drawn-out flight of stairs until reaching the top, where they approached an open door sporting a black plaque on which was etched, *Dr. Molech*.

Lynn walked inside the office authoritatively. Against the left wall sat a leather couch and matching chairs. Next to that was a long bookcase filled with medical texts, on top of which rested a record player, a smattering of well-worn vinyl records, and a small metal bowl, resting atop little wooden legs, inside which burned incense smelling of cypress and frankincense. Along the wall hung pictures of Molech's wife and dogs, and medical degrees. In the middle of the room was a long oak desk behind which Dr. Molech sat bleary-eyed, slowly turning his gaze beyond the cheap cup of noodles he slurped unhurriedly.

"I thought I told you to get rid of that thing," Lynn quipped as Dr. Molech chewed a mouthful of noodles. "You're going to burn this whole place down. How that incense doesn't set off the smoke alarms is beyond me," Lynn grumbled.

"Take the batteries out, and it's as quiet as a mouse," Dr. Molech chuckled. "Ah—Jayla! How nice to see you," he greeted, happy for a change of topic. "Have a seat, have a seat," he beckoned, motioning to the leather furniture where Lynn had already made herself at home. "How was your weekend?"

"Fine," Jayla lied, smiling back at the doctor but inwardly feeling disgusted. *Toss it in the trash*, she could still hear his voice ringing in her ears as she approached the seats.

"So," Lynn asserted, "thank you both for taking time out of your busy schedules to meet with me. We need to talk about this past Friday night."

"Everything is alright, I hope. Jayla and I made sure everything was done to the letter. The patient should be recovering nicely," Dr. Molech said nervously.

"To my knowledge, everything is great," affirmed Lynn to the relief of the room. "That being said, her father would like for us to fill these out," she said, opening the folder and handing a sheet and a pen to both Jayla and Dr. Molech. "A *tying up loose ends* sort of thing."

Jayla looked at the form labeled *Nondisclosure Agreement* and waded through the opaque legal terms and multi-syllable words. Finally, at the bottom of the document was a place for her to sign her name. "What is this for?"

"It's so you don't share anything about the patient you looked after Friday evening or about the people or circumstances that may have brought her here. You didn't recognize the girl. She came in alone and on her own recognizance or something like that. It's all there. Just sign it," Lynn explained.

Jayla's eyes returned to the form. "It says breaking this could result in being sued or being subject to an *injunction*? What is that?" Jayla queried as Dr. Molech handed Lynn his autographed form.

"Read the document for yourself. Basically, it just says that if you tell people what happened to *her*, bad things will happen to *you*—and if you keep your mouth shut, then everything will be great. It's not much different than the one you signed when you were employed, they just want their own version signed," Lynn replied impatiently. Then, seeing Jayla's hesitancy to sign, groaned. "What's the problem here?"

"I'm just not sure I should sign it," Jayla expressed. "The girl from Friday, Miss Crix, she—"

"You told her *her name*!?" Lynn snapped at Dr. Molech, who sputtered in his chair.

"She—you—I had to call the young lady *something*!" he weakly defended, swiveling back and forth from one woman to the other. "You—you never said *not*—"

"It was *implied*," Lynn condescendingly interrupted.

"She said she didn't want the abortion. That her dad made her do it," Jayla divulged. "That's so *wrong* on so many levels. And, you're saying, if I sign this, I can never legally tell anyone what he did, ever?"

"This deal gets better and better," Lynn laughed to herself. "He forced her to do it? Did she tell you that? That's a *huge* win for us. Tell me that was caught on camera."

A win? Jayla parroted to herself in disbelief as Dr. Molech affirmed, "Yes, their conversation happened in the operating room, so it was on our security cameras."

"And they say good things don't happen to good people," Lynn grinned, placing that vital information into the safety deposit box of her mind. Obviously, this information was of some value to her somewhere—somehow.

"How is this good? Are you even hearing what I'm saying? He *hurt* her," Jayla emphasized emotionally.

"Yes, and the more he hurts her, the better it is for us," Lynn replied calculatingly. "This is ammunition for our cause, don't you see, if we ever had to use it. And in the right hands, at the right time, it could be absolutely explosive. Crix has changed party platforms before. He rides the fence as a social liberal with a pro-life bent. For him it is all about the votes." Lynn's eyes took on an evil look.

"So we don't care anymore about if a woman is brought in here against her will? I thought you were pro-women? I thought we were helping people here?" Jayla accused.

"I *live* for the women who come into this clinic!" Lynn reprimanded ardently. "A part of me *died* Friday when I heard the terrible news of what this country's high court had done. But that all changed with a little phone call from the governor's personal assistant. That teenager and her abortion just saved this election for us! And for that, we can expect the governor's behind-the-scenes support. And if he doesn't, then we have our own Plan B pill for him now, don't we?"

"What are you talking about?" Jayla asked, as Lynn rolled her eyes.

"Are you kidding me? You really don't see it?" Lynn asked, then staring at Dr. Molech continued, "tell me you see it. That *procedure* was a blank check with our names on it! We can use it to negotiate whatever deal we want. If he loses the re-election, we win because this state can finally become totally liberal and free. If he wins the election, we win because he won't be able to make any real change, not that he or any of his former conservative cronies ever wanted the vote to go this way in the first place. Goodbye *30 percent of the vote*! Goodbye *only reason for you being in office*! So yes, one girl got hurt, and I hate that. But that one girl may have just ransomed all the women in this state for the next four years!"

"Two girls," Jayla corrected. "Two girls were hurt. The teenager *and* her baby."

"Oh, don't you start growing a conscience on me," Lynn sneered. "You knew what we did here before you even applied for the job. Don't lose your appetite just because you've seen how the sausage gets made."

"I quit," Jayla announced, dumbfounding the rest of the room. "I don't want to do this anymore."

"You *quit*. You . . ." Lynn shook her head, falling back into her chair in disbelief. "I'm *disappointed* in you, Jayla. I really am. I can't believe how absolutely childish you're being."

"Perhaps sending in a pregnant woman to help with a procedure of this nature was a touch—insensitive," Dr. Molech offered.

"Come on, Jayla. Stay with us. You're on the smart side. The winning side. Don't let one ten-ounce blob of tissue derail your whole career."

"You can't talk me out of it. I've made up my mind," Jayla stated adamantly, proudly, as she smoothed over the front of her shirt. "I quit."

"Fine. But you can't go until you sign the form," Lynn said in frustration as she pushed the form and pen closer to Jayla. "And Molech, will you please blow out that incense. It's giving me a headache and making the whole room smell like smo—"

Suddenly the sound of the downstairs fire alarms began blaring beneath their feet, muffled by layers of concrete and moldy insulation.

"What is that?" Lynn asked in a panic, looking around the room. "Is that the fire alarm? Why isn't it going off in here? You freakin' moron! The building is on fire!" she shrieked.

Jayla sprang from her chair and raced to the exit as the others followed at her heels.

"Move, move, move!" Dr. Molech shouted from behind as they ran through the dingy hall, the smell of smoke intensifying. Flinging the door to the stairwell open, a plume of black smoke hit Jayla in the face, stinging her eyes. "Move it! Go! Go!" he barked again the sensation of heat grew hotter as she descended the stairs.

Feeling the side of the wall for support, Jayla scurried down the narrow stairs as quickly as she could. Then Lynn squeezed past her in the tight space, ramming her with her shoulder as she advanced. Jayla felt her center of gravity shift as she struggled to maintain balance, Dr. Molech prodding and bumping her from behind with every step. The air was hot, the stairs were narrow, the smoke was heavy as Jayla felt Dr. Molech begin to make a move to pass her. An elbow clumsily knocked into the back of Jayla's head as the doctor's hips connected with her lower back, pushing her completely off balance, as she tumbled face-first down upon the hard steps.

Stair after stair impacted Jayla as she plummeted with outstretched arms down the remainder of the staircase. Her legs and stomach careened full force down onto the blunt stair edges. Her vulnerable frame flailed and twisted, scarcely missing Lynn as she plunged to the bottom, where she lay motionless, dizzy, and bleeding. As the bawling of the fire alarm shattered the air, Jayla felt a pair of clumsy shoes trample her. As the door to the hall was opened, a fresh gust of fumes entered the stairwell, and for the first time, Jayla could see the inferno. Hands of orange and fingers of yellow beckoned and stretched in discontent, tongues of flame licking the skin off the walls until the bones of the building were exposed.

It was then, in the deepening darkness, Jayla's eyes finally closed, and she lost herself in a backdraft of unconsciousness.

CHAPTER 38

GET WELL SOON

The sound of nurses gossiping nudged Jayla back to consciousness. Every inch of her body ached. Her ribs felt bruised, her stomach was cramping, her lungs felt like they had been turned inside out. Slowly, barely able to open her eyes into a squint, Jayla was blinded by brightness of her surroundings.

"She's *awake*," one of the nurses whispered, followed by the hushed sound of footsteps pitter-pattering out of the room.

"Oh, so *now* you care about what happens to my baby," Jayla heard a raspy voice crack as a withered, cold hand touched her forehead and cheek. Unable to believe what she was hearing, Jayla squinted her eyes open further and found Amarika leaning over her attentively, caressing her hair. "I'm so glad you're awake now, baby," Amarika doted warmly, then snapping to the nurse, growled, "Why don't you be helpful for once and get my daughter a glass of water?"

Gradually, the room came into focus. The walls were white as far as she could see, while a few flower arrangements were scattered around the room. Protruding out of her wrist was an IV. She could feel the prongs of an oxygen tube in her nose as the beeping sound of her heart rate began to rise. "Where am I?" Jayla asked faintly.

"You're at the hospital, baby. You were brought in two days ago," Amarika said tenderly. "You've been through so much, baby, but you gonna be alright. Mom is here to take care of you."

"Two days?" repeated Jayla, feeling like she was in a dream.

"Two days. Um, that's right. You've been in and out, but mostly out. I bet you're thirsty," Amarika soothed and then shouted, "Where is that water for my daughter? Don't you know she's been through enough already! Where's that nurse call button?"

Jayla moaned as she tried to move in bed, the pain all-encompassing. "What happened?" she asked.

"You don't remember?" Amarika asked, surprised. "Baby, it's all over the news." Reaching for the TV remote attached to the hospital bed, Amarika turned up the volume as Jayla heard her name being pronounced over the morning news report while a video of firefighters hosing down her torched workplace flashed into view.

"This is just one of a frightening number of attacks on abortion and anti-abortion clinics across the country since the unprecedented Supreme Court leak. Well—and now full overturn. What has made this incident of particular interest is that Jayla Cadel—the viral sensation better known as the *Abortion Angel*—was inside when her workplace was set on fire," a news anchor revealed, as clips of the shaky footage of a disguised Jayla wielding two umbrellas came onto the screen.

"*Set on fire?*" asked Jayla, images of that night flooding her mind. "Someone did it on purpose?"

"Police are urging anyone from the public to come forward if they have any information on the whereabouts of this man in connection with the suspected act of arson," the reporter announced as a cropped picture of a tall, lanky man in a ball cap and a familiar uniform came into view.

"Is that . . ." Jayla paused, doubling her focus on the image in disbelief. "Darla's *husband?*"

"You know that man?" asked Amarika, turning down the volume on the TV as a nurse returned with a cup of water. "Can we maybe get some lunch too? Look at my baby. She hasn't eaten in days! We're nothing but skin and bones over here."

As the nurse fled the room, a tall female doctor entered. "Good afternoon, Miss Cadel. I'm so glad you're awake," she greeted, grabbing Jayla's chart from the foot of her bed. "Do you know where you are?"

"I'm in—the hospital," replied Jayla, the moment feeling too surreal to be happening.

"That's right. The firefighters and paramedics got to you right in time. You might not be here right now if they were even just a few minutes later to respond," the doctor advised gravely. "Do you remember anything about what happened?"

Jayla thought for a moment, reliving the event. "There was a fire; I was running down the stairs when I fell."

"It's amazing you haven't suffered any fractures with a fall like that," the doctor remarked, consulting the medical folder. "Although, you do have severe bruising and a few lacerations over your body. It probably feels like you've been in a car accident right now."

"Yeah."

"I also have some unfortunate news to share with you," the woman said, putting Jayla's chart to the side. "The impact to your abdomen on the stairs caused you to have a miscarriage while you were unconscious."

"Miscarriage?" Jayla and Amarika repeated as Amarika's eyes turned to her daughter in surprise.

"Sadly, yes. Because of that, over the next two weeks, you will be experiencing some cramping and bleeding like a period. This will gradually get lighter over time until it stops. So don't be concerned when that happens, as it's part of your body healing itself."

"Okay," Jayla winced, waves of guilt and remorse and relief washing over her.

"I also wanted to tell you, should you need to talk with someone, we have several grief counselors and a chaplain on site you can talk to," the doctor delicately said as she returned the chart to the foot of the bed.

"I didn't raise no weak daughter," Amarika declined, scoffing at the idea of counselors or chaplains. "You tell everybody that my daughter doesn't want to talk to nobody."

"That's not for you to decide. It's up to her," the doctor countered, unfazed by Amarika's toxic nastiness. Then, looking again to Jayla, she continued, "And there actually is someone else you'll need to talk to. There's a police officer waiting outside who would like to talk with you about what happened Monday night whenever you're ready."

"The girl just woke up! Give her time to breathe," Amarika erupted. "All these doctors and nurses and ain't nobody looking after my baby but me."

Completely ignoring Amarika's tantrum, the doctor's gaze remained steadfast on Jayla. "No rush, just whenever you're ready."

A few moments after the doctor left the room, Amarika turned to her daughter, a look of confusion on her face. "A miscarriage?" she asked, her eyebrow raised, holding back a smile. "You told me you weren't pregnant," she reminded. "Listen to me, child, you shouldn't be talking to the police, you hear. You get a lawyer first. You're a bi-racial girl, and to them that means black. But when it all hits the fan, the man always sees you on the colored side. They'd try to pin this on you in a minute. You hear me? *Abortion Angel* could become the *Abortion Arson* in a heartbeat."

"I need some time to myself," Jayla replied, turning her head away from Amarika, hoping for some time to process the news free of scrutiny or shame. Would they find out she was working for a pro-life pregnancy center too? This could easily look very bad, very quick.

"Okay, baby. I'll tell those nurses to leave you alone," Amarika said, taking a sip out of the water brought for her daughter.

"No, I want to be *alone*, alone," demanded Jayla, her face still away from Amarika.

"What? Now that you're awake I can't stay?" Amarika seethed. "I've been sleeping in that chair next to you, never once leaving your side since I found out what happened to you."

Jayla slowly rolled her head back to Amarika, and said, "You've been here the whole time?"

"Of course, Jay," Amarika smiled. "Momma is always there for her baby."

Something didn't sit right with Jayla. "Why are you here, *really*?" she asked suspiciously "Staying here overnight, being sweet to me, calling me *baby*. Something is up."

Amarika grinned as she set aside the façade of an attentive, affectionate mother. "There's a friend of mine I want you to see. A lawyer named Morgansberg or Morganstien. Yes, that's it. He called me up when he saw what was on the news, and he told me—" Amarika held back a squeal of excitement. "He told me we can sue that abortion clinic you were working for. We might could even sue the whole corporation! Unsafe workplace, he said, or something like that. He said this is our big break! And he doesn't charge any money, only if he wins."

"Big break?" Jayla repeated. "Whose big break?"

"Ours, Jay! This is what we've been waiting for! All those years of triple shifts and slumming, and now we are about to get what's ours!"

"I'm not suing anybody," Jayla stated as Amarika scooted closer.

"Then you a fool and not the woman I raised you to be. Either you take the offensive, or you—you might be on the defensive for something I know my baby would've never done."

"And who did you raise me to be, exactly? You didn't raise me to be anyone because you never raised me at all! All you did was leave me alone with your boyfriends or come home and punish me for doing nothing wrong!"

"Who were all those shifts for? Huh? Why were all those men around? It was to keep a roof over your head, and clothes on your back, and food in your stomach."

"They hurt me!" Jayla wailed, freshly drudged-up memories spewing over. "They touched me, abused me! Me, your daughter. Raped me! And you—you did nothing! You took their side. You picked those men over me *every time*. You were supposed to protect me! You were supposed to—"

"Let you starve? Live on the streets? This world ain't easy. I did what I had to do to keep you safe!"

"You did what you had to do to keep *yourself* safe."

"How do you think I felt? Have you ever once stopped to ask how I felt knowing you were getting hurt and there was nothing I could do about it? Or how it felt to have those same men with me after knowing what they did to you? Me working triple shifts, being manhandled from the moment I got home, never sleeping, always worrying, all so my ungrateful daughter could grow up and say I never raised her. Poor women don't have nobody to call."

"Then why didn't we leave?" the little girl inside Jayla pleaded. "If you were so miserable, why didn't we go? Just disappear?"

"Because that's not how real life works! That's how fairytales work. That's what rich people do. We can't do that. People like us can't leave one branch before we find another to hold onto. And now—now we finally have a big branch in front of us that we can grab! Now we can finally be safe, be settled. If we're smart about this, we can cash out and never have to work another day in our lives. Then we can be family again," Amarika bargained.

"I had a family once," Jayla stated as Amarika popped out of her chair and threw her hands in the air.

"Oh, don't start with this again."

"Mrs. Neidringhouse loved me. She and her husband cared about me—really cared. There was nothing in it for them, and they still loved me. When I screamed at them and tore pages out of their Bibles or purposefully wouldn't come home days at a time. They didn't leave me, and they never laid a hand on me. They loved me through it all. That's who my family was. Not you. Never you."

"Then where is your family now? Hmm? If they were so good to you, how come they're not here with you now?"

Jayla knew the reason her beloved Auntie and Uncle were out of her life. She remembered vividly how she ran away from their home when she was sixteen years old, just hours after they told her they wanted to adopt her. She recalled the leap of her heart at being told she was someone worth wanting, and the crushing, crippling fear that one day, maybe someday soon, she might wake up to find they had changed their minds. She could still see the moment she came to the decision that it was better for her to leave the love extended to her than to have something so precious, so wonderful taken from her.

"If they're so perfect, why is it only me who's here?" Amarika pushed, looking around the empty room. "You know how you got out of that fire? How you've survived all these years? It's because I made you a survivor. I made you a fighter. All gold has to go through the fire, baby. But you the stronger for it."

"I'm the gold?" Jayla clarified as her mind worked through Amarika's analogy.

"That's right, Jay," Amarika smiled, getting closer, seeing her words penetrating Jayla's heart.

"Then what does that make you?" Jayla asked rhetorically, a mixture of hurt and malice in her eyes. "I want you to know that whatever happens—whoever I sue or don't sue, for however much it is or isn't—you won't see a single penny from this gold."

Amarika grinned with a mixture of pride and disappointment as she smoothed over the front of her wrinkled blouse. "Okay. You need your rest. I get it. I'll come back by tomorrow to see how you're doing."

"I don't want you to come back," Jayla declared as Amarika opened the door to leave.

Amarika turned around and looked at her with genuine sympathy. "You know, we're a lot more alike than you might like to admit. You may hate me for what I did to you. But that's okay. A mother's job is a thankless job. I get it. But whether you like it or not, you and I are the same, Jay."

"I'm nothing like you!" Jayla called out through a hoarse voice as the door closed behind Amarika.

That last exchange rang through Jayla's ears for the next several hours. She was still trying to process the tangled emotions of the miscarriage and the last few days. Of course, there was the ever-lingering shadow of fear of what could go wrong at any minute in her new narrative.

After her conversation with the police detailing everything she could remember about the arson, Jayla settled into a restless nap, each twitch of her body ushering in a fresh sensation of pain. Half awake, half asleep, Jayla stirred as nurses scuttled in and out, their sneakers squeaking against the polished floor, checking her vitals and scrawling notes.

"Jayla?" a familiar Spanish voice rang softly from the doorway. Jayla opened her eyes to find Renee peeking in with a bouquet of pink and red flowers in her hand. As soon as it became obvious Jayla was resting, Renee quietly began backtracking. "Oh, I'm sorry. I'll come back later."

"No, no. It's okay. I haven't been able to sleep much anyway," Jayla maintained as Renee meekly re-entered the room.

"We've been praying for you ever since we heard your name on the news," Renee shared, presenting Jayla with the flowers and a little note with the LifeLine Pregnancy Center watermark that read, *We love you, Jayla! Get well soon!*

"This is really nice, thanks," Jayla remarked, handing the bouquet back to Renee who found a spot for it against the window ledge.

"How are you feeling?" Renee asked.

"Sore. Like I've been hit by a Mack truck," complained Jayla as she used the remote to her electric bed to sit up a little more.

"I'm so sorry to hear that, that sounds really rough," Renee sympathized as she took a seat in the chair where Amarika had allegedly spent the night. "Has the doctor said if you'll be in here long?"

"I'm not sure," Jayla said. "I only woke up a few hours ago."

Renee nodded. "The last twenty-four hours have been such a mess of confusion and heartbreak for me—for LifeLine—I'm still trying to wrap my head around it," she lamented. "So you were at the abortion clinic across town?"

Jayla's eyes grew large with the recognition that her two lives had messily converged while she was unconscious. Fear gripped her heart as the wheels of deception worked hard to spin. "Yes," she said succinctly. Her mind walked a razor's edge, knowing she didn't really know what was public knowledge yet.

"Why were you there? Was it to get an abortion?" Renee asked, gently prying.

"No," Jayla answered again.

"So then what were you doing there? Were you somehow there with Darla's husband?"

"What was Darla's husband doing there?" Jayla redirected, changing the subject to her favor.

A look of heartache broke across Renee's face. "I still can't believe. It all just seems unreal, like how can any of this be happening? Darla's in pieces, as you can imagine."

"*Darla* is in pieces? What about me?!" railed Jayla. "Her crazy husband tried to *kill* me!"

"But why were you there in the first place? Some of us thought you might be somehow working with him," Renee asked again. "On the news they're saying that you *worked* for that place; is that true?"

"And if I was, does that give Clem the green light to set me on fire?" Jayla replied, finally seeing she had nothing left to hide behind. "I did work there. Yes. For a while," her mind still racing to find the best spin.

"At the same time you worked for us?" Renee questioned, astonished to hear the confession. "Were you one of those people they send over to spy on what we are doing and saying?"

"No— uh—I was—spying on them," Jayla replied. "You know, keeping an eye on how they do things and ways that Lifeline could do better." As the words flowed from her mouth, she realized what a poor narrative she had spun.

Renee stared dumbfounded at Jayla. "Why are you lying? It's all on the news—all of it."

"Well, if it's ALL on the news, why ask me in the first place? It ain't never ALL on the news."

"Jayla, I came here today as your friend because I care about you, but seeing you like this—have you been lying to us the whole time?"

Jayla was silent as she turned her eyes away from Renee and onto the flowers behind her—guilt, anger, remorse, fear flooding through her.

"What about your college classes, was that a lie too?" Renee asked, standing to her feet, but again was answered with a reply of silence. "The paper receipts? Aren't you going to say anything to me?"

"It sounds like you've made up your mind," Jayla said dismissively, counting the number of petals in a bouquet of tulips, as her mind chose to lean on the anger.

"I don't want to do this, but as you're leaving me no other option. Unless you can somehow make sense of all this for me, I have to terminate your employment with the center effective immediately," she then pleaded, "*but give me something to work with, and I'll take it back to the board.* Help me here. *Please.*"

"What about Darla? Are you going to terminate her?" Jayla confronted. "Or do the donors like arsonists now?"

"Okay," Renee concluded. "Okay. I think we know what has to happen."

"I guess we do," Jayla replied, her eyes still distracted as Renee walked to the foot of Jayla's bed.

"Sam's outside worried sick about you. She let me come in first since you're only allowed one visitor at a time. Be more courteous to her than you were to me. She's taking all this really hard," Renee implored. "And if you ever need anything, or if you ever want to help me understand what happened, I'll be there for you. Employee or not, I want you to know I'm there for you. Jayla, I do love you."

Jayla knew she could look away from the flowers when the sound of Renee's small strides became inaudible. Then, bracing herself, she heard another set of quick steps approaching as Samantha stuck her head through the door, her eyes puffy and red.

"Oh, sweetheart," Sam soothed, seeing Jayla lying in bed. "You poor, poor thing. Are you okay? I have been praying non-stop for you."

Jayla nodded, feeling unable to speak. Samantha came closer to the hospital bed, a used tissue in hand. "And the baby?" she whispered in anxious fear.

Jayla's eyes couldn't meet Samantha's. Despite the pain, she shook her head, and Samantha began to cry, her hands covering her mouth as she perched on the corner of Jayla's bed. "Oh no," she shook, gasping, choking on her sobs. "*My baby*," she mourned softly to herself. "*My baby.*"

Jayla felt her own eyes begin to fill with tears. "So—you would have . . ." she began. Before she could finish, Samantha was nodding her head.

"Ricky and I finally agreed on something. But now, I guess the Lord had other plans," Samantha swallowed, wiping her nose with the used tissue. "I just—I don't know how I'll tell him the news."

The taste of sadness Jayla was finally able to access soured inside her, churning on Samantha's statement and frothing to the surface as indignation. "Rick!" she fumed, thoughts of his affair and of her past abusers coalescing in her mind. "Some dad he would have been!"

Samantha looked at Jayla through wounded eyes, the salt of her words doused over her open heart. "What's that supposed to mean?"

"Oh, wake up, Sam," Jayla quipped. "He didn't want to be a dad in the first place. This will probably be the best day of his life when you tell him the news."

"I don't know where this is coming from," Samantha began softly, "and I know you're in a lot of pain right now, and probably this wasn't the best time to come and visit."

"Yeah, why did you come and visit, Sam? Did you come to find out how I was doing because you care about me? Or because of the baby?" Jayla spat out, sensing a pattern between Samantha's and Amarika's visits. Her thoughts became wild and unsteady as an oddly possessive jealousy intensified within her. "You don't care anything about me at all, do you?"

"Of course, I care about you!" Sam defended, blindsided by the accusation. "I'm your friend. You know I—."

"This wasn't *your* baby, Sam. It was mine! You didn't see any of the hurt I was going through because you didn't care. Nobody cares! No wonder your husband is cheating on you!" Jayla shouted, punishing Samantha for being more distraught over her unborn baby than she was.

"Now that is enough!" Samantha exclaimed, jumping to her feet. "I don't know what's gotten into you. We're both grieving, but this—this has gone too far!"

"Go home and ask him. Look him in the eyes and ask him. The man's been cheating on you for months! Are you Christians just blind?"

Samantha opened her mouth to speak but couldn't as anger, fear, and grief overwhelmed her. Without a word, her face crumbled as she rapidly left the room.

As the door clicked shut, Amarika's words replayed in Jayla's mind like a prophecy coming to fruition. *Whether you like it or not, you and I are the same.* "We're not the same," Jayla declared loudly to the silence of the vacant room. "Sam needed to know. I'm protecting her. Maybe now she won't be weak and get used anymore."

As the sun began to dip lower into the southwestern skyline outside Jayla's hospital window, her sense of restlessness heightened. Jayla rotated mindlessly through the TV channels for any distraction. She was surprised by the interviews these news broadcasts were garnering. First, there was the segment featuring Dr. Molech, in which he gave a vivid first-hand description of what it was like to be trapped inside the burning building. Then there was the dialogue one reporter had with a sunburned, camera-hungry Nikole in which she not only called Jayla her best friend but said she wanted to kick-start a fundraiser in her honor. Finally, there was a news conference outside the hospital where Lynn appeared.

Jayla watched as Lynn rained down acid upon the radical right, dangerous pro-lifers, and crazy Christians. "The wacky-religious-zealot-pro-lifers have opened up a can of worms they can't swallow. Mark my words; this overturn will be the greatest victory ever for a woman's right to choose. And what they did to my center will be the nail in their casket!" Then the piece cut to protesting going on across the country for women's right to choose. Though much of it was old stock footage, the clip appeared as if the entire female world had risen in revolt.

"Do I look good on the TV or what?" Lynn smiled, giving Jayla a fright. "Oh, I'm sorry! I didn't mean to scare you."

"What are you doing in here?" Jayla winced, confused, disoriented, and in anguish.

"It's still visiting hours," Lynn explained as she looked at her watch. "I still have forty-two minutes that I can be in here, and I only need five of them. So, how are you feeling? The last two days have been pretty unreal, wouldn't you say?"

"I'm alright," Jayla murmured, her body racked with pain. "You know, Dr. Molech is the reason I'm in here. He pushed me down those stairs."

"Pushed you down the stairs? Why, that's absurd. We were all doing what we could to escape. It's that awful crazy man's fault—the right-wing religious firebug. I just have no idea how someone can call themselves *pro-life* and try to kill me at the same time," Lynn mused before perking up. "You'll be happy to know that we've been invited to New York to speak at the Unplanned Incorporated National Convention!"

"We?" asked Jayla. "Why?"

"Because, my dear, we're famous! You're the *Abortion Angel* conservatives tried to set on fire and send to hell! And as they say, hell hath no fury like a woman's scorn. We might even get a book deal out of this. I could even get a promotion," Lynn exclaimed. "That redneck has most likely just lost the re-election for Crix. That's a fact, an absolute fact. And he's helped the whole country see how we are on the right side of this issue. And, on top of all that, if my commissioner comes through, that little pregnancy resource whatever on the other side of town will be forced to move in two months. This is the best-case scenario possible."

"What?" Jayla responded.

"Because of *Roe*, and all the other stuff going on, cities across the country are creating ordinances to remove these pro-life fake clinics from their towns. They will have to sell their precious buildings and move out to the country. Their business is over. Their shot around the world was into their own foot." Lynn giggled like a schoolgirl invited to her first dance.

"But, ah, how about the. . . ." Jayla tried to form a thought, but Lynn was on one of her rants.

"You know how all these fake clinics have those fake ultrasound stork buses? Well, I have three motor homes coming in next week. Fire or not, we are back open using their own mobile clinic playbook to keep a woman's right to choose."

"I'm in the *hospital, and you are talking about book deals and motor homes?*" Jayla chided in disgust.

"But you're *alive*," Lynn reminded her.

"And in a lot of pain!" Jayla asserted. "And they told me I had a miscarriage."

"You lost the baby?" Lynn asked, pausing to consider the additional ramifications. "That's even better!" she proclaimed, eliciting a torrent of profanity from Jayla. "What I mean is, not only will this lowlife creep get jail time for setting the fire, but he'll go to jail for killing your baby as well. Isn't that good news?"

"How is it a crime that I lost my baby but not a crime that the Crix girl lost her baby?"

"They're not babies! They're fetuses!" Lynn snapped. "And that fetus of yours is going to help us protect a whole bunch of women who want to have a life."

"I want you to leave now," Jayla warned, lowering her bed and pushing the call button on the rail next to her for assistance.

"But we have more to talk about," Lynn deflated as the nurse stepped into the room.

"No, we don't," Jayla asserted. Then, turning to the nurse, she said emphatically, "I want this woman out of here. And I need pain medication. Lots of pain medication."

CHAPTER 39

KNOCK-KNOCK.
WHO'S THERE?

When the time came for Jayla to be discharged from the hospital two days later, she had no one to call to give her a ride home but Uber. Entering her empty apartment, she sat her prescription of Tramadol on the counter along with the flowers she was gifted during her stay. Her body was stiff and rigid and aching with every step. Hobbling to the kitchen, she unpacked the small bag of groceries waiting on the doorstep that included little more than a few packs of chips and a bottle of brandless whisky she took with her back to her bedroom, leaving the cups in the pantry.

Settling down upon her coil mattress that squeaked and protested under her repositioning weight, Jayla unscrewed the whisky cap and, for the first time in nearly five months, took a drink, followed by half a bottle more. Jayla measured the rest of her first day home in gulps and swigs, eventually venturing to the living room to endure some reality TV through a broken screen as she gradually nursed herself to sleep.

The following morning Jayla awoke on the carpet beside her couch, her head splitting and her body racked with pain. The smell of unflushed vomit emanated from the toilet. Since her vehicle was still in the parking lot of what remained of her former smoldering workplace, Jayla spent the day sequestered at home, splurging on DoorDash takeout and having more choice liquors catered to her home via her iPhone.

A jarring knock at the door woke Jayla suddenly. *Did I order something?* she wondered to herself as she unevenly rolled out of bed, another severe hangover tugging her head in opposing directions. Stumbling to the doorway, haphazardly kicking an empty bottle along the way, she cracked open the door to find a bronzed man in a suit behind whom hovered two bodyguards.

"Jayla! It is so good to finally meet you!" the man greeted with a luminant smile, wearing a pin with his face on it that read *Re-Elect Governor Crix.* Jayla slammed the door in his face, stupefied as to what was happening. Then, opening the door again to the startled governor, Jayla, disheveled and smelling of puke, blurted out, "One minute," and slammed the door for the second time.

Am I still drunk? Jayla asked herself as she tidied up the apartment, trying to move speedily but restrained by her bruised mobility. Then, changing her clothes for the first time since coming home and fixing her hair, she cupped her hand, breathed into it, and winced. By the time she had transformed herself and her home into a state just north of awful, the one minute she promised Governor Crix had stretched to five.

Re-opening the door for a third time, Jayla found the governor concentrating on his phone. Then, noticing Jayla, he reactivated like a triggered automaton. "Jayla! It's so nice to finally meet you!" he restated, sticking out his hand for a handshake as Jayla heard a camera snapping pictures in the background. "Mind if we step in for a moment?"

Jayla held the door open as the governor, his two bodyguards, and personal photographer stepped inside.

"My, what a lovely home you have here, Jayla," Governor Crix complimented through impeccably whitened teeth. "Or do you prefer Miss Cadel?"

"Jayla is fine," Jayla said, her head feeling flattened by a hammer and in much need of some caffeine. "What—uh—why are you here?"

"I heard about what happened to you on the news, and I wanted to come by personally to see how you were managing," Governor Crix explained sympathetically.

"You're here to check on me? Jayla asked, remembering bits of her last conversation with Lynn. "Are you sure you're not here because your number one fan burning down the abortion clinic has made you drop in the polls?"

Governor Crix was impressed. "Well, maybe that too," he chuckled, then, leaning closer, said with regret, "And, may I say, on a personal level, I am so very sorry for your loss." Memories of his daughter, her abortion, her admission, and his hypocrisy came rushing to her mind. "I might say the same thing to you," she countered, catching the politician off guard, his thousand-watt smile going rapidly ashen.

"Jayla, can we, uh—" Crix began and then, looking around at his people, insisted, "Guys, can we have the room, please?" Jayla listened as the bodyguards fussed over the irregular and unsafe request before being sterned into submission by the red-faced independent conservative. "I'm not asking! I'm telling you. Wait outside until I come out."

Suddenly it didn't seem like such a good idea to Jayla to be left alone with the politician, and her nervous heart was hoping for the agents to remain at their post for her own safety. Nevertheless, the room cleared against her will.

"Well, Jayla, I must admit I expected for us to dance around this for a while, but it seems you're the type of person to cut straight to the chase. And I appreciate that about you," Governor Crix recognized as he pulled out a white form and extended it to Jayla, the top of which read *Nondisclosure Agreement*. "You're the only one left that I need a signature from."

"I'm not signing that," Jayla obstinately rejected, crossing her arms authoritatively and refusing the paper.

"Why? What's in this for you?" the indignant man chortled in disbelief. "How do you *possibly* benefit from not signing this?"

"Because I want everyone to know what you did," Jayla glared.

"What *I did*? What did I do?" demanded the governor, confused by her remark.

"Your daughter told me everything," Jayla said.

"Oh, she did, did she?" he asked, an amused expression on his face. "And what is *everything* exactly?"

"She told me she never wanted to get the abortion. That you made her do it so you wouldn't look bad," Jayla revealed, unsure if she shared too much.

"Of course, she wanted to get it done. Why wouldn't she? She's seventeen and has her whole life ahead of her. It's the best decision she could have made—at least, from what she thinks." The governor began to falter as his impassioned explanation stumbled over the lowered bar of his professed ideals. "I, on the other hand," he course-corrected, straightening out his crimson tie, "I tried my best to talk her out of it. As you know, my personal belief is abortion isn't the answer, but teenagers don't often listen to their parents. Sadly, in the end, I felt like it was her mistake to make, and like your other job always says, Jesus heals and forgives. Yes. I know all about your double-life, Jayla. Don't be self-righteous with me."

"But she *didn't* make the decision. You took that from her. You *made her* get the abortion," Jayla shouted. "And that's—that's abuse! And people need to know that."

"I've never laid a hand on my daughter in my life!" Crix reeled at the accusation, raising his voice to Jayla's volume.

"Forcing someone to have an abortion *is abuse*! Even if Jesus forgives," Jayla declared, breathing heavily.

"You know what," Governor Crix began, pulling out his latest-generation smartphone and holding it up to his ear. "Send her in."

The pair glowered at one another in silence as the front door to the apartment creaked open. Jayla anticipated seeing Lynn strutting into her living room. Instead, to her dismay, a young, beautiful blonde-haired teenager entered wearing a modest red dress.

"Hi, Daddy," the girl addressed respectfully as she walked up to the governor and gave him a kiss on the cheek, planting herself next to him. "Hello, Jayla. It's so nice to see you again. Thank you again so much for the excellent care you gave me the other night."

"Princess," the governor said to his daughter, "Jayla here is under the impression that I somehow forced you into getting a pregnancy reversal against your will. Is that true?"

The teenager looked back at her dad and then at Jayla, hurt in her eyes. "No, Daddy. Of course, that isn't true."

"There. See," Crix clapped his hands. "You heard her. Now, will you sign the form already?"

"But," Jayla pushed back, "the other night, you said—"

"Yes, I'm afraid I wasn't quite feeling myself that evening. The medicine I took was making me a little loopy. It sounds like I was saying things I should never be saying," the teenager reasoned, a smile on her lips but pain resonating through every other inch of her face. "I feel so silly about it. I'm so sorry if I gave you cause for concern."

"There you have it," the politician concluded, wrapping a powerful arm around his daughter. "And, Princess, I'm sorry to say, but Jayla is thinking about telling more people about your pregnancy reversal."

"Why would she do that? That could ruin my reputation," the girl asked, sounding scripted and hollow.

"She thinks she's helping you by speaking up for you," her daddy explained somberly. "But you don't want that, do you?"

"No, Daddy," the teen declined, looking at Jayla. "I don't need anyone else telling my story. My life is my private life."

With a smug look, the politician continued his line of questioning. "And would I ever do anything to hurt you?"

"No, Daddy. You're pro-life, pro-family, and pro-business," she said robotically. "It was my body, and it was my choice. You wanted me to stop, but I insisted. And now, I wish I hadn't." Tears began to fill her eyes.

"See, Jayla, you've got it backward. I tried to stop my daughter. I believe pregnancy reversals, um, abortions are terrible, godawful things. My time in office reflects that, I have attempted to deliver a number of bills to stop abortions. Recently I brought to the floor the six-week abortion ban bill, which I tried tirelessly to introduce months *before* the Supreme Court leak stirred up the battle. But what can I do? I am a loving father. I want to see my daughter protected," the governor said as Jayla witnessed a future TV ad played out in real-time in her living room. "And that's why I want you to sign that form. To protect my daughter. She made a mistake. Will you hold that against her and ruin the rest of her life? Or will you choose to help me protect her? Two wrongs don't make a right."

Jayla searched the teenager's face and then looked up at her impeccably anguished father.

"Alright," Jayla finally relented, seeing that there was no fight to be had. "I'll sign."

"Excellent!" Governor Crix cheered, extending the form back out to her.

"Is there anything else you need from me, Daddy?" the teenager asked, like a trained circus animal asking if there were any more hoops to jump through.

"No, Princess," the politician reassured, kissing the top of her head. "You did great. I'll meet you in the car."

Jayla's eyes skimmed the form with the appearance of diligent study, but her mind was wrapped up in a tangle of malice and manipulation as she repeated a list of the governor's sins to herself. *You introduce the six-week bill knowing it will actually cause women to race to the abortion providers. You say you're pro-family and forced your kid to get an abortion.* "You're such a hypocrite," Jayla muttered, reluctantly signing the document and smashing it down on the arm of the chair.

Governor Crix almost smirked as he stuffed the signed form into his suit jacket pocket. "No. A hypocrite is someone who gives parenting advice when they couldn't even take care of their own baby."

Jayla smacked her hand across the governor's leathery white cheek with such force it left a hand mark red enough to match his tie. Lifting her hand to do it again, she saw the politician wince and lift his arms in wimpish defense, a look of terror replacing his trademarked overly confident demeanor. "You're a coward," Jayla spat, staying her hand. "And I want you out of my home."

With the lingering cologne of the retreated, wounded governor scenting the air, Jayla went to her kitchen and filled a glass with tap water. She looked in her cupboard for some aspirin for the worsening headache grinding her brain to pulp, still shocked by the events of the morning. Unable to find any medicine, Jayla noticed the bottle of Tramadol left unopened on the counter. *You're for pain, right?* Jayla said to herself, briefly gazing over the prescription label. *I guess you will have to do.*

Tossing the chalky tan pill into her mouth, Jayla swallowed and walked back over to her bed as she waited for the medicine to take effect, overwhelmed with different frequencies of pain. Sitting by herself in the empty apartment, Jayla was consumed with loneliness—a loneliness that didn't seem to go away no matter how many shots of whisky she had in her system or how loud her TV was turned up. There was now officially no one in her life. She no longer had a community, let alone family, to call her own. Every friend she had, every memory, all carved in past tense.

"I'm not alone," Jayla defended to herself out loud. "I'm *independent*."

Suddenly, Jayla realized her declaration of self-sufficiency was actually a quote she heard Amarika repeatedly say during her childhood. In an instant, she realized the transformation she had long feared and resolved would never happen had, at last, come to pass. She had become her mother—friendless, relationshipless, used, abused, angry, empty, calloused, numb, and alone.

An unexpected thudding on Jayla's front door put a pause on her bleak self-evaluation. Crossing her fingers in hopes another order of alcohol and microwavable snacks was being delivered, she cracked the door and discovered a small package left behind. The sender listed was Samantha, no doubt mailed before Jayla ruined their friendship. *Don't open it until we talk*, Jayla roughly remembered her saying. But since they likely would never talk again, she took the liberty of opening the package. The first item she drew out was a soft little baby onesie. On the front of the white shirt was a yellow softball with red laces, around which was written, *Having a Ball with Mommy*. Accompanying the onesie was a small handwritten note, which read:

Looks like there will be a second player on the Goodall Team!
Thank you for choosing to make me a mommy.
Love always,
Samantha

Jayla dropped the onesie and the card back into the box and closed the flaps. Then, turning on her living room TV to almost full blast, she attempted to drown out the words she told herself. *You never wanted that baby. You're glad it's dead. This is what you deserve. No one wants you. Everyone is better off without you. No one would even notice if you were gone.*

Grabbing the bottle of pain medicine, Jayla walked to her room and popped another three into her mouth, the incessant bantering of the television begging to distract her from the stones of condemnation she mercilessly heaved onto herself.

Life is always going to be like this. Life is never going to get better. You're worthless. You're weak. You're a waste of breath. You're a waste of space. Once you go to sleep, do everyone a favor, and don't wake back up.

Jayla's throat burned, her mouth dry, as goosebumps fell and rose across her shivering skin. She could feel the hollowness inside her, where a baby should be, where a heart should be. She remembered how awful she was to Samantha. She remembered how unforgiving she was with Brittany. She remembered how abused she was by Marcus. She remembered how abandoned she was by Amarika. She remembered how loved she was made to feel by her Auntie Neidringhouse.

You don't deserve love.

At the end of her rope, Jayla grabbed the tawny bottle of promises and guzzled down the rest of her prescription. Though the rest of her body became tingly and tired, her mind, sharp as ever, mounted guilt upon her until she was suffocating in it.

Maybe this is hell, she thought, hearing her phone ring as she teetered on the edge of consciousness, slipping.

CHAPTER 40

ONE OLD LETTER

For the second time in less than a week, Jayla awoke in a hospital bed, feeling somehow worse than her last visit. Within seconds of identifying her surroundings, she hastily glanced over to the seat next to her. *Alone*, Jaya thought, repeating the word with finality as the vultures of self-condemnation swarmed, swooping inward, scenes of the overdose bombarding her mind.

"You're awake!" a sweet Southern voice gasped from the doorway, breaking into Jayla's thoughts. She was dumbfounded to find Samantha holding two cups of coffee in her hands, a stunned, thankful expression on her makeup-less face. She looked more ragged than normal, the effortless shine of joy now replaced with sleepless purple eyes, a baggy T-shirt, and unattended hair. "Praise God! We have been praying for this," she exclaimed with such relief and devotion Jayla questioned if their spat really happened or was just a part of an elaborate fever dream. "I'll call Renee and let her know. She'll be so relieved."

"Sam? What are you doing here?" Jayla asked pensively. "How did I get here?"

"You don't remember?" questioned Samantha, setting the coffees down on the over-bed. "Oh, sweetheart, you accidentally *overdosed*. I was really worried we were going to lose you."

Accidentally, Jayla reflected to herself, quietly confirming the reality of her overdose and, by association, the spiral that prompted it. "I remember the overdose. I don't remember calling for an ambulance."

"That's a total God thing. Renee was calling you to check in on you, and it must have been a miracle you answered when you did because, a few minutes later, and you would have been unconscious, and no one would have known what happened until—" Samantha paused. "Until it was too late."

"Renee called *me*?" Jayla clarified. "Didn't I get fired? What happened the last time I saw you?"

Samantha took a coffee and moved to the chair next to Jayla's bed, considering her response before speaking. "Yes," she began, both hands snugly warming themselves against the disposable cup sitting on her lap. "You no longer work at the LifeLine Pregnancy Center. You and Renee had a falling out, of sorts, and the last time I saw you, you were taking it out on me."

"So why are you here right now?" Jayla pressed, confused. "Why did Renee call me in the first place? Who checks in on someone they fired?"

"Renee does," Samantha smiled softly. "She just wanted—we all just wanted to know how you were doing. We have been praying for you every day. And when we found out about what happened, the overdose, I volunteered to come and stay until we knew you were okay." Then, bending below Jayla's eye level, Samantha grabbed something and placed it on the bed. It was a get-well card. "This is from everyone at LifeLine," she explained as Jayla took the card in hand. "We all signed it." Inside she saw a slew of names and well wishes from everyone she knew, Brittany included. The only name suspiciously missing was Darla's. "It was the first thing we did when we were able to get the place up and running again."

"Thanks," remarked Jayla, unsure how she felt about receiving this token of affection.

"Didn't want you to think all that pro-abundant life talk was all for show," Samantha added, taking a sip of her coffee. A few moments of uncomfortable silence later she combed a loose strand of hair behind her ear. "You were right, you know—about Rick."

Jayla looked over at Samantha who was staring despondently at the floor, the coffee in her hand the only warmth in her body. Jayla remembered the last argument she had with Samantha, unprovoked, full of malice. "Sam," she whispered hoarsely as she gazed upon the only person who, despite everything, stuck with her. "When I—I shouldn't have said that," she offered lamely, unable to articulate a full apology.

"You said what I needed to hear, even though I didn't want to hear it. No one else would tell me how blind or stupid I was," Samantha shook her head as Jayla cringed, confronted by the bile in her own words. "So, thanks. Thanks for telling me like it is; that's what a real friend does."

Jayla was shamed by the way Sam was constantly assuming the best about her, filtering kindness out of bitterness, mining good intentions from harmful slights. Somehow, someway, Samantha embraced Jayla's brokenness, holding tight even when she was pierced by the pieces, unflinchingly bearing all things, believing all things, hoping all things, enduring all things, until love prevailed above all else. It wasn't that Samantha had a lack of sight, as Jayla accused. Rather, she possessed a *supernatural* insight—a faith, which saw things not as they were but as they were in the process of becoming.

Looking at her only true ally in the world, Jayla willed two unnatural words out of her mouth. "*I'm sorry*," she admitted, the words tasting like tar. "You're not those things, and I shouldn't have said you were. Only one of us has been a good friend, and it isn't me."

Samantha looked up with glistening eyes as Jayla felt an unseen hold on her begin to loosen. The once inescapable mold of her mother's image began peeling ever so slightly at the edges.

Samantha gave a small smile as she reached over, took Jayla's hand, and gave it a squeeze. "Yeah, this week has been pretty much the worst for me. Not to complain. I know you've been going through a lot as well," Samantha relented, releasing her hand in order to dry her eyes with a baggy sleeve. "The center gets trashed, my friend is calling me saying the police have her husband in handcuffs, another friend is mad at me and telling me my husband is cheating—and then she turns out to be right," Samantha shook her head again, her lower lip trembling. "And then the *baby*," her voice cracked. "I'm sorry. I'm sorry. I know— I know it was *your* baby and not *mine*," she withdrew, referencing their last conversation.

"I—I got your package," Jayla disclosed as Samantha let out a burst of tears.

"Yeah?" Samantha sniffed, wiping her nose on her sleeve. "When I saw that little onesie, I just . . ." she stopped and let out a crushing moan. "How is it one week ago I was a wife and was going to be a mom, and now . . ." she heaved, seeing how instability had infiltrated her safe, certain life.

Sitting in Samantha's silhouette was an invitation for Jayla to break free of the cycle of self-preservation, loneliness, and heartache that had swallowed her. It was a fearsome decision that went against every defense mechanism and coping strategy that promised safety in retreat and strength in isolation.

Jayla looked at her friend, her only friend, and fully aware of all she had to lose, slid her hand across the bed toward Samantha. "Now—we have each other," she offered, opening her hand like a blossom.

Samantha clasped Jayla's hand. She held it tight, making a sacred, unspoken oath between them. Then, letting out a small smile through her tears asked, "You don't happen to have a spare room I could stay in, do you?"

"No," Jayla laughed, inducing Samantha into an unexpected chuckle. "But I have a bathtub you're welcome to sleep in."

"I'll take it," Samantha blurted, her cheeks red, her eyes bloated and tired. Then, with the face of a sudden bug bite, she stuck her hand in her pocket and pulled out her phone. "Oh! Oh! Great!"

"Things with Rick?" Jayla probed curiously.

"No. Rick's not calling anyone unless he got his phone off the neighbor's roof," Samantha stated casually, then, with a glint in her eye, alluded, "It's something else."

For a moment the old Sam was back. "Uh—what aren't you telling me?" Jayla asked.

"Well," Samantha began mischievously. "While you were unconscious, I had some time on my hands and I was thinking of ways to cheer you up, hoping to find a little project to keep me preoccupied and not dwelling on the dumpster fire of my life, and that's when I remembered this name you told me the other day—Mrs. Neidringhouse."

Jayla's heart froze, her eyes bulging. "*Sam*—"

"Jayla, the God I serve is a God of restoration and recovery. And so, I kinda, sorta, did some snooping and social media stalking, and one thing led to another and I *found* her," Samantha insisted, her face a mongrel cross between a smile and a grimace. "And she just got here." Then, pausing and evaluating her friend's horrified expression, clarified, "Is that good? Did I do good?"

Jayla's considered her ragged appearance and smoothed out the front of her gown. "When does she get here?"

"Now—she's coming up now."

"Oh lordy, lordy, lordy," Jayla repeated nervously, smoothing out the front of her gown faster, wishing for some place she could hide.

Samantha began to worry she made a huge mistake. "Should I tell her not to come?"

"No, yes! It's fine," Jayla assessed. "Just let me think."

Immediately Jayla's mind latched onto the last time she saw her beloved mother figure. She thought about the love on her Auntie's face as she was broaching the topic of adoption and imagined the hurt, the anger, the resentment she must have felt from Jayla's abrupt exit from their lives. She thought about how she looked back then and wondered how age would have changed her over the years. By now, the woman would be around seventy years old. *What if she hates me now?*

Without warning, there was a knock on the door. Jayla looked at Sam and then threw her attention to the doorway. "Come in," Jayla invited, preparing for the worst.

In walked a young Hispanic woman, a little older than Jayla, wearing black-rimmed glasses and a gentle demeanor. "Jayla?" she confirmed as she made eye contact with the scarecrow in the hospital bed.

Jayla stared confused. "Samantha, who is this?" she asked before turning again to the woman. "Who are you?"

"I'm Kendal. Kendal Neidringhouse," the woman said, her voice kind and melodious. "I have to say, it's really amazing to finally meet you after all these years."

Samantha's face, which had been buried beneath the glow of her screen since Jayla's question, emerged with an inquisitive look. "This isn't your Mrs. Neidringhouse?"

"That *Mrs. Neidringhouse* was my mother," Kendal shared, stepping forward. "That's who Jayla knew, I'm *Miss Neidringhouse*."

"Where is she?" Jayla asked, looking over Kendal's shoulder. "Is she here too?"

"No, I'm so sorry. She and Dad passed away a few years ago," Kendal confessed sadly, elaborating when she saw the dazed look on Jayla's face. "Mom from cancer, and Dad had a heart attack in the rose garden soon after. That must have been who you were expecting. I'm so sorry."

"Oh," Jayla sighed, letting the news sink in, realizing the reality of never getting closure on that chapter of her life. Now she would never have the chance to explain what prompted her to leave or to apologize, to share her gratefulness or to disclose how she really felt about her Auntie.

"She talked about you *all* the time," Kendal said, smiling. "She and Dad would tell me stories about the three of you, and even during the cancer treatments, just the thought of you made her light up."

"She talked about me?" Jayla asked, stunned.

Kendal's eyes turned to beaming moon slivers as a delicate smile formed. "Of course, she did— she loved you. They both loved you."

Tears of regret streamed uncontrollably down Jayla's cheeks as her hand covered her mouth.

"You don't know this, but I have a lot to thank you for," Kendal said, her eyes glistening with tears. "I was in foster care all my life. I was so old it was almost time for me to age out, and I knew, I just knew, I would never get adopted. No one ever wanted to adopt the older kids. But one day," she began to cry. "One day, Mom and Dad showed up. And of all the kids they could have picked, they picked *me*. And I asked them why—why me when no one else would have picked me. And they told me about *you*." Kendal smiled through the tears. "You are the reason I got the most amazing parents in the world. You're the reason I had a home to grow up in. The love they had for you spilled out and opened their hearts to take the kid no one else wanted." Reaching into her canvas bag, Kendal pulled out a letter. "Before Mom died, she wrote this and gave it to me in the event I ever found you," she explained, putting the card into Jayla's shuddering hands.

Unfolding the aged letter, Jayla held it to her face, struggling to read it through her wet eyes. The scent of the paper smelled like her Auntie's floral perfume, and the elegant flowing cursive script flooded her mind with memories.

Dear Jayla,

If you are reading this letter, one of my deepest prayers has been answered. As I write to you, I am sitting here at our family dinner table, the one my grandmother gave me. I can still see the imprints from where you did your homework all those years ago, pressing your pen too hard through the page. I remember being so frustrated at you for doing that, but now, from time to time, I catch myself running my hands over the indentions, wishing I could go back. I close my eyes, and it's as if you're still here. Like you'll walk through the door any minute and raid the fridge on the way to your room. Like you never left.

This table, of course, was the last place I saw you all those years ago as we spoke about your adoption. You have reasons, of course, for why you left. It was your choice to come here and your choice to leave; we only ever wanted to hold our time with you with open hands. But while I respect your decision to leave, for years, I've wanted to say that if there was ever anything we did to hurt you or break your trust, you have my sincerest, most heartfelt apologies. I know we weren't perfect guardians, and we fell short every day in so many ways. And I know I'm not supposed to replay how things happened or what I should have done differently, but that hasn't stopped me from contemplating everything over the years, and if I'm honest, there is something I wish I could go back and change.

I would have told you more how much I loved you. I would have started each day by saying it and ended each evening with it. I would have written it to you in notes and slipped it into your pocket on your way to school. I would have embarrassed you with it at the bus stop and carved it into this silly oak table if it meant you knowing how much you meant to me. I would have told you how I loved you from the first moment I saw you in my class. Shirt untucked, nose runny, a crooked smile the size of the solar system. You were so precocious and so brave, especially with the hurt you carried inside. I would have told you that you stole my heart then and every single moment after. And, while you weren't the daughter of my womb, you were the daughter of my prayers, born in my heart, bursting it to overflowing. I loved you then, and I love you now.

Things weren't always easy, of course. Often times we felt like we were in over our heads. But how can we learn to love unconditionally if our love is never tested? You taught us how to love with no strings attached. Thank you for that. Thank you for letting me experience what it was like to be a mother. Thank you for giving me many of the best years of my life, even though they came with many more gray hairs. And thank you for helping me understand better what God is like—the God of adoption who welcomes into His family anyone who believes in the death and resurrection of Jesus. He is a Father to the fatherless and gives rebels like me a place to call home. I got to uniquely experience His love for me in loving you. I can't thank you enough for that.

There's not a single day that's gone by when you haven't been on my mind and I haven't wondered about you, where you are, how you are, and if you have a family of your own by now. I like to imagine you are loved like you deserve. I wish you every joy, peace, and kindness that this life has to offer and some this life can't.

Always and forever,
Your Auntie

Jayla pressed the paper against her chest, weeping. "Did you read this?" she asked Kendal as Samantha extended a tissue to her.

"It wasn't mine to open," Kendal replied, "but whatever she said, I know she meant every single word. Mom was the best, wasn't she?"

"Yes . . ." Jayla said softly, avoiding getting tears onto her newest and most cherished item.

"Mom always put her heart into what she said. Because of her, I decided to become a teacher too. I've even begun the adoption process with another foster care child, trying to pass on her and Dad's legacy," Kendal shared proudly, adding, "There's so much paperwork, some days I want to scream, *Why is there this much paperwork? Why is it easier to have an abortion than an adoption in this country?* But I know it will be worth it when it happens."

"Is your husband excited about that?" asked Samantha, her mind seeming to gravitate to Rick and their current situation.

"I'm not married," Kendal clarified, "I might very well be by the time this paperwork gets done, but I didn't think I should wait on a man to do the right thing for a child."

CHAPTER 41

YOU DID MATTER

Three months later, Jayla stood outside the recently refurbished LifeLine Pregnancy Center, now renamed CareNet Women's Center, the result of a much-needed remodeling and rebranding. The remodel was the result of another *Jane Gets Revenge* vengeance leveled against them. Jayla grasped a folded piece of paper she tapped nervously against her black dress as her heart thumped in her throat. *Come on, come on*, she said to herself, waiting for Samantha to arrive. Then, spotting her new yellow Jeep pulling into the parking lot, she let out a sigh of relief and quickly walked in her direction.

"Sorry I'm late," Samantha apologized, getting out of the car.

"That's okay. I'm just glad you didn't forget," Jayla said, letting Samantha give her a hug.

"No! Of course, I wouldn't forget. This is the most important day in October!" Samantha encouraged. "How are we doing on time?"

"Fine," Jayla replied. "I took the rest of the afternoon off not knowing how long—or how I'd be doing." Jayla began as she peeked anxiously into the backseat of Samantha's Jeep.

"Did you bring it?"

"I was working on it all night," Sam said, reaching onto the floorboard and pulling out a beautifully stained small rectangular wooden box. "I hope you don't mind, but I put this inside," she said, lifting the lid and revealing the tiny white softball onesie inside. "What did you bring?"

"Just my letter," Jayla answered. "Do—do you think I should have brought more?"

"Nope. Just the letter is perfect," Sam comforted as the two began walking up to the building.

"How are things going with Rick, anyways?" Jayla asked, averting her attention from the morning's ceremony.

"Ups and downs; some days it seems like he's trying to make it work more than others, but he might say the same thing about me. It's hard to make forward progress in a car when half the wheels don't feel like working," Samantha sighed, reaching for the door handle to the entrance. "Our marriage counseling sessions with Pastor Steve are helping a lot, though. But, you know, still separate beds, still separate bedrooms, taking things slow like we're starting to date again. You ready?" she asked, pausing before opening the door.

Jayla took in a deep breath and nodded her head affirmatively.

Entering the building, she was greeted by some new volunteers whose names she almost remembered, new faces serving as replacements for many of the former paid employees due to a large decrease in giving following the Supreme Court ruling. Rumor had it the entire center would have closed if not for the rallying of several churches in the area and a large anonymous donation. She knew the five hundred dollars she repaid the center helped a little as well, but it was hard for her not to wonder what the community would be like—what she would be like—if Lifeline were to close from a lack of support, especially now that she was benefitting so greatly from the abortion support group Renee invited her into.

"Good morning, Jayla," Brittany called out in a friendly tone, a shimmering gold and black headscarf around her head. "Nice to have you visit!"

"Thanks, Brittany," Jayla replied, finally at a point in her life where she could appreciate any second chances at relationships she was given.

Walking through the halls, Jayla greeted women that, before, she never saw the need to acknowledge, let alone talk to. She passed by the supply closet and break room, her heart quickening the closer they got to the conference area.

"Jayla," Renee called out as Samantha and Jayla were passing by her office. "It's a good thing what you're doing today. A hard thing, but a good thing," she affirmed. "We're all proud of you and are praying for you, and Jesus is going to be with you."

"Thanks," Jayla said, forcing a smile. "Wish me luck."

Before she was ready, the pair reached the conference area, the phrase *Memorial Service* spelled out on the felt letter board. Entering the room, Jayla could see where each participant signed a pair of baby shoes and placed them on the ornate wooden display table. These would be left as an encouragement for others recovering from abortion. Jayla paused and scribbled a single name onto the tag and tucked it deep into one of the shoes.

An acoustic guitar was playing gently in the background. The circle of chairs she had grown accustomed to were doubled and already filled with attendees, some coming as friends and supporters, others being the grieving mothers. Even if Jayla hadn't attended these sessions over the last few months, it would still have been easy for her to spot who the mothers were, as each one held their own little wooden casket close to their chest.

Gradually Jayla made her way to the group, Samantha right by her side. The two sat just as a suit-wearing Pastor Steve stood from his chair and began to address the room.

"Good morning," he started, pausing for the audience to reciprocate. "We have come today to celebrate the lives of eight babies, eight image-bearers of God, whom we had the privilege of knowing but never meeting. Today we remember their lives. We honor them. In so doing, we honor ourselves as we give back to God what was always and already His." Then, looking around the circle, compassionately asked, "Who would like to go first?"

Jayla watched as one by one the women around her took their turns, tearfully reading handwritten letters and explaining what little items had been carefully selected to fill their babies' caskets. A small fuzzy teddy bear, a golden necklace, a hand-knitted blanket, a picture of the child's mother and father. Some of the women who shared lost their baby decades ago, while others, younger than Jayla, had their abortions more recently in the mass panic following the overturning of *Roe v. Wade*. A few women mentioned in their letters the circumstances under which they had their abortions. One woman couldn't stop repeating the word *sorry* over and over again to the empty little box in her arms.

By the time it was Jayla's turn to share, everyone present was already emotionally overextended.

Resisting the urge to smooth over the front of her black dress, Jayla stood from her seat, all eyes glued on her. Jayla looked at the letter in her hand and read the words repeatedly in her mind before speaking anything aloud. Then, having firmly made up her mind, broke precedent and folded the letter in half, placing it gently in the wooden box Samantha held on top of the softball onesie.

"I— uh—" Jayla began, clearing her throat. "I just wanted to say—" she paused, digging deep into her soul for something authentic to say, she thought, *Please, help me, God.* "I know I'm probably not supposed to say this at a funeral or anything, but I know I didn't always want you; that's the truth. For most of the twenty weeks you were inside me, I didn't. I acted like you weren't even there. So why is it that for someone I didn't want, I miss you?" Jayla stopped and shuffled her feet as she looked at the little box cradled by Samantha. "For someone I didn't love, I feel such *loss*; maybe I don't deserve to feel this way. I don't know—I never saw you or held you. I was not conscious when you passed. You never even had a name," she said, struggling to fight through the feelings of inadequacy and discomfort as Samantha offered her hand.

"But even though I didn't always love you, I love you now. And even though you never got a name, I—I want to name you now. So I can remember you—so the world can remember you. So it can be like you mattered—because you did. You did matter, and—I don't know if I fully believe there's a God or heaven, but over the past three months, I have been trying my best to believe. Oh, how I want to believe. And if there is a God, I don't know what He calls you up there, but for me, I am going to name you *Someday*. Because I think—I hope—someday all this will change. All this pain and messed up stuff in the world— someday it will change, and it will be down here like it is where you are now—peaceful—full of love—and, so, I name you *Someday*, because you are not hurting.

"Someday, you are at peace. Someday, I will join you, and I will hold you, and we will be together. You are free, Someday. You are free, and maybe, God-willing, someday I will be totally free as well."

Stepping outside the service, Jayla followed the women to a plot of grass where eight small holes had been dug underneath the shade of a protective juniper tree. Pastor Steve stepped up meekly behind Jayla and whispered, "Thank you for your vulnerability and honesty back there. What you said—was so meaningful. If you have a few moments after the service I would love to talk more with you. I think your some-day might start today."

Jayla nodded her approval, a faint brushstroke of hope shading her face.

Before Jayla put the tiny casket in the ground, she gave it to Saman-tha who hugged it and kissed its lid, handing it back with tears. Then Jayla placed the box into the desert ground and grabbed a handful of dirt. "*Be free, Someday,*" she whispered, speaking as much to herself as to the box she was burying. And, as she opened her hand to scatter the soil, she at last began to be.

ABOUT THE AUTHORS

Mike G. Williams is an author and comedian. For three decades he has toured with the most memorable names in the CCM music industry, written comedy for some nationally known television acts, won the GMA Dove Award for Comedian of the Year, recorded a Dry Bar Comedy Special, a Bananas Television Special, is played almost daily on SiriusXM, recorded eighteen audio/video projects, and written twenty books while flying over 5 million miles on Delta and American airlines.

Mike's own story is that of a rescue adoption in 1962. Mike and his wife chose to pay it back, adopting the first of their four children from a rescue situation similar to his own. The life of this book's lead is not far from his own upbringing. Much of Mike's work these days is helping Women's Health Centers around the country raise money for their important work. He is the most repeat-booked fundraising speaker in the United States. When not on the road, Mike and his wife of thirty-nine years, Terica, operate a mission program in the Dominican Republic, rescuing young girls from human trafficking. All Mike's proceeds from this book will go to fund that CupsMisssion.com project.

W. R. Ponder is the husband of an incredible wife and father to three amazing little girls, none of whom would be alive if not for the bravery of a woman named Nancy. Because of Nancy's selfless decision to choose life, three generations of brilliant, wonderful women have the chance to make the world—and W.R Ponder's life—better.

Similarly, your decision to purchase this book is providing aid to women in urgent need around the world as W.R. Ponder's proceeds from this book are going to amazing charities, such as CarePortal and Open Doors US. This good read is making a good impact thanks to wonderful readers like you.